THE
FOXGLOVE
KING

By Hannah Whitten

THE NIGHTSHADE CROWN

The Foxglove King

THE WILDERWOOD

For the Wolf

For the Throne

THE FOXGLOVE KING

The Nightshade Crown: Book One

HANNAH WHITTEN

orbit

orbitbooks.net

Copyright © 2023 by Hannah Whitten

Cover design by Lisa Marie Pompilio
Cover illustration by Mike Heath | Magnus Creative
Cover background image by Shutterstock
Cover copyright © 2023 by Hachette Book Group, Inc.
Map by Charis Loke

Orbit
Hachette Book Group
1290 Avenue of the Americas
New York, NY 10104
orbitbooks.net

First Edition: March 2023
Simultaneously published in Great Britain by Orbit

Orbit is an imprint of Hachette Book Group.
The Orbit name and logo are trademarks of Little, Brown Book Group Limited.

The Hachette Speakers Bureau provides a wide range of authors for speaking events. To find out more, go to hachettespeakersbureau.com or email HachetteSpeakers@hbgusa.com.

Orbit books may be purchased in bulk for business, educational, or promotional use. For information, please contact your local bookseller or the Hachette Book Group Special Markets Department at special.markets@hbgusa.com.

Library of Congress Cataloging-in-Publication Data
Names: Whitten, Hannah, author.
Title: The foxglove king / Hannah Whitten.
Description: First Edition. | New York, NY : Orbit, 2023. | Series: The nightshade crown ; book 1
Identifiers: LCCN 2022034979 | ISBN 9780316434997 (hardcover) | ISBN 9780316435192 (ebook)
Subjects: LCGFT: Novels.
Classification: LCC PS3623.H5864 F68 2023 | DDC 813/.6—dc23/eng/20220721
LC record available at https://lccn.loc.gov/2022034979

ISBNs: 9780316434997 (hardcover), 9780316435192 (ebook)

Printed in the United States of America

LSC-C

Printing 1, 2022

To anyone who chose themselves.

APO

LA VIE ET LE JOUR

CALDIEN

BURNT
ISLES

RATHARC

Kettleburgh

GOLDEN
MOUNT

LA MORT ET LA NUIT

CALDIENAN-CLAIMED
TERRITORY

Farramark

OURISH PASS

Huverraine

ROUSKA

Dellaire

BALGIA

EROCCA

KALIACH

KIRYTHEA

Laerdas

MYROSH

MALFOUR

KADMAR

NUX

THE
FOXGLOVE
KING

The world is too much with us; late and soon,
Getting and spending, we lay waste our powers:
Little we see in nature that is ours;
We have given our hearts away, a sordid boon!
This Sea that bares her bosom to the moon;
The Winds that will be howling at all hours
And are up-gathered now like sleeping flowers;
For this, for every thing, we are out of tune;
It moves us not.

—William Wordsworth

CHAPTER ONE

No one is more patient than the dead.

—Auverrani proverb

Every month, Michal claimed he'd struck a deal with the landlord, and every month, Nicolas sent one of his sons to collect anyway. The sons must've drawn straws—this month's unfortunate was Pierre, the youngest and spottiest of the bunch, and he trudged up the street of Dellaire's Harbor District with the air of one approaching a guillotine.

Lore could work with that.

A dressing gown that had seen better days dripped off one shoulder as Lore leaned against the doorframe and watched him approach. Pierre's eyes kept drifting to where the fabric gaped, and she kept having to bite the inside of her cheek so she didn't laugh. Apparently, a crosshatch of silvery scars from back-alley knife fights didn't deter the man when presented with bare skin.

She had other, more interesting scars. But she kept her palm closed tight.

A cool breeze blew off the ocean, and Lore suppressed a shiver. Pierre didn't seem to spare any thought for why she'd exited the house barely dressed when mornings near the harbor always carried a chill, even in summer. An easy mark in more ways than one.

"Pierre!" Lore shot him a dazzling grin, the same one that made Michal's eyes simultaneously go heated and then narrow before he asked what she wanted. Another twist against the doorframe, another seemingly casual pose, another bite of wind that made a curse bubble behind her teeth. "It's the end of the month already?"

Michal should be dealing with this. It was his damn row house. But the drop he'd made for Gilbert last night had been all the way in the Northwest Ward, so Lore let him sleep.

Besides, waking up early had given her time to go through Michal's pockets for the drop coordinates. She'd taken them to the tavern on the corner and left them with Frederick the bartender, who'd been on Val's payroll for as long as Lore could remember. Val would be sending someone to pick them up before the sun fully rose, and someone else to grab Gilbert's poison drop before his client could.

Lore was good at her job.

Right now, her job was making sure the man she'd been living with for a year so she could spy on his boss didn't get evicted.

"I—um—yes, yes it is." Pierre managed to fix his eyes to her own, through obviously conscious effort. "My father...um, he said this time he means it, and..."

Lore let her expression fall by careful degrees, first into confusion, then shock, then sorrow. "Oh," she murmured, wrapping her arms around herself and turning her face away to show a length of pale white neck. "This month, of all months."

She didn't elaborate. She didn't need to. If there was anything Lore had learned in twenty-three years alive, ten spent on the streets of Dellaire, it was that men generally preferred you to be a set piece in the story they made up, rather than an active player.

From the corner of her eye, she saw Pierre's pale brows draw together, a deepening blush lighting the skin beneath his freckles. They were all moon-pale, Nicolas's boys. It made their blushes look like something viral.

His gaze went past her to the depths of the dilapidated row house beyond. Sunrise shadows hid everything but the dust motes twisting in light shards. Not that there was much to see back there, anyway. Michal was still asleep upstairs, and his sister, Elle, was sprawled on the couch, a wine bottle in her hand and a slightly musical snore on her lips. It looked like any other row house on this street, coming apart at the seams and full of people who skirted just under the law to get by.

Or very far under it, as the case may be.

"Is there an illness?" Pierre kept his voice hushed, low. His face tried for sympathetic, but it looked more like he'd put bad milk in his coffee. "A child, maybe? I know Michal rents this house, not you. Is it his?"

Lore's brows shot up. In all the stories she'd let men spin about her, *that* was a first—Pierre must have sex on the brain if he jumped straight to pregnancy. But beggars couldn't be choosers. She gently laid a hand on her abdomen and let that be answer enough. It wasn't technically a lie if she let him draw his own conclusions.

She was past caring about lying, anyway. Lore was damned whether or not she kept her spiritual record spotless. Might as well lean into it.

"Oh, you poor girl." Pierre was probably younger than she was, and here he went clucking like a mother hen. Lore managed to keep her eyes from rolling, but only just. "And with a poison runner? You know he won't be able to take care of you."

Lore bit the inside of her cheek again, hard.

Her apparent distress made Pierre bold. "You could come with me," he said. "My father could help you find work, I'm sure." He raised his hand, settled it on her bare shoulder.

And every nerve in Lore's body seized.

It was abrupt and unexpected enough for her to shudder, to shake off his hand in a motion that didn't fit her soft, vulnerable narrative. She'd grown used to feeling this reaction to dead things—stone, metal, cloth. Corpses, when she couldn't avoid them. It was natural to sense Mortem in something dead, no matter how unpleasant, and at this point she could hide her reaction, keep it contained. She'd had enough practice.

But she shouldn't feel Mortem in a *living* man, not one who wasn't at death's door. Her shock was quick and sharp, and chased with something else—the scent of foxglove. So strong, he must've been dosed mere minutes before arriving.

And he wanted to disparage poison runners. Hypocrite.

Her fingers closed around his wrist, twisted, forced him to his knees. It happened quick, quick enough for him to slip on a stray pebble and send one leg out at an awkward angle, for a strangled "*Shit!*" to echo through the morning streets of Dellaire's Harbor District.

Lore crouched so they were level. Now that she knew what to look for, it was obvious in his eyes, bloodshot and glassy; in the heartbeat thumping slow and irregular beneath her palm. He'd gone to one of the cheap deathdealers, one who didn't know how to properly dose their patrons. The veins at the corners of Pierre's eyes were barely touched with gray, so he hadn't been given enough poison for any kind of life extension, and certainly not enough to possibly grasp the power waiting at death's threshold.

He probably wasn't after those things, anyway. Most people his age just wanted the high.

The dark threads of Mortem under Pierre's skin twisted against Lore's grip, stirred to waking by the poison in his system. Mortem was dormant in everyone—the essence of death, the power born of entropy, just waiting to flood your body on the day it failed—but the only way to use it, to bend it to your will, was to nearly die.

If you weren't after the power or the euphoric feeling poison could give you, then you were after the extra years. Properly dosed, poison could balance your body on the cusp of life and death, and that momentary concession to Mortem could, paradoxically, extend your life. Not that the life you got in exchange was one of great quality—half-stone, your veins clotted with rock, making your blood rub through them like a cobblestone skinning a knee.

Whatever Pierre had been after when he visited a deathdealer this morning, he hadn't paid enough to get it. If he'd gotten a true poison high, he'd be slumped in an alley somewhere, not asking her for rent. Rent that was higher than she remembered it being, now that she thought of it.

"Here's what's going to happen," Lore murmured. "You are going to tell Nicolas that we've paid up for the next six months, or I am going to tell him you've been spending his coin on deathdealers."

Fuck Michal's ineffectual bargains with the landlord. She'd just make one of her own.

Pierre's eyes widened, his lids poison-heavy. "How—"

"You stink of foxglove and your eyes look more like windows." Not exactly true, since she hadn't noticed until she'd sensed the Mortem, but by the time he could examine himself, the effect would've worn off anyway. "Anyone can take one look at you and know, Pierre, even though your deathdealer barely gave you enough to make you tingle. I'd be surprised if you got five extra minutes tacked on for *that*, so I hope the high was worth it."

The boy gaped, the open mouth under his window-glass eyes making his face look fishlike. He'd undoubtedly paid a handsome sum for the pinch of foxglove he'd taken. If she wasn't so good at spying for Val, Lore might've become a deathdealer herself. They made a whole lot of money for doing a whole lot of jack shit.

Pierre's unfortunate blush spread down his neck. "I can't— He'll ask where the money is—"

"I'm confident an industrious young man like yourself can come up with it somewhere." A flick of her fingers, and Lore let him go.

Pierre stumbled up on shaky legs and straightened his mussed shirt. The gray veins at the corners of his eyes were already fading back to blue-green. "I'll try," he said, voice just as tremulous as the rest of him. "I can't promise he'll believe me."

Lore gave him a winning smile. Standing, she yanked up the shoulder of her dressing gown. "He better."

Pierre didn't run down the street, but he walked very fast.

As the sun rose higher, the Harbor District slowly woke up— bundles of cloth stirred in dark corners, drunks coaxed awake by light and sea breeze. In the row house across the street, Lore heard the telltale sighs of Madam Brochfort's girls starting their daily squabbles over who got the washtub first, and any minute now at least two straggling patrons would be politely but firmly escorted outside.

"Pierre?" she called when he was halfway down the street. He turned, lips pressed together, clearly considering what other things she might blackmail him with.

"A word of advice." She turned toward Michal's row house in a flutter of faded dressing gown. "The real deathdealers have morgues in the back. Death's scales are easy to tip."

Elle was awake, but only just. She squinted from beneath a pile of gold curls through the light-laden dust, paint still smeared across her lips. "Whassat?"

"As if you don't know." Lore shook out the hand that had

touched Pierre's shoulder, trying to banish pins and needles. It'd grown easier for her to sense Mortem recently, and she wasn't fond of the development. She gave her hand one more firm shake before heading into the kitchen. "End of the month, Elle-Flower."

There was barely enough coffee in the chipped ceramic pot for one cup. Lore poured all of it into the stained cloth she used as a strainer and balled it in her fingers as she put the kettle over the fire. If there was only one cup of coffee in this house, she'd be the one drinking it.

"Don't call me that." Elle groaned as she shifted to sit up. She'd fallen asleep in her dancer's tights, and a long run traced up each calf. It'd piss her off once she noticed, but the patrons of the Foghorn and Fiddle down the street wouldn't care. One squinting look into the wine bottle to make sure it was empty and Elle shoved off the couch to stand. "Michal isn't awake, we don't have to pretend we like each other."

Lore snorted. In the year she'd been living with Michal, it'd become very obvious that she'd never get along with his sister. It didn't bother Lore. Her relationship with Michal was built on a lie, a sand foundation with no hope of holding, so why try to make friends? As soon as Val gave the word, she'd be gone.

Elle pushed past her into the kitchen, the spiderweb cracks on the windows refracting veined light on the tattered edges of her tulle skirt. She peered into the pot. "No coffee?"

Lore tightened her hand around the cloth knotted in her fist. "Afraid not."

"Bleeding *God*." Elle flopped onto one of the chairs by the pockmarked kitchen table. For a dancer, she was surprisingly ungraceful when sober. "I'll take tea, then."

"*Surely* you don't expect me to get it for you."

A grumble and a roll of bright-blue eyes as Elle slinked her way toward the cupboard. While her back was turned, Lore tucked the straining cloth into the lip of her mug and poured hot water over it, hoping Elle was too residually drunk to recognize the scent.

Still grumbling, Elle scooped tea that was little more than dust into another mug. "Well?" She took the kettle from Lore without looking at her and apparently without smelling her coffee. "How'd it go? Is Michal finally going to have to spend money on something other than alcohol and betting at the boxing ring?"

"Not on rent, at least." Lore kept her back turned as she tugged the straining cloth and the tiny knot of coffee grounds from her cup and stuffed it in her pocket. "We're paid up for six months."

"Is that why you look so disheveled?" Elle's mouth pulled into a self-satisfied moue. "He could get it cheaper across the street."

"The dishevelment is the fault of your brother, actually." Lore turned and leaned against the counter. "And barbs about Madam's girls don't suit you, Elle-Flower. It's work like any other. To think otherwise just proves you dull."

Another eye roll. Elle made a face when she sipped her weak tea, and sharp satisfaction hitched Lore's smile higher. She took a long, luxurious swallow of coffee and drifted toward the stairs. There'd been a message waiting for her at the tavern—Val needed her help with a drop today. It was risky business, having her work while she was deep undercover with another operation, but hands were low. People kept getting hired out from under them on the docks.

And Lore had skills that no one else did.

She'd have to come up with an excuse for why she'd be gone all day, but if she woke Michal up with some kissing, he wouldn't question her further. She found herself smiling at the idea. She liked kissing Michal. That was dangerous.

The smile dropped.

The stairs of the row house were rickety, like pretty much everything else in the structure, and the fourth one squeaked something awful. Lore winced when her heel ground into it, sloshing coffee over the side of her mug and burning her fingers.

Michal was sitting up when Lore pushed aside the ratty curtain closing off their room, sheets tangled around his waist and dripping off the mattress to pool on the floor. It was unclear whether it was the squeaking stair or her loud curse when she burned herself that had woken him.

He pushed his dark hair out of his eyes, squinted. "Coffee?"

"Last cup, but I'll share if you come get it."

"That's generous, since I assume you need it." He grumbled as he levered himself up from the floor-bound mattress, holding the sheet around his naked hips. "You had another nightmare last night. Thrashed around like the Night Witch herself was after you."

Her cheeks colored, but Lore just shrugged. The nightmares were a recent development, and random. She could never remember much about them, only vague impressions that didn't quite match with the terrified feeling they left behind. Blue, open sky, a churning sea. Some dark shape twisting through the air, like smoke but thicker.

Lore held out the coffee. "Sorry if I kept you awake."

"At least you didn't scream this time." Michal took a long drink from her proffered mug, though his face twisted up when he swallowed. "No milk?"

"Elle used the last of it." Lore shrugged and took the cup back, draining the rest.

Michal ran a hand through his hair to tame it into submission while he bent to pull clothes from the piles on the floor. The sheet fell, and Lore allowed herself a moment to ogle.

"I have another drop today," he said as he got dressed. "So I'll probably be gone until the evening."

That made her life much easier. Lore propped her hips on the windowsill and watched him dress, hoping her relief didn't show on her face. "Gilbert is working you hard."

"Demand has gone up, and the team is dwindling. People keep

getting hired on the docks to move cargo, getting paid more than Gilbert can afford to match." Michal gave the room a narrow-eyed survey before spotting his boot beneath a pile of sheets in the corner. "The Presque Mort and the bloodcoats have all been busy getting ready for the Sun Prince's Consecration tomorrow, and everyone is taking advantage of them having their proverbial backs turned."

It seemed like Gilbert was doing far more business during the security lull than was wise, but that wasn't Lore's problem. That's what she told herself, at least, when worry for Michal squeezed a fist around her insides. "Must be some deeply holy Consecration they're planning, if the Presque Mort are invited. They aren't known for being the best party guests."

Michal huffed a laugh as he pulled his boots on. "Especially not if your party includes poison." He rolled his neck, working out stiffness from their rock-hard mattress, and stood.

"Be careful tonight," Lore said, then immediately clenched her teeth. She hadn't meant to say it. She hadn't meant to *mean* it.

A lazy smile lifted his mouth. Michal sauntered over, cupped her face in his hands. "Are you *worried* about me, Lore?"

She scowled but didn't shake him off. "Don't get used to it."

A laugh rumbled through his chest, pressed against her own, and then his lips were on hers. Lore sighed and kissed him back, her hands wrapping around his shoulders, tugging him close.

It'd be over soon, so she might as well enjoy it while it lasted.

Despite Michal's warmth, Lore still felt like shivering. She could feel Mortem everywhere—the cloth of Michal's shirt, the stones in the street outside, the chipped ceramic of the mug on the windowsill. Even as her awareness of it grew, a steady climb over the last few months, she was usually able to ignore it, but Pierre's unexpected foxglove had thrown her off balance. Mortem wasn't as thick here on the outskirts of Dellaire as it was closer to the Citadel—closer to the Buried Goddess's body far beneath it, leaking the magic of death—but it was still enough to make her skin crawl.

The Harbor District, on the southern edge of Dellaire, was as far as Mortem would let her go. She could try to hop a ship, try to trek out on the winding roads that led into the rest of Auverraine, but it'd be pointless. The threads of Mortem would just wind her back, woven into her very marrow. She was tied into this damn city as surely as death was tied into life, as surely as the crescent moon burned into the bottom curve of her palm.

Michal's mouth found her throat, and she arched into him, closing her eyes tight. Her fingers clawed into his hair, and his arm cinched around her waist like he might lift her up, carry her to their mattress on the floor, make her forget that this was something finite.

The fact that she *wanted* to forget was enough to make her push him away, masking it as playful. "You don't want to be late."

He lingered at her lips a moment before stepping back. "I'll see you tonight, then."

She just smiled, though the stretch of her lips felt unnatural.

Michal left, that same step squeaking on his way down, the windows rattling when he closed the door. Lore heard Elle heave a sigh, as if her brother's job were a personal affront, the thin walls making it sound like she was right next to Lore instead of all the way on the first floor.

Lore stood there a moment, the light of the slow-rising sun gleaming on her hair, the worn silk of her gown. Then she dressed in a flowing shirt and tight breeches, made her own way down the stairs. She had a meeting with Val to attend.

Elle was curled up on the couch again, a ragged paperback novel in one hand and another mug of tepid tea in the other. She eyed Lore the way you might look at something unpleasant you'd tracked in from the street. "And where are you going?"

"Oh, you didn't hear? I received an invitation to the Sun

Prince's Consecration. I wasn't going to go, but rumor has it there might be an orgy afterward, and I can't very well turn that down."

Elle rolled her eyes so hard Lore was surprised she didn't strain a muscle. "There is something deeply *off* about you."

"You have no idea." Lore opened the door. "Bye, Elle-Flower."

"Rot in your own hell, Lore-dear."

Lore twiddled her fingers in an exaggerated wave as the door closed. Part of her would miss Elle when the spying gig was up, when Val had a different running outfit she wanted watched instead of Gilbert's.

But not as much as she'd miss Michal.

She couldn't miss either of them for long. People came and went; her only constants were her mothers—Val and Mari—and the streets of Dellaire she could never leave.

That, and the memories of a childhood she was always, always trying to forget.

With one last glance at the row house, Lore started down the street.

CHAPTER TWO

Those born to darkness will carry it in their nature;
they will carry sin in their very selves, body and mind
and soul.

—The Book of Mortal Law, Tract 7

Dellaire was easy to navigate. Lore had heard tales of other cities—chaotic and winding, byways butting into themselves—and the concept seemed entirely foreign to her after half a lifetime spent in Dellaire's well-organized roads. The Four Wards at ordinal directions, the western two coming up against the sea while the eastern led to Auverraine's rolling farmland. The Church in the city's center, built in a circle, guarding the Citadel within.

But if Dellaire was a grid, the catacombs beneath were a tangled web.

Weak sun radiated over the back of Lore's neck as she stood at the entrance to a dilapidated building a few blocks from Michal's row house. It had the look of a construction that had been many things in its time, so many that they'd all canceled one another out, so now it was nearly featureless. A slight wind off the sea rippled the torn cloth hanging in the windows.

Lore cursed softly. Being this close to the catacombs always made her twitchy.

They were empty. She could sense it, even now, standing yards away from their entrance. There was no one in the tunnels, at least not for a couple of miles.

Still, her skin prickled.

This was the skill that made her invaluable. The one she'd shocked Mari with on that day ten years ago, when she was a thirteen-year-old wandering in the streets with blank eyes and a fresh burn scar on her palm. Val's wife had been heading to the market and had come across a young Lore staring at a ragged hole in the side of a derelict building, one that led to the catacombs.

Lore still remembered it. She'd blocked out nearly everything that came before this moment, thirteen years of life spent almost entirely underground, but her recall of meeting Mari was crystalline, perfectly preserved, as if her mind could wash over everything that had come before by saving this memory in vivid detail.

"Are you all right?" Mari's voice was soft and low, her long, dark braids twisted up on top of her head. A moment of hesitation before her golden-brown hand settled on Lore's shoulder. "Is something wrong?"

Lore had stared at the hole and concentrated on the sting of the still-healing burn on her palm, on the darkness beyond and how it stretched out into what had been her forever. She blinked, and the layout of the tunnels overlaid the back of her eyelids. "No one is coming," she'd said. "Not right now."

In the present, Lore shook her head. She'd gotten better at only tapping into her awareness of the catacombs when she needed it—even now, as the strange skill seemed to be growing in strength alongside her sense of Mortem—but standing so close made it nearly impossible to ignore, made it seep through her thoughts like ink in water. She felt the tunnels like phantom limbs, like the catacombs and the Mortem within them were part of her. Sometimes Lore thought that if you peeled off her skin and turned it inside out, there'd be a map on the slick underside, pressed into the meat of her.

With a sigh, she leaned against the side of the building. She was a little earlier than Val had told her to be, and Val was nothing if not punctual.

A minute later, Val was striding down the street toward her, with the same determined gait that equally served for a casual stroll or a charge into a knife fight. A middle-aged woman more severe than traditionally pretty, with a paper-pale face, bottle-green eyes, and a scarf that had faded to near colorlessness holding back her gold hair.

Lore raised a hand in greeting. Val took hold of her fingers and pulled her into a hug instead. "You keeping out of trouble, mouse?"

"Only the kind you don't want me in." Lore hugged her back, the familiar scent of beeswax candles and whiskey a soothing weight in her lungs. Val and Mari had raised her since that day when she'd emerged from the dark into a world she didn't know. They'd protected her and given her purpose, even when it was a risk. Even when the effects of her strange childhood had manifested in terrifying ways.

None of them talked about that, though.

Val snorted and straightened her arms, hands still on Lore's shoulders. Her gaze had always cut like a scalpel, and now was no different. "I'm pulling you out," she said with no preamble.

Lore's brow knit. "What?"

"We have all the info we need on Gilbert's outfit; if he's moving as much contraband this week as you say, he won't be running poison for much longer, anyway. There's always a rush of religious feeling after a royal Consecration. The Presque Mort might be distracted now, but after that ceremony, they'll have their noses to the ground like you won't believe."

For all that Lore loved her surrogate mothers, there was no denying that they were cutthroat. Val and Mari had visions of being the only poison suppliers in Dellaire—once they were, they'd be nigh untouchable. Bloodcoats took any bribe you threw at them, and even the Presque Mort and the rest of the Church turned their backs sometimes. The criminal underbelly of Auverraine was only criminal until the right amount of gold crossed the right palm.

Still, Lore shook her head, telling herself that her reluctance to leave was a business decision that had nothing to do with Michal. "I don't think that's a good idea. There's still more I can learn."

One pale eyebrow rose. Val cocked her head, that scalpel look delving deeper. "You like him."

"No." Yes. "That doesn't have anything to do with it."

"Oh, mouse." Val sighed. "I've told you before. You have to keep yourself apart."

But she was *always* apart. The power in her veins, the awful things she was capable of kept her always, always apart. And it was nice to let the pieces of herself that could be liked—loved, even—have just a little comfort, sometimes.

Val patted her on the shoulder again. "It's for the best, Lore. Trust me." A pause, her teeth digging into the corner of her bottom lip. "It's all for the best."

And she was right. Val always was. Lore sighed, nodded.

It wouldn't be difficult. She had scripts for this, lists of excuses she'd given other lovers over the years, lovers she'd similarly been cautioned against taking when she infiltrated their lives to find the secrets of their employers. There was the sick aunt she had to tend, the jealous spouse who'd finally found her, the sudden desire to move to a new city and start over. Typically, the excuses weren't questioned, and Dellaire was big enough that she rarely saw those people again. On the rare occasions she did, they didn't notice her. Lore kept her affairs quick, and poison runners moved on even quicker.

"Tell me about this drop," Lore said, eager to change the subject.

"It's simple." Val's eyes flicked away from Lore's. "Normally, I wouldn't bother you with it. But the client requested that the boxes be left at the catacombs entrance in the Northwest Ward's market square."

"So you need me to watch it and make sure no one comes near before the client can pick it up." Vagrants often used the outer tunnels of the catacombs to move around Dellaire. Leaving anything in them was a risk.

"Shouldn't take long," Val said. "If you leave now and cut by the dock roads, you should get there by the time the guard is changing. It'll be chaos, since it's the day before a royal Consecration. Jean-Paul is bringing the contraband to the square, and if he arrives during the changeover, he should be able to slip through without getting searched. Then you can help him unload."

Get to the square, unload the drop, watch the poison until it gets picked up. Clients didn't like to leave their contraband sitting for long, so she shouldn't have to be there for more than an hour. Then she could go back to Michal's row house, jump in the rusty claw-foot tub to wash off the itchy feeling of being near the catacombs, and decide which of her lies she was going to use to break whatever they'd built between them.

She gave Val a decisive nod. "I'll head that way, then."

The old poison runner watched her for a moment, expression unreadable. Then she pulled her forward again, a crushing hug that made Lore nearly yelp in surprise.

"We love you like our own daughter," she murmured into Lore's hair. "Mari and I do. You know that, right?"

Bewildered, Lore nodded, though she couldn't move her head much. "Of course I do."

"And whatever we do, we do it because we have to." Val stepped back, keeping her hands on Lore's shoulders, her green eyes uncharacteristically soft. "I'm sorry to make you leave him, mouse."

Lore jerked another nod, swallowing past the curious tightness in her throat.

One more squeeze of her shoulders, then Val let her go. "Now get on with you," she said. "Don't want to be late." She turned and started walking back the way she'd come.

Lore closed her eyes. Sighed, the sound of it shaking only slightly. Then she turned and headed in the opposite direction, toward the dock roads.

❦

The dock roads were a mistake. Lore had barely gone a mile before she caught a glimpse of gilt on the horizon, and at a mile and a half, it became clear that preparations for the Sun Prince's Consecration had overtaken nearly all of the street space between here and the Northwest Ward. Colorful stalls lined the usually deserted paths, hawking figurines of the Bleeding God and greenish-copper replicas of the Sainted King's sun-rayed crown. Bloodcoats in their crimson jackets milled around the growing crowd with shining bayonets, and Lore even saw one or two Presque Mort, clothed head-to-toe in oppressive black.

"Stupid," she hissed beneath her breath. "Gods-damned *stupid* to do a drop right before a Consecration."

She could probably weave through the crowd, but it'd take time to work around the traffic, and that would leave the contraband sitting unattended. With a string of curses, Lore turned around and started jogging back toward the building where she'd met Val.

If she couldn't go overland, the only way to get to the drop site on time was to go through the catacombs.

Shit.

The dagger at her hip was a comforting weight as Lore ducked cautiously beneath the sagging door's lintel, keeping an eye out for revenants. Revenants weren't really a threat, made slow by the physical effects of too much poison and too-long lives, but Lore still wasn't keen on meeting one. They tended to congregate around entrances to the catacombs, and her inconvenient talent only told her if someone was actually inside the tunnels.

There was always the risk of encountering leaking Mortem around catacomb entrances, too, which made going near them at best unpleasant, at worst dangerous. Unchanneled Mortem could eat straight through a body, and at the rate it leaked from the Buried Goddess's corpse beneath the Citadel, sometimes there was too much for the Church to handle, even with the Presque Mort.

Thinking of the Mort made Lore's mouth tighten. The elite cadre of Mortem-using monks had been created specifically to channel all the leaking Mortem and keep it from overwhelming Dellaire, but sometimes there was simply too much. And then there was the problem of what to do with it. Presque Mort usually channeled Mortem back into stone, since it was already dead matter, but it opened sinkholes all over the roads. Dellaire's dead goddess issue was hell on infrastructure.

The other option was to channel Mortem into something living, usually plants—rumor was they had a garden full of stone flowers and rock-hewn trees. When the leaks got especially bad, the Presque Mort sometimes had to turn to the farmlands, razing entire fields, though a leak that dire hadn't happened in ages.

The catacomb entrance was toward the back of the building, over a collection of graffitied rock and broken floorboards. Someone had helpfully painted a face with *X*s over its eyes on the wall, with an arrow pointing the way.

Lore didn't need the direction. The farther she went, the more her skin buzzed, her innate knowledge of the underground kicking to life with a sickly lurch. This close, if she shut her eyes, she could see the black lines of the catacombs in her head—a tangled maze of tunnels overlaying her thoughts, tinting them dark.

The effect always unsettled her, so she tried very hard not to blink as she approached the dilapidated door, taking deep breaths in through her nose and out through her mouth to keep her mind clear. Pushing a poison lode into the catacombs to get picked up was one thing; it was wholly another to walk through them, to feel them pressing down from all sides. It made the moon-shaped burn mark on her palm ache, and was distraction enough that she didn't notice the person behind her until they were too close for her to escape.

An arm curled around Lore's neck, the bite of dirty fingernails in her skin chased with the sweet, herbaceous scent of belladonna. Choking out a curse, Lore brought up her elbow, jabbing it backward into a frame that felt horribly bony.

Revenant, had to be. They always looked like walking corpses.

The revenant laughed, a breathy, wheezing sound that brought another waft of poisonous flower scent. The arm fell away, their slight weight lurching back—Lore spun on her heel, dagger drawn and held against the grimy throat.

Definitely a revenant, and one that should've been dead long ago. Skeleton-thin, not many teeth left, eyes sunken inches into a face the color of a fish belly and crossed with stone-gray veins. Too emaciated to make a guess at their sex. The revenant wheezed another laugh, and Lore could see the work of their lungs through their skin, laborious in a body that was more rock than flesh.

"Thought you'd hide, did you?" The revenant's lips parted in a rictus grin. Their bottom lip split, but no fluid came out. "I could smell the death on you miles away, sweetling. Such a wealth of it. How are you so hale, so whole? A girl born to house oblivion shouldn't be so."

"Guess the mind goes quick even when the body lingers," Lore hissed.

The revenant laughed, a rough, painful sound. "I got close, a few times. So close to being able to touch eternity." One shoulder lifted, fell. "I never quite got there. But you...you have that power without even trying. How novel. How rare." Chipped yellow teeth, bared in a smile. "They should've killed you when they had the chance."

Lore's knees locked. The tip of her dagger wavered.

"I went down there, you know." The revenant smiled again. "Wandered for days. They're filling up, all nice neat rows, ready for the war."

Nonsensical rambling, the obvious sign of a mind long-gone. She felt briefly sorry for the should-be corpse, and it broke her murderous resolve. Lore sheathed her dagger and started back toward the door, legs slightly shaky. She could run. If she ran the whole way, she might be only a few minutes late to the rendezvous point.

Behind her, another laugh, a creak as the revenant laid their skeletal body on the floor. "Run, run, sweetling," they sang softly. "You can't outrun yourself."

❦

She knew she was too late before she even saw the guards.

They were hard to miss. The Protectors of the Citadel wore bright-red doublets and kept their bayonets polished to a shine, clean enough that one might doubt how many people met the business end. Lore knew better—they weren't called *bloodcoats* for nothing. She also knew that with her hair tucked beneath a cap and her generous curves hidden in loose boy's clothing, she could escape their notice as long as she kept her head down. Clearly, the guard had already changed, and she could only hope Jean-Paul had made it through while the checkpoint was unmanned.

The crowd here was even thicker than it'd been on the dock roads. Lore stood on tiptoe to watch the gate, searching for Jean-Paul's distinctive red hair and the large, placid horse they used for drops within Ward limits. She couldn't see him, and had to fight down a growing knot of panic in her middle as she made her way to the old storefront where they were supposed to leave the contraband. Maybe he'd already gone through the checkpoint, maybe he was waiting for her there...

Lore rounded the last corner before the old storefront came into view. Scarlet jackets, polished guns. A cart carrying mostly empty boxes. Jean-Paul's red hair. He looked up to see her, a stocky middle-aged white man who'd been running for Val since before Lore came along, and though his expression was carefully neutral, fear sheened his eyes and made them nearly animal.

Too late, too late, too late.

For a moment, Lore couldn't do anything but stand there. As one of the guards turned toward her, she ducked into an alley, pressing her back against the grimed brick, breathing hard enough to sting her throat.

"Shit," she spat, quick and hoarse. "*Shit.*"

Holding her breath, Lore peered out of the alleyway. It looked like Jean-Paul had made it through the checkpoint without being searched, but then the bloodcoats had realized their error and caught him right when he reached the storefront. Even if she'd gotten here on time, it wouldn't have made a difference.

Jean-Paul, to his credit, managed to keep that calm expression even as the bloodcoats poked through the boxes. The big man had his hands in his pockets and rocked back and forth on his feet, a simple trader just waiting for the search to be over. He kept his head tipped down under the brim of his hat to hide his terrified eyes.

She should abandon him. She knew that. It was one of Val's earliest lessons. If a job went south, it was every man for himself.

But she couldn't make herself run. Jean-Paul had a husband and a young son, and if he was caught, he'd be sent to the Burnt Isles. Lore couldn't just leave someone to a fate like that.

"Shit." Lore cursed one final time, landing hard on the *t*, then ducked out of the alley and into the crowd.

The bloodcoats didn't pay her any attention as she sidled up, as inconspicuous as she could manage. One of them, a burly man with a curling mustache beneath his small, pale nose, held up a dummy box full of nearly sprouting potatoes and cocked an eyebrow. "If you were making my deliveries, old man," he sneered, "I'd be very concerned you were skimming them."

The boxes with the contraband were always on the top. The bloodcoats never expected it, always checked the boxes on the bottom first, assuming the poison would be as hidden as possible. That way, if you were found in the middle of a job, chances were the lode had already been moved to the drop point.

"Alaric needed boxes," Jean-Paul said, deadpan. Alaric was the name they always used if stopped and asked whose business they were about. "Wanted to store something. The potatoes were just to hold them down on the cart."

All the boxes were off the cart now. Curly Mustache's cohorts started poking through the new ones. One, opened, full of nothing but more mealy potatoes. Two. Three.

"You're telling me a merchant hired a cart to haul boxes of old potatoes from the Southwest Ward to the Northwest?"

Six boxes left. Three of them held mandrake. Sweat slicked Lore's back.

"Not my concern how he spends his coin," Jean-Paul answered.

A fifth box opened. If Lore was going to do something, it had to be now. She just didn't know what. There were too many of them to take with a dagger, especially once she lost the element of surprise, and she'd never been much good at brawling.

A creeping feeling began in her palms, the tips of her fingers.

Pins and needles, an acute awareness. Mortem waited in the stone beneath her feet, the brick and dead wood of the storefront, the cart, the poison waiting in the still-hidden mandrake. It was a low hum, a string she could grasp and pull, and it'd be so easy…

A bloodcoat reached for a sixth box, the end of his bayonet cracking open the lid. In the shadows beneath, Lore saw green.

She rushed forward, banishing the call of Mortem, speaking before she even knew what words were on her tongue. "You found them!"

Jean-Paul and Curly Mustache turned toward her, the bloodcoat she'd interrupted looking up with a curious wrinkle in his forehead. She snatched the box, open lid pressed to her chest. "Father sent me, I'm so sorry I'm late."

Curly Mustache cocked his head. "Would your father perhaps be Alaric, girl?"

Damn her breasts. She thought this shirt would be baggy enough to obscure them, but she'd never had the kind of chest that was hidden easily. "Yes," Lore said, standing up straighter, making her smile wider. "He's been so upset, I've broken too many jars trying to load them one by one, we need the boxes immediately…"

She backed up as she spoke, rapid-fire words and smiles, inching the contraband closer to the old storefront. The trapdoor inside would lead to the catacombs, and the uncanny map in her head said the tunnels nearby were empty. If she could just get the boxes through the door—

Her foot hit a pebble and slipped sideways, throwing her off balance. The box tumbled from her hands.

Mandrake carved a green swath over the cobblestones.

For a moment, they all stood in tableau, Jean-Paul and Lore and the bloodcoats and the big, placid horse Val kept only for poison running, the one Lore affectionately called Horse because no one had ever actually named him.

Then, a heartbeat, and with a cry of triumph, Curly Mustache charged forward.

"*Run!*" Lore threw herself sideways toward the mouth of the alley where she'd hidden, drawing her dagger. Her foot twisted beneath her, made her fall to her knees, the *crack* of it whiting out her vision. Gloved hands closed roughly on her shoulders, hauled her up.

The bloodcoats were a chaos, and Horse responded, rearing and upsetting the cart, sending it careening toward onlookers. Jean-Paul yelled wordlessly, trying to grab Horse's bridle. The creature's whinny sharpened in fear, hooves slicing at the morning sky as bloodcoats surrounded them. Jean-Paul dove for the reins, but he wasn't fast enough to wheel Horse around and away; a bayonet ripped through the animal's throat, and it collapsed into a heap of shuddering meat.

Lore's vision was still watery as she tried to throw a punch at the bloodcoat holding her, swiping out with her dagger blade between the fingers of her fist. Another bloodcoat caught her arm and twisted it back hard enough for her to feel the bones grind, a breath away from breaking. A harsh, choked noise erupted from her throat, a cry aborted by the bayonet's cold muzzle, the pointed end grazing her windpipe. Three of them had her now—two holding her arms, and one with a gun. Not very good odds.

The pricking feeling sparked in her palms again, cold awareness slithering through her limbs.

"Move and I'll shoot," the bloodcoat with the bayonet snarled. "And a shot through the neck doesn't make for a quick end."

Her fingers trembled, the Mortem seeping out from the catacombs and Horse's dying body making them itch. Lore hadn't channeled it in thirteen years, had pressed it all into the back of her mind and left it there to rot. But now, the awareness of it nearly drowned her.

Awareness, and instinct. Her hands burned with the desire to call Mortem up from every dead place where it waited, to channel it through her body and make it do her bidding. Resisting made her head light, her breathing shallow.

Half the bloodcoats went for the spilled mandrake, but their leader was focused only on Jean-Paul. He caught him by the arm; Jean-Paul tried to go for the hidden dagger in his coat, hands stained with Horse's viscera—*poor Horse*—but the bloodcoat brought the bayonet end to his throat before he could reach it.

"Don't make me fire," the bloodcoat snarled through his bloody mustache. "They could use someone like you in the mines on the Burnt Isles." A guttural laugh. "Your girl, too. She looks strong enough for a shovel."

A bullet would be preferable to the mines. Lore had heard of more than one poison runner who slit their own throat rather than be made to live the rest of a cut-short life in the dark and dust of the Burnt Isles.

Dark. Dust. Death. All of it swirled around her, coppery blood and an emptiness that abraded her sinuses. Black mist rose from Horse's body, coalescing into dark threads that only a channeler could see, seeping from the eyes, the slack mouth. Mortem. Calling to her.

Use it.

Lore didn't know if it was truly a voice she heard, or just the firing of her own brain, desperate to do *something*, to use whatever it could.

A distraction, that's what they needed. Something that would allow her to run, something awful enough to pull the bloodcoats' focus so Jean-Paul could escape. It was too late for her. Lore was caught, and what she did in these next few moments wouldn't change that.

The choice was between the Burnt Isles or a pyre. In the end, it didn't make that much difference, if it meant Jean-Paul could go back to his family.

Distraction it was, then. And as soon as Lore made the decision, her body went to work.

She took a deep breath and held it in her lungs, letting instinct take over, drive her as it had before. She'd been born to this, to the magic and the dark, and every part of her but her mind was eager.

One moment everything was bright and lurid, and the next she saw only the barest impression of her surroundings, the world cloaked in grayscale as her lungs began to burn, her body tipped toward death. The bloodcoats and Jean-Paul and the living bodies of the crowd were all surrounded in auras of white light. The outline around Horse's corpse leaked slowly from white to black, life leaving as death took over. Threads of Mortem waved in the air like spider legs, the black corona of an inverted sun.

Lore didn't look down at herself as she slowly let her breath out, keeping her grip on Mortem strong, because she was in it now and the current of instinct had pulled her under. She knew what she looked like—her fingers cold and corpse-pale, her eyes shifting from hazel to opaque white. On her palm, the moon-shaped scar blazed like a beacon, a black glow that was the absence of light and yet so bright it hurt to look at. Over her heart, a knot of darkness swirled, a black star of emptiness hidden beneath her shirt.

She knew what she looked like, and it was death walking.

Her hands curled, pulling the dark matter that was the power of death inward, as if her Mortem-touched heart were a magnet. The threads waving over Horse's body shuddered, then flowed toward her. They braided in the air and attached to her fingers, magic easily breaching the barrier of her skin.

Horse's death danced down her veins, swirled through her like tainted blood. Lore channeled the Mortem quickly through her system, pushing it through every vein like a half-frozen winter stream, fighting against her flagging heartbeat, her gone-shallow breath. Death magic circled her every organ, pausing them all, like frost on a bud at the edge of spring.

This was the part that was supposed to make you live longer, freezing your insides so they moved slower in time, so the years touched you more gently. Those who took poison couldn't channel the death it brought to them back out, couldn't make it do anything but curdle them into twisted immortality as it awakened the dormant Mortem in their bodies. To channel Mortem, you had to embrace death like a lover and hope it let you go, and hardly anyone ever got that far, not on purpose.

At least, that's what Lore assumed. She'd been born with this. Born with death beside her like a shadow.

Slowly, slowly, Lore pushed the Mortem she'd channeled through herself back to her hands, like gathering fistfuls of black thread. Then she thrust all the death she'd taken back out.

Mortem arced from her fingers, death eager for a new home, and Lore had just enough presence of mind to direct it to a flower bed in the center of the road, already browned and limp from an unseasonable lack of rain. The blooms withered and dropped, the roots that held them up going dead and brittle, all of it turning gray. More Mortem cut into the rock, sending cracks spider-webbing beneath scrambling feet. It didn't open into a sinkhole, thank every god dead or dying, but still screams rose into the air.

Her heart seized in her chest, just once, tithing a beat. The instinct that had seized her ebbed away, leaving only fear and panic and disgust.

And with a grunting, pained sound, Horse stood up.

CHAPTER THREE

Death, for mortals, is inviolable: Any who would raise a body from the dead is guilty of the worst heresy and must be executed, so they may suffer forever in their own hell.

–The Book of Mortal Law, Tract 1

Cedric had been a year older than Lore, fourteen and worldly as a prince for it. The son of a runner on Val and Mari's team, he'd been the only child Lore spent much time around, in those months after Mari found her. Warm and kind, with wide brown eyes and messy hair that was always falling in his face. He'd taught her to swim down by the docks.

Then he got run down by a bloodcoat's horse during a raid.

His body was a horror. Lore remembered it in vivid detail. Things sunken where they shouldn't be, other things sticking up, making tents of torn flesh and valleys of mashed bone and organ. But his face had been untouched, those brown eyes staring into the sky as if transfixed.

She hadn't thought. She just acted, gave in to instinct. Lore had wound Cedric's death around her fingers like the games of cat's cradle he'd taught her to play, spun it out of him and into her. She'd channeled it through her body and sent it down into the rock, down to where the roots of trampled grasses strove toward the sun, planting his death in the earth instead of in his body.

And he'd sat up. There'd been a terrible sound when he did— nothing within him was where it was supposed to be, and all of it *squished*—but he'd sat up, then turned to look at her. His eyes weren't brown anymore. They were black, without iris or pupil.

It was clear he wasn't going to do anything until she told him to; he was an automaton that needed winding up, needed direction. So she'd taken the ball of string they used for cat's cradle from her pocket. "Play with me."

That was how Val found them. A girl and a dead boy with thread woven through their fingers, acting as though nothing was amiss.

It was honestly astonishing that Val hadn't killed her then. After seeing what she was. What she could do.

And it was with that memory flashing through her head that Lore watched Horse rise from the ground, clearly dead and yet moving. Animals were different from people, apparently. She hadn't had to tell Horse what to do.

"Shit." It came out of her mouth thin and breathy; Lore's legs felt like limp pieces of string, the death she'd channeled manifesting in numb limbs and a straw-thin throat. She fell to her knees, the cold tip of the bloodcoat's bayonet slipping away from her neck with a slight scratch, not deep enough to draw blood. "Shit on the *Citadel Wall*."

For a second, Lore thought her dear-bought distraction was pointless—the bloodcoats still held her and Jean-Paul, not sparing so much as a glance for the horse rising from the dead in the center of the market square. She'd given in, succumbed to the call of Mortem, and for what?

A broken, furious sound wrenched from her mouth.

The bloodcoat holding her arms tried to haul her back up, but then he caught a look at her eyes, still death-white and opaque. Lore watched him take in her blackened veins and corpse-like fingers, watched the color slowly drain from his face as he put together what it all meant. The guard retreated until his spine met brick, his hands springing open to release her. "Bleeding God save us," he muttered in a tone of quick-rising panic. "Bleeding God save us!"

That was more like it.

The other bloodcoats finally noticed the undead livestock situation. Curly Mustache slashed at the animal's now-fully-risen corpse, but Horse didn't mind, being already dead. If anything, he seemed curious, nuzzling at his gore-caked shoulder with a bloody nose, neck hanging open like a second mouth. The long lashes around his opaque eyes fluttered, dislodging a fly that had landed there.

"Sorry, Horse," Lore mumbled, then heaved up her coffee on the cobblestones.

When she looked up, Curly Mustache was staring at her, at all the ways channeling Mortem had made her monstrous, his face gone nearly as pale as her own.

"Heresy," he said, voice hoarse from shouting. "*Evil!*"

"Melodrama." Lore's lips felt numb, and so did the rest of her.

Chaos erupted then, as if time had suspended for the few seconds after Lore raised Horse from the dead and now had returned to normal. Curly Mustache brandished his bayonet, bellowing for backup, ordering his company to surround the horse and apprehend the deathwitch.

It took Lore a moment to realize that was her. *Deathwitch* was what they'd called necromancers, back before everyone who could channel that much Mortem had been executed or sent to the Burnt Isles. Now there was only her. A deathwitch alone.

Channeling Mortem left her fingers waxy and pale, her skin

nearly translucent, the tracery of her sluggish veins an easy map against her skin—she looked worse than a revenant, which was really saying something. Strands of death tied her to Horse, a dark braid that could be seen only from the corner of her eye, when she didn't look directly at it.

With a sharp, snarling sound, Lore snapped her hands to fists. The strands of Mortem severed, and the horse toppled, the power that had reanimated it slithering into the air like smoke, then dissipating. That's what she'd done with Cedric, when Val saw them, when Val screamed. It hadn't been intentional then. Lore was just startled, startled and scared, and she'd snapped the threads that held them together.

It'd seemed harder then. The raising and the ending. This time, with Horse, she'd barely had to try. Channeling the Mortem out of the body had come to her so naturally, stealing death and sending it away.

The animal's heavy corpse fell on a group of bloodcoats, dead meat once again. The crunch of bone and pained shouts echoed through the Ward, cut through with the screams of onlookers. The guards had forgotten about Lore and Jean-Paul; she saw the lick of his red hair as he disappeared into an alleyway. Curly Mustache had turned around when Horse fell, and the surge of people between him and Lore had carried him away, made him lose her in the crowd. Lore could hear him shouting, but she couldn't see him.

She'd certainly gotten the distraction she wanted. Now if she could just make herself *move.*

Lore levered herself up from the ground on legs that tingled with pins and needles, cursing as she tried to hobble away. Memories of Cedric crashed through the mental barriers she'd trapped them behind, made the past and the present muddle, awful and infinite. She limped as fast as she could into the narrow space between two storefronts, huddling into the shadows. In a moment of clarity, she pulled the cap from her head and let her hair tumble free, twisted the hem of her shirt and tucked it in her trousers so it molded to her curves. Not really a disguise, but it made her look different than she had at the moment she'd raised the horse, and it might buy her enough anonymity to get away.

Someone grabbed her arm.

Lore turned with a snarl in her teeth, hand already raising to strike at whoever had touched her.

Michal.

Clearly, he hadn't expected what he saw when she turned around; he'd seen her running to the alley, but not made the connection between her and Horse. Now she watched every piece of the puzzle lock into place, played out across his features: blue eyes narrowing before going wide and horrified. He glanced over his shoulder at the square, mouth dropping open, a flinch shuddering through his hand before it jerked back from her, fingers splayed.

"Sorry," Lore muttered, her tongue suddenly thick. "I'm sorry."

She shoved past him, out into the square again. Turned down the first alley she came to. Started running and didn't stop, her head down and her vision blurred, picking directions at random and thinking only of *away*.

So when one of the Presque Mort stepped out of a trash-strewn alcove in front of her, she nearly ran right into him.

He loomed over her, hands outstretched, the image of a lit candle inked into each palm. His black clothing fit close to a muscular body, one blue eye gleaming at her, the other covered by the dark leather of an eye patch.

There was something almost familiar about him, a sense that she'd met him before. But that was ludicrous. Lore didn't know any of the Presque Mort, or any other members of the clergy, for that matter.

Not anymore.

"Of *course* the Presque Mort would show up," Lore spat as she stumbled away from the inked hands, fumbling for her dagger again. "Of fucking course."

The Presque Mort didn't respond, just watched her as she turned to run in the opposite direction, trying to backtrack the way she'd come and pick a new route. He whistled, a low note rising higher, and it was echoed by others, ringing off the stone, clear above the grown-distant cacophony of the Ward.

They had her cornered.

The first monk moved slowly forward, tattooed hands held out like she was an unfamiliar dog he didn't want to frighten away. Unusually tall, with a crop of shorn reddish-blond hair and broad shoulders, handsomeness wasted on someone with vows of celibacy.

"We don't want to hurt you." Deep voice, clipped tones, like this refuse-lined alley was a Citadel ballroom.

"You have a funny way of showing it." Lore's feet stuttered over uneven cobblestones as she backed away, nearly sending her stumbling.

The Presque Mort made no response. Others dressed in the same plain, dark clothing emerged from the two mouths of the alley, moving slowly, implacably forward. Too many to fight off, and now there was no livestock to reanimate and call their attention.

Lore's legs buckled; she braced her still-numb hand on the wall. Even predisposed to death magic as she was, the recovery was a bitch.

So distracted was she that when the tall Presque Mort pulled a cloth from his pocket, she didn't have time to react before it was pressed over her airways. Chloroform. There was something almost funny about it, pedestrian chemicals in a city famous for romantic, flowery poisons.

"We don't want to hurt you," he murmured, "but we do need you to come with us, and something tells me you won't do it consciously."

"Whatever gave you that idea?" Lore slurred, then all the world went dark.

The bindings felt familiar; the rasp of rope on her skin was like an echo. For a moment she smelled stone and burning skin. For a moment she was sure there was nothing but tunnels and pale torchlight beyond the veil of her eyelids, an obsidian tomb and hazel eyes that matched her own.

So when Lore opened her eyes and saw a cell, it was almost a relief.

Someone had stuffed a gag in her mouth—it tasted sour, like it'd been used to clean up spilled wine. One rope bound her ankles to the legs of the chair where she sat, another bound her wrists together behind her back, and yet another connected the two. Whoever had tied her up had left enough slack that she wasn't painfully contorted, but there was no chance in any of the myriad hells that she could get out of the chair unassisted.

And all of it—the chair, the bindings, the stone walls—all of it felt like death.

Lore gasped against her gag, pulling the fabric farther back in her throat, making her choke as she pressed her eyes closed. Usually, she could deal with her awareness of Mortem in dead matter. She had to; there was no escaping it. But something had changed when she raised Horse, and now it pressed in on her from all sides, heavy and thick, bearing down with a suffocating weight.

Worse than the rock and rope, things that had never lived, were the things that *did*. The minuscule threads of grass pushing against the cracks in the floor, the people close enough for her senses to pick them up, her own body—alive, for now, but she could feel each individual cell as it collapsed, an eternity in microcosm—

Had this happened after Cedric? If it had, she didn't remember it. It seemed like getting older had made the raising easier and the side effects worse.

Swallowing hard, Lore opened her eyes again, making herself actually look at her surroundings.

Not a cell, technically. Just a bare stone room, with the chair she was bound to and a wooden table as the only furniture. On the wall hung a tapestry, its vibrancy made garish for being the only spot of color. The tapestry depicted a man with gleaming brown hair and milk-pale skin, blood-smeared hands outstretched, blood seeping from a gaping wound in His chest and dripping into the mass of darkness below Him. In the background was something that looked like a fountain, edged in gold, and above the man's head, a message was picked out in silver-gilt thread.

Apollius, may we hold fast Your Citadel, protecting the world from Death and living in purity until Your return, when the world shall rise in the Light of a New Age.

The nebulous form below Apollius's feet appeared to be a shadow at first glance. But if you looked closely, you could almost pick out the shape of a woman, see where the weaver had used threads of varying darkness to suggest a moon-crowned head, feminine curves. The Bleeding God's feet were directly above the points of the vague woman-shape's crescent crown, turned on Her forehead so the points speared up like horns. It gave the impression of the god stomping Her into the earth.

The Buried Goddess, Nyxara.

The Church, then. Of course the Presque Mort had brought her to the Church.

The thought made panic spike anew. The one who'd drugged her said they meant her no harm, but that could be semantics, a cruel game. The Presque Mort might not be authorized to execute her themselves, but the Priest Exalted certainly was. Or maybe the King would want to do the honors. It'd been ages since they'd had a real necromancer to burn. All of them had been killed in the year of the Godsfall and the decade afterward, when Mortem leaked from the Buried Goddess's body like blood from an arterial wound.

A deep breath, an attempt to quell the fear. She wondered how her captors might react if she asked for chloroform again. A drugged sleep was preferable to this churn of anxiety, especially when her fate was all but sealed.

Her stomach gurgled, hunger making it twist in on itself. How long had she been down here? There were no windows, nothing to help her mark the time, but the stiffness of her limbs and the emptiness of her stomach made her think it'd been hours.

Lore barely reacted when the Presque Mort filed in, only two of them: the one who'd drugged her and another she didn't recognize, with a shaved head and walnut-brown arms marked in deep, silvery scars.

The one with the scarred arms looked her way and cocked a brow. "You might've gone overboard with that chloroform, Gabriel. She looks a moment away from losing her lunch."

"I didn't use that much." The tall Presque Mort—Gabriel, apparently—looked curiously at her from his one working eye, then grimaced at the air. "It's still so thick in here, even after a day."

A *day*? Gods dead and dying, she'd been knocked out for a whole day?

"She channeled so much..." Gabriel turned to his companion. "Do you feel it?"

The other's expression darkened. "A bit," he said, almost begrudgingly. "Not as much as you do. Some of us have to pay our dues in Dellaire, instead of out in one of the country monasteries. We're used to Mortem being thick here."

There was a bite of defensiveness to his tone, for all that it sounded like he'd meant it as a joke. Gabriel raised a candle-inked hand. "I meant no offense, Malcolm."

"None taken," Malcolm replied. He rubbed his scarred arms and scoffed good-naturedly, as if trying to lift the mood. "If I'd had to spend my entire training period in one of the country monasteries, I would've gone raving mad with boredom. I nearly did in just the two months a year I *did* have to spend there."

"They certainly aren't barrels of fun," Gabriel agreed. "Though the two days I've spent in the city have me wishing to return."

"You're on your own there. The library in Dellaire is far superior."

"And we all know that's what you care about," Gabriel snorted. "Don't worry, we'll finish this quickly and you can get back to your true love."

"Good. I only agreed to come along since we're short-staffed. Running about the Wards doesn't agree with my constitution."

Gabriel turned his attention back to Lore, a thoughtful crease to his brow. "I think that's the problem here," he said softly, with an air that could be mistaken for sympathy if Lore didn't know better. "If we can sense so much Mortem, imagine what *she* can sense."

"Too much," Lore tried to say, though it came out garbled from behind her gag.

It startled them both, made them flinch back, as if she were a piece of furniture that had suddenly decided to speak. For her part, Lore was barely aware that she'd managed to make a sound. Her head was full of death, her nerves vibrating against the onslaught of so much entropy.

Gabriel nodded, as if something had been decided. Malcolm just looked more confused. "I don't understand," he said slowly. "Does it...can it hurt you? Some of the others report discomfort, but all I ever get it a little numbness—"

"It can hurt," Gabriel said, almost rueful. "It can really, really hurt."

Something flashed across Malcolm's face, halfway between fear and jealousy. He rubbed at his scarred arms again.

Gabriel crossed the room and knelt by Lore's chair. Even on his knees, the top of his head was nearly level with her nose, and his short hair wafted a scent of Church incense. That taut feeling in her middle pulled tight again, that sense that she knew him, somehow.

Gently, he reached behind her head, untied the gag so it fell out of her mouth. "Listen to me," he said quietly, a command. "The sense of death, it's all in your head. You can block it out."

"How?" Her mouth still tasted like sour cotton. Behind Gabriel, Malcolm stood with his arms crossed, expression equal parts intrigued and disturbed.

"It's *your* head." His one-eyed gaze was stern. "Nothing can stay there unless you let it. You make it leave." The words came out like a lesson often repeated.

Lore tried to laugh, but panic still had its teeth in her, and it sounded more like the start of a sob. "You're gonna have to give me step-by-step instructions, Mort."

He nodded smoothly, like this was a perfectly normal request. "Imagine a wall. Make it a thick one, soundproof. Imagine a barrier around your mind until it's so solid you feel like you could touch it. And then don't let the sense of death in. There's no way to *not* be aware of it, not when you can channel so much Mortem. But it doesn't have to take you over. It doesn't have to rule you."

It sounded too simple, but desperate times and all that. Closing her eyes tight, Lore imagined a wall. At first it was stone, and she quickly discarded it—she'd had enough stone walls to last a lifetime, and stone was dead, and she'd had enough of that, too. So trees, instead, thick trunks growing close.

Lore had never seen a forest up close. Her power wouldn't let her get too far from the catacombs, and there were certainly no forests in Dellaire, just ornamental copses of manicured trees in some of the more affluent districts. But she could imagine a forest, a real one, full of green and growth.

So her mental barrier wasn't a wall, exactly. It was just her, in the middle of a forest. A peaceful one, with a blue sky beyond the leaves, and the bizarrely comforting scent of a fire. It felt natural for her head to settle here, like this forest had been waiting for her.

Slowly, the sense of imminent death crowding all around her faded away, became the background buzz she was used to.

Lore opened her eyes. The Presque Mort stared into them with a gaze made fiercer for having only one outlet. His right eye was very, very blue.

"Thank you." She wanted to say something cutting. She should—helping her before turning her over to a pyre was a special kind of cruel. But the *thank you* was all Lore could muster.

Gabriel nodded, once. "It'll be a useful tool for you."

She huffed that half laugh again. "I don't think I'm going to get another chance to channel much Mortem before I get executed for necromancy."

His brow furrowed over his eye patch, an expression she couldn't quite make out, but he didn't comment on her fate. Instead he held up the gag. "This was on the Priest Exalted's orders." Apology was thick in his tone. "I'm going to have to put it back."

She thought about fighting, but she was too tired. Lore nodded.

Carefully, Gabriel refastened the gag, though she noticed it was looser this time. Then he stood, towering over her, and stepped back to Malcolm. The other monk's face remained unreadable.

"Do you have to do that?" he murmured to Gabriel. "To . . . to make the awareness stop?" Malcolm's gaze darted to Gabriel's eye patch, then away, as if he was embarrassed.

"Sometimes. Anton taught me that trick with the wall. Right after my initiation." Gabriel paused, reaching up to itch at his eye patch. "Since my injury was nearly as severe as his own, he knew that the potential for me to channel large amounts of Mortem was high."

Malcolm shook his head and itched at his own eye, almost like an afterthought. "Damn."

Gabriel said nothing.

Lore cringed. The Presque Mort attained their power to channel Mortem the same way anyone else might: dying, just for a moment, and then coming back. Usually, it was due to accident, injury, or illness. Because channeling Mortem was against holy law, someone who'd survived such an experience had two choices—avoid Mortem as best they could, or join the Presque Mort. The manner of the near-death experience mattered, though. Those who'd sought death out—gone to deathdealers—weren't eligible, since the Presque Mort were technically part of the clergy.

In the first few years after the Godsfall, there'd been another option. There still *was* one, far beneath the earth, in the deepest tunnels of the catacombs. But no one talked about the Buried Watch anymore, not since the last Church-recognized Night Priestess went mad.

Malcolm jerked his thumb toward the door. "When should we expect him?"

"Any minute now." Gabriel crossed his arms. "He had to collect the informant first. So she could make sure we had the right one."

"We definitely have the right one," Malcolm scoffed.

Lore frowned, the expression twisted to grotesquerie by the gag. An informant?

The door opened. An older man with iron-gray hair and a long white robe glided in first, a golden pendant formed like a heart with sun's rays hanging around his neck, a large teardrop-shaped garnet at the heart's apex. He turned to face her, and Lore bit down on the gag, hard.

One side of the man's face was handsome, almost angelically so. But the other side was a mass of burn scars, dark purple with age, carving twisted runnels from chin to hairline and turning that side of his mouth to a permanent smirk.

She'd heard of this man's face, though she'd never seen it up close. The Priest Exalted, Anton Arceneaux, leader of the Church and the Presque Mort. King August's twin brother.

And behind him, a woman with graying blond hair under a familiar faded scarf. A woman who wouldn't look at Lore, even when she made a sharp, disbelieving sound behind her gag.

Val.

She must be dreaming. With all the drugs and Mortem still in her system, the Bleeding God Himself must somehow have reached into her brain to play out a nightmare.

Val flinched. "You didn't have to gag her," she snapped, eyes shooting daggers at the Priest Exalted. "Afraid she'll make fun of your face?"

The Priest Exalted simply arched his unscarred brow. "Supplicants are making prayers upstairs in the South Sanctuary." His voice was silk-smooth, cultured tones that made sense for the Sainted King's brother. "And the Church is more crowded than usual as we prepare for my nephew's Consecration this evening. I'd rather not have them disturbed."

"Then tell her you'll stick her if she makes noise." Val stood directly between the Bleeding God's tapestried hands on the wall, as if He was welcoming her home, reward for a job well done. "Don't *gag* her."

A pause, then the Priest Exalted—Anton—nodded. Gabriel moved behind Lore, untying the knot that held the gag in place.

"I'm sorry," he said quietly, then moved away.

Even ungagged, Lore didn't have anything to say. Words had left her. She just sat there, sore mouth agape, staring at Val.

Val, who still wouldn't look at her. "It's her," she sighed wearily. "Just like I said." Her piercing gaze went from the floor to Anton. "Is that all you needed?"

The Priest Exalted nodded once. "Your inventory will be returned to you," he said, "and the certificate of pardon can be picked up from the court justice in the Northwest Ward at your convenience." The side of his mouth that could move quirked up. "The first official crown-sanctioned poison runner. What an honor."

"Eat shit," Val muttered.

"Same to you," Lore spat. She knew how to bury sadness, but anger was a tool, fresh and near at hand. "So you're going to be a *privateer*, Val? You turned me over for a *contract*?"

She expected answering vitriol, but Val's shoulders sank. "I didn't have a choice. They knew about Cedric."

Her fingers were already numb from being tied behind her. But Val's words were enough to make that numbness spread up her spine, through her chest.

Val finally looked at her. Tears brimmed in her eyes. "Mouse, I—"

"Don't call me that." *Tunnel mouse*, Val had called her when she was young, for her hair that couldn't decide whether it was brown or blond and landed somewhere indiscriminate, for the place where Mari had found her, at the mouth of the catacombs. Even after Lore grew up, she was still *mouse*. "Does Mari know? Did she decide that a contract was worth killing me for, too?"

Val's chapped lips pressed flat, her eyes blinking closed before opening again. "I'll explain to Mari," she said quietly. "She'll understand."

"Good for her." The break in Lore's voice was too raw to hide. "Because I sure as fuck don't."

Val sighed. A pause, then she walked over, crouched next to the chair. She raised a hand like she would smooth Lore's hair away, but Lore jerked her head back. "I know what this looks like," Val said softly. "But, Lore, this could be an opportunity. This will keep you safer than Mari and I ever could."

Lore didn't say anything. She stared straight ahead, until the colors in the tapestry whirled together in her wet eyes. Finally, Val stepped away. The door shut softly behind her.

"For what it's worth," the Priest Exalted said, coming to sit before her in the chair Gabriel hastily provided, "none of us have lied to you. We don't want to hurt you, Lore."

"Then what do you want?" Her voice still sounded scraped-up, like her throat was made of rock. Lore swallowed.

A smile crinkled the handsome side of Anton's face. "We need assistance," he said. "And it appears you're the only one who can provide it."

CHAPTER FOUR

The one who can stab you quickest is the one to whom you give a knife.

–Kirythean proverb

Lore paused. Then she laughed.

It was a rough and rasping sound, her mouth still dry from the cotton gag. Lore hung her head and laughed until it ran the risk of becoming a sob.

"My help?" She shook her head, though it made her temples throb. The chloroform had knocked loose a bitch of a headache, worse than any hangover. "I'm sure I don't have to tell you, priest, but wanting *help* from an unsanctioned Mortem wielder is more than a little light heresy."

Anton's expression was almost amused, at least on the side of his face that could show expression. "Heresy can be forgiven, when it's for the greater good."

Behind Anton, Malcolm still stood with his scarred arms crossed, face unreadable. But at the word *heresy*, the line of Gabriel's mouth went flat.

"The Bleeding God knows our plight and gives us benediction

to do as we must in His service." All this in a low, pleasing baritone, as if Anton was reciting a prayer. Maybe he was; the Book of Prayer was thick as every hell and seemed to have an entry for everything. "Indeed, it is a vital part of the Presque Mort's work, the marrow to its bone. We submit ourselves to darkness, knowing that in the end all shadow will be eclipsed in light, as the Buried Goddess was eclipsed by the glory of the Bleeding God."

That didn't seem to have worked out so well, what with the Mortem still leaking from the goddess's dead body and all. "If you're asking me to join your cult," Lore said, "my answer is a resounding no."

It was Anton's turn to laugh, a sound as court-cultured as his speaking voice. "Oh, no," the Priest Exalted chuckled. "That's not what we want at all. It takes a person of a very...specific...temperament to make it as one of the Presque Mort."

She gave him a beatific smile. "And I'm too pretty."

Malcolm turned his face away, fighting down a smirk. Gabriel didn't react at all, that one blue eye blazing at her.

Anton raised a sardonic brow. "You are unscarred, yes. Clearly, your abilities with Mortem didn't come through an accident, not like ours did."

That skated a bit too close to close to the truth for her tastes— they might be willing to overlook her power if they needed her for something, but she'd like to avoid revealing where that power came from. Lore shifted in her chair. "What do you need me for, then?"

All the laughter was gone from Anton now, both the handsome and the scarred sides of his face stoic. "You've heard of the village, I presume."

Everyone had heard of the village by now. Lore nodded.

"And what exactly have you heard?"

"Not much." She lifted her hands behind her as much as she could against the ropes, twiddled her fingers. "I might remember more if you untied me."

Anton's placid expression didn't change. He waved a hand, and Gabriel stepped forward, ducking behind Lore's chair to cut the knots that held her. The Presque Mort moved silently, stiffly. She smelled incense again.

When she was free, Lore sat forward, working her wrists back and forth. Malcolm watched her warily, and she held up her hands like surrender. "No weapons. Relax."

He didn't. "It's not the weapons I'm concerned with."

"You've channeled Mortem before," Lore replied, opening and closing her fists. "You know it's no picnic. I'm not in a hurry to do it again."

Malcolm eyed her for a moment longer, then gave a begrudging nod.

Marginally less sore, Lore sat back. "I heard a whole village died overnight. Shademount, to the southeast." Shademount was one of the smaller villages in Auverraine, more an outpost than a proper town. It was the last Auverrani settlement before reaching what was formerly Balgia, a small duchy now part of the Kirythean Empire. Lore had never been there, obviously, but she'd had Shademount-brewed beer. It was very good. She guessed no one would be making it anymore. "The people had no marks on them, no sign of poisoning or sickness. They just look like they're asleep. Some think it's a sign of Apollius's disfavor."

"And what do you think it is?" Anton folded his fingers across his middle, like a teacher quizzing a student.

"Mostly, I think it's all rumors. Maybe one or two got sick and died in the night, maybe a whole farmhouse full, but a whole village? Horseshit."

"Not horseshit," Anton said levelly. Priest he might be, but he didn't stutter at all over the profanity. "Truth. All of it." A pause. "Though there have been two villages, now. It happened again two nights ago. Orlimar. Slightly bigger than Shademount, nearer Erocca than Balgia."

Another village on the southeastern border, close to another country conquered by the Empire. Lore swallowed.

Anton's eye glinted as he leveled an unreadable look her way, something vaguely sinister in the curve of his mouth. But it was gone quickly, covered by a mask of nondescript pleasantry. Behind the Priest, Malcolm and Gabriel were mostly expressionless. Gabriel kept raising his hand to his eye patch, though, like it itched.

"That's interesting," Lore said finally. "But I fail to see how I can help you with it."

"The same way you helped your unfortunate equine friend in the Northwest Ward this morning," Anton replied. "Reanimation."

The word fell like a stone in the quiet room. Lore gaped, the uncomfortable feeling of returning circulation forgotten. "I..." She stopped, shook her head, jangling free more of that chloroform headache. "Listen, it's not something that I do frequently, and the comedown is really unpleasant, so I'd rather not—"

"You've done it more than once already." Anton nodded and waved a stately hand, as if presenting her with her own success. "It's not an ability you can simply wish away. Wouldn't you rather do it in the employ of Church and Crown, where a pyre isn't imminent?"

That was a threat, despite his genteel tone. She sat back in her chair, instinctually putting distance between the two of them.

The scar tissue massing the left side of the Priest Exalted's face moved as his mouth stretched to a cruel smile. "When you have unholy skills," he said, "it is best to put them to holy purpose."

"Don't you have some *unholy skills* of your own? Surely one of you could do it." Incredulous laughter ticked at the back of Lore's throat. "You can channel Mortem, can't you? All of you can, that's your whole purpose." Her newly free hand cut through the air, jabbed toward Gabriel. "He can *feel* it! There has to be someone in your damn cult that can raise the dead; leave me out of it!"

Gabriel's one visible eye narrowed. "Necromancy is beyond our scope."

"And that is the crux of our issue." The garnet on Anton's pendant winked in the candlelight as he shifted in his chair. "While our order does have the ability to channel Mortem, none of us are capable of resurrection. Not like you."

The logical questions hung thick in the air, the why to the how. But they remained unspoken. The four of them sat in silence, Anton's and Malcolm's faces implacable, Gabriel's slightly pinched.

When it became clear the silence would only break if she did the breaking, Lore sighed. "I still don't understand how me doing...doing *that*...helps you find out what's going on in the villages."

Anton shrugged. "You raise one of the victims," he said, as if the answer was obvious, "and you ask what happened."

The thought made Lore recoil. Raising Horse was one thing— and her throat still burned from the coffee she'd vomited up when she saw the poor animal's dead eyes blinking—but she couldn't raise a person again. Never, ever again. "I don't—"

"Not for an extended time, of course." The Priest Exalted shook his hand and his head, double negation, the movements exaggerated by his shadow on the floor. "They don't even need to be ambulatory."

She didn't have anything else in her stomach to retch up, but it churned just the same.

"All we need," Anton continued, "is for you to bring the victims back to life long enough for them to relay their memories. Tell us what happened before they died, to see how it was done."

"And if I don't?" She wanted it to sound defiant, but it came out small.

"Then you can choose: a noose, a pyre, or the Burnt Isles." The Priest Exalted shrugged again, as if it was all the same to him. "They're mining more and more coal out of the Isles recently, I hear. Going deeper, on the off chance we lose our stronghold there to Kirythean raiders. They can always use extra hands."

He said it so smoothly, nonchalant, with those rounded royal vowels. Lore clicked her teeth shut and swallowed again, trying to settle her stomach.

"Think of all the people you'd be helping." Gabriel stepped forward from behind Anton, blue eye locked on Lore, jaw tight. It seemed almost like the Mort begrudged the fact that he was trying to convince her, that he'd been reduced to cajoling a poison runner, fished out of the gutter and brought into his Church.

"This has happened twice now, and we have every reason to believe it will again," Gabriel continued. "Both villages were along the border we share with the Kirythean Empire. I don't have to spell out for you what that means."

He didn't. Relations with Kirythea had always been tense. The previous Emperor, Ouran, had conquered everything up to Auverraine's southeastern edge before his death—more than half the Enean continent. Now Ouran's son Jax had taken his throne, and no one knew whether or not he'd continue his father's uneasy truce.

The raids on the Burnt Isles—hotly contested territory that Auverraine had held for the entirety of Ouran's reign—made continued peace seem unlikely.

Anton nodded, shooting Gabriel a pleased look from the corner of his eye. "Gabriel is right. This isn't just a matter of strange happenings or morbid curiosity. It's a case of maintaining our country's security."

"I think you're overestimating my patriotism," Lore said.

"It isn't a question of patriotism. It's a question of keeping war from our doorstep." Anton's scars pulled as he narrowed his working eye, a motion that looked painful. "You know who bears the weight of war. It won't be the nobles in the Citadel. It will be the peasants in their villages, the poison runners in the streets. People like you."

He said it like it bothered him. She hoped it did.

Gabriel appealing to her sense of greater good—did she even have that? She wanted to—and Anton appealing to her sense of self-preservation. Death on one end, blackmail at the other.

"This leads us nicely to the second part of your assignment," Anton said, as if following a carefully constructed script. "Necromancy is not the only skill you possess that is useful to us. You are also an accomplished spy."

"*Accomplished* might be pushing it," Lore muttered.

Anton continued as if he hadn't heard. "We have reason to believe that someone within the Court of the Citadel is passing information on to Kirythea. Possibly the Sun Prince himself."

Lore's eyes widened until they ached. "You want me to spy on the fucking *Sun Prince?*"

"We just want you to stay near him," Anton said. He gestured to her. "You're a pretty enough woman, and Bastian likes pretty people. Insinuating yourself into his good graces once you're established as part of the court shouldn't be an issue."

She knew what all those words meant individually, but strung together like that, she had a hard time following. "I don't—what do you mean, part of the court—"

"Things will be clearer once we speak to my brother." Anton glanced upward, as if he could see straight through the ceiling to the sunshine outside and use it to tell the time. "Which we should go do as soon as possible. The Consecration ceremony begins in just a few hours." His eye came back to rest on her, the handsome side of his face perfectly peaceful. "So what will it be, Lore? The Isles, or the court?"

Put so baldly, it wasn't much of a choice at all. "Fine. I'll do it."

Gabriel almost looked relieved.

Anton inclined his head, like her answer was exactly what he expected. "Come on, then," he said, headed toward the door. "The Sainted King doesn't like to be kept waiting."

Chapter Five

And Nyxara, hungry for power, did attempt to take
Apollius's rightful place–thus, He cast Her down, over
the sea and the Golden Mount where They dwelt,
and over the Fount that had made them gods. Where
She landed, the earth blackened into coal, and where
He bled, the ground grew jewels like fruit. And They
were known from this point as the Buried Goddess
and the Bleeding God.

—The Book of Holy Law, Tract 3

Apparently, Lore's oversize man's shirt and muddy breeches
weren't suitable for an audience with His Royal Majesty,
August Arceneaux, the Sainted King and Apollius's Blessed. Outside
of the interrogation room, Anton had waved her down a small hallway. "Donations," he said simply, gesturing to Gabriel that he should
follow. "Find something that fits. Preferably on the conservative side."

Now Lore stood in a giant closet, stuffed to the brim with
sumptuous clothing that no one outside of the Citadel could
possibly use. *On the conservative side* must mean something completely different to Anton than it did to her.

A froth of pale-lavender tulle seemed promising, the rest of the dress hidden in the cascade of ridiculous wealth. But when Lore pulled it out, the bodice looked fashioned after a peacock plume, complete with feathers.

Lore gave the dress an incredulous look, then turned to the doorway, brandishing the skirt like a dagger. "These are *donated*?"

Gabriel nodded. He stood with his back to her, right outside the closet's open door. His broad shoulders nearly spanned the frame, the top of his reddish-gold hair disappearing beyond the lintel. "The Court of the Citadel knows that things are... less than ideal, outside the walls. They try to help."

Less than ideal was a kind way to put it. Taxes on common Auverrani citizens climbed every year, paying for security against the Kirythean Empire and who knew what else, while those in the Citadel paid next to nothing.

Lore pulled out another dress, this one tight to the hips before flaring out in panels shaped like iridescent fish scales. "Unless one of these is made of something edible, they won't do shit for us. Have any of them considered donating coin rather than evidence of their sartorial crimes?"

Gabriel snorted. "The peerage likes to do just enough to think they're helping without inconveniencing themselves. What's in fashion moves fast, and it's easier to donate clothes you wouldn't be caught dead in after a season than it is to keep them in storage."

Her brow arched. There was a low poison in Gabriel's voice, made more potent by the way he tried to hide it. "You seem to know the court well."

A long pause. Gabriel shifted uncomfortably, his impressive shoulders inching toward his ears. "Better than I'd like," he said finally.

Lore pulled the least offensive dress she could find from the rack, a dark-green affair in velvet that looked to have enough room in the breast and hips for her to wear. Her shirt made a small sound as it hit the floor, and Gabriel stiffened.

She smirked.

The dress was still too tight, but Lore was fairly certain it was the best she could do. Once clothed, she tapped Gabriel on the shoulder to sidle out of the room.

"Such a gentleman," she remarked, starting down the hall to where Anton and Malcolm waited, unfamiliar velvet swishing around her legs. "Celibacy has got to be a drag, but you didn't even try to peek."

The Mort made a choked noise.

❦

The Citadel was bright enough to hurt her eyes.

She'd seen the tops of its four corner turrets before—they were just barely visible over the wall of the Church, built in a circle around the Citadel itself—but seeing them up close was another thing entirely. They gleamed in the sun, arrows pointing toward the sky, flocked with silver that traced the tower's sides like frosting on a cake. In the walls that connected the turrets, windows glinted jewel-like at equidistant points, some stained glass and some diamond-clear. A domed glass roof arched up in the center of the square the turrets made, throwing off rainbow prisms. The building was a behemoth of marble and precious metal, polished wood and gemstone, large enough to house the entire court in the summer months. Lore thought she could wander around in there for a year without finding the way out.

The ground around the Citadel was a garden, at least here, between the southern wall of the Church and the Citadel's main entrance. On the other side of the Citadel, there were fields, stables, an entire world the size of at least two city Wards. And all around it, the Church, built more like a fortress. As much a structure to keep out the rabble as it was for worship.

Anton led them from the Church's arched doorway out into the garden. Lore glanced back, shading her eyes—they'd come from the South Sanctuary, the one meant for common worshippers. Miles away, on the opposite side of the Citadel, was the North Sanctuary, meant for the court. The large stone walls that split the grounds in two were filled with storage and cloisters, topped with battlements prepared for the possibility of siege.

A white marble statue rose from a tangle of pink roses beside the path. The Bleeding God, again, wearing a crown like sun rays—a holdover from when the pantheon had been whole and He'd been merely the god of light, life, and the day, instead of everything. Plinths circled the statue, now empty, but Lore counted five. One for each elemental god of the former pantheon, dying one by one, Their bodies found in strange places all over the world. And one beside Apollius, slightly taller than the others, for Nyxara.

Anton and Malcolm walked before her, Gabriel behind, though none of them necessarily seemed to be on guard. It wasn't like she'd run, and there was nowhere to go but back inside the Church, anyway.

"Keep your head down if you see anyone." Gabriel's voice came low enough to tickle her shoulder blades. "Unless you want to be the subject of rumors for years to come. New faces in the court are rare."

Lore kept her voice low, too. "Maybe they'll come up with something interesting."

"More interesting than the truth?"

"Fair." She glanced over her shoulder. "If your boss wants me to befriend the Sun Prince, though, I think rumors are probably inevitable."

Gabriel didn't respond, but his eye narrowed.

Trees were planted throughout the garden with just enough randomness to seem unplanned, and thickly flowering arbors covered the benches beneath them almost entirely from view. Movement under one of the arbors caught her eye. Lore squinted between a froth of yellow roses, curiosity immediately overriding Gabriel's directions.

A dark-haired man had his head bent low, whispering to a lady whose back was turned. Lore could make out little of his face through the flowers, but what she could see was almost ridiculously handsome—strong jaw, sun-bronzed white skin, dark eyes. The lady she could see even less of, only enough to surmise that her hair was light brown and her clothes were elegant. The man seemed to be trying to talk her out of them, if the insolent hand on her thigh and the brush of his lips against her shoulder were any indication.

As if he could feel her watching, the man raised his eyes, staring at Lore through the lattice of roses. His lips continued their gentle path along his companion's shoulder blade as, slowly and deliberately, he winked.

Lore whipped her head around to face the front.

The guards asked no questions as the Presque Mort approached the entrance to the Citadel proper, great double doors inlaid with large golden hearts like the one Anton wore as a pendant. The guards inclined their heads to Anton as the doors opened, sun reflecting off the tiny garnets in the wood, nearly the same color as their coats.

Up until now, Lore had kept her nerves well in hand. Necessity made her shrewd, and she needed to keep her head. But as the Citadel doors closed behind her, Lore's heart leapt in the direction of her throat, thrumming so quickly she could nearly taste it.

The inside of the Citadel was even more luxurious than the outside. Knaves set into the walls held small icons of Apollius, sun rays over their arched tops breaking gold on the rich mahogany. The ceilings were painted with lush garden scenes, nude figures reclining among green trees and beside rushing blue streams, interrupted occasionally by the gold chains of heavy chandeliers, light catching the hanging gems and splashing rainbows across the walls.

The iron crossbars bisecting the floor seemed brutally out of place.

The bars were flush to the marble, but Lore still didn't want to step on them. She lengthened her stride as much as the too-tight dress would allow. "Interesting décor decision." Something about all this opulence made her want to keep her voice quiet.

"They're symbolic," Gabriel murmured back. "Supposed to remind everyone that the Citadel is here to keep Mortem contained, and that the Arceneaux line rules through divine right."

"Gaudy."

"Quite."

A huge tapestry hung on the wall to her left, nearly wide enough to span the length of the hallway. In the top corner, the pale, chestnut-haired figure of Apollius hovered, wings of light spread behind His back, one hand thrust forward into the chest of a dark shape careening toward the ground. Just like the tapestry in the Church, the figure was vague, more smoke and shadow than concrete lines, but the crescent crown on Her brow was clear. Below, azure thread was interrupted by circles of brown and green, seven stylized islands in a stormy sea. The one at the end of the archipelago, farthest from the viewer, was the biggest by far. The Golden Mount. Where Apollius and Nyxara had lived before this moment.

This was the Godsfall, how the Burnt Isles had gotten their name. Apollius cast down Nyxara when She tried to kill Him and take His place, creating a deep crater in the second island and rupturing the others. According to the Book of Holy Law, that was why so many gemstones and precious metals could be mined from them. Gods bled riches, apparently. Convenient.

Lore stopped for a moment, studying the tapestry. It was strange to see all seven islands depicted. The smoke from the Godsfall obscured all but the first two from view, now, and the Golden Mount was functionally a myth, with countless voyagers lost as they searched for it in the smog. Five hundred years, and the ash still hadn't cleared.

A soft touch on her elbow. Gabriel nodded forward, where Malcolm and Anton were about to turn a corner. Lore lurched forward to follow, tearing herself away from Apollius and Nyxara.

Around the corner, a huge set of double doors appeared, even more gilt-and-jewel-encrusted than the Citadel's main entrance. Bloodcoat guards lined the hall, all of them inclining their heads in a bow when Anton appeared. The Priest Exalted paid them no mind, facing forward as the bloodcoats at the end of the line pushed the double doors open.

The throne room beyond was even more impressive than the rest of the Citadel, large enough to hold a ball. The walls were covered in sculpted golden friezes, curving up into graceful arches beneath a domed window. Those iron bars still covered the floor, but seemed more polished here, shining almost silver. They coalesced around the bottom of the throne in a sharp, cresting wave, their pointed ends mirroring the rays of the gilded heart set at the top of the throne, right over the head of the man sitting at its edge, deep in thought.

"Anton," King August said, glancing up from his steepled hands. "You took longer than anticipated."

"I had to inform the lady of our expectations. She took a bit of convincing." For all his brother's brusqueness, Anton seemed unruffled, though he toyed with his pendant again, one fingernail digging into the garnet. "Unless you'd rather I left that to you? You do excel at negotiation."

His tone made it clear this was not a compliment.

"No need." August stood up, stepping deftly over the iron bars bristling the base of the throne with the ease of practice. He and Anton were twins, but August wasn't quite as good-looking—at least, he wouldn't be if Anton weren't so horribly scarred. Their hair was the same iron gray, their eyes the same deep brown.

August kept a short, well-trimmed beard framing his sharp jaw, where Anton stayed clean-shaven.

For all the extravagance of his palace, the King was dressed rather simply. Dark pants, dark doublet over a creamy white shirt, supple leather boots, all of it clearly the best Auverraine had to offer. The understated clothing made August's crown that much more ostentatious, the same design Lore had seen sold in the stalls on the dock roads yesterday—a band that rested on his brow, studded with winking rubies, and another band over the top of his head that supported thick golden sun rays, making him look like Apollius himself.

Lore supposed that was the point.

Maybe she should've felt some sort of awe at being in the presence of the Sainted King. But the day already felt so surreal, so difficult to hammer into the borders of the life she knew, that all she felt was annoyance and the distant thrum of dread.

"So," the Sainted King said. "This is our deathwitch."

Lore fidgeted a moment, wondering if she should curtsy, quickly deciding that it would only lead to falling on her ass. Instead she lifted her chin and clenched her hands in her skirt. "In the flesh."

The corner of the King's mouth flickered up and down again, a smile only in shape. "They tell me you've fallen in with poison runners. How did that happen to a woman of your prodigious talent?"

"Too mean to charge for my company, too clumsy for barkeeping, and I'm a terrible cook. That rules out most gainful employment." She said it pleasantly enough, an answer that gave away nothing important. "My *prodigious talent* isn't good for much, honestly."

The King sniffed. "Your former employer tells us you're an accomplished spy, in addition to your...less common qualities. Surely that's a skill that can earn quite a lot of coin."

The mention of Val made something twist in her chest. "Being a good spy mostly comes down to knowing when to lie and when to stay quiet," she responded. "And there's not much coin to go around out there, regardless of how good you are at what you do."

"An unfortunate predicament," August conceded with a nod. "Made worse by the threat of the Kirythean Empire at our doorstep. There are shortages all over the kingdom."

It seemed no shortages of any kind were felt within the Citadel walls. Lore bit her tongue against that particular observation. She was a commodity that couldn't be replaced, as far as she was aware, but she knew better than to press her luck.

"Since Anton has given you the broader picture of what we need from you," August said, "I will give you the specifics." He turned back to his throne and sat more gracefully than the iron spikes around it should allow. "We believe that Kirythea is attacking villages along our border, using some kind of lesser magic to kill our citizens in the night. Something left over from one of the minor gods."

Her brow furrowed. "There's still lesser magic to go around?" When the minor elemental gods died, Their bodies had leaked power, just like Nyxara's still leaked Mortem. But all that power had dissipated long ago. At least, that's what everyone assumed.

August's lips flattened. "Jax is canny."

Which wasn't really an answer.

"Currently, it's only been two small villages, and the timing is random—the second was eliminated two nights ago." August crossed one leg over the other, nonchalant as he spoke of so much death. A chalice balanced on the arm of his throne; he took a long sip. "We need to neutralize the threat before Kirythea moves on to more profitable targets."

More profitable targets. As though the lives lost in the outer villages were worth less than cattle. Lore's eyes narrowed. "So you want to find out what's happening before it kills someone that *matters.*"

The poison in her voice was apparently lost on the King. "Precisely."

Gabriel stood behind her, but close enough that she could see his face from the corner of her eye. He looked like he was fighting a frown, as if the comment angered him as much as it angered her. She wondered how much dissent the Presque Mort were allowed to voice. The Church and the Crown were two legs of one government, but from the little Lore knew of court politics, it seemed they didn't always walk in the same direction.

"If Kirythea is responsible," August continued, "we need to identify the threat immediately, and take appropriate action."

That could only mean war. Lore sneaked a glance at the waiting Presque Mort. Gabriel's eye narrowed; Malcolm's mouth pressed into a tense line. But if Anton was disturbed by the implication that war loomed close, he didn't show it, his scarred face serene.

The Sainted King clasped his hands, eyes flashing beneath his heavy crown. "You will stay in the Citadel," he said to Lore. "And in addition to using your...skills...to assist us in finding out what is happening to the outer villages, you will be my eyes and ears."

"I'll watch your son, you mean."

August grinned, giving his face a predatory cast, and took another long drink of whatever was in his cup. "It seems my brother did give you some relevant details. Yes, you will stay here with the express purpose of getting close to Bastian. We have reason to believe he might be informing Emperor Jax of our weaknesses, acting as a spy from the inside."

"Why?" Lore crossed her arms, holding them like a shield. "Why would the heir to the crown want to turn his country over to the Kirythean Empire?"

"Because the crown sits heavy," August said quietly. "And my son has never demonstrated himself to be strong enough for that weight."

Anton's hand spasmed around his pendant, but when Lore looked at him, his scarred face was still blank.

"While Bastian is our main concern," August continued, "we also wish for you to insinuate yourself into the court. My courtiers will be eager to gossip about you, but also *with* you."

"All of that sounds great, but how exactly am I supposed to enter the court without making everyone suspicious?" Lore gestured to her ill-fitting gown. "I'm not sure if you've noticed, but it's extremely obvious that I'm not a noble."

"On the contrary." August's grin widened. "We'll tell them you're the cousin of the Duke of Balgia."

Behind her, Gabriel's face went nearly white. Next to him, Anton sighed, as if he'd come to his least favorite part of a task.

"Balgia?" Lore's brow arched. The tiny duchy to the southeast had fallen to the Kirythean Empire fourteen years ago, conquered by Jax while his father was still the Emperor.

August nodded. "Balgia." He gestured to Gabriel. "It seems it's time for you to take up your title again, Gabriel Remaut."

CHAPTER SIX

The sins of the father are visited upon his heirs. Children inherit both shame and glory.
                                    –The Book of Mortal Law, Tract 24

Gabriel's face was corpse-pale, his jaw clenched tight, like the sound of his surname had turned his stomach. The scars around his eye patch stood out stark as lightning.

A duke. Gabriel was a *duke*? Why in every myriad hell would a duke join the Presque Mort, even the duke of a place that didn't technically exist anymore?

And how had a duke lost an eye?

The Sainted King either didn't notice Gabriel's distress or didn't care. "It seems your lineage will finally come in handy, Gabriel," he said nonchalantly, the ruby rings on his hands winking as he drank once more from his chalice. "When Anton pursued you so relentlessly after...the incident...I was hesitant, but apparently my brother knew what he was doing, recruiting you into the Presque Mort."

Every line of Gabriel's body was tense as a violin string, his muscles held so still Lore half expected them to vibrate. "Your Majesty, I can't...I don't know..."

For all his even tones, Gabriel clearly didn't have words for what he meant. His face said it all, though. He was furious. He was terrified.

"Son." Anton stepped forward, his hand settling lightly on Gabriel's shoulder. "I know this is a shock."

So the Priest Exalted had known. He'd known this was going to happen, and he'd let Gabriel be blindsided anyway. Lore felt a rush of contempt for the scarred old man.

"But this is Apollius's will," Anton continued. "You have hidden away from the court for years, healing. Now it is time to reenter. Time to play the part Apollius has chosen for you."

At the sound of his god's name, Gabriel closed his one eye.

"You will escort Lore," Anton said, all his focus on the still-tense, silent Presque Mort before him. "You will help her in the tasks she's been given. And you will be rewarded, Gabriel. The mantles we are given are not always what we would choose, but Apollius, god of all, knows what is best, and He honors those who choose Him, even when we must go against our nature to do so." He paused, his hand tightening. "This is how you atone."

"I thought becoming a Presque Mort was how I did that," Gabriel whispered hoarsely. "Isn't that what you told me? What your vision said?"

The vision that had given Anton his scar. Even Lore had heard the story. Anton Arceneaux had been so overcome with holy fervor as he prayed that Apollius had given him a vision, one so sacred it was kept deep in the Church, its contents a secret. In the ecstasy of speaking with his god, Anton had fallen into the brazier, and after nearly dying from his wounds, he woke with the ability to channel Mortem. August, newly crowned, had made him the Priest Exalted, forcing the former holder of the title into retirement. No one had heard from him since.

"My son," Anton murmured, "I could not tell you everything."

Hurt lived in the ridge of Gabriel's jaw, and in the way he stepped out from beneath the Priest Exalted's palm. But he didn't refuse, didn't rail against unfairness. He didn't say anything at all.

August smiled, then, and turned his full brilliance on Lore, continuing as if Anton and Gabriel hadn't interrupted him with their murmured conversation. "Besides, the girl is from the streets, Remaut. Don't rob her of her rags-to-riches fairy tale. She's probably dreamed of the opportunity since she was a girl."

"I'm not sure the opportunity to lurk around the Citadel in the hope someone would tell me something useful ever occurred to me, really," Lore said.

"You'll do more than lurk. You'll make friends. Insinuate yourself into society." August saluted her lazily with his chalice. "And above all, you will stick as close to my son as you possibly can. If this proves too much for you...well. There's always room in the cells."

Nerves twisted her middle. Lore tried very hard not to let them show in her expression.

The Sainted King took a long drink, draining the cup, then set it back down on the arm of his throne. "Time grows short. Bastian's Consecration will begin soon, and all of us must be there." August flicked his fingers at Gabriel like one might gesture to a well-trained dog. "Gabriel! Step forward, please."

The look on the duke-turned-Mort's face was drawn and tense as he stared at August. But Gabriel followed orders, stepping up to where the Sainted King waited. He kept his head down, eyes trained on the floor.

His docility rankled her, for reasons she couldn't quite name. That strange feeling of familiarity she had toward the Mort told her that he wasn't supposed to be like this, placid and easily led, smothering the flames of his anger. He was someone who should let it burn.

August stood and descended from his throne of spiking iron.

The throne was on a slightly raised dais, and he remained on the bottom stair, putting him right at eye level with Gabriel—clearly deliberate; the King didn't want to look up at someone he deemed beneath him.

The Sainted King stretched out his jewel-scabbed hand to place it on the Mort's shoulder. "I know you wish to leave your title behind," August said softly. "I know it has brought you nothing but trouble and shame." Lore's eyes narrowed. She was very familiar with the way people wielded pity like a bayonet, hiding the desire to make sure you knew your place behind false concern. August wasn't trying to comfort Gabriel; he was trying to intimidate him.

"But you've always known that someday you would be expected back in court," August continued. "This is your chance to redeem yourself. To show the Citadel that the Remaut family isn't made wholly of traitors who give up at the slightest hint of conflict. You know the Tracts as well as I do: Parental sins are passed on to the children. Your father's treason is carried in your blood."

"I was *ten*." Gabriel's voice didn't waver, showed no emotion but for the slight emphasis on the number. The look in his one blue eye was far away, unfocused. "I was ten, and Jax had just killed my father and carved out my eye. I didn't know what else to do."

So *that's* how he'd lost the eye. Jax had taken it. Anton had used the maiming to bring Gabriel into the Presque Mort fold, and now August used it as proof Gabriel carried sins that weren't his.

Lore decided, then, that she really hated both of the Arceneaux brothers.

"And that's how they remember you." August changed the course of the conversation smoothly; he was practiced at this, apparently, feeling out the cracks in someone and working them open. "As someone who hid."

Almost absently, Gabriel reached up and touched his eye patch. "Anton gave me a place," he said quietly. "Anton told me I could work to cleanse my line, if I joined the Presque Mort."

"You reentering the court doesn't make you less of a Presque Mort. Think of this as one more way to atone for your father's mistakes. To make his name an honorable one again." August released Gabriel's shoulder with one final clap. A small smile, nothing kind in it. "So many of them would love to see you again, Gabriel. Alienor Bellegarde, in particular."

The name stiffened Gabriel further. He stepped back, that blank look still on his face, staring carefully at nothing.

"I will make official introductions tomorrow, when the court gathers for morning prayers in the North Sanctuary. Wardrobes of appropriate clothing will be provided, but in the interest of discretion, no servants will be assigned to the upkeep of your quarters." The King's dark eyes slid to Lore. "Do try to keep it tidy."

She resolved to pour an entire bottle of wine on the carpet the first chance she got.

August looked to his brother. "Show them to their apartments, but do hurry. We don't want to keep everyone waiting."

With a smooth inclination of his head—not a full bow, Lore noted—Anton glided through the now-open double doors. Gabriel and Malcolm followed, Gabriel still with a dazed look in his eye.

Lore glanced back at August before following. The Sainted King was resplendent on his throne, sunlight gilding him like a statue. "Welcome to the Court of the Citadel, Lore. I'll see you at my son's Consecration in an hour."

❧

Bloodcoats were waiting outside the throne room. Wordlessly, they escorted the four of them through shining hallways that Lore would have no chance of navigating on her own, through open atriums that could be museums in their own right, covered in icons and tapestries and frescoes. The halls were empty, the gathered courtiers apparently still abed or preparing for the ceremony. The light through the windows put the time at around midday.

Anton walked in front, right behind the bloodcoats with Malcolm on his heels. Lore and Gabriel trailed them, as if some invisible partition had cut them off, separated them into factions of court and Church.

The guards led them up a wide, carpeted stairway, lined in marble statues of buxom figures in varying states of undress. The staircase ended in a short hallway full of identical arched doors; the bloodcoats walked to its end, where another door opened on another staircase, this one smaller and shabbier, though still ornate.

"The southeast turret," Gabriel murmured, as if he could tell Lore was having a hard time keeping her bearings. "The least fashionable one in the Citadel. Everyone who's important lives in the northwest turret during the summer."

His voice was deceptively even, but when Lore looked at him, his face was pale, his eye distant. Her hand was halfway raised before she realized it, ready to land on his arm in comfort.

Lore snatched it out of the air before it could, fingers in a fist. Gods, that odd familiarity was inconvenient. Misplaced softness for a sad Mort was the last thing she needed right now.

The stairs evened into landings every few steps, but the bloodcoats led them farther and farther up. Finally, they came to a stop, on a landing whose carpeting looked far more worn than any of the others.

The bloodcoats pushed open the door. Another hallway, dimly lit, the only illumination provided by a golden candelabra on the wall. Another Bleeding God's Heart; the candelabra was shaped like a heart inside a sun, with one flickering oil lamp in the center.

Small candles studded the ends of the sun rays, but most of them had burned out.

Across from the light fixture, a heavy wooden door.

"Apologies, Duke Remaut." The nearest bloodcoat inclined his head to Anton, then Gabriel and Malcolm as he inserted a key into the door and turned the lock over. Lore, he ignored entirely. "Our Sainted King was insistent that you both stay in these apartments. They formerly belonged to Lord and Lady Grosjean, but they both passed away this past winter."

Of course August would put them in a dusty hallway, far away from the rest of the peerage. It'd make them easier to keep an eye on.

Gabriel paled, as if the guard had just given him a live rat. "You mean...you mean both of us are staying here?"

A nod from the bloodcoat. "On orders of the King, you and your cousin are both to stay in these apartments for the duration of the season."

Malcolm's dark brow rose. Gabriel swallowed.

Lore rolled her eyes. "I promise not to impugn your virtue."

Malcolm made a noise that might've been the choked beginning of a laugh. Gabriel made none at all, but his already-pale face went whiter.

Anton gave her a slicing look, then waved an imperious hand at the bloodcoats. "Leave us." His voice wasn't harsh, but it brooked no argument.

They obeyed almost as quickly as if the order had come from the King. Shaking his head, Anton pushed open the door.

The apartment was nearly twice as large as Michal's row house. The first room was furnished with a low couch and two chairs before a cold fireplace, the upholstery luxurious, if a few seasons out of fashion. Beyond the sitting room, three open doors revealed two bedrooms just as sumptuously appointed, with a tiled room housing a gleaming copper washtub between them. A door beside the fireplace led to an enclosed balcony, full of spindly wicker furniture, and another small study opened off the main sitting room. At least four people could live here comfortably.

Anton sighed, turning to Gabriel. "I know this is overwhelming, especially after your cloisters at the Northreach monastery. But I specifically asked that August put you in the apartments farthest from the rest of the court, so you'd have the space you need to be comfortable." The unscarred side of his face softened, though it looked forced. "Truly, I've done everything I can to make this as easy on you as possible, Gabe."

Gabe. It should've sounded gentler, Lore thought, for being a nickname. But coming from Anton, something about it had edges. She recalled what Malcolm had said before, about Gabriel being from the country monasteries. Apparently, he'd been brought back to Dellaire for the Consecration, and he'd gotten all *this* in the bargain. A vague, dangerous assignment and betrayal from the man he appeared to trust above all others.

She shot a look at Gabriel. The monk had his arms crossed, eye on the floor. The wrinkle of his brow above his eye patch said he was deep in thought, his shoulders tense as if waiting for a blow.

"Well, *I'm* satisfied with these accommodations," Lore announced, sprawling on the couch. It sent up a tiny cloud of dust, proof it hadn't been disturbed in a while—so much for August asking her to keep it tidy; it looked like the Grosjeans hadn't done a great job of that themselves. "Seems better than a cloister to me, in Northreach or otherwise."

Malcolm eyed the room dubiously. "I think the cloisters have more recently updated upholstery, but this place *does* have more furniture."

Anton shot him a dark look. "The Consecration begins in less than an hour," he said, "and both of you must be there."

Gabriel's arms tightened across his chest. His one eye slid to

Lore, and then away, like someone trying to keep an eye on a horse they thought might kick. "I was unaware you needed my presence at the Consecration."

"Of course we do." Something in Anton's voice sounded...not *shrill*, but close to it, as if the idea of Gabriel and Lore not being at the Consecration was unfathomable. "You two are to get close to Bastian, so of course you must attend."

"Will the Sun Prince not find it strange that a random duke's cousin is suddenly stuck to his ass?" Lore asked from the couch. "If you want me for my spying experience as well as my unfortunate Mortem affliction, let me give a word of advice: Staying on someone like a burr on a pant leg isn't always the best way to find out the information you want. Sometimes you have to use a bit more subtlety."

Anton approached the couch and glared down at her. Lore wanted to sit up, but it would feel like a capitulation, so she stayed sprawled over the pillows and gave him an inane smile.

"You will follow the orders you've been given." Anton's voice was cool and smooth. "To the letter."

Lore didn't respond. She shifted on the lumpy throw pillows.

The Priest Exalted stepped away from the couch and turned to Gabriel. "There is appropriate clothing for the girl in one of the bedrooms. For you, as well. Go change, and we will escort you to the Consecration. Bleeding God help us all."

CHAPTER SEVEN

In their twenty-fourth year of mortal life, the gods
ascended: Apollius to the rulership of life and the day,
Nyxara to rulership of death and the night, Hestraon to
rulership of fire, Lereal to rulership of the air, Braxtos to
rulership of the earth, and Caeliar to rulership of the sea.
                              –The Book of Holy Law, Tract 7

Lore wasn't exactly sure what she was supposed to wear
to a Consecration, having never been invited to one. They
occurred on your twenty-fourth birthday, but only the nobility
made a fuss over them—everyone else would just go get blessed
at the South Sanctuary by whatever priest had the time, if they
bothered with observing it at all.

The mass of clothes she'd been provided would be overwhelming even if she wasn't trying to dress for a holy holiday. None
of the dresses were as ridiculous as the things she'd seen in the
donation closets, thankfully, but they were far finer than anything she'd worn before. In the end, she chose the one that looked
easiest to get into by herself. If she asked any of the Presque Mort
for help, they'd probably keel over.

The sage-green dress fit too nicely to be a coincidence. Lore studied herself in the full-length mirror hanging on the wall by the closet door. A high neck, short, gathered sleeves, and a floor-length skirt that just brushed the top of the matching slippers she'd found lined up beneath the canopied bed. Either the seamstress who'd made it had a dress form exactly her size—unlikely, as she was a good deal curvier than most mannequins she'd seen—or it'd been tailored to her measurements.

Gooseflesh raised the small hairs on the back of her neck. The Presque Mort had known about her since she raised Cedric years ago—Val had told her as much. Still, the knowledge that she'd been *watched* didn't settle easily.

Thoughts of Val didn't settle easily, either. Lore swallowed, hard, forcing down the constriction that wanted to close around her throat, the liquid heat gathering in the corners of her eyes. No time for all that. Letting go was a skill she'd had extensive practice developing. Val and Mari weren't part of her life anymore. Her life now was silk dresses and matching slippers and a golden leash held by the Sainted King and Priest Exalted.

She tilted up her head, blinked until that prickly feeling in her eyes was gone. All she'd ever done was adapt; this was just one more thing to get used to. She'd survive. She always did.

Lore hastily braided her hair in a crown around her brow, the fanciest hairstyle she knew how to do, and pushed open her door with a sarcastic flourish. "Behold, a lady."

"Close enough, at least," Anton said drily.

Behind him, Malcolm tapped at the side of his head. "You have a braiding mishap, *my lady*."

"Shit." Lore turned to an age-spotted mirror hanging on the wall behind the couch. A strand of hair stuck out of her quick braid, making it look like she had half a set of horns. Scowling, she took her hair down and braided it again.

The other bedroom door opened, and Gabriel stepped out,

looking decidedly un-monk-like. Dark-blue breeches were tucked into shining black boots, and a trim torso was covered in a close-fitting white linen shirt with a matching midnight vest. The clothes were almost nice enough to distract from the thunderous scowl on his face, highlighted by the rough leather of his eye patch.

Malcolm made a noise that might've been a laugh, but swallowed it down when Anton shot him a pointed look. "You clean up nicely, Gabe," he said instead.

Gabriel shifted his weight, the new leather of his boots squeaking. "Father, are you sure that—"

"I am sure. More important, so is Apollius." Anton narrowed his eyes. "Do not continue to question Him, Gabriel."

The Presque Mort nodded. There was a faraway look on his face, like he was trying to pretend he was somewhere else.

That chord in Lore's chest twinged, the one that seemed attuned to him. She pressed a hand against her collarbones, rubbed. The Mort's hurting was hard to watch.

Malcolm didn't care to witness it, either. "I'm headed back to the library." He clapped Gabriel on the shoulder. "You'll be all right," he said softly, then slipped out the door, his tread fast on the hallway carpet beyond. Apparently, the other Presque Mort wasn't overly fond of time spent in the Citadel. Lore wondered if all of them were that way, the delineation between court and Church drawn thick and obvious.

With a nod at the two of them, Anton turned to leave the spacious apartments. Lore followed, and Gabriel took up the end of the line. "I would rather walk over hot coals than attend this," she heard him mutter under his breath, clearly not intending for anyone to hear.

"That makes two of us," Lore muttered back.

The Mort didn't respond, but his mouth softened, just a bit.

The Sun Prince's Consecration took place in one of the rolling fields behind the Citadel. A golden dais stood on the green, canopied in billowing white gauze that flowed tide-like in the breeze. In the center of the dais, a lectern, studded in garnets. A golden-handled knife rested on its surface.

The knife made Lore's eyes widen. As far as she knew, Consecrations didn't require bloodletting, but maybe royals did things differently.

The dais was surrounded by polished wooden pews on all sides. Anton led them to one of the pews in the back, nodding for her and Gabriel to sit before gliding toward the dais. From this angle, Lore could see the hollow inside of the lectern, and the huge book on the shelf there. The Compendium, combining the Book of Holy Law, the Book of Mortal Law, and the Book of Prayer.

Lore craned her neck to see around the dais. Other courtiers filed in slowly, all elegantly dressed, some clutching feathered fans or half-eaten pastries. They seemed more like they were attending a picnic than a holy ceremony. A few of them cast curious glances at her and Gabriel, but for the most part, they were ignored.

So much for August's bluster about new faces. But maybe the courtiers of the Citadel didn't care about a person until it was proven they were important.

Their back pew wasn't a popular one, thankfully. The rest of the Court of the Citadel slowly filled the pews at the front of the dais, the soft sounds of their voices rising and falling like birdsong. Lore vacillated between staring at them and staring at the ground. Her line of work didn't allow her to be anxiety-ridden, but the sight of so many nobles in one place still made her stomach knot up. All the spying she'd done for Val had been on smaller scales; poison runner crews weren't large, so she only had to lie to ten or so people at a time. But a whole damn *court*—

Warmth on her hands, stilling them, stopping her from twisting mindlessly at the fabric of her skirt. Gabriel's palm was laid across her fingers, rough with calluses. His eye patch was on her side, so he wasn't looking at her, but he still took his hand away when her head whirled his direction.

"You'll tear it," he said. "And that will attract far more attention than just sitting here will."

With effort, Lore straightened out her fingers, placed her sweaty palms on her knees.

She stayed like that even as the later courtiers arrived, filling in the spaces in the pews around them because the better seats had been taken. Up on the dais, Anton had pulled the Compendium from its place beneath the lectern and was quickly turning the pages, putting scarlet ribbons into the spine to mark relevant passages. Another clergyman—wearing a white robe instead of the Presque Mort's dark colors; must be a run-of-the-mill Church acolyte—lit wide braziers of incense at the corners of the dais. Herbal smoke twisted into the sky, staining it gray.

Next to her, Gabriel snorted softly. "If every Consecration was this involved, the priests wouldn't have time to do anything else. All they did at mine was recite Tract Seven and sprinkle some ash in my hair."

Lore suspected that the only reason the Mort was speaking to her was for a dearth of options, but she'd take the distraction. "So all this isn't normal?" That explained the knife, maybe.

He shifted so he could look at her from his one eye, brow arched over it. "You haven't had yours yet?"

She shook her head. "I turn twenty-four in the middle of the summer."

"Hmm." He looked forward again, hiding his eye, and that was the extent of the conversation. The man was not much of a talker.

Deep breath in, deep breath out. Stare straight ahead. Try not to notice if anyone is looking at you.

But Lore's careful composure was shattered by the overwhelming feeling that she should turn around, *right now.*

It was enough to make her press her hand against her collarbones. The feeling wasn't physical itself, but the reaction it inspired was—the hairs on her arms rising, her head going strangely light.

So she turned around.

Behind the pews, yards away, stood a young man with shoulder-length black hair held back from his face with a golden circlet. His clothes were all eye-searing white, down to the leather of his boots. He was too far away to see clearly, but his shape seemed familiar. Similar to the way she'd felt when she saw Gabriel, like this was a person she should know, though surely it wasn't someone she'd ever met before.

A string quartet had gathered off to the side of the pews, all dressed in bright colors, instruments gleaming as if they'd been polished for the occasion. The maestro stood and raised his baton; a slow, stately processional began. Behind them, the distant figure in white started strolling toward the dais as if he had all the time in the world.

Oh. That was the Sun Prince.

Gabriel stood up next to her, and Lore hurriedly followed suit. Her heartbeat felt faster, her veins almost too full.

The Sun Prince grew closer. Gabriel grew stiffer.

When he came level with their pew, shining like a god himself, Bastian Arceneaux glanced their way. White skin gilded in sunlight, sharp jaw, dark eyes. When he winked, a memory snapped into place.

The man she'd seen in the gardens. The one who'd watched her enter the Citadel flanked by Gabriel, Anton, and Malcolm, in an ill-fitting dress one of his paramours had probably donated.

Shit.

Bastian mounted the dais, walking elegantly through the billowing curtains and sinuous trails of incense smoke. Applause and whoops greeted his entrance, and he took an exaggerated bow. By the lectern, Anton stood stiffly, the Compendium opened to the first of the scarlet ribbons. August had been seated directly in front of the dais, in a golden throne only slightly less ostentatious than the one inside the Citadel. His ruby-ringed hand clutched another chalice, and he sipped from it quietly as he watched his son, stoic and nearly unmoving.

"Seems like bad form to be drinking at your heir's Consecration," Lore muttered.

"August drinks all the time," Gabriel replied.

The crowd settled, and Anton began to speak, reciting Tract 7 first—a list of the gods who'd ascended from their mortal forms to their holy ones on their twenty-fourth birthdays: Caeliar, Braxtos, Hestraon, Apollius, Nyxara, Lereal. After that, an entry from the Book of Prayer, about stepping into your power when it is time and knowing when to cede it. Bastian shifted back and forth on his feet through the entire recitation, clearly bored. At one point, he smirked at someone to the left of the dais, and Lore wondered if it was the woman he'd been kissing in the garden.

The ceremony seemed to reach a natural conclusion, the gathered courtiers growing restless in their seats as they anticipated dismissal. But Anton turned to another scarlet ribbon in the Compendium, one near the back. The Book of Holy Law, then.

Anton picked up the knife, golden blade glinting in the sun. Lore was too far away to see Bastian's expression, but the Sun Prince took a tiny step back.

She shot a look at Gabriel. A frown drew at the Presque Mort's mouth.

"The Book of Holy Law, Tract Fourteen," Anton intoned. "Powers that oppose each other sharpen each other in turn. The presence of darkness increases light, and light drowns the darkness. But my children, have caution, for neither can be wholly tamed except by your god. Life cannot exist without death, and to hold the whole of them is holiness."

Lore's lips twisted. The Book of Holy Law was a conundrum:

Parts of it had been written pre-Godsfall, but a majority hadn't been recorded until the year of the Godsfall itself, the year between Nyxara's death and Apollius's disappearance. Those Tracts contradicted earlier ones, stating that Apollius was the only true god. Right before He disappeared, Apollius dictated the Book of Holy Law to a man named Gerard Arceneaux, whom He then appointed the Sainted King.

The Arceneaux family had ruled ever since, handpicked by Apollius Himself.

The crowd was silent. Courtiers glanced at each other, some trying to hide bemused grins, others just confused.

"Is that not normally part of it?" Lore whispered to Gabriel.

He shook his head, still frowning.

"Bastian Leander Arceneaux," Anton said, raising the golden knife. "You are the scion of a holy house. You are the vessel of holy power. And today, you step into your Consecration with a heart that will be made ready to carry us forward into a new age."

The bemused smiles faded, every courtier wearing an expression of confusion, Bastian included. He didn't speak—he hadn't through the whole Consecration—but he didn't step closer to his uncle, either.

Anton gestured. "Come, nephew." His voice was the gentlest Lore had ever heard it. "Today you become who you are meant to be."

In his golden chair, August leaned forward, clutching the chalice in his hand like a lifeline.

The Sun Prince hesitated a moment. Then he gave a forced laugh, clearly attempting to break the strange tension. "Well done, Uncle," he said, in a rich baritone voice that rang over the pews. "You've started a trend. I'm sure every Consecration from here on out will include room for improvisation."

The gathered nobles laughed gaily, the sound somewhat strained, as if their prince had given them permission not to be discomfited by the unusual ceremony. By the lectern, Anton remained expressionless, the knife outstretched.

August did nothing, still staring at his son.

Bastian approached the Priest Exalted, held out his hand. Anton grabbed it and carved into his skin with the point of the knife. It happened quickly, too quickly for anyone to do anything but let loose a polite gasp. Bastian grimaced, a spasm going through his shoulders, but he didn't pull away.

When it was over, Anton turned to the crowd, his back to Lore and Gabriel and the others unfortunate enough to sit behind the dais, holding up Bastian's hand. Even from here, Lore could see the blood on the Sun Prince's palm, though she couldn't see what exactly Anton had carved into it.

For a moment, the sky brightened, as if the sun had decided to burn hotter for a heartbeat. Appreciative murmurs rose; maybe it was just a bit of stagecraft, something else to make the Sun Prince's Consecration as dramatic as possible.

But across the dais, August looked stricken.

"Behold, Bastian Leander Arceneaux, the scion of House Arceneaux and future Sainted King of Auverraine, who has today been consecrated in the sight of our Bleeding God!" Anton sounded nearly jubilant. The golden knife still dripped with scarlet in his hand.

"Hail!" called the crowd, and the word dissolved into thunderous applause. Bastian laughed, giving another sweeping bow, then purposefully wiped his bleeding hand on his white doublet.

"Come on," Gabriel grumbled next to her. "Let's get out of here."

The courtiers mobbed the dais, laughing and trying to get as close to Bastian as possible; he let them. Someone handed him a glass of wine, and he took a long, hearty gulp to the sound of more cheering.

August said that he suspected Bastian of betraying Auverrani secrets because he didn't want the weight of rulership. But it looked to Lore like he was just fine with being the center of attention.

She stuck close behind Gabriel as he made his way back to the Citadel doors, trusting Bastian to hold the courtiers' attention. The only other people moving away from the dais were Anton, the other clergymen, and August.

The Sainted King still held tight to his chalice as he walked, flanked by bloodcoats. He raised it to take another drink, a slight tremor in his hand. Dark wine spilled from the cup as Lore and Gabriel passed him, splashing onto the ground and barely missing Lore's hem.

Lore glanced over her shoulder before following Gabriel inside. Bastian stood on the dais still, surrounded by beautiful people in colorful clothing, leaning in close to whisper in the ear of a young man who looked thrilled to be the object of his attention. But his eyes were on her. She wasn't sure how she could tell, across so much space, but she knew with a pull in her gut and no hint of a doubt that the Sun Prince was staring right at her.

CHAPTER EIGHT

The Night Witch said she'd watch the tomb
But lost her mind instead
She tried to let the goddess out
But the goddess got in her head
                    —Auverrani children's rhyme

T hink they left any wine in here?"

Their apartments felt cavernous with only the two of them inside. Lore toed off her slippers by the door—they pinched something awful, which meant in all the years the Presque Mort had been watching her, they'd still managed to get her shoe size wrong—and sat heavily down on the couch. "I need some, after all that."

"If they did, it will be in the sidebar." Gabriel waved toward a small table next to the empty fireplace. He leaned against the wall by the door, one hand reaching up to readjust the leather patch on his eye. "Hopefully August tells someone to send us food."

"He can't expect me to spy on an empty stomach." Lore rummaged through the sidebar until she found two dusty wineglasses and a small bottle of red. "That was strange, right? I mean, I haven't attended many Consecrations—any, really—but that seemed strange."

"It was," Gabriel conceded. "Malcolm told me Anton was planning more Tract readings than a typical ceremony, but I wasn't expecting..."

"A bloodletting?"

His mouth quirked, somewhere between a smirk and a grimace. "Precisely." He rubbed at his jaw. Slight reddish stubble grew there, the sign of a long day. "But there was a purpose, I'm sure. Anton always has a purpose. And an Arceneaux Consecration is a special occasion; I shouldn't expect it to be the same as others I've seen."

It sounded like Gabriel had gotten very good at rationalizing whatever Anton did. The man could probably strip naked and waltz around the South Sanctuary, and Gabriel would think it had some higher spiritual purpose.

Lore pulled off the cork of the wine bottle with her teeth. It smelled vinegary, and her nose wrinkled when she poured it. "It's shit," she warned, handing a glass to Gabriel, "but so is this day."

She half expected him to refuse—she wasn't clear on how the Presque Mort felt about alcohol—and for a moment, it looked like he would, eyeing the glass balefully.

"If you don't help me drink this, I'll just throw back the whole bottle," Lore said. "I promise you don't want that. I sing when I'm drunk, and I'm a *very* bad singer."

Gabriel studied the glass a moment longer before plucking it from her fingers. "Fine." He tossed back a swallow, pulling a face. "Apollius's *wounds*, that's awful."

"But it is better than thinking about the situation in which we find ourselves." Lore sat back on the carpet with her own glass, crossing her legs beneath her borrowed skirt. "I still don't know how I'm supposed to get close to Bastian. Or why we had to attend his extremely...eccentric...Consecration."

"It won't be hard," Gabriel said darkly, taking another sip of wine. He avoided the subject of the Consecration entirely. "Like August said, Bastian likes pretty people. Just let him come to you."

"That could've been a compliment, if you didn't say *pretty* with the same tone that most people say *pus*." Lore tossed back the rest of her vinegary wine and poured more. "But this is the most words you've said to me since yesterday, so I suppose I should be grateful."

Gabriel said nothing, staring down into the crimson depths of his glass. "Being here is...difficult," he said finally.

They sat in silence for a moment. "I'm sorry," Lore murmured.

He looked at her, then, brows lowered. "Sorry for what?"

"That you have to stay here. With me."

He snorted. "You're not the worst company in the Citadel."

"You really need to work on your compliments."

Gabriel lifted his wine her direction, a mock toast. She raised her glass in kind, and they both drank.

It was strangely easy, being with the Mort. He wasn't one to talk, but his silence was soothing, like sitting with an old friend, someone you'd known for ages.

Lore frowned into her wine. She'd barely known Gabriel for two whole days; their relationship began with a fight in an alley. And he was obviously deeply loyal to Anton, while Lore didn't really trust the Priest Exalted or his brother. Getting too comfortable with the one-eyed Mort was surely not a good idea—and she knew better, besides. What was it about him that made her want to toss out years of experience teaching her trust was a commodity to be hoarded?

It was probably nerves. Nerves and desperation, making her cling to whatever seemed solid. When Lore was cast adrift, she wasn't the type to let the current take her. She was the type to scramble for an anchor, no matter how ill-advised it may be.

She waved a hand toward her face, eager for something else to think about. The wine made her land on a less-than-tactful subject. "So. You have one eye."

"Astute observation."

"How badly did it hurt?"

His fingers lightly touched the patch again. "Bad," he said, after a stretch of quiet. Then, low and vehement, "Really fucking bad."

"You drink and you curse." Lore arched her brow. "They apparently aren't sticklers in the Presque Mort about anything other than celibacy."

"Oh, no, they're sticklers. But fourteen years of holy life hasn't refined all the worldliness out of me just yet. A personal defect." He tossed back the rest of the wine and strode to the fireplace. Cut wood was piled on a golden stand next to it, and he threw a few logs on the bricks, then set about searching for a match. "Holiness takes a while to set in, apparently."

"If ever." Lore watched Gabriel's fruitless search for a match a moment longer, then set down her now-empty glass and headed for the doorway into the hall. "Hold on, there's an easier way."

In the hall, Lore grabbed one of the lit candles from the Bleeding God's Heart candelabra. "Put this in the fireplace, then feed it wood," she instructed as she came back in the room, passing the candle off before sitting back down on the couch. "Unfamiliar with setting fires?"

"Not necessarily." Gabriel removed the wood he'd already set, then chose some smaller pieces, holding one above the candle's flame. "Unfamiliar with stealing candles from depictions of the Bleeding God's Heart to do it, though. That's technically a sin."

"Five minutes, and I have wholly undermined your divine sensibilities. And most of the candles had burned out, anyway, so clearly no one in this turret was feeling pious."

"That's the Court of the Citadel for you. If the piety can't be seen, it doesn't matter." Gabriel sat back on his heels, watching flames lick up the kindling, catch on the logs. "So what's your story, if that's the game we're playing? I'm assuming it's nothing quite so dramatic as having your eye ripped out by the heir to the Kirythean Empire. So was it a more mundane near-death experience? Some accident that left you with power and your family afraid?"

And Bleeding God help her, for a moment, Lore considered telling him the truth. Her mouth was open to let it all spill out— *well, you see, I was born in the catacombs and I've been able to channel Mortem for as long as I can remember*—and she choked the words back just in time.

Dammit. That feeling of familiarity that plagued her when it came to this man was more than irritating. It was dangerous.

She recovered with a sip of wine. "Fell off a bridge, drowned for a minute. Came back. Family wasn't into it, so they kicked me out when I was thirteen."

Vague details. Easy lies.

"Some family," Gabriel muttered to the flames. He stood, went to sit on the couch. "Though, granted, I have no room to judge on that front."

"What about you?" Lore asked, eager to turn the conversation away from herself. "How'd you fall in with the Presque Mort, after..."

"After my father betrayed August to the Kirythean Empire and gave them a stronghold directly on Auverraine's border?" Gabriel's voice was flat and inflectionless. "Anton found me. Told me it was my destiny to join the Presque Mort, to make something holy out of something terrible."

He'd been ten. She remembered him saying so in the throne room. He'd been ten, newly orphaned and horribly injured, and Anton had twisted that into loyalty. Her distaste for the man grew teeth.

She didn't ask Gabriel how it happened, but he continued as if she had. Sometimes all you needed was a sign that someone was listening. "My father pledged fealty to Kirythea when they approached the Balgian border. August had denied military help; all his extra troops were guarding the Burnt Isles." A pause. "They still killed my father, though. The Kirytheans. Jax said a man who'd betray one country would easily betray another, then cut off my father's head." He made a rueful noise. "Jax was sixteen. Still a child, and already ruthless."

"You were there?" Lore murmured. Then she shook her head. "I mean, of course you were there, since then he..."

She didn't finish, and swallowed against sudden dryness in her throat. Gabriel Remaut had watched his father beheaded, and then the person who'd done it had plucked out his eye.

Gabriel nodded. In the dim light, she could almost see the vestiges of that scared boy in the scarred man. "I'm not sure why Jax let me live, to be honest. He wasn't the Emperor yet, and killing us all certainly would've made his point about traitors. But he sent me back to Auverraine—in a bad state, certainly, but alive." A shrug. "Anton found me soon after. I was inducted into the Presque Mort, then I stayed in the Northreach monastery—I could sense too much Mortem to make staying in Dellaire a possibility. Anton traveled back and forth as often as he could, to help me learn to block it from my mind. The plan was always for me to come here, when I was ready." He made a rueful noise. "It took until after my Consecration."

She thought of him in that room beneath the Church, telling her to make a barrier around her mind. *It's your head.* It'd sounded like something he'd repeated to himself over and over, a lesson long-ingrained.

Lore leaned forward, fingers knotted. "So Jax spared you after killing your father," she said. "And knowing that this court is full of assholes, I assume that only made them more suspicious of you."

Gabriel stayed silent for long enough that Lore wondered if he'd decided dissecting his history for her was something he didn't want to do after all.

"Sometimes," he murmured finally, "I wish he'd just finished the job."

A rustle outside, in the hall. Something slid through the crack beneath the door and the floor—a creamy white envelope.

Lore stood, her legs only slightly wine-loose, and picked it up. *Remaut*, read twirling golden script across the front. She ripped it open, read the letter inside, then brandished it at Gabriel. "It's an invitation."

He stood and crossed over to her, frowning. "To what?"

"A masquerade. Hosted by Bastian, in the throne room, at sunset."

They stared at each other, wearing similar guarded expressions. "Well," Lore said finally, "I *am* supposed to get close to him."

Gabriel grumbled, then took the invitation, reading it for himself. "August hasn't introduced you to court yet. How does he know we're here?"

"He might've seen me coming into the Citadel," Lore said, then quickly told Gabriel about spotting Bastian in the garden. She glossed over what he'd been doing there, thoughtful for his monkish sensibilities, but the way he rolled his eyes said he knew without her saying.

"Wonderful," he muttered. "So your cover might be blown before you even begin."

"Not necessarily." The specter of a cell to wait in between raising villagers' bodies loomed large in her mind still, the reality that would become hers if she couldn't spy on Bastian. "I'm a good liar; if he asks about what we were doing this morning, I'll say I had a night on the town and you had to escort me back."

"I still don't like that he knows you're here. It means he's paying more attention than August thinks. I knew us going to the Consecration was a bad idea."

It was the closest she'd heard him come to naysaying Anton, and Lore assumed it was the closest he ever did.

Gabriel gave the invitation another once-over, then cast it on the couch. "And what are we supposed to wear to a masquerade?"

A light knock on the door. "Your Grace? I have a delivery. From His Majesty."

"Gods, I hope it's dinner," Lore said, opening the door.

Not dinner. Instead, a rolling cart with two garment bags, hastily brought in by a slight serving girl who looked at Lore with wide, curious eyes. She ducked a curtsy and was gone before they could ask her any questions.

Lore unbuttoned one of the bags and peered inside. "Looks like clothes won't be a problem."

Gabriel groaned.

CHAPTER NINE

No transformation cuts more deeply than that of a
friend to an enemy.

–Auverrani proverb

I deeply hate this dress."

Gabriel shot her a sideways glance. His new clothes
amounted to a rich-green doublet embroidered over with gold
vines and breeches to match, topped with a billowing white shirt
whose sleeves could probably hide an entire roast turkey. The
refined clothes made the scarred leather of his eye patch stand out,
vicious and out of place. "You look nice," he hedged, though the
way his eye darted quickly away somewhat belied the statement.

"I look like a plum pudding." The long skirt caught beneath
one of her heels; Lore swore, kicking it away. "A plum pudding
that is apparently meant to be stationary." Her bodice slipped
downward, and Lore yanked it up. "A plum pudding meant to be
stationary and possibly eaten."

"Compared with some of the things the courtiers wear, *this* is
demure."

Lore itched beneath the domino mask that had come with her

costume, a lavender bit of silk speckled with darker purple. "This party should be quite the education for you, then."

Gabriel scoffed. His costume hadn't come with a mask, like whoever had sent the clothes wanted his face uncovered. They could only assume it was the Sun Prince's doing. Not only did Bastian know Gabriel was here, Bastian wanted Gabriel to be *seen*. Seen and recognized by the court who thought him a traitor, the heir to his father's sins.

The skirt of Lore's dress caught under her foot again. "Bleeding God and his bloody *wounds*."

"Yes, good, get it all out of your system now." Gabriel rolled his eyes. "Dukes' cousins generally keep a civil tongue. Match the script to the costume."

"I'll be sure to start peacock squawking, then." The narrow, twisting stairs the bloodcoats had led them up would be entirely impossible in Lore's heeled violet shoes, and so they took the long way, walking down each hall to the wide steps at their ends, twisting back in on themselves to funnel down the turret. "That is what I'm supposed to be, right? A peacock? Not *actually* a plum pudding?"

"Are we supposed to *be* something?"

"It's a masquerade, Mort, the costumes are the whole point." But she couldn't quite puzzle out what their costumes were. The tulle of her skirt was layered shades of purple, wine-dark on the bottom and a nearly white lavender on the top. Embroidered threads of green lined the deep-violet bodice, ending in wide leaves around the plunging neck. Some kind of flower? Gabriel's costume didn't give any clues—regular court clothes, only odd for being all in shades of green.

"You should probably refrain from calling me *Mort* once we arrive," Gabriel said. "Doesn't exactly sound familial."

"Just Gabriel, then?"

He paused. "Gabe."

"Gabe," she repeated, feeling out the word on her tongue.

He gave a solemn nod, a tiny tick of a smile in the corner of his dour mouth. Lore returned it, then reapplied herself to the arduous task of walking in her ridiculous dress.

Earlier, it had seemed like their rooms were miles from the center of the Citadel, but as the candelabras became more ornate and the iron-barred floor more polished with each descended stairway, Lore felt like they were getting there too fast. Her heart beat a nervous tattoo and sweat misted her skin, making the already-itchy tulle nigh unbearable.

"What's your full name?" Gabriel—*Gabe*—asked after a moment. They'd turned a corner and found themselves in a wide atrium that she vaguely remembered from earlier. Rosebushes grew profuse in ceramic pots, traced in golden gilt, hiding delicate wrought-iron tables and tiny statues of frolicking nymphs. "Is Lore short for something?"

"No." She shrugged. "It's the only name I have."

"We'll have to make something up, then. Something that sounds like the cousin of a duke." He looked down at her, brow thoughtfully knit. The gentle light of the fading sunset through the atrium's huge windows strobed over his face, then pitched it to shadow as they turned into another hallway. "Eldelore."

Her nose wrinkled.

The brow over his eye patch rose. "You have approximately two minutes to come up with a better one."

"Two minutes?"

They turned another corner, and the doors of the throne room loomed up ahead. Gabe gave her a chagrined look from the corner of his eye. "I *did* say approximately."

The entrance to the throne room somehow looked even more intimidating than it had this morning, the sunset light burnishing the Bleeding God's Hearts on the door with pink and crimson and orange. Five bloodcoat guards stared straight ahead, swords sheathed at their sides, not a bayonet in sight. Lore assumed the weapon wasn't elegant enough for inside the Citadel. Such slaughter was saved for outside the walls.

These guards weren't the ones who'd been there earlier, though. "New bloodcoats?" Lore whispered out of the corner of her mouth, only loud enough for Gabe to hear.

"I'd imagine the ones who saw you this morning won't be making an appearance again," Gabriel murmured. "August is thorough. The guards who caught you in the Ward are probably gone, too. Keeps the circle of people who know who you really are as small as it can be."

"So the guards were reassigned?"

"If you want to call sent to the Burnt Isles *reassigned*."

So the Citadel was just as violent as the streets of Dellaire, even if the blades were polished and the blood was mopped up more quickly.

"Name?" the bloodcoat at the door asked as they approached. Clearly, it was a formality. His eyes were wide as he looked at Gabe, like someone might look at a ghost.

"Leif Gabriel Remaut, Duke of Balgia," Gabriel announced, voice strong and sure as if he'd done this a thousand times. "And my cousin, Eldelore Remaut."

Lore dug her nails into Gabriel's arm. His lips twisted against a smirk.

The bloodcoat nodded, then opened the door.

And revealed the kind of sumptuous chaos that could've been the dead gods' Shining Realm or any one of the myriad hells.

Opulently dressed courtiers whirled to mad music from a small orchestra. Hair was done up in spirals and towers, powdered impossible colors—deep greens and gem-bright blues and light blush-pinks. Some of the dancers appeared to be dressed like animals, with half masks covering their eyes and false ears on their heads, made of expensive fabric. A thin slip of a person wore shimmering butterfly wings on their back, the same bright yellow as their hair. Another had what looked like actual swan feathers attached to the back of her diaphanous gown, and her dance partner wore nothing *but* feathers around her waist and breasts.

If Lore's eyebrows climbed any farther, they'd disappear into her hairline. "You weren't exaggerating about my dress being tame."

"Positively chaste." Gabriel looked like he'd rather be walking into a jail cell than this party. His jaw was a tight line, and the muscles under Lore's slack hand were tense as a fence post.

A familiar scent itched at Lore's nose. Belladonna.

She whipped around, searching the crowd anxiously. There, in the corner—a group of courtiers took turns drinking from a tiny ceramic cup, not even trying to hide it. Their faces were flushed, their legs unsteady, their eyes glassy with a euphoric poison high. Flashes of gray showed at wrists and throats, stone working its silent way through veins as just enough Mortem was pulled forth to slow the ravage of time. Painful years added to pampered lives.

"They'll kill themselves if they drink too much," she muttered. "The key is moderation, and nothing about this party tells me these people know anything about that."

"Citadel physicians are highly skilled at treating overdoses." Gabriel's blue eye flashed as he turned away from the knot of poisoned nobles. "It happens all the time. There are laws in place that force a nobleman to step down in favor of his heir if he lives too long."

"I haven't seen anyone that looks like a revenant."

"Citadel physicians are skilled at treating that, too. Take a good look at some of the older nobles next time you get a chance. Cosmetics and padding go a long way to hide stone veins and emaciation."

Lore's jaw tightened as she watched the extravagantly dressed courtiers pass the poison, giggling. She didn't realize she'd taken a step toward the group until Gabe's hand landed on her shoulder.

He shook his head. "Just leave it, Lore."

And what could she do, even if she did go over there? It wouldn't make a difference.

So Lore sighed, and shook her hands out of their fists, and turned to observe the Court of the Citadel in all its debauchery.

Knots of revelers stood drinking between dances, gathered in bursts of bright clothes, as ornate as the golden frescoes they stood before. Those who weren't kissing or drinking were gossiping—heads bowed as close together as elaborate hairstyles would allow, whispering and then breaking into whoops of laughter. Cosmetic-lined eyes scanned the room, as if making sure their mirth was marked, and hopefully envied.

A man wearing a sea-green mask with golden scales turned his eyes lazily to Gabe, then away. A moment, and his gaze snapped back, disinterest becoming openmouthed surprise. He leaned to the ear of the person next to him, their hair coiled into something resembling a beehive, whispering furiously.

"And thus our new faces are noticed," Lore said. They still stood by the door, neither of them keen on venturing into the sparkling milieu.

"Mine isn't new, which seems to be the problem." Gabriel sighed. "I'd hoped that ten years and one less eye would make recognizing me more difficult."

"You're hard not to notice," Lore murmured, then clamped her lips shut.

"And you say *I* need to work on my compliments." Gabe shook out his shoulders. "Well. Into the breach."

He tugged them into the party.

Dancers spun past them, their costumes wearable displays of wealth. Jewels encrusted bodices; clouds of gold-threaded tulle swept the ground. The dancers paid no mind to the iron bars crossing the floor, the reminders of holy responsibility covered in sweat and spilled champagne.

Lore's heart thrummed, and not just from nerves. This reminded her of the wilder venues down by the docks, though it felt more dangerous than those ever had. Money and power gave it weight, made it heady.

Made it exciting, and part of her hated herself for that. The part that kept thinking of those people drinking brewed belladonna in the corner.

In the scents of whirling dancers and strong perfume, there was also the scent of food. Lore's stomach twisted in her too-tight bodice. "Any idea where the buffet is?" she asked Gabriel, pitching her voice to carry over music and laughter.

"On the right side, I think," he said, eyes shifting like prey in a predator's den. Other courtiers had noticed them now, gazes flickering their direction and then away with practiced nonchalance.

The ebb and flow of the party revealed a table set up before the golden depiction of a fox hunt, baying dogs and howling hunters chasing the ruby-encrusted animal across the wall. Two fountains in the center of the table flowed with wine, red and white, with crystal goblets set in precarious gleaming pyramids next to them. Bowls of bright fruit sat beside artfully stacked pastries, jewels on an expensive necklace.

Her stomach rumbled. Lore stepped forward, ready to weave her way through to the table, but the parting crowd revealed the throne at the front of the room, and for the first time, she noticed someone was on it. One leg was tossed over the arm, booted foot swinging in the air, and an elbow was propped on the opposite side, head leaned against a clenched, ring-studded fist.

Even in the decadent chaos of his own party, Bastian Arceneaux somehow managed to look bored.

That sense of familiarity came again, looking at him. Almost like déjà vu. Like Bastian fit perfectly into a place in her head that she hadn't even known was empty.

"Gabriel?" The woman's voice coming from behind them was light and musical. And from the way the Presque Mort froze beside Lore, it seemed he recognized it.

"Gabriel Remaut?" A questioning lilt, a hint of nervousness. "I'm sorry, maybe I'm mistaken—"

Lore tugged on Gabriel's arm and turned him around to face the person speaking.

A diminutive woman stood on the edge of the dance floor, with an anxious expression and hair the color of white marble in a cloud of airy curls. Pearlescent dust gleamed across warm copper-brown cheekbones scattered with freckles, sparkling like the wings attached to her white tulle gown, and her eyes matched the delicate dark-green embroidery across the sheer neckline. She looked like a flower fairy, straight from a children's book, and the smile she broke into was nearly as bright as the rest of her.

His arm somehow tenser than before beneath Lore's palm, Gabriel inclined his head. "Alienor."

"It's really you!" The sparkling woman laughed aloud, clapping her hands together. "Bastian told me you were coming back from the north for a while, to introduce your cousin to society, but I thought he had to be joking!"

"Bastian is less than trustworthy at the best of times, true."

"Fourteen years of holy service and you still harbor the sin of jealousy." Alienor mockingly shook her head, making glitter fall from her false wings.

"I was never *jealous* of him, Alie."

"Of course you were; every time he'd tell me I looked pretty you'd tell him to watch his mouth around your betrothed. He only did it to get a rise out of you, you know." Alienor said it lightly, like something funny, but there was a shadow around her eyes that dimmed the illusion.

Betrothed. It explained the tension in Gabriel's stance. Only ten years old when his father's betrayal and Anton's vision pushed him to the Presque Mort, but people were betrothed early in the Court of the Citadel, their lives laid out practically from birth.

Gabe reached up and touched his eye patch self-consciously; Alienor's gaze followed his hand, her mouth falling a fraction.

"It's good to see you, Gabe," she murmured, all teasing gone.

Gabriel lowered his hand. "And you."

Lore shifted her weight, feeling very much like an intruder.

For the first time, the smaller woman seemed to notice her. Her smile brightened. "And this is your cousin, right? I didn't know you had one."

"Third cousin." Lore offered her hand, reciting the backstory she and Gabriel had come up with in their apartments while he buttoned the back of her dress and tried not to faint at the sight of feminine shoulder blades. "Distant and obscure, social climbing by way of my esteemed relative."

"Alie, meet Eldelore." Gabe's mouth twitched as he said the full name, almost a smirk.

"Just Lore, if you please." The wide skirt of her dress gave her cover as Lore slipped her foot over Gabe's and pressed the heel of her shoe into his toe, just enough to make him jerk.

Alienor smiled, taking Lore's hand and giving her a tiny bow. "Lovely to meet you, Just Lore. And you must call me Alie, all my friends do."

Alienor's face was open and kind, with no trace of artifice. Lore found herself desperately hoping it was real, though everything about the Citadel called for caution. "Alie," she repeated.

The three of them lapsed into uncomfortable silence. The music stopped, then swelled, going from a lively jig to something even more upbeat.

Gabriel frowned. "This music," he said, twisting his head. "It's Kirythean."

"Is it?" Alie looked puzzled, but not disturbed. "Well. That's interesting."

"If by interesting you mean traitorous."

"That seems a bit dramatic." A new voice, from behind Lore—smooth, courtly, with an upturned edge like it was on the verge of a joke. "I prefer *daring* to *traitorous*," the voice continued.

Gabriel's one visible blue eye was stormy, teeth clenched tight in his jaw. But Alie grinned, waving a glitter-dusted hand. "Speak his name and he appears."

Lore turned.

The Sun Prince of Auverraine stood behind her, one brow arched over his domino mask. He'd been handsome from far away, clothed in gleaming white at his Consecration and seen from behind roses in the garden. But up close, wearing all black to match his hair and eyes, he was near to devastating.

And the grin he gave her said he knew it.

"The return of the Remaut family to the Court of the Citadel is a momentous occasion indeed," Bastian Arceneaux said, clapping Gabe on the back; Gabe stiffened and didn't move, a tree refusing to bend to a gale. "My father is very excited to have you here, and suggested most strongly that I make you welcome, though I doubt a masquerade was what he had in mind. Technically, we're all supposed to be at evening prayers, but since I was just Consecrated, I think the Bleeding God will give me the evening off from piety."

"As if you've ever been pious," Alie scoffed.

"You wound me." Bastian pressed a hand to his chest, then looked back at Gabe. "I must say, I'm thrilled that I beat out Apollius for your attentions this evening. Sorry about the mask, old friend. I wasn't sure how it would interfere with..." He waved a hand at his eyes. "All that."

Lore had known it was Bastian behind the lack of a mask for Gabe, but hearing it still churned her middle. A flippant cruelty, making Gabe the center of attention for people he had no desire to be around. She tried to keep her eyes from narrowing.

Bastian's lips curved in a mischievous smile that didn't tell her if she was successful or not. His voice dropped low as he bent and took Lore's hand. "Pleased to make your acquaintance from up close this time. Believe me, had I not been otherwise occupied, I would have stopped to speak with you at the Consecration. It's rare to get new blood in here."

She was thankful for his leather gloves; they'd hide the clamminess of her palm. "I'm pleased to provide," she said, giving him the best coquettish smile she could muster.

Apparently, it wasn't a good one; she saw Gabe's mouth twist before he looked away toward the wine table, like he was fighting back a laugh. Lore darted him a quick glare from the corner of her eye. She was supposed to get close to the prince, right? In her experience, this was how the game was played.

But there was something calculating in Bastian's eyes, a spark of steel that his smile couldn't hide. Something that said he was just as good at playing games as she was.

Alie crossed her arms, shedding more glitter from her dress. "You told everyone it was supposed to be a costume party, Bastian, but all you wore is black."

"I'm a *night*." The Sun Prince straightened, releasing Lore's hand and gesturing to the shining sword by his side. For being part of a costume, the blade still looked sharp. "Get it?"

"Bleeding God." Alie rolled her eyes, but she was grinning. "Everyone will think they're overdressed, as opposed to you just being lazy."

"Oh, no, they all know I'm lazy." Bastian's eyes hadn't left Lore's. She held his by instinct, as if she'd unwittingly entered a battle of wills by meeting his gaze. A battle she now refused to lose.

A courtier approached, dressed in layers of pastel rainbow tulle, eyes lined in shimmering dust. She swayed on her feet, a glass clutched in her hand. More poison, the assault of it making Lore's nose wrinkle and her fingertips go numb. Instinctively, she backed up, nearly stepping on Gabe's foot again. The awareness of Mortem was just a tingle, a prickle of unease and slight nausea. That mental trick Gabe had taught her must really be something.

The courtier grinned and held out the cup. "Want some, Bastian?" Her eyes cut over to Lore and Gabe, her grin going subtly cruel. "Or how about you two? Think of it like an initiation."

"Come now, Cecelia." Bastian's voice was light, but his eyes were a dark glitter behind his mask. "This is bad manners."

Tulle fluttered as Cecelia swayed on her feet. "Suit yourself," she said, taking another tiny sip from her cup before wandering off.

Bastian laughed, low beneath the whine of violins. "Forgive them," he said, eyes still cold. "Idle hands turn to sin as naturally as flowers to the sun. The Book of Mortal Law, Tract Forty-Five."

Gabe said nothing, but his jaw tightened.

The Sun Prince drained his wine and handed the glass to a passing courtier, who seemed simultaneously confused and delighted. "Aren't you going to introduce me to your charming cousin, Gabe?"

"Do I need to?" Gabriel's voice sounded like his teeth wanted to close around it. "You seem to know all about us already."

One hand hung in a fist by his side. Lore lightly brushed her fingers against it. She didn't think knuckles-to-cheekbone was the kind of closeness August and Anton wanted her and Gabriel to cultivate with the Sun Prince.

Gabe's hand splayed, the exaggerated opposite of the fist it'd been before.

"It *is* considered polite." Bastian finally dropped Lore's gaze, turning to Gabe instead. "But you have been out of court for a while, toiling with my uncle up in Northreach. So in the absence of politeness, I suppose I will have to introduce myself."

The band whipped up, violins and cellos sighing out a plaintive note before launching into a faster tempo. The dancers clapped gleefully, yelling their encouragement.

"Over a dance," Bastian continued, and laced his fingers with Lore's, tugging her out into the bright whirl.

CHAPTER TEN

To my chosen, I bequeath my power—Spiritum, the
magic of life. May it be used to bring about the world
as it should be.

—The Book of Holy Law, Tract 714 (green text;
spoken by Apollius to Gerard Arceneaux)

Lore the poison runner felt slightly nauseous, between the hunger and the smell of poison and the anxiety that numbed her
limbs. But Eldelore Remaut would be thrilled to be pulled out into
a mad Kirythean dance by a handsome prince, and it was Eldelore
Remaut who needed to be here tonight, getting close to the Sun
Prince and learning if he was currently committing treason.

If he was, the choice of Kirythean music was a bold one.

The deep-purple tulle of her skirt caught under her heel again,
and Lore swore soundly, kicking it away. Bastian arched a brow,
an amused smile picking up the corner of his mouth.

Eldelore Remaut probably wouldn't do that.

The cousin of a duke would also be expected to dance well, a
skill Lore didn't possess. She'd tried, once, with a job at a tavern like the one Elle had, keeping patrons dancing, drinking, and

spending their coin. She'd knocked over two barmaids and hadn't lasted the night. Poison running was the only thing she'd ever been good at.

Poison running, and spying. She could do this.

Lore pulled back on Bastian's leading hand. There were calluses on his knuckles, she noticed, which seemed strange for a prince, and the nose beneath his black mask looked slightly crooked, like it'd been broken before.

He glanced at her over his shoulder, mouth twisted in a wry smile. "I won't bite." Then, the smile twisting higher, "unless you decide you want me to."

She supposed she should blush, but she'd heard much worse, and dealt it, too. She tried for an answering smile she hoped was demure. "I'm afraid I don't know this dance." The Kirythean music careened wildly from the violins, a match for the cavorting of the crowd. The dance appeared to involve jumping and clapping, neither of which Lore thought she could do in her dress. "I'm not familiar with Kirythean customs. Are you?"

A leading question: Start easy, and see how hard they were going to make you work.

"Not necessarily."

Harder than that, apparently.

Bastian pulled her to the center of the floor, through courtiers that parted like a jewel-toned wave. He raised a hand and gestured to the band in the corner. Abruptly, the music changed, moving to something slow and measured.

"But I've decided I'm over the *katairos*." Bastian grinned, placing one hand on her waist. A beat, and he swept her into something Lore thought was a waltz. Hopefully, her guise as a country cousin would be ample cover for her lack of grace.

"So the Kirythean music was just for Gabriel's benefit, then?" Lore cocked her head, smile still in place, though there was a hint of venom behind the question. The Mort was stuffy and overimportant and built like he could take care of himself, but their odd circumstances made her feel almost protective of him.

"It wasn't for Gabe's benefit at all." Bastian spun her out, then pulled her back in, close to his black-clad chest. He was shorter than Gabriel, but only just, and Lore's forehead would've knocked into his chin if he didn't lean gracefully away, making it look like part of the dance. "The Kirythean music was because I like it."

"I'm sure that thrills your father."

His eyes sparked behind his mask, the slight smile on his mouth going sharp. "Nothing I do thrills my father. He's decided I'm worthless, and I don't particularly care enough to try and change his mind."

Another spin, under his arm this time, his hand staying on the small of her back to guide her through.

"And just so we're clear," he murmured as she passed close again, "I wouldn't taunt Gabe about his family. I know he thinks I'm awful, and he has his reasons, but even I'm not *that* heartless."

Lore hoped her laugh didn't sound as false as it felt. "But you'd make sure he doesn't have a mask, so that everyone here can see his face."

"I wanted the court to know he was here. To give him an opportunity to see what he's missing, maybe decide to stay instead of slink back to the Presque Mort." Bastian's voice was pleasant, but the ridge of his jaw could carve stone. "My uncle has been half mad since his accident, even if everyone wants to pretend like it's something holy, and he's controlled Gabe's life for fourteen years. I saw an opportunity to set him free, at least for a few weeks, and I took it. He should thank me."

Lore wondered what Bastian would think if he knew that Gabe was only in the court because of Anton. That his uncle's control was still ironclad.

"How exactly would making sure the court sees him here make him want to stay?" she asked.

Bastian waved a hand at the party. "Stick a man in a den of iniquity after he's been cloistered for over a decade, and it's likely he'll fall into sin. If it was public enough, Anton might not let him come back into the monkish fold. That was the hope, anyway." The Sun Prince snorted. "Though I've probably underestimated Gabe's piety. He always was predisposed to martyrdom."

They swayed in silence for a moment, the air between them filled with violins and the scent of spilled champagne.

"I suppose the fact that Gabe joined the Presque Mort was fortunate for you." Bastian's eyes were so dark a brown as to almost be black, and lit with prying curiosity. "As it was your ticket into the Court of the Citadel. I can't imagine the third cousin of a disgraced duke being invited for the season if said disgraced duke hadn't become the Priest Exalted's pet project."

He said it with a purposeful sort of condescension, like he was trying to bait her into disagreeing, and as if that disagreement would give something away.

She gave a closed-lip smile. "I would've found a way in," she answered.

A country cousin hungry for power and placement, eager to be here. It was as far from what Lore felt as possible, but she could play the part.

Bastian stared at her a moment, inscrutable beneath his mask. Then he laughed, spinning her around again.

Gabriel still stood with Alienor at the edge of the ballroom. The two of them spoke with their heads bowed toward each other to hear, but his eye, bright with nerves, kept straying to find Lore and Bastian.

She was better prepared when Bastian spun her out this time. And when everyone stomped their right foot to the beat, Lore was perfectly in sync.

Bastian grinned. "A fast learner, are we?"

"I'm certainly trying to be."

They came together again; Bastian slipped a hand around her waist, and she did the same as they circled each other, a movement that would've looked predatory without the softness dancing brought it. "That dress suits you," Bastian said, not trying to hide the turn of his eyes up and down her form. "I didn't get a very good look at you during the Consecration—or yesterday morning in the gardens, occupied as I was—but I thought it might."

So he *did* recognize her from the gardens. Lore gave him a self-deprecating smile. "That was you? How embarrassing. My belongings didn't arrive on time, so I had to borrow a dress from the Church's donations."

Hands left waists, came to face height and hovered within an inch of each other, palms flat as Lore orbited around him. "How fortunate," Bastian murmured, "to have such a close contact in the Church."

The dance ended. Around them, other couples were in a pose with their right hands together and the other curved above their heads, but Bastian and Lore still stood with their palms facing between them, almost touching but not quite.

"I look forward to having you around, Lore." His voice was low, breath brushing her temple as he leaned forward to speak into her ear. "It certainly has the potential to be interesting."

"Do you think so, Your Highness?"

He was close enough that she felt the brush of his lips curving. "I know so."

Across the room, Alie watched them, giggling behind her hand. Next to her, Gabe caught Lore's eye, arched a sardonic brow. She tried to make a face that communicated *what else am I supposed to do?* but mostly just succeeded in looking nauseous.

Bastian stepped back. He reached into his coat, and for a wild moment, Lore thought he was going to pull out a dagger or one of those tiny pistols, prove himself the Kirythean informant his father thought he was by taking care of her right here in the middle of his own party. The courtiers would probably love it. They'd all bring in peasants to murder at their own balls; it'd be the next big trend in masquerade hosting.

But all Bastian pulled from his coat was a pressed flower, a line of pale-purple blooms on a green stem.

"A foxglove for a foxglove." Bastian handed it to her with a bow and a flourish. "Beautiful and poisonous. Much like yourself, if I may be so bold as to make an assessment after our brief acquaintance."

Gingerly, Lore took the bloom. The dry petals crunched slightly between her fingers.

"Until next time, Lore." Bastian turned and walked away, a drop of ink in a sea of color.

❦

Lore closed the door to the apartments behind her and leaned back against it. "I suppose that went about as well as it could."

"You performed your assignment admirably," Gabriel said, sitting down on the couch with a long sigh.

"It seems ingratiating myself with Bastian won't be the hard part." Lore pulled off her mask and let it drop. "Getting any kind of information out of him will be. He's not going to tell me he's a traitor just because he thinks I'm pretty; he's smarter than his father or his uncle gives him credit for."

Gabe snorted.

Lore toed off the heeled slippers that had come with her costume, pale purple and embroidered with serrated leaves. Foxglove leaves. The dried bloom Bastian had given her was still in her palm. If she'd been found with something like this on the streets of Dellaire, it'd be at least three days in the Northwest Ward stocks if it was a first offense, and a ticket to the Burnt Isles if it wasn't. But here, in this gilded palace full of money and excess, it was a prince's idle gift.

She thought of the courtiers in the corner with their bella-donna tea, physicians on call and no reason to worry. Her fist closed, crushing the flower into pastel dust. She brushed it from her hands and let it fall to the floor with her mask.

Feeling coming back into her feet now that her slippers were off, Lore walked over to Gabe and stood in front of him, gesturing to the buttons down her back. "Help me out here, I can't reach."

He hesitated a moment before setting to work. For a monk, he was a clever hand at undoing a woman's buttons, a thought that flashed across her mind unbidden before she resolutely shut it out.

"Did he say anything important while you were dancing?" Gabe asked.

The only things she'd learned while dancing with Bastian were about Gabe. But some tug of intuition told her that if she tried to talk about that, he'd shut down. She'd only known Gabe for two days, but it was enough to know that he wouldn't take lightly to disparaging Anton or the Presque Mort. People who thought they'd been saved tended to deify the savior.

"Not really. Certainly not anything that made it seem like he's a Kirythean spy." With a sigh, Lore flopped on the opposite end of the couch and propped up her aching feet on the ottoman. "I don't understand why August is so convinced the informant is Bastian."

"He told you. Because Bastian doesn't want to be King." Gabriel stared into the dying embers in the fireplace, head propped on his hand. He'd loosened his cravat, revealing a triangle of pale, freckle-dusted skin. "When we were young, he used to tell me he wanted to be a pirate."

It was strange to think of the man across from her as the boy he must've been, cavorting around these halls with the Sun Prince and pretty Alie every summer. Not knowing that his life would crash down around his ears, that he'd have to rebuild it into something holy in order to survive.

"As someone who was maybe one degree removed from being a pirate," Lore said, "I would like to disabuse anyone of the notion that it's a great time."

"A better time than being a King, I'd think."

"Doesn't seem like a good enough reason to start a war."

"It might seem like one if you had the responsibility of being an Arceneaux King hanging over your head," Gabe murmured to the fire.

She gave him an incredulous look. "For someone who clearly dislikes the man, you seem very in tune with how his mind works."

He frowned at that. "I'm just saying I know Bastian well enough to understand that he'd see a war—especially one that seems all but inevitable eventually—as a small price to pay for leaving behind the responsibility his lineage brings him. Holy and otherwise."

Lore scoffed, thinking of the iron bars on the marble floors, what they symbolized. The Arceneaux family's divine right to rule came with the caveat that they'd have to control the Mortem leaking from Nyxara's body. Establishing the Church and Citadel on top of Nyxara's tomb kept Mortem contained, mostly, but according to the Tracts, the Arceneaux line could also wield Spiritum, Apollius's power—the magic of life.

But not one Arceneaux had ever actually been able to do it.

"Do you believe that part?" she asked. "The Spiritum bit?"

Gabe stayed quiet for a moment, thinking. "I believe that the presence of the Arceneaux family in the Citadel is what keeps Mortem from overwhelming the continent." He spoke slowly, piecing together a tapestry of belief and doubt. "That's just history; we have records of what it was like before the Citadel was built, before Gerard Arceneaux made it the seat of his power."

"But there's no records of him actually *using* Spiritum, like it says in the Tracts."

"It's possible that was a misinterpretation. It's happened

before." He looked her way. "Did your parents ever scare you with tales of the Night Witch?"

Her throat went dry. "The mad priestess?"

She said it like a question, like she wasn't sure if she had it right. Like that story wasn't an indelible part of her history.

"Exactly." Gabe shifted on the couch, scratching at his eye patch. "The Night Witch was just a priestess, leader of the Buried Watch, a holy order tasked with guarding the Buried Goddess's tomb and monitoring how much Mortem leaked out. They were a sister sect of the Presque Mort, actually, another group of Church-sanctioned channelers, though after the Citadel was built and Gerard Arceneaux crowned, that requirement was waived. By the time the Night Witch came around, she was the only channeler in the Watch."

Lore made herself nod along.

Gabe continued. "Eventually, she went mad and tried to open the tomb. She claimed she was the goddess reborn, because she'd misinterpreted some Tract in the Book of Holy Law. It's been stricken from the Compendium since." He shook his head, almost in pity. "That's why we need men like Anton, who can read the Tracts and help us know what they mean. The consequences can be horrific."

Her fingers knotted in her lap, cold and numb.

They sat in silence, except for the crackling fire. After a moment, Gabe stood. He went into the bedroom that had been designated as his and came out with blankets and pillows, then began piling them by the door.

"You know there's a perfectly serviceable bed in there, right?" Lore asked.

"I'm sleeping in front of the door." Gabe glanced at her, a calculating shine in his visible eye, before stripping off his doublet and shirt. His chest was well muscled, covered with reddish hair darker than the gold-tinged shade of his head and beard. "I don't trust anyone in this Citadel as far as I can throw them."

"It looks as though you can throw them rather far," Lore muttered.

"Let's hope I don't have to demonstrate." Gabe nestled down into his makeshift bed, back against the door. If anyone tried to enter, they'd be blocked by a pile of one-eyed holy man. "If I were you, I'd go to bed. First Day prayers are at sunrise."

First Day prayers—she'd forgotten that August was officially introducing them to court then. With a groan, Lore rose and walked to the bedroom that Gabe hadn't ransacked. "Good night, Mort."

"Good night, heretic."

She had barely enough energy to laugh. Lore stepped out of her foxglove gown, leaving it in a lavender pile on the floor, and fell into sleep and darkness.

CHAPTER ELEVEN

The goddess whispered in the Night Witch's ear,
"It'd be so nice to see you, dear,
Open the door and let me go
There's many stories you don't know."
                                        —Children's skipping rhyme

Lore sat by the ocean and felt, for the first time she could
remember, completely fine.

The water was warm; it lapped against the white rim of the
shore, splashing up her calves and wearing away at the sand she sat
on. This wasn't the beach by the harbor docks, cold and rocky—
no, this was more like one of the beaches she'd heard about in
the southernmost cities of Auverraine, where the rich sometimes
went when winter bit too hard. There was no salt scent to the air.
It smelled like nothing.

Like nothing.

Someone sat next to her. Lore couldn't see who. When she
turned her head, there was only a dark void, a person-shaped gap
in the world.

A void, but if she looked too long, there were flashes of

things in the dark. An obsidian block of a tomb. An iron brand, crescent-shaped, glowing orange. A woman with hazel eyes, just like hers.

Lore didn't try to look again.

In the sky above the warm ocean, smoke twisted sinuously, gray against blue. It took Lore a moment to notice that the smoke was coming from her, streaming out from her chest, reaching dark tendrils over the water. As she watched, it stretched farther and farther, arcing over the sky.

Perfect, said the figure next to her, the one she couldn't see. *Much easier, this time.*

❦

Lore shot up from the too-soft bed, pressing her knuckles against her eyes until stars danced behind them. The mental barrier Gabriel had helped her make had finally failed, as if the strange nightmare even now fading from her memory had burned through her forest. She sensed Mortem in everything—the walls, the bedding, the furniture. It made her every limb feel leaden, made her head pound, the symptoms of suffocation even as she heaved lungfuls of air. The moment of death, crystallized and endless, all the pain with none of the peace.

Lore stood on shaky legs, hissing against the throbbing in her head. Between her mad dash away from the Northwest Ward, being tied to a chair for all of one night, and nearly dancing through another, her body felt like the end of a fraying rope.

With a lurch, she forced herself forward, through the bedroom door and into the shared sitting room. She nearly hit the wall, reeled back, gritted her teeth. Touching anything felt like a punch to her brain, and part of her wanted to claw off her perfectly tailored nightgown. She stayed her hand, but only just. Gabe would have to help her with this, and he wouldn't be much assistance if his celibate heart gave out at the sight of her naked.

The one-eyed monk was still half propped against the threshold that led to the hallway, like a human doorstop. She prodded his shoulder with her foot; her head hurt too much to crouch down, she'd probably be sick all over him if she tried. "Gabe. It's back."

He went from sleep to wakefulness in an instant. Gabe sat up, his sheet slipping down to his waist, concern scrunching the skin around his eye patch—he slept in the thing, apparently, at least when he was guarding doors. His one blue eye flickered over her, took quick stock of the situation, thankfully knowing exactly what she spoke of without Lore having to explain. "Did you ground yourself before you fell asleep?"

"Did I *what?*"

"I'll take that as a no."

"How the fuck would I have known to do that?" Pain made her sharp; Lore's teeth were nearly bared.

Gabe took it in stride. He shifted his position so he sat cross-legged on the floor, palms on his knees. A sweep of his hand indicated he wanted her to do the same.

Lore did, slowly, hissing a string of curses. Her legs prickled with pins and needles; trying to move them felt like hauling sacks of unresponsive meat.

"Grounding," Gabe said when she was settled, "is visualizing your barrier, setting it in place. Making it as real as possible in your mind, so that you don't have to be actively concentrating to keep it up."

"I haven't concentrated on it all day, and it held up fine." It'd only been a problem since her nightmare. Lore could still feel it tugging at the edges of her mind, at her *heart*, as if she hadn't really woken up at all. As if the nightmare were a living thing, full of malice and trying to trap her.

But she couldn't quite fix it in her mind. When she tried to recall exactly what happened in the dream, all she got were flashes—white sand, blue water.

His brows drew together, a fleeting expression of puzzlement. "That *is* odd."

"Can we discuss the oddness later, please?"

A troubled light still shone in Gabe's eye, but he nodded. His hands relaxed on his knees. "Think about your barrier," he said, low and calm. "Every detail, no matter how small. Settle into it, so it seems as real as anything else."

The only thing Lore felt like settling was her fist into her own face—anything to stop this headache. But she gradually calmed her breathing, unclenched her jaw. Untangled her thoughts from the unpleasant sensations of head pounding and a sweaty brow and death on every side, and thought instead of a forest.

Trees. Lots of them. Growing around her in an impenetrable green wall. She heard Gabe breathing in a deep, even cadence; her breath came in counterpoint, like she took in what he let out.

Slowly, slowly, the awareness of omnipresent death dimmed, faded. Not entirely, never entirely. But enough that Lore didn't feel like she was drowning in it. In her state of deep concentration, where the forest in her head seemed as real and present as the dusty carpet below her, she could almost see something moving beyond her wall of trees. Smoke drifting sinuously in a blue sky.

The image itched at her mind, but she couldn't fit it to a memory.

When the pounding in her skull subsided and her nightgown felt merely like cotton instead of a chthonic shroud, Lore opened her eyes.

Gabe was looking at her. He'd looked at her a lot over the course of their two days stuck together, but in light made only by a fire's embers and with so much freckled skin visible, it seemed heavier now. Like he could really *see* her, a person, not a Mortem channeler or a pretender in a foxglove gown or a stone hung around his neck. Just a woman.

"Has it always been this bad?" His voice was hushed. "The awareness?"

Lore swallowed. "No."

He stayed quiet, expecting her to go on. But when she kept silent, he didn't press. "Our minds are most vulnerable in sleep," Gabe said. "They're more open, more receptive." His eye fixed on her, shining with empathy in the moonlight through the window. "It's nothing to be ashamed of."

As if *this* was what she'd be ashamed of, out of everything she had to choose from.

Abruptly, Lore stood. "Well. Thank you for helping me." She rushed into her room, ready to fall asleep again, to lose herself in tree-shrouded oblivion. Eyes clenched shut, she imagined her forest, filled it out with as much detail as she could.

Branches swayed. Trunks grew thick. Through the emerald leaves, sinuous smoke snaked over an azure sky.

The Church was just as impressive as the Citadel, albeit in a different way. Where the Citadel was all opulence and gilt, the Church was austere, with whitewashed stone walls that nearly glowed, gleaming oak rafters, and pews polished to high shine. Gemlike windows of stained glass cast the gathered congregants of the North Sanctuary in shards of colored light as the sun slowly climbed the sky.

Not for the first time since rising at an ungodly hour—a phrase Gabe had taken as a pun when he woke her up, though she meant it in all sincerity—Lore gave silent thanks that she'd shown restraint with the wine fountain at Bastian's masquerade. Her eyes still felt gritty from lack of sleep, but at least she didn't look as haggard as some of the courtiers silently filing in through the wooden double doors. The parade of red eyes and missed streaks of glitter made an easy-to-follow guest list of who'd spent the night dancing with the Sun Prince and who hadn't.

It would appear that most had. Among the younger courtiers, at least, Bastian was a popular man. She wondered if that was part of the reason why August was so eager to think him a spy. Men in powerful positions were unsettled by popular heirs waiting to take their places. In that regard, the Court of the Citadel wasn't that much different from a poison runner crew. She'd seen more than one upstart assassinated by their own captain.

A yawn stretched her mouth so wide Lore's jaw popped. She'd barely taken in the walk from the back entrance of the Citadel to the North Sanctuary, too tired to pay much attention. It was a good mile and a half, by her counting, the path cobble-paved and smooth, lined with rosebushes—a stark contrast with the rubble-strewn walkways in Dellaire proper leading to the South Sanctuary, the one meant for commoners. On either side of the path, the Citadel's massive green spaces rolled, manicured fields and pseudo-forests, rich land fenced in by the fortress of the Church's walls.

Something nudged her shoulder. Gabe. "Wake up, cousin."

"I'm awake, *cousin*." But another yawn cramped her jaw as she said it. "Why in all myriad hells are First Day prayers right at the ass-crack of dawn? Surely Apollius can still hear them around noon."

Gabe inclined his head to the stained-glass window at the very front of the sanctuary. The Bleeding God's Heart, set out in panels of red and gold and ocher. As the sun rose, its gleam traced up the window, slowly illuminating the glass until the whole thing blazed with color.

"That's why," he answered. She couldn't tell if he sounded reverent or resentful. Maybe a little of both.

For sleeping against the doorframe all night, Gabriel seemed positively refreshed. Dressed in plainer clothes than he'd had for the masquerade—dark doublet, dark breeches, and a linen shirt beneath, this time with sensible sleeves—this was the handsomest he'd looked in their brief acquaintance.

Lore, on the other hand, had carefully avoided the mirror this morning, even as she brushed out her hair. The bags under her eyes were probably deep enough to smuggle hemlock.

The double doors at the back of the sanctuary remained open, emitting the last straggling courtiers. Alienor glided down the thick tapestry carpet running through the center aisle, the sun through the windows making her nearly white curls glow the same colors as the stained glass, a halo-like nimbus around her head. Her eyes were clear and her gait steady as she approached the altar at the front of the sanctuary, knelt, and kissed its polished wood. Lore and Gabe had done the same when they entered. Lore tried not to think about all the lips that had been on it before hers.

When Alie straightened and went to find her seat, her eyes met Lore's. She smiled, threw a tiny wave. Lore returned it with a genuine smile of her own. Gabriel didn't look at Alie at all.

An older man walked close behind Alienor, close enough that they had to be arriving together, though they looked nothing alike. His skin was milk-pale to her warm-copper, his hair wood-brown and pin-straight instead of white-blond and curling. His expression was dour, and the lines around his mouth said that rarely changed. The man's gaze flickered to Lore, as if taking her measure.

"Who's that?" she murmured to Gabe out of the side of her mouth.

"Severin Bellegarde." Gabe didn't have to move to answer the question; he'd been watching Alie already. "Alie's father."

Lore arched a brow. Alie must take after her mother, then, in every way.

She looked away from Bellegarde, made a show of studying the windows. Apollius, again, in various scenes both imagined and taken from the Tracts. Healing a mortal wound with a touch. Stepping through a door of cloud into what she could only assume was supposed to be the Shining Realm, leaving the world behind. Lore frowned and turned her attention to the crowd instead.

For all her resentment at being here, the North Sanctuary glittering with the gathered finery of the Court of the Citadel was certainly a sight to behold. They all knew exactly what to do, where to go, how to sit and wait and look holy, even with their eyes spiderwebbed in red from drink and poison the night before. As a non-noble, Lore had never been permitted in the North Sanctuary, and she'd only been in the South Sanctuary for common prayers a handful of times, mostly when she got caught in the shuffle while doing reconnaissance for a nearby drop.

The last of the courtiers filed in. The double doors leading to the green space and the Citadel beyond closed, booming in the silence.

At the front of the sanctuary, a small door on the raised platform behind the altar opened, emitting Anton, dressed in a robe so white it almost hurt Lore's eyes, his Bleeding God's Heart pendant swinging from his chest. Another of the Presque Mort emerged behind him, dressed in the usual black, holding a thurible spilling with thick incense smoke. She was missing a hand, the stump riven with lurid scars. It was rare to see women in the Presque Mort—before, anyone who wasn't a man and could channel Mortem would've joined the Buried Watch, if they didn't choose to simply try ignoring the call of their new death magic—but it did happen. Anyone of any gender could become a Mort.

And the Buried Watch wasn't an option anymore. At least not officially.

Lore slid her eyes to Gabriel, still and stoic next to her. She probably would've tried to ignore her abilities, were her circumstances more conventional. The Presque Mort didn't exactly make being a monk look fun.

Next to the Mort, a priest Lore didn't recognize stepped up to the braziers lining the front of the dais and lit them with the flame of his beeswax taper. He was dressed in white, and unscarred. Just a general clergyman, then.

She watched Anton carefully as the braziers were lit. She'd think someone who'd been scarred by them so horribly would look at least a little nervous, but the Priest Exalted stepped right up to the smoking embers without so much as a momentary flinch.

Another door opened on the opposite side of the dais, larger than the first, inlaid with a sun's golden corona around the lintel. August strode through, rayed crown on his head, a deep-orange cloak over his shoulders. The inside lining of the cloak was golden cloth, winking as he moved down the short stairs to the altar before the dais and sank to his knees, facing the gathered crowd.

The Sainted King's movements looked slightly unsteady. A tremor in the knee, a tiny quake along his fingers. He scratched once at his neck, concealed by the high collar of his shirt, then clasped his hands in an attitude of prayer.

And behind him, moving at a pace just slow enough to interrupt the rhythm of the ceremony, was Bastian.

The Sun Prince looked like he'd been up all night—there was a slight reddening of his eyes, and tired lines beneath them—but somehow, he made it look good. His hair fell in gleaming waves to his shoulders, and the limning of scruff on his jaw looked rugged rather than sloppy. He was dressed similarly to his father, in a black doublet, black shirt, and black breeches, but his crown was a simple golden band across his brow, ruby-studded, and his cloak was crimson and bronze. He shot a lazy grin to the gathered court as he followed August down to the altar and slumped into a similar posture.

The King's expression was hidden, his face lowered to his clasped hands, but Lore could see his shoulders stiffen.

Bastian shifted and pushed his hair from his face, artful in the way he made a calculated move look utterly nonchalant. Too handsome by half, and he knew it.

As if he could hear her thoughts, the Sun Prince glanced up, catching her eye. A grin curved his mouth.

Lore smiled back. Next to her, Gabe rolled his eyes.

Now that the royals were kneeling, the other courtiers did the same, smoothly going to their knees on the tufted pillows that stretched before the pews. Gabe sank with easy grace, head bowing forward.

It didn't go so smoothly for Lore, who had to adjust the bend of her legs at least twice to keep her skirt from pulling down her neckline. She didn't curse, though. Small improvements.

When everyone was kneeling appropriately, Anton raised his hands at the front of the sanctuary. The light through the window made the scars on his face look fresh. "Apollius, Lord of Light and Life, we greet You with the dawn, as we do at the first of every seven days."

"We greet You and ask Your favor on the days ahead," the gathered courtiers murmured. Lore's tongue stumbled to keep up. She shot a sharp look at Gabriel—he could've told her there was audience participation here.

He gave a tiny shrug.

Up front, the one-handed Presque Mort swung the thurible to the rhythm of Anton's voice. Gray smoke swirled around her feet, drifted over the floor to tangle around skirts and heeled boots, twining in the rays of August's crown. The braziers added more smoke, making the sanctuary seem wreathed in heavy fog.

"We ask Your favor and beg Your protection from the dark," Anton continued. "We ask that You shine the light from Your Shining Realm upon us, where You wait in glory."

Lore's lips twisted. The Shining Realm was the Church's concession to death, the place where they thought Apollius was waiting, where He'd gone when He disappeared. If you were pious and followed the Tracts, you'd meet Him there after death. Lore could think of few things that sounded more boring.

"We beg Your protection and pledge our loyalty," the nobles answered. "We seek the light of the place where Your undying body resides."

The incense smoke reached them, heady and thick. Lore fought not to sneeze.

Anton lowered his hands, then his head, bowing with his chin toward the golden-rayed heart on his chest. A ripple as the gathered courtiers did the same. August and Bastian bowed, too, but the positions of the court before them and the Priest Exalted behind made it look almost like they were all bowing to the Arceneaux family.

She felt eyes on her. Anton, peering across the bowed heads to her own, with something unreadable in his expression.

Lore ducked her chin.

"We pledge our loyalty," Anton said, "and tolerate no other sovereignty but Yours. We acknowledge none others as gods, and denounce those who'd claim it."

"We tolerate no other sovereignty," the courtiers murmured, "and accept none other than Apollius and those He's blessed."

Those he's blessed. The Arceneaux family. Royalty and religion tangled up in an inextricable knot.

Lore shifted again, her legs going numb as they pressed into the hard floor.

"We bask in Your light," Anton said, his hands coming down from their outstretched position to rest on his chest. He looked like the statue of the Bleeding God in the garden, and Lore was nearly certain it was intentional. "And we wait faithfully for Your return, when our world is cleared of darkness and made ready. We ask that You make a vessel for Your light."

"We ask that You return and make us holy," the gathered nobles murmured. "Return from Your Shining Realm and make it here."

The thurible made one more rotation, swinging smoke in a spiral through the air. Then Anton, the Presque Mort, and the Priest with his candle stepped back.

The Sainted King stood. The light of the window behind him burnished his graying hair, illuminated the rays of his crown.

Anton inclined his head to his brother, passing off the leadership of the ceremony.

There was a slight tremble in August's hand as he raised it. "Gabriel and Eldelore Remaut, come forward please."

Gods dead and dying, had it not occurred to anyone to give them an idea of how this was supposed to go? Gabe had told her that they had to be officially introduced, that it would look strange if they weren't, but they'd received no instructions on how the actual introduction was supposed to take place.

August arched a brow, like he was irritated at their apparent confusion. Lore briefly considered wrenching one of those garnets off his crown and stuffing it in his nostril.

Gabe seemed just as surprised as she was. The two of them took a beat, looking at each other in lost silence. Then, ever graceful, Gabe offered her his arm and slid out into the aisle, leading her up to the altar and the smug faces of both Arceneaux men waiting there.

Curious gazes followed them. Lore couldn't tell if any were friendly, but her money was on *no*.

August gave them a smile as they walked toward him, a cold one that came nowhere near his eyes. He didn't say anything, instead flicking his fingers in a motion that told them to face the congregation.

Gabe's cheeks burned, making the slight freckles across his nose stand out. But he did as he was bidden, taking Lore with him, and faced the court. The first row of nobles could probably hear her teeth grinding.

"At long last," August said from behind them, voice lifted to carry across the North Sanctuary. "The Remaut family returns to the Citadel."

He paused, and after a moment of needle-drop silence, the gathered courtiers gave a round of polite applause. Gabe's arm was so tense beneath Lore's hand that it nearly shook.

She squeezed, hoping to offer some kind of reassurance. But

Gabe's face didn't change, like he barely registered her presence at all.

"Gabriel is on a brief…hiatus…from his holy duties to the Presque Mort," August continued, "and will be residing with us for the season to introduce his cousin Eldelore to polite society. Please make them welcome."

The courtiers all inclined their heads, faces inscrutable, blurred by the rapidly increasing sunlight through the windows lining the sanctuary. Lore nodded back, mostly because she wasn't sure what else to do, and flicking both her middle fingers at them didn't seem like proper duke's-cousin behavior.

"Go in peace," August said, and with that, First Day prayers were dismissed. Courtiers rose, making their way back toward the double doors leading to the path and the green. Voices murmured and laughed, the solemnity of religious ritual disappearing as the sun rose higher in the sky.

Lore looked to Gabe, but he still seemed far away, expression distant. After a moment, he drifted toward the doors with the rest of the nobles. With a weary sigh, Lore went to follow.

Gabe seemed so lost here. Almost as lost as she was.

August's hand came down on her shoulder before she took a second step. "I'm afraid the court's diversions will have to wait," he said quietly. "You have a task before you, Lore. Come with me."

CHAPTER TWELVE

The Emperor was rumored to drink a cup of hemlock tea each morning, so that he might live longer. Still, he died in the night, though most think it was his son rather than his sickness.

    —Last report of Gaspard Beauchamp, Auverrani spy in the Kirythean Empire, executed by Emperor Jax two days after message received

Gabe looked behind him at the moment August gripped Lore's shoulder, like some extra sense told him to pay attention. When he saw August, he stopped, a rock in the eddying sea of courtiers, brow furrowed.

August waved a dismissive hand, speaking just loud enough for Gabe to hear him in the rising babble. "Your services are unneeded, Duke Remaut. We're only going to the vaults."

Lore shifted under August's hand. "Could he come anyway? I'm—"

"I've made myself clear." For all the force of his words, the way August took her arm was still polite. To anyone watching, he'd be the picture of a benevolent King, welcoming to even the lowest new noble in his glittering court. "You come with me. The duke does not." He chucked a finger beneath her chin as if she were a wayward child. "The sooner we make progress on this, the sooner you'll reunite."

Her lips pressed into a white line, but Lore fought the urge to jerk away. Instead she ducked her head, as gracefully as she could. "Lead on, Your Majesty."

August gave a surprised snort. "Well then," he murmured, "it seems a weed can become a rose, if you move it from the gutter."

She was going to wear her teeth to nubs if she kept grinding them this hard.

Gabriel watched August lead her down the aisle, worry clear on his face. Lore tried her best to look confident and reassured. This was the price of staying out of the Burnt Isles, and she could manage it without his worry.

When her eyes left Gabe, they found Bastian.

The Sun Prince loitered near the doors, joking with a knot of people she vaguely recognized from the masquerade—one of them being Cecelia, the woman who'd offered them belladonna. Her eyes were glazed this morning, but other than that, she seemed fine. Those court physicians must really earn their keep.

The now-risen sun gilded Bastian's skin, highlighted a scar through one brow, made his eyes look closer to golden than black. There was something solemn in them as he watched his father lead Lore away.

She had no idea where the vaults were supposed to be. They were yet another mark of privilege. It was exorbitantly expensive to be laid to rest within the Citadel rather than in one of the lesser vaults on the edges of Dellaire—little more than stone boxes with bodies stacked inside. Particularly pious commoners were known to start saving for a place in the city vaults from the moment their children were born.

The Sainted King strolled slowly enough to look casual, but his jaw was tight beneath his trimmed gray beard. "Most of the bodies from the latest attack have been examined and disposed of," he said. "But the Presque Mort were working all night, and rode hard to bring one of the bodies here, for you to . . . try."

Her palm was clammy. She wiped it on her skirt. "The latest attack?"

August nodded. "There was another last night."

Three villages, all dead. Lore swallowed past a sudden lump in her throat.

They fell into uneasy silence as August led her down the path and back into the Citadel, the double doors closing behind them. The interior dim was disorienting after the summer-morning sunlight.

Once inside, August stopped, breathing labored as if the trek across the green had worn him out. He reached inside his glimmering cloak and pulled out a flask, taking a quick nip.

An herbal scent itched at her nose, immediately familiar. It seemed like sipping poison for fun wasn't confined only to the younger nobles.

"I hope whoever is dosing you knows what they're doing," Lore said quietly.

Dark eyes swung her way, cold and calculating. "You mind your affairs, deathwitch," August said, tucking the flask away, "and I'll mind my own."

The Sainted King strolled down a hallway, then took a sharp turn to a small doorway between two huge oil paintings of Apollius. The paintings were pre-Godsfall—the god's chest was whole, His heart not yet carved out by His vengeful wife.

With a quick glance around the hall, August pushed the door open to reveal a narrow corridor beyond, lined with arched recesses crowned in golden sun rays. Statues of Apollius stood in the alcoves, plain white marble, each in a different pose. Hands outstretched. Hands to chest. Head tilted up, or looking down with a benevolent smile.

Words in swirling calligraphy had been carved over the arched doorway at the hall's end, almost too ornate for Lore to make out. She squinted in the dark.

"Our deaths remain our own," August intoned quietly, reading it aloud.

The numb, nervous feeling at the back of her neck extended down her shoulders.

The door at the end of the hall swung soundlessly inward onto thin gray light and a bare stone staircase, leading down only a few steps before leveling out into a tunnel.

The Sainted King offered a courtly hand. "Come along."

Lore took the King's hand and let him lead her into the gloom.

She *hated* tunnels. Thankfully, this one was short. Up ahead, a lone bloodcoat guard stood at the lip of where the tunnel opened up into what looked like full sunlight.

Not just any bloodcoat, Lore noticed as they approached. Gold lapels gleamed on his red jacket, the bayonet and sword by his side polished to a high shine. He made no indication that he noticed them at all, but when August approached, he inclined his head and stepped aside.

"The Sacred Guard," August said as they passed. "A highly sought-after position, only granted to those who show themselves worthy both physically and spiritually, and whose loyalty I can be assured of." He gave her a sidelong look. "They don't get much chance to use their weapons, but they certainly know how."

If she wasn't so completely distracted by the sight of the vaults, Lore might've wondered if that was a threat. The room at the end of the tunnel was wide and circular, but the ceiling soared miles above their heads, topped with a cut-glass skylight that filtered the morning sun into faceted shards. It must've been what Lore had seen gleaming in the center of the Citadel yesterday.

The skylight was impressive, but not nearly as impressive as the vaults themselves. They climbed like stone towers, stretching nearly all the way to the glass above. Stairs were cut into the sides of the vaults, twisting upward, broken by platforms that led to small doors—the only way to get to the bodies inside. At the tops of the vaults, overgrown rosebushes reached for the sun. The roses were the only living things inside the vaults, other than August and Lore and the guard in the tunnel.

Lore took a moment to concentrate on her mental wall, all those trees blocking out the awareness of Mortem. Trunks and leaves and blue sky beyond.

Some of the doors in the towering vaults were closed, but most remained open, small windows into the darkness inside. Those were empty. Even nobles couldn't always afford a Citadel vault. Most of the open doors were near the top—those were for the Arceneaux family only.

"We've tried to keep one body from every village," August said. He strode purposefully toward the nearest tower and the closed door at its base. Of course. No one would waste a top vault on a villager, no matter how strange their death. "The rest are destroyed."

"How much does one of those run?" Lore asked quietly, still staring at the vaults.

The King looked up, snorted. "More than you've ever seen or ever will, girl. Keep your sights set on one of the body boxes outside the city." He rapped on the stone wall. "Anton? We're here."

The Priest Exalted opened the door, squinting against the light. He didn't say anything, merely stood to the side to let his brother enter. He gave Lore a polite nod, but a muscle feathered in his jaw as he did it.

Inside the vault was dark and cool. It took Lore's eyes a moment to adjust, but when they did, she took an involuntary step back, knocking into the wall. Another stone Apollius stared down at her. The statue's feet were placed at the rear of the vault, his back bent against the ceiling so his empty chest gaped over the plinth, eyes level with the door. His face was eerily devoid of expression, and garnets studded his palms, gesturing to the slab in the room's center with handfuls of jeweled blood.

And on the slab lay the body of a child.

Bile clawed at the back of Lore's throat, her vision blurring. The child on the slab looked nothing like Cedric—he was younger, nine or ten at most, and his body was whole and unblemished. But when she looked at him, that's who she saw. Her friend, whom she'd just wanted back for a while.

Gods, and she was about to do it again.

"Horrible business," August murmured. She couldn't quite read his expression in the dim light, but true regret thickened his voice. "Apologies that this must be our first experiment, Lore. We thought maybe a child would be...easier...to reanimate. Since you've done it before."

She winced.

Anton shook his head sadly. "So much wasted potential."

When she raised Horse, it'd been all instinct, following a pattern that felt as ingrained into her as the map of the catacombs she could sense behind her eyes. All she had to do was follow that pattern again. Let her body take over, try not to think.

Lore clenched and released her fists, and blinked until she could be sure she wasn't going to cry. She didn't let herself cry about anything, as a rule. If she started, she didn't know if she could stop.

Anton ducked out of the door for a moment, then returned carrying a rosebush in a large pot. He set it down—it was heavy for someone his age to carry, but he didn't appear to have an issue—and stepped back between Apollius's stone hands.

"Now, don't worry yourself with asking the questions," August said. "Simply command it to follow my orders, and then you're free to wait outside."

Lore wasn't listening, but she nodded anyway.

The King swept a hand toward the body on the slab. "And so we begin."

Mortem was thick here; she could almost smell it—empty, ozonic. The smell of the sky during a storm, she'd always thought. The space between thunder and lightning. Lore closed her eyes tight, imagining her forest again, a touchstone to hold on to.

The child's corpse conflated with Cedric's in her mind, and it constricted her thoughts, made it more difficult to concentrate. She'd been betrayed, imprisoned, conscripted into using an awful power she'd rather forget about to help a King who didn't seem to give a shit about anyone outside his gilded walls.

But Lore had been born with the ability to channel Mortem. Born with the dark running congruent to her bones. It'd only ever been a wound, a fault, a thing to fear and run from. Maybe now she could use it for something good.

Lore opened her eyes, took a deep breath, let it empty from her lungs. Slowly, almost without her direct thought, her arms reached out, turning pale, cold, necrotic.

"Bleeding God hold us in His wounded hand," Anton murmured. The words were shaped for fear, but his tone wasn't. It was almost eager.

Lore didn't have time to dwell on it. Her vision went grayscale, white light in the shape of the King and the Priest, nothing but a yawning void where the body of the child lay on the slab. The huge statue of Apollius looked monstrous in shades of gray and black, the dead stone unilluminated by any shard of light.

The moon-shaped burn on her palm glowed dark as Lore held her hands over the slab. The child's death was distant, the instant, awful power of it long gone. She could sense it but couldn't touch it; dim threads wavered in the air above the body, but they weren't thick enough to grasp.

Death had gone deeper.

Lore stepped closer, until her palms hovered just barely above the corpse, almost touching. In life, there was a ring of energy around a body. Spiritum, which Apollius alone could channel—the same power He'd allegedly given the Arceneaux line. It surrounded a person like the corona of a miniature sun, and in the moment of death, it burned out, exploded, a dying star. That's what she'd seen when Horse died, what she'd grabbed onto. Spiritum turned to Mortem, seized at the very moment of its alchemizing, the same precarious balance that could make poison lead to horrible immortality.

But that explosion of energy dissipated soon after death, sank deep into the body and eventually withered away. If Lore wanted to raise this corpse, she'd have to search out that tiny spark of Mortem still within it. Take hold of death and pull it out.

It took her a moment, her teeth clenched tight in her jaw, her necrotic fingers lowering until they rested on the still chest. For a moment, Lore didn't think she was going to find it at all.

Then—the barest slink of darkness, a thin thread of latent death.

Lore grabbed it like a lifeline, and wound the strand of Mortem around her hand, tugging it out as deftly as threading a needle. It flowed from the body and into her, twisting through her veins, braided into herself.

Her heart froze. Tithed a beat.

Her hand thrust sideways, Mortem flowing out of her and into the rosebush Anton had brought into the vault. The blooms withered instantly, leaves dropping, the soil turning dry and pale.

Lore's eyes opened, banishing the grayscale world in favor of the true one. Her veins were blackened to the elbow, her fingertips white and corpse-cold. The body on the slab was still, with no visible change to mark what she'd done.

This was a human, not an animal. She had to give him a direction. And though August had told her what to do, she couldn't remember what it'd been, so she asked the question they all wanted the answer to.

"Tell us what happened," Lore whispered, the sound hoarse and broken through her death-dry throat.

August started, rounding on her with his brows drawn low. "You are not performing this interrogation," he said, with every scrap of regal authority he had. "I gave you instruction. Do *not* overstep your place."

But it was a moot point. The body on the slab stayed still and silent.

She'd failed. She'd been the only one who could help, and she failed. "I'm sorry," Lore said, inane in the face of the King's displeasure. "I did the same thing as before, I think, but it's been too long—"

She was interrupted by a the deep, rasping noise of a breath being pulled into desiccated lungs.

The sound was unmistakable. Lore and August and Anton stared at each other over the body, beneath Apollius's impassive watching face, the gaping maw of his stone chest.

A rustle as the corpse moved. A creak as it sat up.

The dead body opened his eyes, and Lore couldn't help but meet them, no matter how awful—her gaze was drawn there, even as terror set deep in her bones, even as the power that made this possible kept her eyes opaque and her veins inky, looking just as dead as he did.

The child's eyes were wholly black—no white, no iris. Darkened veins stood out around them, like the veins around her own, like the scars around Gabe's eye patch. The child opened an empty, yawning mouth.

And though his lips didn't move, he began to whisper.

CHAPTER THIRTEEN

To reach for power beyond what has been given to
you is the greatest sin.
                              –The Book of Mortal Law, Tract 78

At first, the whispering was just a soft susurrus, the bare sug-
gestion of language without any detail filled in. The sound
reminded Lore of flies buzzing, of suffocating dirt, the soft fall
of flesh rotted from bone. But after a moment, words conjured
themselves from the shapeless noise.

Just one phrase, over and over and stopping abruptly, stuck in a
replicating loop. The words started slurred, then grew sharper edges,
became crisp as an elocution exercise despite the stillness of dead
tongue, dead lips. "They've awakened," the unmoving corpse whispered. "They've awakened they've awakened they've awakened—"

The King's face was pale. He looked surprised, almost, surprised and nervous, like he hadn't entirely expected this to work.
His head swung to his twin. "Does that mean—"

Anton held up a hand, and his brother closed his mouth, swallowing the end of his sentence. The Priest Exalted's gaze flickered
from the corpse to Lore's face, calculating.

Lore stared into the not-dead child's black eyes, the gape of that unmoving, whispering mouth. "Stop," she rasped. "Please stop."

The body fell back, eyes still open, limbs slack.

She snapped her hands closed, just like she'd done with Horse, just like she'd done with Cedric, breaking the threads of Mortem that bound her to the corpse.

Then Lore bolted.

August's voice chased her out the door, echoing in all that stone, but Lore paid the King no mind. She tripped over her hem, hit her knees, skinning them beneath her skirt. A heaving breath in and another out, trying her best to keep the bile in her throat from surging. The white, necrotic skin on her fingers slowly leached back to living warmth, the gray of her veins fading with each breath. Her heart lurched in her chest, beating so hard it almost hurt.

"Get up, girl."

Anton's voice was as cold as the stone against her palms. Lore rubbed the back of her wrist over her mouth, deliberately taking her time before she straightened and glared up at the Priest Exalted. The sun through the skylight blazed his gray hair into a halo, obscured his features.

"Ready for round two?" Lore nearly spat it. As humanity suffused her again, chasing out death, so did a righteous anger she couldn't totally explain—the thought of that child, of how she'd disturbed his peaceful rest after something terrible happened to him, made shame prick up and down her spine. "Are there any other corpses you want to disturb while we have the time? Maybe we can climb up to the top and see if I can get some dead marquess to sing the national anthem—"

"That's quite enough," Anton murmured, his expression still hidden in shadow. "This is exactly what we brought you here for. Don't start having a conscience now."

"Rich, coming from a priest."

"I told you before. The Bleeding God understands that sometimes the rules must be bent for the greater good. For the glory of His promises to be fulfilled." Anton's hand lifted, a finger tracing over one of the golden rays on his pendant. "He forgives His faithful, always. For everything."

Lore swallowed. Tightened her fists in her skirt. The shame didn't dissipate, but she managed to shove it down, push it somewhere to stay until she dealt with it later.

"I failed," she said, shaking her head, returning to the matter at hand instead of an existential one she couldn't parse yet. "We learned absolutely nothing about what's happening in the villages."

They've awakened. It still reverberated in her head, that awful whisper from a dead mouth. *They've awakened.*

She'd asked the dead boy what happened to him, and she didn't think the dead could lie. It was an answer of some kind, but not one that made any sense.

"It doesn't matter, on this first attempt." August waved a hand as he stepped through the small door of the vault, ducking so his crown didn't knock into the lintel. Despite his look of confused near-terror when he heard the corpse speak, he looked in good spirits now, almost excited. "You made it talk. That's what we wanted."

Her brows knit. "But I didn't—"

"In time," August said. It might've been reassuring coming from anyone else. From him, it sounded like the extension of a sentence. "We'll try again."

"The body won't keep," Anton said quietly. "It will have to be moved."

"Burn it." Another wave of August's hand, careless. "There will be another."

"Yes." August's eyes flickered to Lore, then away. "Now that Kirythea has begun, I don't expect them to stop."

"So you're still convinced it's Kirythea?" Lore asked.

"Who else could it be?" August pulled his flask from within his cloak and took another sip. Anton's nose wrinkled, but the Priest Exalted didn't comment on his brother's indiscretions. "And speaking of Kirythea—did you attend Bastian's soiree last night?"

"Sure did." Lore stared at the door to the vault behind him. It gaped open enough for her to see the body prostrate on his plinth. "But I didn't find out anything important, so it wasn't exactly a success."

"In time," August repeated. "You'll learn something in time."

Anton's pendant swung, the garnet blood drop sparkling. "Well," he said, redirecting the conversation away from Bastian, "not to worry. We'll try again. Perhaps a different corpse will have more to say. This one *was* just a child."

August nodded, once.

Lore felt sick again. "So I…what do you want me to do while…"

"Enjoy the Citadel, Lore." August turned around, headed back the way they came, to the narrow tunnel and the alcove-lined hallway beyond. "You're an officially introduced member of the court. Make friends, find lovers, amuse yourself as you see fit. Just make sure you do it all while staying near my son."

Behind August, the muscles on the unscarred side of Anton's face tightened.

"And I'll let you know when we have another corpse for you to raise," August continued. "I'm sure it won't be long."

Lore followed the King back into the tunnel, unsure of what else to do. The Sacred Guard, she noticed, once again didn't acknowledge them at all. The end of his bayonet gleamed wickedly sharp in the sun through the skylight.

She picked at the threads in her tailored gown. "Your Majesty, I know I'm supposed to get close to Bastian, but if I had a directive, any clue at all to what kind of information you think he's passing on..."

"You've been given your directives." The Sainted King mounted the short staircase at the end of the tunnel, pushed open the door. The hallway beyond glittered, the alcoves holding all those Bleeding Gods shimmering like miniature suns. "Are you implying you aren't up to the task?"

The implications of *that* didn't need to be spelled out. Burnt Isles if she was lucky, pyre if she wasn't.

"No." Lore shook her head. "No, I'm up to it."

"Good." August turned his back on her and strode down the hallway, the orange-and-gold cloak he'd worn at morning prayers fluttering behind him. He didn't give her a deadline for a report, she noticed. Apparently, he was content to wait until she had something concrete to tell him.

The doors to the vaults closed softly behind her. When Lore turned, Anton peered at her from his one gleaming eye. Then, with a tilt of his chin, he asked, "How old are you, Lore?"

Her brows drew together, confusion bringing a quick answer. "Twenty-three."

"And your birthday is near midsummer, correct? Your year of Consecration."

It still made her uneasy that he knew so much about her. Lore nodded again and started walking toward the end of the gilded hall, toward the rest of the Citadel.

Anton fell into easy step beside her. "We'll have to make sure you're given a proper ceremony, since you're part of the court now. Even if it is currently under false pretenses."

"That's really not necessary."

"Oh, I think it is." He swept past her in a rustle of pale robes, opening the door before she could reach it. "Bastian is probably out on the green somewhere. Go find him."

With that order, Anton glided away into the depths of the

Citadel, headed to whatever holy duties occupied him during the day, leaving Lore alone in the vault corridor.

For a moment, she just stood there, among all those stone Apolliuses with empty chests and hands full of garnet blood. Then, Lore drifted to the end of the hallway, out into the expanse of the Citadel proper. She retraced her steps, going back to the door that led to the green space and the North Sanctuary. No one else was in the halls, all the courtiers dispersed to wherever they spent their innumerable leisure hours. Just as well. Her mind was too tangled up to make a convincing duke's cousin.

She'd been given a direct order to find Bastian, but she'd take her time. She had scads of it, apparently.

The sun was high in the sky, now, and bright enough to make her squint. Lore wandered off the path immediately, her feet pointing toward the manicured forest to the left of the cobblestones. Not a real forest—it was planned down to the leaf, designed just so, nothing wild about it. But it was close enough.

Lore stopped once she was under the trees, closed her eyes, took a deep breath of green and dirt. It smelled so *clean* within the walls of the Citadel, a difference she hadn't really noticed until now. She was used to the scents of people crowded together, of sea brine, of soot and trash and grime. But here, the air smelled crisp and sharp, as if it were fresh-scrubbed every morning.

With a sigh, Lore sat heavily down on the grass. Green stains marred her knees nearly instantly, and she cursed, situating her legs in front of her though the damage was already done. Another sigh, and she let herself fall back, head cradled by the soft loam. Her eyes closed; the summer sunlight filtering through the branches above lit the network of veins in her eyelids, a lurid map of capillaries.

It reminded her of the catacombs. Of that awareness waiting at the edge of her grasp, pushed just far enough away to let her function. She almost couldn't believe she'd lived so long without the barrier Gabe had helped her build. It was as if by finally channeling Mortem when she raised Horse, she'd opened a floodgate. Being within the walls of the Citadel tempered it a bit, but her sense was still stronger than it had ever been before, increasing as the days marched on.

Each day that drew her closer to her twenty-fourth birthday.

Raising the dead child had battered against her mental shield, and though it still held fast, she could almost *taste* Mortem at the back of her throat, empty and ashlike. Her fingers itched, as if the threads she'd wound around them had left an indelible burn on her skin, as clear as her moon-shaped scar. It pushed on her from all sides, an encroaching void, a vast and terrible storm of *nothing*.

That's what was so awful about it, really. The lack of anything. Death was a yawning chasm, a hole with no bottom. Lore wished she was capable of the easy faith the Church taught, capable of thinking there was a Shining Realm waiting once this life was through.

Pointless. Even if there was, she'd never see it.

Lore shuddered. Despite the clean air and the nice clothes and the plentiful food, despite the illusion of safety being here under the King's protection brought her, the prospect of raising another dead body was nearly enough to make her run for the docks, for Val and Mari, and beg them to take her back. She'd forgive them everything, if she just didn't have to use Mortem again.

"Fuck me," she swore softly.

"You'll have to ask more nicely than that."

Her eyes flew open—a dark human-shape bent over her, the sun behind it blurring their features. But then the unnamed shape sat back, and she caught the edge of an irreverent grin, the toss of a dark curl.

Bastian's eyes went to the grass stains on her knees. "Though perhaps someone already took you up on it?"

Well, she wouldn't have to go looking for Bastian. The Sun Prince had found her.

Lore scrambled up, brushing grass out of her hair and trying in vain to find a position that hid the green stains. "My deepest apologies, Your Highness—er, Sainted—"

"Just Bastian, please," the Sun Prince supplied, cutting short her stuttering search for the proper honorific. "And no apologies needed. One's first season in court is generally laced with indiscretions."

"I'm afraid my only indiscretion here was...was falling asleep." Lore waved a hand at the bower the trees made, lit in soft golden light from the sun above. "It's such a nice day, and we were up so late only to wake at sunrise..."

"You'll get used to it." Bastian's smile crinkled his eyes. They weren't black, like she'd first thought. Up close, they were maybe a shade lighter than his dark hair, whiskey-colored. "I heard my father took you to the vaults. I'm surprised he indulged your curiosity, to be honest—many courtiers want to see them when they first arrive in the Citadel, but generally, August denies requests for tours."

He was far more observant than was convenient. "He was asking me about my mother," Lore said quickly, barely thinking the words through before they left her mouth. "She's...she's in poor health, and was considering the possibility of a Citadel vault when she passes."

Bastian's brow arched. "I'm sorry to hear it," he said. "Pardon me for being so uncouth as to speak of money, but I didn't know the Remaut family had relatives well-endowed enough to consider a vault within the Citadel. Most minor nobles opt for the common vaults just outside the Northeast Ward—they're by far the nicest of the exterior burial grounds."

Lore gave him what she hoped was a confident smile, though the inside of her head sounded like the horns they blew on the docks when the weather took a turn. "We've been saving."

He still grinned, but there was something calculating in those gold-brown eyes. "You and everyone else. What a pious woman your mother must be, to be such a good citizen even in death."

The blade in his tone made her feel safe to answer in kind. "A shame, really, that one must pay an exorbitant price to be a good citizen."

The Sun Prince chuckled, still an edge to it—an edge turned away from her, though, a sword they both wielded. "A shame, indeed. Enough to make one think the Church didn't care so much about ensuring all the pious reach the Shining Realm, bodies intact."

"Only the pious who can pay."

"Precisely." Bastian offered out his arm. "Come. Walk with me to the stables. If anyone asks about the grass stains, we'll tell them you fell off a horse."

She thought of the woman she'd seen him with in the gardens yesterday, his lips on her shoulder. If anyone saw her with Bastian and grass stains on her skirt, the conclusion they drew would have nothing to do with *that* kind of riding.

When she took the prince's proffered arm, she could feel his muscles move beneath his silken sleeve. More defined than she'd expect from a pampered royal; an incongruous roughness, like the scar through his eyebrow and the calluses on his hands.

Lore and the Sun Prince strolled casually down the clear paths cut into the forest, winding trails carefully designed to look natural while being anything but. A slight breeze fluttered at Bastian's hair, worn down, waving dark against his shoulders—just on this side of too-long to be in current fashion, though she assumed that however Bastian wore his hair was how the entire court would in a month's time. He smelled like red wine and expensive cologne, one that Lore's untrained nose couldn't pick out the notes of.

"I've petitioned my father over and over again to waive the fees associated with a vault burial," Bastian said as they took another turn, the edge of the manicured forest appearing up ahead, "but he's adamant that we need the money for the upcoming war with the Kirythean Empire."

Lore's shoulders tensed, but she kept her face impassive. "Oh?" she murmured. "Does he think a war is imminent, then?"

"He's thought a war was imminent for as long as I can remember."

"The Empire *has* drawn steadily closer." Close enough that she'd heard hushed talk of possible war down on the docks for years, fears of conscription and bottlenecked trade.

"And yet," Bastian said, "they've never invaded."

"Perhaps they're waiting for something." Lore kept her eyes ahead and her voice light. "Information, maybe. An opportune moment."

"Information would be difficult to acquire." His eyes slid her way. "August only trusts a select few with military secrets. I don't even know most of them."

She forced a laugh. "Surely that's not true. You're his heir."

"And how he hates that."

They ambled along quietly for a moment, Lore's palm clammy on Bastian's sleeve. The fabric was soft and billowing and would probably show sweaty prints when she lifted her hand away.

"Imminent war or not, I think it's deplorable to charge your citizens for a decent burial. There should at least be exceptions for extenuating circumstances." Bastian glanced at her from the corner of her eye. "All this mess with the villages, for instance."

Her teeth clamped on the inside of her cheek, stirring her mind for a way to pry that wouldn't seem suspicious. August had said that most of the bodies from the villages were disposed of—that had to mean burned, regardless of what their personal choices for burial had been in life. Shademount and Orlimar were both small villages where most of the citizens were subsistence farmers. According to the Tracts, you entered the Shining Realm in whatever state your body was left in, so being burned meant you didn't enter at all. The Church wouldn't concern themselves with absorbing the fees of a vault burial for poor villagers.

"I'm rather surprised the Church doesn't advocate for more equitable burial practices," Lore said. "Entry to the Shining Realm should hinge on piety, not money."

"Especially since most of the nobles won't see the Realm's lintel, whole-bodied or not." Bastian smirked. "The Church and the bloodcoats might close their eyes against the amount of poison coming into the Citadel, but I doubt Apollius will."

Lore gritted her teeth, thinking of Cecelia and her cup of belladonna, of the flask always by August's side. "Ah, the justice system."

Bastian's snort became a full laugh. "It's certainly a system. Unsure if justice has much to do with it."

The forest opened on another garden, smaller and less regimented than the one on the other side of the Citadel. Similar to the forest, it was a careful pantomime of wildness, a contradictory illusion of free nature. Colorful birds nested in the bushes, and a few peacocks strutted through the foliage.

They strolled on past banks of brightly colored flowers and tiny gleaming pools full of shimmering fish. A few other courtiers were out taking morning constitutionals or playing lazy games of croquet, but beyond inclinations of heads, they didn't interact. Lore assumed most of the court had fallen back into bed after sunrise prayers.

"Speaking of the villages," Lore said, redirecting the conversation to something that might actually get her information instead of just make her angry, "I heard they were all dying overnight, with no sign of sickness or poison. But surely that can't be the case?"

"It is as far as I know. But I have my own theories." Bastian reached out and stroked a passing peacock's violet head. The bird pecked at his hand, and he gave it a halfhearted swat. "I think the Mortem problem is to blame."

Her toe stubbed on one of the cobblestones; Lore clenched Bastian's arm and regained her footing, just barely managing not to curse. His forearm was rock-hard under her palm, a fact she was irritated with herself for noticing. "Oh?"

"No poison, no sickness, no trace of attack?" He shrugged, making the muscle beneath her hand ripple distractingly. "Sounds like Mortem to me. Why, would you not agree?"

"Not really, no." Lore shook her head. "The bodies wouldn't be whole, if it was unchanneled Mortem. They'd be in advanced stages of decay, or gone altogether." Mortem leaks had been a problem during the first few years after the Godsfall, though they weren't really a threat anymore. Not since the Presque Mort were founded and the Arceneaux line built the Citadel over Nyxara's tomb.

Bastian gave her a considering look. "You know more about Mortem than the average courtier, Lore."

So casual, so even. But she knew it wasn't. Dammit. He'd handed her a shovel and she'd happily started digging. "I find it an interesting topic."

"Morbid, too."

"Interesting and morbid often coincide." She shrugged. "Besides, anyone who pays attention to their history will come to the same conclusion. The accounts of the Godsfall and the years after are well documented. We know what a body looks like after coming in contact with raw, unchanneled Mortem from an outside source."

"Fair." Bastian plucked a lone peacock feather from where it'd gotten tangled in a bush, sticking it behind his ear at a jaunty angle. Another trend in the making, she was sure. "But couldn't it be channeled into something that caused the deaths? Something that descended on a village, killed them, and left no trace?"

"I don't think so. The Spiritum in a person wouldn't allow it." Lore had never heard of channeled Mortem being used to outright kill someone. Channeling death into a living body was difficult—the aura of Spiritum, of vitality, that surrounded every living thing made it next to impossible. Weaker auras could be overcome, like those of plants or very ill humans, but not healthy ones.

If someone was using Mortem to kill those villages, it was in a way that Lore had no context for. And she had a good amount of context, all things considered.

"Clearly, I've been remiss in not consulting another scholar." The peacock feather apparently itched; Bastian pulled it from his ear and twirled it between his fingers instead. "No one else I've discussed this with has been as learned as you."

Lore gave him a small, shy smile, conjuring *country cousin*, conjuring *no threat* and *don't take me too seriously*. "There isn't much to do at home. I find my amusements where I may."

He cocked a brow and looked pointedly at the grass stains again. Lore pinched his arm, fighting a genuine laugh.

"Lore!"

Gabriel walked hurriedly down the path, like he'd been trying to catch up without running. Still, he was slightly out of breath when he reached them. His eye darted to Bastian, then to her, brow rising as if he was annoyed that she was following her orders so closely.

"Remaut, nice of you to join us." Bastian took the peacock feather from behind his ear and swiveled it flirtatiously beneath Gabe's chin. "I was just taking your cousin to the stables. Don't worry, she already had the grass stains when I found her."

Gabe's eyebrow climbed farther. Lore gave him a smile that felt more like a grimace.

"Come along." Bastian tightened the bend of his arm, trapping Lore's hand. "I have a curious new acquisition. You two will be the first I've shown it to." He gave Lore a brilliant smile. "Honestly, between this and inviting you to the masque last night, I've been quite the social director. Perhaps I should hire myself out to the mothers of spinsters."

"I'm sure August would love that." Gabe fell into step on Lore's other side. It felt somewhat like being escorted by two abnormally tall cats, twitchy and standoffish.

"Probably as much as Anton loves you coming back to court. I'm sure he wasn't pleased about losing his star channeler for a season."

Gabe said nothing, arms politely behind his back, though those polite arms ended in fists. Lore thought of the conversation she and Bastian had as they danced, about how Bastian had attempted to orchestrate Gabe's freedom for the summer, not knowing that Anton had planned it already.

But the awkward transition gave her an opening, a place to speak about the two ruling brothers of Auverraine with someone who would know more about their relationship than most. "August and Anton..." she began, feeling out how she wanted to word it. "They don't seem to get along. Why is that?"

"Anton didn't become the Priest Exalted until after his vision." Gabe jumped in to answer, though he had to know she'd meant the question for Bastian. The man was apparently incapable of not immediately rising to Anton's defense. "But August has been the heir since he was born, Apollius's chosen. Naturally, it led to some tension."

"Like children fighting over being Father's favorite," Bastian scoffed. "Anton's vision was certainly convenient."

Gabe shot him a dark look. "Are you implying it wasn't true?"

"Remaut, I don't even know what the vision *was*, and neither does anyone else." Bastian reached across Lore to clap Gabe on the back. "I'm just saying that it'd have to be quite the fucking thing to make me fall face-first into a brazier. Though I suppose Anton did get magic in the bargain. You win some, you lose some."

A muscle twitched in Gabe's jaw, but he didn't comment further on the veracity of Anton's vision. "The Arceneaux line had magic already, according to the Tracts."

"Which is one of many reasons why I don't waste much time on the Tracts." Bastian held up one hand, exaggeratedly flexed his fingers with a wicked glint in his eye. "I *have* been told I possess magic fingers, but the context wasn't anything holy."

Gabe rolled his eyes.

The gardens slowly tapered off, giving way to a wide green field. Horses wandered placidly, not held in by any fence but the Church wall about a mile away, cutting up into the blue sky. It seemed even the livestock in the Citadel were creatures of luxury.

The stables were up a slight hill, a structure of shining wood nicer than anything Lore had ever lived in. Purple-liveried servants guided muscled mounts in exercises around a gleaming ring. Another man-made pond shimmered in the pasture like a jewel.

"Gods dead and dying," she murmured.

"A devotee of the equestrian arts?" Bastian asked, a lilt in his voice that said he was teasing.

"I could certainly be persuaded to become one."

The prince laughed, pulling her toward the stables. "That's one of you. Gabe hates horses."

Lore glanced back at the man in question. His eye was narrowed at the side of Bastian's head, since the Sun Prince still wouldn't face him. "I don't hate horses."

"You told me so."

"Yes, when I was eight. After falling off a rather formidable stallion that *you* dared me to ride. Most people mature between eight and twenty-four, and their particular hatreds change."

"I hated roast peahen when I was eight, and I still hate it now."

"I said *most* people."

Bastian waved a flippant hand.

The inside of the stables was just as well made as the outside.

Horses whickered at Bastian as he passed, and he patted their noses absently, headed toward the very back of the building.

A gaggle of children were crowded around the last stable in the row, some dressed like the offspring of courtiers, others as if they were employed by the stables. None of them spoke, all with wide eyes, staring at whatever was housed there. "Move along," Bastian said, but it was soft. Lore expected the children to scatter when they realized who he was, but they just stepped aside, eyes still glued to the creature in the stall.

When they approached close enough to see, Lore understood why.

Horse. It was Horse.

But it couldn't... it didn't make *sense*, didn't follow any of the rules of Mortem she knew. Dead was dead, and unspooling the magic of it from a body couldn't change that, there was no possible way to pull *all* of it out. A dead thing couldn't regain a semblance of life, couldn't exist on its own. She'd seen the animal fall after she snapped the threads, seen death come back over the corpse.

But something must've changed between then and now, because here Horse was.

Lore was frozen. Her hand was still on Bastian's arm, but she couldn't feel it. Horse's eyes shone milky and opaque, his throat still gashed. He nuzzled at Bastian's outstretched hand and made a sound that would've been a whicker, had his vocal cords been intact.

"Quite a specimen, isn't he?" Bastian's eyes slid to her, dark in the shadows of the stable. "I call him Claude."

CHAPTER FOURTEEN

Secrets breed themselves.

                                            –Caldienan proverb

During storm season in the Harbor District, the tide pounded on the shoreline like a drum. It beat against the rocky sand in an endless rhythm, smelling of salt and fish and rain, ceaseless and inescapable and nearly enough to drive you mad in those first few weeks, before it became part of the background noise.

That's what Lore's pulse felt like. An endless drumming in her ears, pushing at her throat. If she looked down, it was probably visible, throbbing against the tender skin of her wrists.

Horse—*Claude*—looked at her curiously. When his head tipped to the side, the gaping wound on his neck yawned open, the edges gummy with blood and pus. She could see the work of dead, grayish muscles beneath his cut skin, the chipped ends of ivory bone.

"Curious, isn't it?" Bastian petted the horse's muzzle. The beast nickered again, and the sound was *awful*, ragged and wrong. "He should be dead. But it's like he doesn't know that, and has refused to acquiesce to it." The Sun Prince chuckled, though something sharper than amusement glittered in his eyes. "Maybe that's the true secret to eternal life. Just refusing to die. Much easier than slowly turning yourself to stone."

Before, Lore's feelings had always been slightly hurt by the fact that Horse never seemed to hold her in high regard. He mostly ignored her, unless she brought apples. Now she was thankful that the creature didn't act like he recognized her at all. Horse bent his gory head and flicked a fly off his haunch. The bones in his neck ground together.

This wasn't how Mortem was supposed to work. Not for a normal channeler, even those who'd been strong enough to raise a body from the dead before they were all executed. Animal lives were less complicated, so they didn't have to be given specific instructions to go about some semblance of living. Still, corpses were marionettes, only active while the channeler held the strings of their death. A fully independent one like this...it shouldn't be *possible.*

But she wasn't a normal channeler, was she?

Lore squashed the thought with physical force, her teeth digging into the meat of her tongue until she tasted copper.

Bastian pulled an apple from within his coat and offered it to Horse. *Claude.* The animal sniffed it, then shied away.

"He doesn't eat," Bastian said, tossing the apple to one of the stable boys, who bit into it with gusto. "Doesn't drink, doesn't eliminate. Doesn't sleep, I don't think. But other than that, he appears fully alive."

Long lashes fluttered over cloudy eyes as Claude blinked.

Lore's stomach cramped. She looked to Gabe, hoping he didn't look as panicked as she felt. The Presque Mort seemed to be keeping his shock under wraps, though the skin around his mouth had gone pale. "An interesting specimen," he said, and sounded almost nonchalant. "Where'd you find him?"

A half heartbeat of silence, Bastian's lips twisting to the side.

"Some guards I'm particularly friendly with found him wandering through the Southwest Ward," he said finally. "They brought him here because they didn't know what else to do with him. Must be some kind of rogue magic, don't you think? Left over from one of those dead minor gods, something elemental. Earth, maybe. That power lingered longer than the others, and Braxtos's body was found in Auverraine."

It had been, in a cave in the eastern hill country. Parts of Braxtos were still in there, turned to stone, a rocky effigy in the vague shape of a man that backwoods farmers prayed to sometimes. But the excuse was bullshit. None of the magic of the minor gods was left.

It didn't matter; Bastian was clearly lying, and he knew that she knew it. It was in the curl of his mouth, the slow blink of his dark-honey eyes. The way he reached out and tucked a strand of hair behind Lore's ear as she stared at the dead horse she'd raised, face blank.

"Forgive me," Bastian murmured. "I thought you'd find Claude diverting, but it appears your constitution wasn't quite as hardy as I thought."

In his stall, Horse nosed at a pile of hay. It made the skin around his cut neck gape. A gnat landed on an empty artery.

Lore shuddered.

"My apologies if you've taken a fright, Eldelore dear." Bastian shrugged. "I thought you might find it interesting, is all."

She didn't speak. He was as good as shouting that he'd caught her, a trap laid at the very beginning of a trail, but Lore couldn't pull any words up her pulse-pounded throat.

If this had been an assignment for Val, she'd be out in an hour. As soon as someone even hinted they knew she was a mole, she was gone, back to the warehouse on the docks, back to the safety of her mothers.

Safety. She winced. She'd never see that warehouse again.

Even if she could get out of the Citadel, she wouldn't go back to Val and Mari. It hurt too much.

A soft flurry of voices, Gabe's and Bastian's both, fluttering around her ears like moths around a candle wick. Genteel apologies that fooled no one, acceptances of such that could be carved from ice. Gabe's hand on her elbow, leading her away, *I think my cousin could do with some rest.*

As they approached the entrance to the stables, Lore looked back over her shoulder. Horse stared at her, slashed neck rubbing against the wood of his stall door, grating against dead muscle and bone. Bastian stood next to the undead beast, watching.

He caught Lore's eye. He smiled.

❦

Gabe sat on the couch, hunched over folded arms. "He knows something."

"He does." Lore paced back and forth behind the couch, a fingernail clamped between her teeth. She'd shaken off her shock as Gabe led her through the forest, the gardens, the labyrinthine corridors of the Citadel to their suite. The shock was still there, and the fear, but she'd managed to smother it under a burning layer of fury. "Nothing like confirmation via dead horse."

Disgust twisted Gabe's face as he shook his head. "How in all the myriad hells is that horse still... still..."

"Walking?" Cold seized the back of her neck, as if someone had laid their freezing palm on her skin. "Acting like it's alive?"

"It's not someone else channeling," Gabe said. "I'd be able to tell. *We'd* be able to tell. Wouldn't we?"

Lore shrugged nervously, still pacing. He was right, as far as she knew—the few times she'd been around one of the Presque Mort when they were channeling Mortem, it'd felt like an uncomfortable pull in her veins, as if her blood had coagulated and her heart hadn't caught up to the fact. It was hard to miss.

Her teeth broke through her nail, sending a wave of pain shooting up into her gums. She cursed lightly, frowned at the now-jagged nail. "Yes, we'd be able to feel it."

Gabe's doublet rasped over the brocade couch as he turned to look at her. "If it's not anyone actively channeling," he said slowly, "then it has to be something left over from when you did it."

"No." The denial came quick. "Mortem doesn't work that way. It only—"

"I am well aware of how Mortem works." He rose from the couch, towering over her even though she stood at least a yard away. There was something different in his tone, his stance. He looked like the Mort who'd cornered her in the alley, prepared for violence if necessary, not the man she'd started counting as something like a friend. "And I'm well aware that the way you use it has no precedent, not since they killed all the necromancers." His one eye narrowed, fingers curling into a fist to hide the candle inked on his palm. "Even then, nothing dead could stay risen on its own."

Lore narrowed her eyes to match his. Straightened, found the spine that belonged in the Harbor District, not the Citadel. "If you're accusing me of something, Gabriel, say it plain. Don't dance around it like you're at another one of Bastian's parties."

Something about the other man's name seemed to startle him. Shake him out of the Presque Mort and back into the man. A reminder of a common enemy, a common goal; a reminder that he and Lore couldn't afford to be on opposite sides.

Gabe ran a weary hand over his face. "I'm not," he said finally. Snorted. "You seem just as confused about how your magic works as the rest of us."

"I'm glad that's comforting to you." Lore leaned against the wall, tipped her head back. The chandelier hanging in the center of the ceiling was dull with dust. "I find it rather terrifying, myself."

He made a noise she couldn't interpret. When she looked away from the chandelier, Gabe was sitting again, elbows on his knees. "That might be our explanation, then," he said. "I guess this is just...part of it. Part of your power."

"If it's any consolation," she said, sitting down next to him, "I would tell you how it worked if I knew."

"If you happen to figure it out anytime soon, that would be most excellent."

"Noted."

They sat in the gloom for a moment before Lore's mind circled back to their other problem, the potentially bigger one.

"If Bastian knows who I am," Lore said, "then why not just tell me? Or kill me? Isn't that what he'd do if he was really a Kirythean informant?"

Gabe rubbed at his eye patch. "Bastian gets spied on quite a lot. Just because he knows you're spying doesn't mean he knows *why*."

"His big show of revealing the dead horse makes it seems like he has an idea," Lore said. "Surely he's smart enough to make the connection that his father bringing in a necromancer has something to do with the villages. And if it's Kirythea that's responsible, it's not a leap to deduce that said necromancer is likely to expose him."

"Maybe he's just really excited about his pet dead horse and hasn't made all the connections yet."

"Or maybe he's not working for Kirythea, no matter how much August and Anton think he is. They have no real reason to suspect him; at least, not one they've told us."

"Anton wouldn't be so insistent that you investigate Bastian if he didn't have a good reason." Gabe propped his elbow on the arm of the couch and his forehead in his hand. "And what other reason would he have? Just because they haven't shared all the information with us doesn't mean they don't have it."

Clearly, she wouldn't get anywhere with Gabe. The man had

been programmed to march to whatever tune Anton played. Her thoughts turned again to Bastian, to what he'd shared while they danced. *My uncle has controlled his life for fourteen years.*

With a sigh, Lore pressed the heels of her palms against her brow, rested her elbows on her knees, and changed the subject back to something that didn't have the potential to become a fight. "How did he even get the horse? I know the story he told us was bullshit."

"Maybe not," Gabe said. "Bastian does have friends in the Citadel guard. Some lovers, too. They carted the body away from the Ward to be burned, but someone might've told him about it as an idle curiosity. He must've been intrigued enough to have them spirit it away, and the other guards just let it happen."

"Truly stupendous minds in that garrison. Just the best of the best." She dropped her hands, looked at him. "Should we tell them?"

Them: August and Anton. She didn't have to spell it out. Silence strung bowstring-tight between her and Gabe, waiting to see who'd slice it.

If she was useless to the Arceneaux brothers as a spy, she'd be kept in a cell until they needed her to raise the dead. And once that was finished, she'd get a one-way ticket to the Burnt Isle mines.

"No," Gabe said softly, as if he could read the thought in her head. "No, we don't need to tell them. Not right now."

"Thank you," Lore murmured.

He gave one quick, firm nod.

A stack of envelopes sat on the table before the couch, gleaming bright in the gloomy glow of the fire. They'd been pushed beneath the door when she and Gabe reached the suite, and he'd gathered them up, tossed them all here. Lore picked up a stack and idly flipped through the fine paper.

Invitations. Teas, dinners, dances, even a night of card

games—Bastian had declared them relevant by inviting them to his masque, and the court followed suit. Just the thought of so many social engagements made Lore's head pound. "Surely we aren't expected to attend all of these?"

"All, no. Some, yes." Gabe continued his moody survey of the banked fire, pointedly not looking at the pile of envelopes. "And all of them aren't for both of us, you'll notice."

"Is that why you're in such a sparkling mood? Feeling left out?"

Another grunt. "The court is eager to talk with you. You're a new commodity. Not as many of them want to socialize with a Presque Mort on hiatus." He grinned, then, tossing it her way with a sarcastic edge. "A fact that I am thankful for, actually. You'll be begging for holy orders after two teas."

"Yes, especially since you make holy orders look *so* appealing." She flipped through the envelopes, selecting one at random. The handwriting was thin and flourishing, addressed to them both, but only by first names. *Lore and Gabe*, with a tiny flower drawn after the last *e*. Her brow furrowed as she opened the flap, trying her best not to tear it. The paper felt more expensive than anything she'd worn before coming to the Citadel.

An invitation to a croquet game. From Alienor. "We should probably attend this one."

Gabe reached for the invitation; Lore handed it over. His jaw went rigid, but he said nothing, handing it back with the gravitas of a judge handing down a sentencing.

Lore turned the silky paper over and over in her hands and fought between tactfulness and curiosity. Curiosity won. "How did you two...I mean, what..."

"Our parents agreed to the match when we were both barely untied from leading strings." Gabe's voice was low and monotone, his answer coming like something rehearsed. He stared at the window across from the couch without really seeing it. "We were childhood friends, as much as two children can be friends with an eventual marriage hanging over their heads. It ended when I was ten, for obvious reasons. That's all there is to tell."

A quick sliver of pain—she'd given herself a paper cut on the invitation's edge. "Is she engaged to someone else now?"

"Not that I know of. Not that it matters."

It seemed to matter, if the set of his shoulders was any indication. And it made something unpleasant prick in the center of her stomach, that it mattered to *her* if it mattered to *him*.

The connection she'd felt between them had faded, no longer a constant feeling of déjà vu. Faded, but not gone. There was still the disconcerting sense that she knew Gabe, that they were something more than tentative allies thrown together mere days ago.

It didn't mean anything. When she first started spying on other poison runners, Mari had warned her against trusting feelings of quick closeness born from strange situations. The mind looked for connection in such cases, wanting something to cling to.

Lore placed the invitation on top of the table with all the other unopened envelopes. "Well. I hope you know how to play croquet, because I certainly don't."

"I'm rather rusty. We didn't play croquet much at Northreach."

"No, you were too busy staring dewy-eyed at paintings of Apollius and reading the Tracts until you could recite them in your sleep."

"Precisely." Gabe stood in a flurry of motion, stretching his arms over his head. "Are you as tired of this room as I am? I have a deep desire to be elsewhere."

"Do you have an *elsewhere* where we won't run into curious courtiers or ex-fiancées or asshole princes with dead horses?"

"As a matter of fact," Gabe said, walking toward the door, "I do."

Chapter Fifteen

Nyxara's power was death, but death made concrete—the essence of un-living, independent of a host. Only someone who has touched death can channel its raw form, cycling it through themselves and then into something else, rendering it dormant. Channeling this raw death—which we have elected to call *Mortem*—into living matter can kill weaker hosts, such as plants, but cannot kill stronger hosts, such as healthy humans and animals. However, there is a way to carefully channel Mortem into a living host that does not kill it, but rather makes it appear as stone, balanced somewhere between life and death through an equilibrium of Mortem and Spiritum. This method appears to work on all living matter, if the channeler is skilled enough to do it correctly.

—From the notes of Hakem Tabbal, Eroccan naturalist, dated two years AGF (after Godsfall)

Elsewhere turned out to be a garden made of stone.

Not entirely made of stone—there were a few living flowers twined among their rocky counterparts. Bloody-crimson roses blooming out of a bank of granite doppelgängers; green ivy climbing up the statues of their fellows. But mostly, everything was stone.

But not dead.

Lore couldn't make sense of it, not at first. Rock was something in which she always reliably felt Mortem: unalive and with no hope of being different. But the stone plants had a buzz of life around them, muted yet undeniably there, threaded through with just the barest hint of Mortem.

It felt...peaceful. The aura of the garden was one of rest, of sinking into a soft bed at the end of a long day.

Next to her, Gabe's shoulders loosened, tension sieving out of him like rain down a gutter. Maybe she looked relieved, too. Maybe both of them were always walking around like there were weights tied to their feet, and they'd never even noticed until someone cut the strings.

The garden he'd brought her to was in a courtyard against the Church wall, guarded from the interior Citadel grounds by a tall, ornate fence with a tall, ornate gate. It was small enough for Lore to see every corner from where they stood by the entrance, the walkways between the flower beds laid out in a neat grid that reminded her of Dellaire's streets. In the center stood what looked like a well beneath a peaked golden roof. The well was closed, covered with a large circle of wood. A small statue of Apollius stood on top of the wood, as if to hold it down.

Looking at the well interrupted the sense of peace from the rest of the garden, made a chill crawl down her spine. She averted her eyes.

Tentatively, Lore reached out and touched one of the stone roses. The texture was surprisingly smooth, still petal-like. "So this is what you channel all that Mortem into?" She'd heard the tales, how the Presque Mort were skilled enough to channel Mortem into plants without killing them. But hearing about a stone garden hadn't prepared her for how uncanny seeing it would be. The expectation was harsh and brutal; this was beautiful instead.

Gabe nodded. Next to him, flowers layered on top of one another, striations of rock and leaf, the new garden continuously grown atop the old.

"How?" A gust of wind made a living rose bend her way, tiny thorns catching on her sleeve. Gently, Lore unhooked them, let the rose bob back upright. "I mean, I know *how*, but how did you make them...I mean..."

"Carefully." Gabe snorted. "We channel the Mortem into the barest surface of the thing. It doesn't overwhelm the Spiritum, just...shrouds it. Puts it in stasis, somewhere between life and death." He gestured to the garden, almost proudly, meandering down the path. "We could reverse this, if we needed to. Channel the Mortem through us again, put it back into something dead, and release the flowers to what they were before. It's a kind of death, but it isn't permanent."

Lore stared at the roses a moment longer, watching them wave back and forth in the sunlight. Then she caught up with Gabe, who was still ambling good-naturedly along the cobblestones. He walked like a different person here, like he carried less. She wondered if he looked like this all the time when he was just a monk, when he was able to exist without reminders of who he could've been in the eyes of every courtier.

"Seems like cheating." Lore couldn't match his stride, but she did her best to keep up, two steps to one of his. "Going back and forth from death to life with no consequences."

"Consequences like what happens when you take poison?" Gabe shook his head. "Anyone who does that deserves what they get. Humans have been given the time they're supposed to have; trying to cheat it isn't part of Apollius's plan."

Lore wondered if he'd noticed the smell of August's flask.

What he made of it. "Have you ever tried this with a person, then?" She waved her hand at the garden.

He froze, a horrified light in his blue eye. "No one would do this to a person."

Her brow furrowed, and Lore stepped back, guilt teased to life by his stricken expression, resentment rising to meet it. "I'm not implying that you have. I'm just curious, Gabriel." She swallowed. "You've had years to learn about this power, with someone actually teaching you. I've just been trying to survive it."

The monk looked at her for a moment that stretched, face inscrutable. Then he turned, started walking again, though it was stiffer than before. "No one knows how channeling Mortem this way into something souled would affect them," he said finally, sidestepping the matter of Lore's ignorance entirely. "The position of the Church is that it would send your soul to the Shining Realm—or one of the myriad hells, I suppose, depending on how you'd lived. Once you were brought back, it'd pull you out of your afterlife, with knowledge no mortal should have."

Raising a person from the dead didn't bring back their soul, just their body—that's why you had to give them direction. But an insatiable curiosity about the afterlife had been what led to a rash of practicing necromancers right after the Godsfall. People who could channel enough Mortem to raise the dead did it to find out what happened after. To know the secrets of where you went once your body was done.

The Church hadn't liked that, even though it never really worked. No one had ever gotten a straight answer from a corpse.

Her eyes flickered to Gabe. "You really believe in the Shining Realm?"

"I'm a member of the clergy. Believing in the Shining Realm is quite literally in my job description."

Lore knocked her shoulder into his, companionably. After a moment, he gave her the smallest edge of a smile.

The path took them by the well. The statue of Apollius was more austere than most, plain stone with no garnet adornment. Lore eyed it warily. "What's that?"

"Catacombs entrance." He said it with such nonchalance, Lore was convinced for a moment she'd heard him wrong. But he shot her a wry look, shrugged. "We open it every eclipse, let out the Mortem, channel it into the flowers. It's efficient, and probably why we haven't had a significant leak in so long."

The mention of an eclipse made her press her palm to her thigh, hiding her scar. "When's the next one?"

"Midsummer. A solar eclipse, so the Mortem will be particularly strong. Nyxara blocking Apollius, and all that." He raised a brow. "Isn't that right around your birthday?"

Her twenty-fourth birthday. Her Consecration. Lore masked her unease with a guileless grin. "Are you planning to get me a cake?"

"Maybe. Depends on if you're nice until then."

She rolled her eyes and took his arm, falling into step with him again as they walked away from the well. Still, pensiveness made her chew her lip. "Does it worry you? When there's a solar eclipse and the Mortem is stronger?"

"I try not to worry until Anton tells me to."

That soured her stomach. But she kept her tone light. "You seem far closer to the Priest Exalted than any of the other Presque Mort."

"Anton was like a father to me. I know some of it was because of his vision—that I needed to be in the Presque Mort, that it was Apollius's will—but he was also kind. Helpful. He traveled back and forth to see me, to make sure I was doing as well as I could." Gabe shrugged. "If it weren't for him, I wouldn't be here."

She didn't know if he meant *here* as in part of the Church, or *here* as in the land of the living. She didn't really want to.

"Why did you ask if I believed in the Shining Realm?" Gabe

asked, after a long few minutes of not-exactly-comfortable silence. "Do you not?"

Lore shrugged. "I don't often think about what happens after we die, really. There's enough to worry about right now."

He made a rueful noise of understanding.

"But if I *do* think about it..." Lore kicked at a stray pebble. "No. I don't think I believe in the Shining Realm. At least not the way the Church teaches it."

Gabe raised a brow, wordlessly asking for further explanation. But he didn't brand her a heretic and run to find Anton, which seemed promising.

She sighed, tipping her head up, as if the summer sky would give her language to explain it. "Mortem, to me, feels like the absence of everything. An end. So I guess it doesn't make sense that I would believe in an afterlife at all...but I do, I think. I believe in *something*, anyway. But in all honesty, the idea of the myriad hells makes more sense to me than the Shining Realm does. I think that whatever comes after this, it's of our own making. Whatever we sowed in life is what we reap in death, good or bad."

"The worst part of the myriad hells would be the loneliness," Gabe said quietly. "Being trapped in the world your own sins made, and utterly alone. I understand your point, but I can't believe that someone who lived piously would be alone in death. And it wouldn't make sense for anyone else to be caught up in the place your own actions made."

She trailed her hand along a bank of stone geraniums. "I don't know. But if Mortem feels empty—lonely—doesn't it make sense that death would be, too?"

They lapsed into silence. Voices called in the distance, courtiers at play in the inner walls of the Citadel, sowing things they must eventually reap.

"I don't think how Mortem feels and how death feels are the

same," Gabe said finally, almost to himself. "One is twisted magic leaking from the body of a dead goddess, and one is something that awaits us all. The first comes from the second, but they aren't the same."

"Why is *Her* magic called twisted?" If it weren't that they were alone, that the hushed stone garden felt like a place removed from reality, Lore wouldn't have spoken. But as it was, the words came tumbling from her mouth nearly dripping venom. "She and Apollius were equals. Her magic might've been dark and night and death, but it wasn't *twisted*, not any more than His was, or any of the elemental minor gods you like to forget existed. It was just different."

Gabe made a *hmm* sound, brows drawn thoughtfully down. "Do you know the Law of Opposites?"

A Tract teaching, a simple one that children were taught soon after learning to walk. Well, children that weren't Lore. Still, she knew of the law and gave him a curt nod.

"If something is good, then its opposite must be evil." Gabe shook his head. "I don't believe that."

"*You* don't believe in something from the Tracts? You're rapidly careening toward a vacation on the Burnt Isles."

It was his turn to knock into her shoulder. "I believe the Tracts are up for interpretation," he said. "And in this, I feel like our interpretation has to be wrong. Opposites are not always in *opposition*; the day and night are equals. One isn't good and the other bad." He paused, mouth pursed. "But one does illuminate things, while the other obscures. And that has to mean something, too, I think."

Lore didn't respond. She crossed her arms, stared at her feet as they walked over the cobblestones.

"I don't think Nyxara is evil," Gabe continued. It sounded like he had to push it through his teeth, though, like calling the Buried Goddess Her actual name was a difficult task. "She made a mistake by trying to kill Apollius, for reasons none of us know, and She was struck down for it. I can't think She's in the Shining Realm with Him—that wouldn't make any sense—but I hope, wherever She went after Her life here was done, it's not too terrible." He paused. "And I wish She'd taken Her magic with Her, instead of letting it leak out all over Dellaire. But I suppose that wasn't a choice She could make."

Lore slid her eyes toward Gabe. "I feel like hoping Nyxara's afterlife isn't terrible might be some kind of blasphemy."

"If grace is blasphemous, build me a pyre."

He said it half like a joke, but they both knew it wasn't. They walked on in silence, both lost in thought.

"Are you hungry?" They'd made their way around the perimeter of the garden, and now Gabe headed for the gate again, the one that would lead them back into the Citadel. "If lunch still happens the way it did back when I was a child, there should be food for the taking in the front hall."

Gabe was right. A long table stretched the length of the hall when they entered through the Citadel doors, piled with more food than Lore had ever seen in one place. The wine fountains from Bastian's masquerade were back, and stacks of small sandwiches, and what looked like an entire roasted boar, complete with an apple in its mouth.

She gaped. "They just leave this out here?"

"Most courtiers send their staff to come make them a tray," Gabe said, picking up a plate and carving off a piece of the boar. "But since we don't have staff, we're on our own."

"Such a hardship," Lore lisped around the macaron she'd just shoved in her mouth.

Not all courtiers delegated their lunch preparations—Alie stood at the bend of the hall, dressed in a long dress of lavender chiffon, understated and elegant. She waved when she saw them, gracefully breaking away from the other ladies she stood with to come give Lore a very tight and very unexpected hug. "You two! Where have you been? We just came from a croquet game on the back lawn; I was sure I'd see you there." She wiggled her pale brows. "You'll need to practice if you're going to make it a good game when we play."

"We were taking a walk," Gabe answered, just as Lore said, "Bastian took us to the stables."

Gabe's one eye shot daggers. Lore gave him an apologetic look over Alie's shoulder. She'd always been told that lies were more believable when you laced them with truth, so didn't it follow that lying about as little as possible would serve them well here?

Alie's eyes widened. "Well, then. I don't blame you for picking Bastian over croquet." She raised a delicate brow at Gabe. "And I assume you felt you had to go along as a chaperone? Probably wise."

"Oh, no, it's nothing like that," Lore said. "He was just being courteous."

The other woman grinned mischievously. "Bastian doesn't really do courteous. He does, however, like to begin illicit propositions by leading his hopeful paramour to the stables."

Lore fought down a mad giggle. Bastian might be in the habit of taking people he wanted to sleep with to the stables, but she was absolutely certain his seduction didn't usually involve an undead horse.

Still, the mere implication was enough to give Gabe a long-suffering expression similar to the boar on the table. "Thank you for the information, Alie."

"Anytime. I have years of court gossip to catch you up on." Alie turned her grin from Gabe to Lore. "I'll tell you all the best bits at our game next week. I find rumors go down best when you have a mallet to swing."

Lore, who had not actually decided on any of the invitations in the stack back in their suite, swallowed a mouthful of wine and nodded. "We'll be there."

"Excellent." Alie waved over her shoulder as she turned back to her friends, a gaggle of beautifully dressed women whom Lore was trying very hard not to make eye contact with. Cecelia was not among them, and she didn't recognize anyone from the group taking poison at the masquerade. "See you then!"

The smile melted off Lore's face as she turned back to the food. "At least we know Bastian wasn't taking me to the stables for his usual reasons."

It was a joke, and she expected Gabe to react to it with his usual eye roll, but the Presque Mort just stabbed another strawberry and knifed it onto his plate. "I wouldn't be so sure," he muttered.

CHAPTER SIXTEEN

To each person is given knowledge according to their station; it is not holy to try to rise above the lot the gods have given you.

—The Book of Mortal Law, Tract 90

The afternoon whiled away in a sunlit haze. After eating, Lore made Gabriel give her a tour of the Citadel—somewhat difficult, as he hadn't spent significant time there in years, but their shared unfamiliarity almost made it better. Two interlopers in a thick fog of luxury they didn't belong to. When thoughts of Bastian and what he might or might not know loomed in her mind, Lore thrust them out, behind that wall of trees Gabriel had helped her grow. She needed time to make a plan, to frame her possible compromise to August in a way that wouldn't land her in a cell.

She also needed distraction, and Gabriel obliged. Their wanderings took them through gilded halls with soaring painted ceilings, celestial scenes scabbed with glittering chandeliers. One room was full of nothing but statuary, gleaming marble bodies caught in sword fights and kisses and dances. Another room, circular and made almost entirely of glass, held a reflecting pool with a fountain in the center and rose petals floating on its surface. They didn't spend long there—a handful of courtiers lazed around the pool's edges, and more than one was swimming in it, naked as the day they were born. Gabe's cheeks turned scarlet beneath his eye patch as he turned on his heel and marched back into the hallway. Lore managed to swallow her laughter until they were far enough away from the door that none of the courtiers would hear it.

After that, entirely by accident, they ended up in a library.

The Citadel was a study in opulence, dripping excess in every corner, but this was the room that really made Lore's jaw drop. The library had three levels, all of them visible from the bottom floor—balconies ringed the walls, accessible by small, polished-wood staircases set into the shelves. All three levels were filled to bursting with books, glowing in the gentle light through the solarium window above. Small chairs upholstered in brocade were grouped in various places on all levels, ready-made reading nooks that held no readers.

"There's got to be buckets of gold in here," Lore breathed. "Do you know how expensive books are?"

"I do." A scowl darkened Gabe's face. "All that money, and hardly anyone here reads."

"No one, really? What a waste."

Gabe shifted uncomfortably. "Bastian used to. When we were children. He read voraciously."

"*That's* surprising." Lore trailed her hand over the top of the nearest chair. The fabric was down-soft and silky, far too fine for furniture.

"He's not stupid," Gabe said. Then cocked his head, amended. "Well. He is, but not in a books way. Just a general-common-sense way."

Lore chewed the corner of her lip as she wandered over to one of the shelves nearest the door. In true Citadel fashion, it appeared to be full of erotic poetry. "You two seem to know each other well."

"Better than I'd like."

"Were you close, when you . . . when you spent time here?"

Gabe paused before answering. When he did, it was quiet. "We were. Bastian and Alie and I were thick as thieves."

Were. The past tense had a heft to it. She and the grumpy monk were probably the closest thing to a friend the other had, now. Wasn't *that* a kick in the ass to think about.

Lore idly pulled a book from the shelf, flipped through the lurid illustrations. "Were your parents close, too?" Her context for childhood friendships might be skewed, but from what she'd seen of other, more normal childhoods, it seemed like most of them were initially predicated on parents being friends.

Another pause, longer this time. She probably shouldn't have asked, not when the subject of parents was such a fraught one for Gabe, but she found herself almost insatiably curious about him. Gabriel Remaut was a mess of contradictions, opposites all knotted up into one man, and she wanted to pick the knots apart.

"Our fathers were too busy for friendship, it seemed," Gabe said. "But our mothers were. Friends, I mean." He rubbed absently at his eye patch. "Bastian's mother, Ivanna, grew rather sickly after Bastian was born, and couldn't often leave her apartments. My mother and Alie's—her name was Lise—would take us over there to spend time with her, let us run wild with Bastian while they talked and drank wine."

"That sounds nice," Lore murmured.

He shrugged. "The three of them were—well, not outcasts, but they didn't really fit into the court. Alie's mother was as Auverrani as anyone else, but she had the look of her Malfouran father, and that made some ignorant courtiers treat her differently. My mother wasn't rich enough to be part of the upper crust—Balgia was such a small duchy, never very profitable, nearly insignificant but for the fact it was a holdout between Auverraine and the Kirythean Empire. And Ivanna was so quiet. People tried to get close to her, since she was the queen, but she didn't seem interested." His mouth flattened. "August was not kind to her."

Gabe turned away abruptly, making a show of perusing the books on a different shelf. Since that one was also erotic poetry, Lore assumed it was more to end the conversation than out of any real interest.

"What was your mother's name?" she asked after a long stretch of quiet.

"Claire," Gabe murmured. "Her name was Claire. She died when I was eight."

"I'm sorry."

"Me too." A pause. Then, softer: "But I'm glad she went before everything happened with my father. I'm glad she didn't have to see it."

Lore glanced back at him. Gabe's shoulders were tight beneath his dark doublet, his hands clasped behind his back. One hand faced palm-out, showing the candle inked across life and heart lines. The wick reached the base of his fingers, the meat before the knuckles covered in a semicircle of lines to imitate light. The candle's base started right at his wrist, detailed with lumps of melted wax. She wondered how much getting that needled into him had hurt.

Probably not as much as losing his eye.

His hand lifted, rubbed across the one-eyed face she couldn't see. "By every god buried or bleeding, I'm tired."

He said it so quietly, she wouldn't have heard if she wasn't studying him. Gabe kept his exhaustion and his anger and everything else he felt packed tight and stowed away.

Lore turned, the book she'd idly picked up still clutched in her hands. "I found one to read. Let's go back to the suite. We could both use a nap, I think."

It wasn't a lie. Between Bastian's party and waking up at the first snap of dawn, she was tired, too.

Gabe turned, brow arched. His one blue eye dipped to the book she held, then widened. "*That's* the one you're taking?"

The gilt cover glinted up as she turned the book around to study it for the first time. More erotic poetry. The painting on the front depicted a randy satyr chasing a nymph wearing nothing but lots of long blond hair.

Her smile grew wicked edges. "What's the matter with it, Mort?"

"Nothing at all." He strode toward the door, stiff-legged.

"Maybe you could read it, too. Learn something. Since you've been celibate your whole life—"

"You're so sure I've never broken my vows, then?"

She tilted her head curiously. "Have you?"

Gabe gave her a cool glance over his shoulder, chin lifted. "Wouldn't *you* like to know."

The door opened as Gabe was reaching for it, letting in a rather harried-looking Malcolm dressed head-to-toe in Presque Mort black. He straightened, clearly ready to bring down the force of a holy stare onto flighty nobles, then started when he recognized them, his flinty expression dissolving into a smile. "Good afternoon, Lore. And *Your Grace*."

"Spare me," Gabe muttered, but he clapped the other man companionably on the back.

"Didn't expect to see you two here without your royal charge." Malcolm held a pile of books in his hands; he passed them to enter the library and headed to one of the small staircases that led to the upper floors. "Anton made it sound like he wants Lore sewed to the Sun Prince's ass."

"I'm actually on my way to find him now," Lore said quickly. Gabe and Malcolm were obviously friends, and she liked the man from the little time she'd spent with him, but she assumed he was just as conditioned to report everything to Anton as Gabe was. "Gabe thought Bastian might be here, but it appears he's spending his leisure hours elsewhere." *Like in the stables, trying to feed apples to a dead horse.*

Malcolm looked down from the second story, leaning over the gilded railing just long enough to see the cover of Lore's book. His dark eyes widened as he snorted a laugh. "Taking *get close to Bastian* very seriously, I see."

"I always follow orders," Lore replied.

Gabe grimaced, but was too preoccupied with what Malcolm was doing to make a snide comment. "Is Anton moving more books out of the Church library?"

"Not quite." Malcolm set his book pile down on the floor, then hefted one of them into an empty space in the shelf. The thing was thick, and Malcolm's muscles strained as he pushed it into place. Truly, it was a waste how good-looking all the Presque Mort were. "He asked for these to be brought to him for study. Newer editions of the Compendium, some translated from other languages and then back into Auverrani." Another over-thick book was pushed into its space. "No idea *why*, since there are literally hundreds of Compendiums in the Church library, including the original. Especially since from what I've seen, he's only looking at the Book of Holy Law. But what do I know! I'm just the librarian." He shoved the last book into the shelf and turned to face them, bracing his hands on the railing. "Compendiums are easy to find, at least. A couple of months ago, he made me look for a book on dreamwalking. I had to write to a university all the way in Farramark, and it took ages to get here, even by sea. Of course he just had to have it when the Ourish Pass was frozen over."

"He must be looking for something specific in the translations," Gabe murmured. "Any Tract in particular?"

"When he left them all open yesterday," Malcolm said, making his way down the stairs, "it was to the Law of Opposites." He shrugged. "Who knows. I certainly couldn't tell a difference."

"Are differences common?" Lore asked.

"Not really." Malcolm pushed the door open for them, this time, waving them gracefully into the hall. "The Compendiums are the least interesting thing in the Church's catalog, to be honest. The firsthand accounts of the Godsfall and the notes on experiments with elemental magic are much more entertaining."

"I'd bet," Lore said softly.

He caught the gleam of interest in her eye, smiled to see it. "You're welcome to come look at them sometime. Just let me know beforehand, so I can make sure Anton isn't going to be around. He's picky about the Church library."

A scowl flickered at the corner of Gabe's mouth, but he didn't say anything.

"I'll take you up on that." Lore turned in the direction she thought would take them toward the southeast turret. "Assuming I can find the time to un-sew myself from Bastian's ass."

Malcolm snorted. "Let me know if you need a seam ripper."

❦

The sun was low in the sky by the time they made their circuitous way back through the shining halls of the Citadel to their suite. Gabe was quiet the whole time, his face drawn into pensive lines. Any attempt Lore made at a joke was rebuffed with silence.

The silence did not alleviate when they got to their apartments. Gabe sighed when he entered the sitting room, hands hung on his hips, before turning right and entering the smaller study off the dining area. She heard a chair creak as he lowered himself into it.

Lore went to the sidebar, found a bottle of wine, poured herself a glass. Still vinegary, but passable. She couldn't find another wineglass, so she poured Gabe's helping into a small mug clearly not meant for the purpose.

A large oak desk dominated the study, empty except for a cut-glass paperweight housing a blood-red rose in its center. Bookshelves lined the walls, but they were mostly empty, too, holding only a dusty copy of the Compendium and a potted fern in desperate need of a good watering.

The study was small enough that Lore didn't have to enter all the way to hand him the cup. For a moment, he just looked at it, but then he took it from her.

She leaned her shoulder against the jamb. "Your mood has taken a drastic turn for the dour."

He huffed, sipped the wine. "Being reminded of the excess in this place will do that."

Understandable. It had itched at her, too, wandering through the museum-like halls, seeing all the accumulated wealth while knowing firsthand the lack felt outside the Citadel. Lore had never worried about starving—Mari and Val made sure of that—but hunger was a sleeping wolf crouched at the door, a continuous threat that you learned to live with and did your best not to wake.

Lore stared into the depths of her glass. "Our guilt isn't helping anyone, Gabe."

He stiffened.

Her foot tapped against the floor, a nervous rhythm to order her thoughts around. "I mean, part of me feels guilty for enjoying it, too. For wanting all this for myself, when I know how little most people have. But we don't have time for the luxury of guilt. Not if there's an actual war coming, and not while we're stuck here either way."

Gabe still didn't look at her. He slumped back in his chair, an inelegant pile of monk. "I didn't think I missed it. But here, in a place where I was...was *happy*, once..." He trailed off. Sighed. "I remember when it was like a home, before I knew it was rotten. The Citadel was easy to love, then. And hating it was just as easy, once I learned how corrupt it was. But hating it is only easy from far away."

He wanted that ease back. Wanted simple answers, clear delineations. And if it weren't for Lore, he'd have them.

"It's shameful," he murmured. "It's *shameful*, how much they have, how much they steal."

"It is," Lore said. "I want to do something about it. To fix it, somehow. But I..." She trailed off, shrugged. This was something she'd thought about so often, and never quite been able to translate. "I don't know how, I guess? I'm one person. One fairly insignificant person, and against so many years of so much power, I feel completely useless. Like...like trying to dam up a river with a pebble."

"It would take a lot of pebbles," Gabe agreed. He picked up the glass paperweight and twisted it in his hands, making the rose inside stretch and refract into odd shapes.

Lore crossed to him. Took the paperweight and placed it gently back on the desk. "Give yourself some of that grace you were prattling on about, Mort," she said softly.

And with that, Lore went into her room, still carrying her book of erotic poetry, and left the one-eyed monk staring into the dark.

She tried reading for maybe an hour or so, lighting the candle by her bedside when the sun completely slipped past the horizon. But the poetry was too flowery to really be titillating, and instead Lore found herself staring into the embroidered canopy over her head and thinking of the vaults.

The memory of the small body on the slab still made her chest tighten. The open mouth, the whispers, the black eyes—it was both like and unlike Cedric, and she couldn't quite wrap her head around that. Maybe her magic had changed, become darker, become somehow worse.

And they wanted her to do it again.

Bastian said he thought that the tragedies in the villages were caused by Mortem. She'd told him it was impossible, but after seeing Horse—Claude, she reminded herself, nose wrinkling—Lore wondered if maybe she didn't know that much about Mortem after all. Maybe she didn't really know *anything*.

As much as she hated the idea of attempting to raise someone from the dead again, the idea of just walking away and letting her failure stand wasn't an option. Wouldn't be even if the other option wasn't the Burnt Isles. Whole villages, whole *families*, were dead. She'd known that, in the abstract. But to know it and to see it were two different things, and to know that she was apparently the only one who could figure it out was still another.

Her failure felt as damning as blood on her fingers.

And it wasn't until then—thinking of her failure, of Claude/Horse, of how they collided—that she realized how the two things fit together.

Lore sat bolt-upright in bed. "Shit."

CHAPTER SEVENTEEN

Nothing binds people together better than desperation.
—Eroccan proverb

Gabe was still awake when Lore burst through her bedroom door, though he'd moved out of the dusty study and was now staring into the fireplace with his usual pensive expression. He'd taken off his shirt and piled his bedding in front of the door, and the flame-light played over the muscled planes of his chest.

He whipped around as her door banged open, brows knit. "Lore?"

She cast a look at the clock on the wall—nearly midnight. Hopefully everyone would be either sleeping or involved in other distracting endeavors. "I have to go back to the vaults."

"You *what*?"

Lore shoved her feet into her boots and tied a quick knot in the sash of the dressing gown she'd found in the wardrobe. Perfectly tailored, once again, and a pretty blush-pink that she never would've chosen for herself. "The body I raised from the dead today—I channeled Mortem with him the same way I did with the horse."

She didn't pause as she spoke, rushing to her boots and shoving her feet into them, moving as quickly as she could. Behind her, Gabe stood slowly from the couch. "I don't understand the problem."

"The problem," Lore said, sitting down hard on the ground to tie her laces, "is that he might wake up, just like the horse did."

Cedric. Gods, had it happened to Cedric, too? They'd burned him after Lore snapped the strings of Mortem animating his corpse; had he been awake for that, his mouth an open maw like the child in the vaults, a scream with no sound?

Lore didn't realize she was hyperventilating until Gabe's hand landed on her shoulder, a calming weight. She fought to control her breathing as the shirtless Mort knelt in front of her, brow creased in concern.

"But you have to tell a human corpse what to do, right?" he murmured. "It's not like an animal; he won't get up and walk around. We can go in the morning."

"No." She shook her head. When her eyes closed, she saw Cedric, his body a horror, his eyes open. "No, I have to try and fix it now, I can't leave him like that. I can't."

Gabe looked at her, his one eye searching both of hers. Then he nodded, once.

Lore made for the door, not giving him time to change his mind. Gabe cursed at her speed, grabbing a shirt and pulling it over his head, hopping on one foot to tie his boots. "Slow down, Lore, it's not—"

"I have to fix it before August or Anton sees." She wasn't sure why. But she knew, with that same deep, primordial sense that told her how to raise the dead, that neither the King nor the Priest should see what her magic could really do. Horse was one thing, humans another.

And even though the body on the slab would never be truly alive again—never truly conscious—the thought of leaving him alone in the dark turned her stomach.

"No one should've been in the vaults since you and August and Anton left, other than the Sacred Guard," Gabe said, nearly toppling over as he tied his second boot. He hadn't quite managed to pull his shirt all the way down in his attempt to catch up with her, and the hem was caught high on his rib, showing a distracting amount of abdomen. "They aren't a place you visit casually. If he woke up, no one will have seen."

Relief flooded her, relief and warmth. There was no guarantee Gabe wouldn't tell Anton about this eventually, but for now, he was choosing her. She'd take it.

They went to the tiny staircase at the back of the turret, rather than the wide steps toward the front. The coils of the stairs were tight enough to make seeing more than a foot or so in front of you impossible, and Lore kept craning her head to look at Gabe, hands on the railings to keep from falling over. "Will the guard let us by?"

"It changes at midnight, so if we hurry, we can get there while the entrance is unmanned."

"Good. So we'll head to—"

Lore was interrupted when her shoulder smacked into something that felt disconcertingly like another human.

"Hmph," said the other human.

Slowly, she turned around.

Alienor's father frowned at her.

Standing on lower stairs put him right at eye level with Lore, but Lord Bellegarde still managed to look like he was looming, peering down a straight nose with eyes a near-acidic shade of green, his dark hair caught in an orderly queue at the back of his neck. He smiled, but it was as thin as the rest of him, and did nothing to warm his eyes.

Lore caught hold of herself, dipped into as passable a curtsy as she could muster in a dressing gown. Behind her, Gabe was stiff as a board. "Pardon me, I wasn't watching where I was going."

"I take no offense." Bellegarde inclined his head to her, then his eyes darted to Gabe. If the sight of them both in states of dishevelment and running down the back stairs threw him off, he did a remarkable job of hiding it. "Gabriel Remaut. I never thought I'd see you in court again."

His voice was cold enough to raise goose bumps. Lore's brow knit, and she fought the anxious urge to chew a fingernail.

The quick spasm of a grimace across Gabe's face showed he noticed the chill, but he didn't react in kind. He nodded smoothly, as if he were in a ballroom rather than half dressed in a servant's stairway at midnight. "Lord Bellegarde. I must admit, I never thought I'd be back, either."

"Fourteen years, this past spring." Alienor's father clasped his hands behind his back. Despite the late hour and the odd location, he was still dressed in Citadel finery—white shirt with billowing sleeves beneath a doublet of cream silk and cloth-of-gold, breeches to match. Where Gabe and Bastian both wore boots, though, Bellegarde wore small heeled shoes in the same white as his shirt. They were not flattering, but even ridiculous footwear didn't lessen the gravitas of his presence.

"Fourteen years," the lord continued, "and only now have we undone all the damage your family caused. The Bellegarde reputation was besmirched along with yours, though you and Alienor had said no wedding vows."

Lore looked from Bellegarde to Gabriel, fingers tightly wound in the long tie of her dressing gown. Good thing, too, because she felt a strong urge to smack Bellegarde in the mouth.

But Gabriel weathered the low blow with nothing but a flicker of his eye to the floor. "I know," he said simply, low and earnest. "Please believe me, Severin, I would never have knowingly ensnared Alie in my family's troubles. I knew nothing of what my father planned with Kirythea."

Using Bellegarde and his daughter's given names was a gamble, and one that didn't pay off—Bellegarde's eyes went flinty.

"And yet you were present in Balgia when the betrayal occurred, when there was no reason for you to have left the court. You can see how such a thing invites ideas of collusion."

Gabe's jaw was a straight line of hard-won restraint. "There were extenuating circumstances," he said stiffly. "I was sent back to Balgia, I didn't choose to go."

That didn't seem to deter Bellegarde. "And when Anton brought you back, you still did nothing to call off the betrothal, leaving it to our house to correct the paperwork—"

"He was *ten*." Lore straightened, trapped between the two of them on the stairs, glaring at Bellegarde with every bit of her considerable contempt. "He was a child."

She stood close enough to smell his aftershave, but Bellegarde looked at her like he'd forgotten she was there. "And now this," he said with a humorless chuckle, mirroring all that contempt right back. "Leaving the defense of your honor to a country cousin I wasn't even aware existed. Truly, Gabriel, bravo."

Lore's fingers tightened to a fist. Gabe's hand clapped around it like a shackle. "Is there something you wanted, Severin?" He should've sounded angry, but Gabe just sounded tired. "It's late, and I assume if you were coming up the southeast turret, you had a particular item you wanted to discuss with me. Your seasonal accommodations are no doubt somewhere more fashionable, and I doubt you'd lower yourself to speaking to anyone else relegated to the far corners of the Citadel."

Lore glanced at Gabe from the corner of her eye, but the monk didn't look suspicious. It seemed as though it was perfectly in character for Severin Bellegarde to come to one's room for the sole purpose of an upbraiding at nearly midnight.

Nearly midnight. Bleeding God in a bandage, they had to *go*.

Bellegarde's face gave away nothing, but his hand twitched by his side. Lore looked down just as the man crumpled what looked like a small piece of paper into his palm.

"I merely wanted to welcome you back to court, Gabriel." There was nothing like welcome in Bellegarde's tone. "You and your...cousin."

"Rather late for a social call," Lore said.

But Bellegarde just shrugged. "The hours kept in the Court of the Citadel are not the hours kept outside. And while I wanted to be polite, I admit that calling on you came dead last on my list of daily priorities."

Gabe heaved a weary sigh. "Thank you for the welcome, my lord. I regret to tell you that my cousin and I are running late—"

"Yes, I gathered when I interrupted your mad sprint down the stairs." Bellegarde narrowed his eyes at Lore's dressing gown. "Where might you be going with your cousin half dressed?"

"A party, of course." Lore answered before Gabe could try, mostly because she saw the panicked look on his face that said he was completely at a loss. "One I don't plan to return from until at least dawn. Might as well be comfortable."

Bellegarde raised an eyebrow. "It appears you fit into the court just fine."

That, apparently, was his goodbye. After an awkward moment of maneuvering, Bellegarde passed them on the stairs, continuing up as Lore and Gabe climbed down. Lore frowned after him. So he *was* doing something other than trying to find Gabe. That, or the idea of walking all the way to the main floor in their company was not a pleasant one.

The feeling was very mutual.

Right before Bellegarde took a turn of the stairs that would take him out of sight, he looked down at her again. His mouth flattened, and his hand curled into a tighter fist by his side. The hand holding that small piece of paper.

Neither she nor Gabe spoke until they reached the bottom of the servants' staircase, emerging into the scarlet-carpeted corridor that marked the first floor of the turret, branching off the Citadel's front hall.

"What a horrible man," Lore muttered, starting down the corridor with more stomp in her step than before. "What a vicious, small little man."

"Don't think too ill of him."

Lore's eyebrows shot high.

"Bellegarde has no love for the Presque Mort. He thinks that channeling Mortem is an unforgivable sin, that there must be another solution to the problem and we should wait for Apollius to show us what it is." Gabe shrugged, following her down the hall at a quick pace with significantly less stomp than her own. "If I'd taken a prison sentence instead of Mort vows, he'd have no problem with me. Or less of one, at least. Honestly, he probably would've preferred if I'd just died from my wounds in the first place. Then dissolving my betrothal would've been less paperwork."

Lore's scowl deepened. "And yet I saw him in the North Sanctuary this morning. Which makes him not only small and vicious, but also a hypocrite. I will continue to think very ill of him, thank you."

"For all his issues with the Church, he'd never miss prayers," Gabe said. "That would be an insult to Apollius." They reached the wide, shallow staircase at the end of the hall and went quickly down, booted feet making little noise on the thick carpet, their voices dropped to just above whispers. "Bellegarde doesn't like that the Church is separate from the crown, doesn't like that they're two different entities instead of one governing body. He thinks the Church should be under the King's rule, since he's Apollius's chosen."

"A theocrat. Delightful." Lore rolled her eyes. "I can't imagine that makes him and Anton the best of friends."

"They mostly just avoid each other." Clearly just talking about someone disagreeing with Anton made Gabe uncomfortable; he didn't look at her, and shifted his shoulders. "Bellegarde and his ilk are few, and more interested in looking like they smelled a fresh pile of shit than actually trying to change anything. Their identity is in being upset; if they actually got what they claim to want, I don't think they'd know what to do with themselves."

"Does Alie share his views?" Lore fervently hoped not.

"Not at all." Gabe shook his head. "Truth be told, I don't think Alie spends much time pondering religion or politics."

"What a life to lead," Lore said wistfully.

They stopped in an atrium that branched off into multiple hallways, chandeliers sparkling overhead, points of light against the shadows cast by the lone lit sconce. Gabe eyed the hallways, seemingly at a loss. "You know how to get to the vaults, right?"

"You mean you don't?"

"Not everyone gets to go to the vaults, Lore." The slight irritation in his voice had an edge that was almost anger. "Only the wealthiest, the most privileged."

"Or those of us conscripted into necromancy." She didn't like it when he talked to her like she was part of the things he hated. When he seemed to forget that she wasn't here of her own will any more than he was.

He glanced at her, sighed.

"Thankfully for your poor, privilege-deprived ass," Lore said, stepping in front of him, "I have an excellent memory."

Lore led him through hallways that felt more like warrens, the gilt and opulence that lit them in the daytime grown ominous in shadows. They encountered no one, though they heard voices occasionally, laughter and shouting made shivery and spectral.

At least, they encountered no one until they rounded the last corner. There, right in front of the door to the tiny corridor with the vaults at its end, a bloodcoat stood leaning against the wall, bayonet sharp and shining. He yawned, the sound echoing in so much empty space.

With a muttered curse, Lore backtracked, pressing her spine

against an oil painting of some very drunk-looking shepherds. "I thought there was just the Sacred Guard in the tunnel, not one out here."

"A tactical mind for the ages," Gabe muttered.

"Make fun of me after you take care of it."

"Why *me*?"

"Because you're the muscle and I'm the brains."

Gabe shot her a look that said he might debate that point, but then peeled off the wall, started soundlessly forward. For such a large man, he moved like fog, keeping to the shadows.

He was nice to watch, she couldn't deny that. Lore tilted her head for a better angle as Gabe came up behind the bloodcoat. If they taught this kind of stealth up at the Northreach monastery, she could think of a few folks in Val's crew who might benefit from a stint there.

Gods. She had to stop thinking of Val.

The bloodcoat didn't notice Gabe until he was on him. One hand over the guard's mouth, another pressing at a specific spot on the back of his neck. Gabe lowered the guard slowly to the floor, propping him against the wall, careful not to catch anything on the sharp end of his bayonet. "He'll think he fell asleep," he murmured. "We have maybe half an hour. Will that be enough?"

"Let's hope." Lore tiptoed around the sleeping guard and pushed open the door into the narrow hallway beyond, Gabe following swift and silent.

The hall was lit only by candlelight; darkness lay deep in the corners. A taper burned in every alcove, slashing harsh light across Apollius's face, making the garnets in His hands glitter.

Briefly, Lore worried that the door to the tunnel would be locked, but it opened soundlessly when she pushed it—she guessed a lock was moot when you had guards. And if Gabe was any indication, only a few people knew how to get to the vaults, anyway.

The short stairs into the tunnel were black as pitch. Lore hesitated on the threshold, remembering the hallway, the Sacred Guard standing at the end. She looked back over her shoulder at Gabe. "The guard... the way this is set up, I don't think there's a way to sneak up on him."

"You're underestimating my sneaking."

"Really, Gabe, maybe I should just try to get back here in the morning. I don't want you to get hurt—"

"Oh, yes, spare all of us *that*," a voice said from behind them.

Lore and Gabe froze, eyes wide. The moment right before the trap's teeth closed on the rabbit's leg.

"Thank the gods I'm here." Bastian stepped out of the shadows with a lazy smile on his face. "Otherwise, you'd be shit out of luck."

CHAPTER EIGHTEEN

Children, strive to be above reproach, for forgiveness
is not easily earned.
                    –The Book of Mortal Law, Tract 403

Lore's tongue felt thick and clumsy in her mouth, her thoughts
packed in wool. She couldn't untangle an excuse from them.

Next to her, nearly invisible in the gloom, Gabriel wasn't trying for excuses at all. A dagger was in his hand—when had he
gotten a dagger?—and it caught the candlelight as he held it to
Bastian's throat.

That broke Lore's paralysis. "Bleeding *God*, Gabe, do you *want*
to hang?"

"You know, I think he might." For having a naked blade at his
neck, Bastian seemed incredibly nonchalant. "The final act in his
endless personal drama."

Gabe's teeth flashed bright as his dagger. "Bold words for
someone at the sharp end."

"Truly, I'm wounded." Bastian made a show of craning his
neck to look over his shoulder at the narrow door. "But not quite
so wounded that I'd wake up the guard outside. Not yet, anyway."

His almost-golden eyes glittered in the dark. "I already paid off the Sacred one in the corridor, so he's probably carousing at some tavern or other. But I'm sure I could find him if I wanted."

As threats went, it wasn't exactly subtle. The three of them stared at one another, Gabe still holding the dagger at Bastian's neck and Bastian looking singularly unbothered by it.

It came to Lore to break the silence, since Gabe and Bastian seemed able to sit in it for hours. She rounded on the Sun Prince. "Do you have someone following us?"

"Of course not. *I* followed you." With a flick of his eyes toward Gabe, Bastian reached up and pushed the dagger aside with one finger. Gabe's knuckles whitened, but he lowered the blade.

"Unlike my father," Bastian continued, "I prefer to do my own spying."

A bead of sweat slid down Lore's back. She'd been a fool to think they could outsmart this man, to think there was a way to stay here unharmed while Bastian knew she was a spy. August's underestimation of his son was going to be the death of her, and of Gabe, too—

But Bastian didn't suddenly produce a sword or shackles, didn't call for guards that would send her to the Burnt Isles before the sun came up. Instead he turned back toward the doorway that led into the Citadel proper, pinching out the flames in the alcoves as he went. He glanced at them over his shoulder, one curling black lock falling over his eye. "You two coming?"

"Absolutely not." Gabe spoke through clenched teeth. The carefully reined deference he'd shown the prince this afternoon was all gone now, nothing but cold rage in its place.

"Pity." Bastian shrugged. "And here I was going to get you into the vaults. After we take a detour, anyway." He leaned a shoulder against the wall, pushed back his artfully mussed hair. The prince wasn't dressed for bed or debauchery; instead he wore a loose white shirt and dark pants, boots that climbed to his knees.

Similar to the clothes people wore out in the Wards. "Think of all the exciting things you'll have to report to my father and uncle, afterward."

Lore swallowed. Gabe's hands tightened to fists.

Bastian grinned. "So, I ask again. You two coming?"

A pause. Then Gabe gave a truncated nod.

"Excellent." Bastian turned to move down the dark hall, extinguishing the last of the candles as he passed.

They fell into step behind the Sun Prince, Gabe fuming, anxiety chewing at Lore's stomach. They were caught, decisively so, and she had no idea what Bastian would do with them now. Turn them over to Kirythea, if August's suspicions were true? Blackmail them into reporting on August and Anton, playing both sides?

She shot a look at Gabe. Going down by herself was bad enough; she hated dragging him along, too.

Warm fingers caught hers. Gabe. He gave her hand a squeeze, gave her a laden look from the corner of his eye. It settled her nerves, squared her shoulders.

Even if the body she'd raised had reanimated, like Horse, there was no one there to give an order. The child might be aware, insofar as something dead could be, but it'd be like he was sleeping, safe inside the vault. As much as she hated to leave him that way, things would hold for however long this detour with Bastian took.

Assuming he kept his word.

Bastian pushed open the door, its corner nudging the still-sleeping bloodcoat on the other side. The guard readjusted but didn't wake, pillowing his head on his bent arms, breathing just this side of a snore.

"You really took him out." Bastian glanced at Gabe. "You'll have to teach me that trick."

"Is that an order?" Gabe growled.

"We'll see." Stepping over the bloodcoat, Bastian led them

back through the winding halls. He took a different route than they had and passed a few courtiers giggling in corners, skin gilded in candlelight. A handsome man with a crimson-haired woman in his arms beckoned to Bastian, wordlessly asking if he wanted to join in, but the Sun Prince waved a dismissive hand. Neither courtier seemed fazed by his rejection.

Lore tensed when they reached the doors into the back gardens—the ones they'd gone through this morning to reach the North Sanctuary—but the guards barely reacted to Bastian's presence, and said nothing when he opened the doors to the chill of midnight.

It appeared the Citadel guards were used to the Sun Prince coming and going at all hours. The knowledge did nothing to soothe the Lore's nerves.

Bastian led them silently through the gardens, walking over grass instead of on the cobblestone. They went the opposite direction Lore had wandered earlier, but still ended up in another false forest with manicured paths. A breeze riffled through the trees, spinning green needles and the scent of pine. An Auverrani summer was scorching in the day, but surprisingly cool at night.

Gabe stopped, planted his feet. "Where are we going?"

"Somewhere interesting," Bastian answered. His hands were in his pockets, his stride almost jaunty. "It will make a great tale for August, since he's apparently so interested in what I'm doing with my free time. And you both need a bit of fun."

"What if we don't want it?" Lore asked.

The prince grinned. He stepped up to her with fluid grace, the night air lifting his dark curls, wafting the scent of red wine and expensive cologne. "I think," he said softly, "that it's *exactly* what you want, Lore. And you strike me as the kind of woman who doesn't waste time denying the things she wants."

She'd spent a lifetime denying what she wanted, denying who and what she was. "You don't know me at all."

He was too close. So was Gabe, glowering behind her. She felt trapped between the two of them, too warm, too charged, too *much*.

Bastian's feral grin widened. "I will, though."

And that felt too *true*, somehow, true in a way that made no sense. It plucked at Lore's chest, made thrumming harp strings of her ribs. The air around the three of them seemed momentarily thicker, as if they'd created their own atmosphere.

Gabe stepped away, out of the pull of their collective gravity, the wind ruffling at his short hair. He crossed his arms over his chest and lifted his chin, stretching the scant few inches he had on the prince for all they were worth. "If we go with you, you'll get us into the vaults?"

"Of course, old friend." Bastian turned and started walking again. The wall of the Church dividing the Citadel from the rest of Dellaire loomed out of the dark, casting deep shadows. "I'll get you into the vaults, you'll tell me what exactly my father is up to. A win for everyone."

Another darted glance between Gabe and Lore, another attempt at communicating without words. They weren't very good at it. Gabe's glare didn't tell her anything other than that he was angry enough to kick a hole through one of these perfectly manicured trees, and Lore's shrug, meant to convey acceptance, only made his jaw clench harder.

A small culvert covered by an iron grate was set into the base of the wall, nearly impossible to see until they were right on it, but big enough for a grown man to climb through. Bastian bent, producing an iron pick from his boot and wiggling it into the lock. It came undone easily, falling to the grass with a soft *clunk*.

"But before all that," Bastian announced, lifting aside the iron grate and setting it carefully against the wall. "The two of you could use an adventure." He ducked into the small tunnel, gesturing for them to follow, and was gone with a slight splash that made Lore wince.

Another fucking tunnel. And this one had *water.*

"He's playing with us," Gabe muttered, barely above a whisper. The heat of him was a beacon against the night air. "This will probably end in both of us bleeding out in an alley after we tell him August's plans."

"I think you can take him, if it comes down to that."

"While I appreciate the sentiment, I don't see that it helps us."

"And I don't see a way around it." Lore ducked down toward the grate, but Gabe's hand vised around her arm.

She looked up at him, scowling. "What exactly do you think he'll do if we don't march to his orders, Gabriel? Just shrug and let us continue on our merry way? Unless you want a one-way ticket to the Isles in less than an hour, we're following the damn Sun Prince into the gutter."

They glared at each other for a moment before Gabe let her go, hand flexing outward exaggeratedly. It made the candle inked on his palm stretch to odd proportions. "Fine."

He dropped through the grate first. Lore followed. A splash, the hem of her dressing gown immediately soaked through. The tunnel was so dark it took her eyes a minute to adjust, and when they did, she made sure not to look down. She really didn't want to see what kind of garbage she might be marinating in.

"I am curious, though." Bastian's voice floated out of the dark right in front of her as if there'd been no lull in their conversation, making Lore jump. A lighter flicked, mother-of-pearl and gleaming, illuminating Bastian's face as he brought the flame to a thin cigarette in his mouth. "What, exactly, do the vaults have to do with anything?"

"You'll find out after you get us into them," Lore said, summoning a bravado she didn't feel. "We can turn around and go now, if you're that interested."

"A negotiator," Bastian mused. He approached the grate on the opposite wall, the orange glow of gas lamps seeping through the metal lattice. Boosting himself up onto the ledge, he pulled the iron pick from his boot again and went to work. "As interested as I am in whatever you have going on at the vaults, I think it prudent to satisfy my other questions beforehand."

"Weren't you going to blackmail all the answers out of us anyway?" Gabe gritted out.

Bastian glanced over his shoulder, a bladed grin tugging up his mouth and coming nowhere near the dark glitter of his eyes. "Don't underestimate yourself, Gabriel. I'm sure you can find a way to give me only half-truths. You learned from the best, after all."

Gabe's scowl deepened.

The Sun Prince gestured to Lore with a courtly hand. "Ladies first."

His hands clasped her waist before she had a chance to move forward on her own, pulling her close enough for his breath to stir her hair. "This opens on a street that leads straight to the docks," he said in a whisper, like he was telling a secret. "Don't stray, there's all sorts of unsavory types who congregate here. But you know that."

He didn't give her a moment to react, boosting her up to the ledge with the grate. The rock was slick enough that she had to grab the iron and pull herself through immediately, if she didn't want to splash back down into questionable water.

The culvert opened up onto a near-abandoned side street. Brine-scented wind pressed the wet hem of her dressing gown against her legs, making her shiver. She pulled the edges of it tighter, tied the belt again. Blush-pink was decidedly not the right color for sneaking out of the Citadel through a storm drain.

This was a street she recognized. She'd run belladonna here once, sewn into the pockets of an old jacket of Mari's, one of the first times she was trusted to undertake a mission on her own.

But you know that.

Her stomach twisted and roiled like an underwater current.

Behind her, Bastian emerged from the culvert, looking hardly worse for wear. He pulled three black domino masks from his pocket, and then a length of white linen. "Here, you'll both need these."

"Another masquerade?" Gabe sounded like the prospect was almost as appealing as gnawing off a finger.

"Hardly," Bastian scoffed. "Everyone wears them at the ring. These fights *are* illegal, technically, and no one wants their identity revealed." He flashed a grin. "Be thankful I'm not making you wear a sack over your head. Half the nobles do."

Scowling at Bastian, Lore tied the mask over her eyes as the Sun Prince did the same. Then he took the length of white linen he'd pulled out along with the masks and began wrapping it around his hands.

Like a boxer.

Bleeding God in a *bandage*.

Gabe's face was a thundercloud as Bastian handed him his own mask, but he didn't say anything. He just tied it on, and loomed, and glared. The mask softened him, almost, hiding the eye patch from view. Made him look less like someone whose life was indelibly marked by violence.

Bastian clapped his wrapped hands together. "Now then. Nothing like a refreshing trip through a storm drain. Onward." He started down the alleyway. Sharing a pointed look through their masks, Lore and Gabe followed.

"You saw his hands, right?" Lore pitched her voice so it wouldn't carry. "Wrapped. He's taking us to the fighting rings, and it looks like he's participating."

"Splendid. The very last thing I want to do this evening is save the Sun Prince's ass."

"You seem certain he'll lose." Lore shrugged. "He looks like he could be a good boxer."

"Oh, does he?" Gabe's voice was low and pointed.

Lore scowled at him.

"Hopefully you're wrong," Gabe muttered. "If he gets knocked out in a boxing match, maybe he'll forget the last hour."

"He also won't be able to get us into the vaults."

"We could ask Anton—"

"No." The very thought made her fingers curl to fists, some cell-deep instinct recoiling. "If something went wrong with that body, I don't want them to know."

If something went wrong, Anton and August might stop thinking of her power as an asset. They might start thinking of it as something too dangerous to keep outside a cell.

Maybe too dangerous to keep alive at all.

Gabe's lips pressed together, his blue eye assessing. Then he nodded.

Bastian ambled easily down the street ahead of them, showing no sign of apprehension. Clearly, this was a regular activity for him. Lore wondered whether he really was a good fighter—people who lost boxing matches on the docks weren't generally eager to return, and tended to carry physical proof of their failure.

And what if she saw someone she recognized? What if her very fine, albeit out-of-fashion, dressing gown, scrubbed face, and clean, brushed hair weren't enough to hide who she was? She didn't look *that* different, even in an aristocrat's nightclothes, and more than one acquaintance of hers spent time at the fighting rings.

She'd just have to lie low. Keep close to Gabriel and Bastian, not make eye contact, hope she didn't attract too much attention.

They exited the mouth of the alley like a reluctant parade, Bastian jaunty in front, Gabe glowering in the back, Lore listlessly caught in the middle. The alley spit them out between two derelict buildings near the harbor front, gas lamps slicking orange light on dark water. A collection of lamps illuminated a shipless dock, the gathering crowd already smelling of beer and sweat. Every one of them wore a mask, some more comprehensive than others. Lore found herself looking at them closely, wondering if she'd passed them in the North Sanctuary.

"Stay close," Gabe muttered, coming up behind her as Bastian went ahead.

She did. The mass of the Mort next to her was comforting.

The crowd parted for Bastian as he approached the hay-bale-lined ring, but not with any reverence that suggested they knew who he was. They wouldn't—beyond the walls, the royal family was an abstraction, something that existed but had little day-to-day bearing, regarded with ambivalence bordering on lazy hostility. There was no reason for them to know what Bastian looked like, and in his simple clothes and wrapped fists, stubble on his jaw beneath his simple black mask, he looked just like them.

Now, if there were any nobles in the crowd, they'd be able to spot their prince. But no one spoke up, and Bastian moved with the surety of someone who'd done this many times before. The Sun Prince did what he wanted, and if what he wanted was to get beat up by commoners, no one was going to stop him or blow his cover.

Bastian peeled off his shirt as he walked, handing it to a rather eager-looking man near the edge of the ring with a wink. The prince was as well muscled as Gabriel, slight scars discoloring his skin, half-healed bruises tinted yellow and faded purple.

Gabe and Lore stayed to the back of the crowd, who paid little attention to them. Thankfully, she didn't see anyone she recognized, and breathed a sigh of relief.

Until she saw Bastian's opponent.

He stood on the opposite edge of the ring, shaking out bound fists. Already shirtless, familiar bunching muscles, familiar rumpled hair.

Michal.

Lore made a strangled sound as she ducked behind Gabe's back.

"What?" He looked around, as if there was some threat he hadn't marked. "Lore, what?"

When Gabe twisted to look behind him, opening a gap between torso and arm that Lore could see through, Bastian was gazing at her, eyes narrowed. Like he'd been waiting for Michal to turn around. Like he'd been waiting to see if she recognized him.

Of course the Sun Prince wouldn't trust a spy to tell him the truth, even under threat. Of course he'd have a layered plan, one that would show him who she really was.

Not just a spy. The girl from the market square. The necromancer who'd raised Horse. Michal knew what she was—her reaction to him would tell Bastian everything he needed to know.

The Sun Prince watched her like a hawk eyeing a mouse, waiting.

Lore bit her lip, made herself straighten. Made herself look right back at the prince like everything was perfectly fine. "Nothing," she said to Gabe, who was still glancing around to find some unknown threat. "It's nothing."

Bastian kept those golden-brown eyes on her, unreadable. Then he smiled, but it wasn't the playful, irreverent grin he usually wore. This smile was sharp. This smile was a knife that had found its mark, even if she pretended she wasn't bleeding.

"You just keep coming back for more." Michal already had his fists up, bouncing back and forth on his feet. There was no real violence in the words; he grinned at Bastian companionably. "Not tired yet?"

"You talk like I haven't thrashed you the last two rounds." Bastian made a predatory circle, with none of the fake sweeps of fists Michal used. No theatrics, just prowling.

"Luck, my friend." Michal's fist darted toward Bastian's face. Bastian bent out of the way, laughing.

Michal and Bastian bobbed and weaved around each other, movements vicious but practiced. There wasn't any malice in the way they fought, just business-like precision. Bastian avoided another swipe of Michal's hand, ducking beneath his arm to come up behind him and land a choppy blow across the other man's back. Michal fell to a crouch but rallied quickly, using the lower vantage to punch out at Bastian's knee. The crowd howled as Bastian almost went down, then regained his balance. He winked at Michal, beckoned him forward with his wrapped and bloodied hands.

"We're going to be here all night," Gabe muttered darkly, arms crossed over his chest. "Longer, if neither one of them gets their shit together and knocks the other out."

Michal circled Bastian, still bouncing on his feet, but his movements had grown more ragged. All his posturing was taking a toll, pointless expenditures of energy. He'd done that in bed, too, Lore remembered. Sometimes acrobatics were just unnecessary.

Bastian, by contrast, looked almost relaxed, dodging punches with ease though he barely threw his own. Still, sweat gleamed on his chest, and there was a tiny cut at the corner of his lip where one of Michal's blows had landed.

The prince looked back over his shoulder, finding Lore again. In front of him, she vaguely saw the shape of Michal readying himself, cocking a fist. The crowd yelled, the young man still holding Bastian's shirt practically jumping up and down, but Bastian paid no mind to their warnings. His eyes stayed locked on Lore's as he reached up, slowly wiped blood from his split lip.

Got you, he mouthed.

Then Michal's fist crashed into the side of Bastian's head. The Sun Prince went down.

Silence. Michal looked almost surprised, glancing first at his fist, and then into the crowd, like he was searching for whatever had so distracted his opponent.

And he found it. Those familiar blue eyes widened. "Lore?"

Michal's mouth kept working, spitting questions, but they were drowned out in the roar of the crowd. The hay-bale ring broke as people rushed forward to congratulate him, and Michal was borne away by well-wishers, shock still stark on his face.

Next to her, Gabe wore nearly the same expression. "Bleeding God and Buried Goddess," he cursed, whirling from the crowd to face Lore. "Who was—"

"An old friend." Bastian was next to them, sneaking up soundless as a cat. The side of his face was bleeding, but he was smiling, that new knife-smile that made all Lore's insides cold. He held his shirt, but instead of putting it on, he used it to wipe up the blood. "If you'll excuse us."

He gripped Lore's arm tight and hauled her forward, and she had no choice but to follow as the Sun Prince led her into the dark, leaving Gabriel behind, shouting and blocked by the crowd.

CHAPTER NINETEEN

A secret is a flame, and it cannot burn forever.
—Auverrani proverb

It only took a moment for Lore to start struggling, pulling against Bastian's inexorable grip with curses that a duke's cousin surely wouldn't know. But that didn't matter, not anymore. Michal had recognized her, and now Bastian knew who she was.

What she was.

Lore twisted, trying to haul herself away, but Bastian pulled her on, toward the mouth of another narrow alley as the shouts of the crowd dimmed behind them.

No dagger, and she'd be no match for the Sun Prince in strength. Mortem was all she had. And though she wasn't sure what she could do with it, in the absence of a dead body to raise, there had to be *something*.

Lore held her breath and waited for her vision to go grayscale, for her fingers to turn necrotic and cold. But it didn't happen.

Instead there was a spark. A flash behind her eyes. The baked, heated scent of high-summer air, so close she expected a singeing. It collided with the sense of Mortem, familiar and empty,

nothingness so compacted it had presence and mass. The two con-
flicting energies felt, for a moment, like they might tear her apart.

Bastian stopped. His grip on her arm didn't loosen, but she felt
his fingers spasm.

Then it was gone, so quickly it could've been the start of an
aborted panic attack.

She could still feel the Mortem surrounding them, but she
couldn't see it, couldn't channel it. Her vision would not change to
the monotone that showed her life and death; the threads would
not connect to her. Something was...was *repelling* Mortem, like
an invisible wall had formed around her, cutting her off.

And as much as Lore hated her ability, it felt like losing a limb.

Whatever had just happened, it seemed not to affect the Sun
Prince. He pulled her into an alley, sooty brick lined with crumpled trash. Then Bastian threw away her arm and spun to face her,
advancing until she was trapped between the wall and his still-
bare chest, not quite touching.

She reached for Mortem, but Bastian's hand closed tight
around her arm, and her sense of death was gone again.

What was he *doing* to her?

"Out with it," Bastian growled, tossing the bloodied shirt in
his other hand to the side. Gone was the casual, almost lazy arro-
gance he showed the court; Bastian's eyes glinted like bayonet
ends, just as sharp. "I was going to wait until we got to the vaults
to demand my answers, but now that I know for sure you're the
girl who raised Claude, I've found I'd rather know it all now."

"Horse," she corrected him, because her brain was stuck in a
hurricane, and it was the only thing that made sense for her to do.

"Yes, Lore, I'm aware it's a horse."

"No, his *name* is Horse. Not Claude."

Bastian shook his head again, straightening; the motion
brought their chests closer together. His hand left her arm and
came to rest on the wall beside her head.

"Call the damn horse whatever you want," Bastian said, "just tell me who you're working for."

"August." Anxiety made her voice sound thin, like her throat wouldn't expand enough to let it out fully. "You know that."

"Is that it?" he asked. "Or are you on Kirythea's payroll, too? You seemed very interested in what I knew about them."

"No, I'm not working for Kirythea. Just your father." Slowly, Lore managed to get her nerves under control. It didn't seem like Bastian was planning to kill her. Not yet, anyway. "August thinks *you're* working for Kirythea. That's why I was trying to find out what you knew."

He glared at her, one curl of sweaty black hair falling over his eye. "Well," he said, after a moment. "Isn't that a fun bit of irony."

Lore set her jaw, still trapped between the prince and the brick. She didn't know what to expect from this other, truer Bastian. Every line of him coiled with anger, the kind often hidden. Now, unfettered, it was so obvious she couldn't believe she'd never noticed before, distracted by funny Bastian, clever Bastian, toying Bastian who seemed fairly easy to handle.

This was furious Bastian, and she had no idea what to do with him.

That strange gravity was back, like she'd felt when she and Bastian and Gabe were at the mouth of the culvert. Falling toward something inevitable.

The Sun Prince stepped back, though not so much that she could run for the alley mouth. His hands remained on either side of her head. "Here's how this is going to go. You're going to tell me *exactly* why my father brought you here. Then you're going to tell me how you managed to channel more Mortem than the entire fucking Presque Mort is capable of."

"Accident," Lore said, latching onto the same excuse she'd given Gabe. "When I was a kid."

His head tilted, a predator's smile gleaming in the dark. "Oh, no, Lore," Bastian murmured. "I think we got off on the wrong foot. See, I know who you are. I know you were a poison runner with Michal. I know you were their watchdog, because of some strange affinity you had for the catacombs. It's remarkable, really, the things people will tell you if you just listen. I like listening."

"Is that why you come here and get the shit beat out of you?" Lore spat. "To *listen?*"

"I come here because sometimes, being inside the Citadel makes me want to claw my own eyes out," Bastian answered. "The listening is just a bonus. It's how I found out about the villages, how I found out how little tax the nobles pay compared to everyone else. How I found out that the necromancer who raised a horse in the market square was just some girl. *Getting the shit beat out of me*, as you put it, is really the only way I know anything. Gods know my father isn't going to tell me."

Lore didn't know if the chill in her limbs was from fear or the still-wet hem of her dressing gown.

"Now, I don't know *everything*." One of Bastian's hands left the wall, went to his boot. Pulled something out. "But I know enough to be reasonably certain that your Mortem affliction didn't come about in the normal way. I know enough to be sure that the truth is far more interesting than a childhood accident. So when I ask you a question, Lore, I expect it to be answered truthfully."

Whatever he'd retrieved from his boot gleamed in the dim light of the alley, brighter than his bared teeth. A dagger, held casually in his hand, but tilted so she could see its shine.

"Let's try again. This time, we can start with the questions about my father, since it seems you might answer those more easily." Bastian leaned forward, close enough to kiss. The blade of his dagger scraped lightly at the silk of her dressing gown. "Why did he bring you here, other than to spy on me?"

"The villages." She could try to lie again, but what was the point? Bastian still didn't seem like he was going to kill her, but any conversation that included a blade seemed best to meet with truth. Gabe had tried to warn her.

Gabe. She hoped he had the sense not to come after her, but she wasn't counting on it.

Lore swallowed, continued. "August and Anton are trying to figure out what happened to the villages. They want me to raise the bodies and ask them."

"And do they have any suspicions?" If Bastian was shocked by the task his father had given her, he didn't show it. "I can guess."

"They think it's Kirythea, using some sort of elemental magic left over from the minor gods. And they think you're working with them, somehow."

Something seemed to shutter in Bastian's face. Not guilt, nothing that simple. Almost…hurt. It softened the lines of the predatory thing he'd become.

"Of course they do," Bastian said quietly. He huffed, the sound too weary to be the start of a laugh. His head dipped just enough for the shadows to hide his eyes. "So that's why you're supposed to stay near me, I take it?"

She nodded, quick and truncated. Bastian held his dagger loosely, almost like he'd forgotten it was there, but *she* certainly hadn't.

"Look what we have here."

A new voice, coming from the mouth of the alley, high and scratchy.

Bastian rolled his eyes. "Wonderful," he muttered.

Lore tore her gaze away from the Sun Prince's gleaming dagger, focused on the figure instead. A small white man dressed in ratty clothes, bruises on his arms and scabs over the side of his face. He didn't look very intimidating.

But the huge man behind him did. Intimidating and glassy-eyed, pale face flushed. He'd been poison-dosed, and recently.

"Gentlemen." Bastian turned, the hand with the knife gesturing politely while his other palm stayed flat on the wall next to Lore's head. "While I admire your enterprise, rest assured that neither I nor my friend has anything of value to offer you."

"For your sake, I hope that's not true." The smaller man spread his hands apologetically. "Or our employer will be even more upset than he already is."

"You lost." The larger man advanced, making his face easier to see. Scarred and rough, with ears swollen from years of fistfights. Lore and Bastian both still wore their black domino masks, but these two didn't, and it did not improve their appearances. "You lost, and you left without paying up."

"A mistake." Bastian didn't sound concerned, but his fingers shifted around the hilt of his dagger, and he had that same waiting stillness he'd had in the ring. "I had a spot of business to take care of, but I assure you, I'm on my way to pay what I owe." His lip quirked. "I assume you bet against me?"

He moved ahead of Lore as he talked, slow and easy enough to be nonchalant, putting his body between her and the two men. Almost protective now.

Gods dead and dying, she could not wrap her head around Bastian Arceneaux.

"Don't worry about it," the scarred man said with an unsettling smile. "We'll collect now."

"It can't ever be simple," Bastian muttered as the scarred man's fist shot toward his head.

He feinted, turning on a bent knee to slam the heel of his hand into the man's back. A grunt, but the scarred man seemed hardly fazed, twisting to meet Bastian from the new angle. His recent poisoning hadn't slowed him down at all, apparently. The man's knee came up, and Lore flinched, but it sailed past Bastian's chin without making contact. The knife hung unused in his hand, like he didn't want to employ a blade unless he had to.

Something else shimmered around his hands, though. Maybe

it was just a trick of dim light and a terrified mind, but to Lore, the air around Bastian's moving fists looked like it swam with gold, trails of soft sun-glow following the path of his skin.

Another dagger glinted silver as the scarred man pulled it from his belt, breaking her concentration on all that odd gold. Bastian didn't seem to notice it, and she opened her mouth to warn him, but a slam of stars exploded in her temple before she could. The scarred man had knocked the hilt into her head.

Lore hit her knees, bones aching against the bite of cobblestone.

Then—something cold and sharp on her neck, and a boot between her shoulder blades, holding her down.

Time slowed. Her ears rang, making everything crystal clear and muffled at once. Lore had been in plenty of situations where the loss of life or limb was a possible outcome, but she'd never been held at knifepoint, never been in a place where the possibility of help was next to none. The sharp edge of the knife almost vibrated with Mortem, her fingers tingling in time.

But she *still* couldn't grasp it.

Lore's eyes met Bastian's. She didn't know what kind of look she gave him, whether it was pleading or defiant. He'd asked why she was here, what his father wanted; those were the answers that mattered, and he had them. The questions about her, about her magic—those were mere curiosity, and curiosity wasn't reason enough to save her, not when there was a perfectly plausible excuse for her death holding a dagger to her neck.

Bastian could let her die and leave her here. He could kill her without even touching her.

"More expensive than just your losses, now," the scarred man rasped, digging his knee further into Lore's back. "You'll pay double for making a fuss. Think how much belladonna I can buy with that, eh?"

Lore watched the calculations spin behind Bastian's eyes. Watched him weigh and measure.

Then the prince reached into his pocket.

The movement took his concentration away from the fight, and the smaller man landed a punch to his stomach. At the moment Bastian bowed forward, hunched over his middle, he thrust out his hand, the thick gold of a signet ring gleaming in the dark.

"If you please," Bastian said, somehow managing to barely sound winded. "Unhand my friend."

The smaller man looked at the ring. Paled. "Milo. Let the lady up."

But the scarred one—Milo—paid no heed. "Don't care who he is. He owes, and my stash is nearly done for." The dagger bit in, just enough to sting, and Lore pulled in a ragged breath.

Bastian straightened, stalked across the alley. His hand fisted in Milo's hair and wrenched the man's neck backward, pointing his blade at the vulnerable artery. They made a deranged chain of threats, Bastian's knife at Milo's throat, Milo's at Lore's.

"I'm the Sun Prince of Auverraine, Apollius's chosen heir," Bastian hissed. "And you will unhand the lady."

A pause. Then Milo's bulk was gone; Bastian shoved his shoulder, forcing him to his knees beside his smaller friend.

Lore dragged in a deep breath and pushed herself up to sit; her legs were too shaky to stand just yet. A tiny cut scored across her neck, a thin filament of pain.

"I really didn't want to have to use that," Bastian muttered, shoving the ring back into his pocket. He didn't look at Lore.

There was no gold around his hands now. A trick of the light, then, her fear affecting her vision. Probably.

"Our apologies, Your Majesty." The smaller man looked terrified. Milo bowed his head too far to see his expression, but Lore could bet it was glowering. "We didn't know, we had no idea—"

"And I would very much like to keep it that way." Bastian sighed. "I was planning to go back and pay my dues, after an... interlude."

He cocked his head at Lore. She was still too rattled to do anything but stare at him. He'd saved her. He'd had the opportunity to dispose of her, a tidy solution to his problem, and he'd saved her instead.

What in all the myriad hells was she supposed to do with that?

The prince turned to the bruisers. "I probably won't be returning, unfortunately, but I would greatly appreciate if you would keep this quiet." Bastian gave them a smile; the sharp one, the predator one. "And if I hear the news get around, I'll know who to blame, won't I?"

They nodded. And when Bastian jerked his chin, dismissing them, they nearly tripped over each other trying to get away.

At the mouth of the alley, Milo looked back, shadows obscuring his face. Then he was gone.

"You let that one off easy, all things considered." Lore's voice was hoarse. She rubbed at her neck.

"Call it magnanimity." The light of the gas lamps beyond the alley limned Bastian in red and orange as he turned to face Lore. He held out a hand. "There's still a question you haven't answered."

Lore hadn't been planning on asking him why he'd blown his own cover to keep her alive. But she thought that if she had, this would be his reason. Unanswered questions, unsatisfied curiosity.

She didn't know whether she believed that or not. There was one more thing to consider, along with that light she might or might not have truly seen around his hands, along with him saving her—that sense of gravity, of things falling together. Of *knowing*, the same knowing she felt with Gabe, like the deep parts of her recognized both of these men, even if her mind and heart couldn't keep pace.

She took his hand.

Bastian hauled her up, then let go. He didn't back her against the wall again, trusting her not to bolt. They'd knit some kind of understanding between them, and neither wanted to be the one to fray it.

"Now," the Sun Prince said. "Tell me how you managed to become such an accomplished Mortem channeler. And don't lie this time, please. Like I said, I'll know."

He would. She knew that like she knew her own name, like she knew the raised edges of the moon scar on her palm. Gabe had bought her lie, even with that sense of knowing, but whatever thread bound her and the Sun Prince was different—thicker, coarser.

He'd saved her once. She had no guarantee that he'd do it again, if she went against his orders. So Lore took a deep breath, and she spoke truth.

"I was born in the catacombs," she murmured. "To one of the Night Sisters, in what's left of the Buried Watch."

CHAPTER TWENTY

There will be two factions to control the power of
the Buried Goddess–the Presque Mort, the Almost
Dead, who will channel Mortem when it reaches the
surface, and the Veilleurs Enterre, the Buried Watch,
who will ensure that what has been struck down by
your god does not rise again.
                                    –The Book of Holy Law, Tract 35

Silence.

Then, a hoarse laugh. Bastian's eyes were a dark glitter in
the gloom of the alleyway, his bloody hands clenched to linen-
wrapped fists. "The Buried Watch? They were disbanded after the
Night Witch went mad. There's no one down there anymore."

"There is." Lore swallowed. Her throat felt like she'd eaten live
coals. "There aren't many of them left; maybe twenty or so. But
they're still there. Still watching Nyxara's tomb."

Still waiting. Still sending someone into the obsidian tomb on
every eclipse to see if the body of the goddess had stirred. Lore
remembered what those people had looked like when they came
back out. Their faces blank, their eyes vacant, as if their very sense

of self had been scooped away.

The moon-shaped scars on their hands a burning, angry red.

"That doesn't make any sense." Bastian spoke slowly, like he didn't trust her capacity to understand him. "The Buried Watch hasn't existed for centuries. The Church would never let a faction persist, not after the Night Witch decided she was Nyxara reborn."

Lore shrugged. "Like I said, there aren't many of them. The Church killed most of them after the Night Witch—they thought the same madness might infect the others. But some of them were able to hide, to keep the order alive."

"How the fuck do they get new members, then? No one goes to the catacombs."

"They do if they have nowhere else to go." Like a merchant's daughter, pregnant with a bastard child that she desperately wanted to keep. Lore's mother had fled to the catacombs when her parents told her they were going to send her to a sanitarium. It'd been panic; she'd only gone there to hide.

But she'd found so much more than a place to hide.

Bastian's eyebrow arched, expression clearly incredulous. "So are the rest of the stories true?" He snorted. "Do they sneak out at night and give naughty children bad dreams? Enchant horses to throw their riders?"

"No." She shook her head. "The true Buried Watch—the Night Sisters who've taken the vow—never leave the tomb, except when some of the younger ones are sent up to get supplies. We stole, or bartered stuff we found in the tunnels. Lost coins, precious stones. You'd be surprised what you can find if you look for it."

Her voice was casual as she spoke of such strangeness. Lore had only ever said these things to Val and Mari, when she told them what she was after she raised Cedric. She'd always thought she'd never be able to find the words again, but they came out of her so easily.

The Sun Prince narrowed his eyes, but he didn't accuse her of lying again. "So they're still doing what the Tracts say?" The question came out guarded. "Watching to make sure Nyxara doesn't rise?"

"They have a Compendium. They read from the same Tracts the Presque Mort do. They follow the Church's laws." Despite herself, anger began its slow burn at the bottom of her stomach. "The Buried Watch was given the worst task possible, sent down to live in the dark, and when their leader predictably went mad from it—from being locked underground next to a goddess's tomb—the Church decided it had incorrectly interpreted the Tracts, and killed them."

Her hair was sticky and wet, clinging to her forehead. Lore reached up to push it away, and didn't realize she'd used her scarred hand until Bastian grabbed it.

She jerked back on instinct—the scar was unusual, but not to the point where she'd felt the need to hide it. At least, not until now. But Bastian held her fast, using his other hand to uncurl her fingers so he could get a good look.

Slowly, he opened his hand next to her own.

A sun. Well, half a sun—carved into the top part of his palm, the edges still fresh and red, only beginning to scab. A half circle arced from just below his smallest finger to his thumb, the short lines of rays cut up to his first knuckle. If they'd pressed their palms together, the upside-down crescent of her moon would fit perfectly as the completed curve of his sun.

She thought of his Consecration, when Anton had taken the knife and carved into his nephew, how everyone watching had seemed shocked.

"That's some coincidence, isn't it?" Bastian murmured.

Lore snatched back her hand.

"Is this how they gave you the ability to channel Mortem?" he asked. "Or was it just a bit of unhinged pageantry, like mine? Anton does love to make things dramatic."

"The Sisters didn't give me the ability to channel," Lore said. "I was born with it. I don't know how, and I don't think they do, either."

They'd never offered her any kind of explanation, at least. Only sidelong looks and whispers.

Bastian frowned at her like a particularly difficult cipher. As if the answers she'd given him only served to make more questions.

And Bleeding God, she'd given him *all* the answers. The Sun Prince of Auverraine knew the truth about her, a truth that she'd never offered to anyone but Val and Mari. And she'd told Bastian even more than that—she'd never told her adoptive mothers that she was a born Mortem channeler, that she hadn't come by her power in the usual way.

"Come on," Bastian said finally, moving away. "Time to be getting back, especially if you want to see the vaults before the sun comes up."

If he wasn't going to talk further about her childhood, she wasn't, either. "We have to find Gabriel first."

"Remaut can take care of himself." Bastian was nearly at the mouth of the alley; with a frustrated growl, Lore hurried to catch up. "And if we go back to the ring, you're likely to run into your former paramour again. I assume that's a conversation you want to avoid, since you were spying on *him*, too." He glanced at her over his shoulder, as if he anticipated her shocked look. "Michal is smarter than you gave him credit for; he knew your game from very early on. He told me all about it when I came down here the other night, after the masquerade. I think he would've forgiven you, had you not turned out to be a necromancer as well as a spy."

She tried not to let that sting. "Do you *ever* sleep?"

"No rest for the wicked, dearest."

Gas lamps glowed on the street corners, casting coronas of sunset-colored light. Now that the threat of imminent death had passed, Lore's thoughts expanded again, covering more than just survival instinct. She frowned at Bastian's back. "You thought I was an assassin."

"Seemed a likely scenario."

"But you knew I was answering to your father. So you think—"

"Yes, Lore, I think my father might be trying to kill me."

"Because he thinks you're working with Kirythea."

"No, actually," he said, his shoulders still bare and going tight. "In fact, I can nearly assure you that my father knows that's bullshit."

Lore gnawed on her bottom lip, letting the necessary pieces fall into place, the things he wasn't saying. "So August just wants to kill you, then. And is using this as an excuse."

"Very good."

"But *why*? You're his only heir. And why not just hire an assassin, if he actually wants you dead? Why go through with some charade of framing you?"

Bastian didn't answer at first. They walked on, in and out of the shadows between streetlights. "My father and I have never seen eye-to-eye on anything," he said finally, softly. "Not ruling, not religion. Frankly, I think it's stupid for the crown of Auverraine to be determined by Apollius's blessing. An absent god shouldn't be the final say in the rule of law."

"That's heresy."

"Quite." Bastian rubbed absently at his side. A bruise was slowly forming there, the edges filling in lurid purple. "I think my father assumes these thoughts are only due to not wanting the crown myself. And he's right. I don't want it. But not enough to turn the country over to Jax and the Kirythean Empire."

"So why kill you?"

"Eliminates the possibility of me changing my mind," he said drily. "As for not just hiring an assassin: August knows this court. He knows that his disdain for me is no secret. If I were to just drop dead, or be *accidentally* killed, there'd always be rumors.

The Arceneaux line is blessed, remember, avatars of our god. It wouldn't do for one of us to be suspected of murder, not when he could frame me as a Kirythean spy and have a perfectly good reason for an execution." He gave her a sardonic look. "He told you to stick close to me, right? He's probably planning to plant evidence for you to find. Then he has the word of a holy man and a *duke's cousin*"—he poked her shoulder—"to back him up. No one would question his motives."

"So why don't you run away?" Lore asked. "If you think your father is one good excuse away from having you assassinated, if you don't even want the damn crown, why stay in the Citadel?"

"Because the Citadel is *mine*." His answer came with a vehemence she hadn't expected. "Even if I don't want it, me running away won't solve anything. I don't want to be the Sun Prince, but I am, and that comes with a measure of responsibility. If I want to see anything change, I will have to do it myself." He glanced at her. "And if my father is able to choose his own heir from the remaining Arceneaux relatives, which he would be free to do with me gone, it will not be someone who is good for Auverraine. I can guarantee it. My relatives are few, and all of them are awful."

Lore thought of what she and Gabe had talked about up in their room, about one pebble trying to dam a river. Bastian wasn't a pebble, though. Bastian was a boulder.

"I'm surprised he's concerned with an heir at all, to be honest." She fell into step beside the Sun Prince, following him down familiar streets. "He's dosing himself with poison regularly, and I assume the Sainted King has a deathdealer who knows the right amounts. Seems like he's trying to make the matter of passing on the crown as moot as possible."

Bastian said nothing, but his eyes cut quickly to her, then away. His mouth firmed thoughtfully.

They rounded a corner, and Bastian took her elbow, steering her toward the culvert cut into the Citadel Wall—she hadn't seen it, hidden in shadow. "You and Remaut are going to have to become better actors," he said, changing the subject. "Everyone in the Citadel has a nose for bullshit, and he doesn't look at you like a cousin."

"How does he look at me, then?" Lore jerked her elbow from Bastian's hold.

"Like he's not especially pleased about that vow of celibacy."

Heat flooded her cheeks.

With a smile, Bastian gestured toward the culvert with his sun-scarred hand. "After you, my lady."

Lore crawled down into the tunnel, re-soaking her hem. Bastian splashed down behind her and took the lead, holding out his lighter.

"Gabriel knows how to get back to the Citadel, right?" Lore asked.

"He's an industrious fellow, he'll find his way." The flame from the lighter shivered over the slick walls. Something rat-shaped scurried into the shadows. "Your concern is touching."

The way he said it belied the words. Lore scowled at his back, gathering her hem high to avoid the water. "He's just as caught up in all this as I am."

"Be that as it may, Gabriel's loyalty is to one person alone. And diverting as you are, Lore, I don't think you can compete with Apollius. If the opportunity arises for Remaut to use you in service to his god, he'll take it." He turned to face her, the flame gilding his dark hair in fiendish light, keeping his eyes in shadow. "In fact, it seems like I'm the only person in the Citadel who knows who you are and what you're capable of, and isn't trying to make you a tool."

It wasn't true, but neither was it comforting. Gabe didn't know what she was, not really. Not like Bastian did.

Bleeding God and Buried Goddess, she hoped that wasn't a mistake.

"Gabe isn't trying to use me," she said softly. "Gabe is trying to keep me safe."

The prince turned around with a rueful noise, shaking his head. "Are you so accustomed to being used that you don't realize when it's happening, as long as it's done kindly?"

She had no answer for that.

Chapter Twenty-One

Nature bends toward wickedness—consider the eclipse. The sky grows dark when it should be light, the moon overtaking the sun. Such is a time when dark power rises. But fear not, for even this can be used.

—The Book of Holy Law, Tract 745[*]

The trip through the short tunnel didn't take long, but Lore was soaked to the waist by the time they splashed up onto the ledge at the other end, and walking through all that water had been taxing enough to make her break a sweat. She desperately wanted to wipe her face, but was afraid of what might be on her hands. "How often do you do this?" she asked, turning to Bastian. "And how in all myriad hells do you hide that much laundry?"

"It used to be once a week or so, but I assume I'll have to cut back now that at least two of the betting enforcers know who I

---

[*]Earliest Compendium translation. Modern Compendiums have eliminated Tracts 690–821; these Tracts can only be found in Compendiums made immediately after being dictated by Apollius (1 AGF).

am." Bastian sloshed up next to her, barely winded. "And I usually just leave all my clothes in the culvert and walk back through the gardens naked. It's refreshing, and whoever finds my cast-offs certainly needs them more than I do."

"Please tell me you aren't planning to shuck off your clothes right now."

"I'll protect your delicate sensibilities, though it is sure to result in agonizing chafing." Bastian grasped her by the waist and boosted her up, out of the culvert and into the Citadel gardens.

Right into Gabriel.

The Presque Mort stumbled back, arms closing around Lore to hold her steady. "You're safe?" he asked, his hands running from her shoulders to her wrists. "He didn't hurt you?"

"Should I be offended?" Bastian climbed out of the culvert, a smile on his face and daggers in his eyes. "I think I'm offended."

"He didn't hurt me." Lore didn't mention the endless moments in the alley when it seemed like he might. She stepped out of Gabe's arms, peered up at his face. A bruise mottled the side opposite his eye patch, and blood crusted beneath a split in his lip. "What happened to you?"

"Ran into some enforcers who thought I hadn't paid up a bet." Gabe rubbed away a fleck of dried blood. It didn't improve the state of his face. "Once I got away, I couldn't find either of you, so I came here to get help from Anton."

Of course he had. Lore wondered if Gabe had planned on telling the Priest Exalted everything, including the possibly reanimated body in the vaults, or if he would've left that out.

She wasn't immediately sure. It made her eyes dart away from him, made her arms cross in front of her as if they could be a barrier.

Gabe didn't notice. He rounded on Bastian, his fists held tight by his sides, like it took monumental effort not to drive one into the Sun Prince's face. "What in all the myriad hells was *that,*

Bastian? You drag us out to the docks to play at being common, get thrashed—"

"On purpose, I feel like I should point out."

"—then kidnap Lore and leave me there?" He'd been advancing the whole time he spoke, and now Gabe stood right in front of Bastian, two inches taller and using it all to loom. "What the *fuck*?"

"Language, Your Grace," Bastian admonished, completely unperturbed by the large mass of angry monk in his face. "I do apologize that you ran into trouble, though it seems like you fought your way out of it just fine."

Gabe ignored him, seething. "You might be the prince, but you can't just—"

"He knows, Gabe."

Lore's voice cut him off midsentence. Gabriel froze, then turned to look at her, shoulders stiff. "All of it?"

She nodded wearily. "All of it."

Gabe mirrored her nod. Then he turned to Bastian and slammed him against the wall.

"*Gabriel!*" Lore snapped, but the Presque Mort was beyond hearing. His palms pressed against Bastian's shoulders, his nose mere inches from the prince's, teeth bared.

"So how are you going to kill us, Bastian?" he growled. "You know why we're here, that your father knows you're sending information to Kirythea, and I'm supposed to believe you'll just let that go?"

Bastian's neck was tendon-tight, but he laughed like this was a game. "They really got to you, didn't they? Made you think the only way to absolve yourself of treason by association was to see it in everyone else."

Gabe's arms trembled slightly. Lore couldn't tell if it was with the force of pressing Bastian to the wall, or with the restraint of not punching him.

"It'll never be enough for them, Gabe." Despite the wicked grin, Bastian's voice was soft. "The Church and Crown don't forget, they don't forgive, not any more than the gods did before them. But they'll keep holding it in front of you like a mirage in a fucking desert. And you'll keep chasing it, even when you know it's not something you can touch."

They stared at each other. Then Gabe slammed him into the wall again.

"Both of you, stop it." Lore gripped Gabe's arm and pulled him back—for a moment, she thought he'd shake her off, but he relented, albeit reluctantly. "Bastian, shut up."

Bastian shook his shoulders out, wincing. But he did shut up.

Lore turned to Gabriel, breathing hard, as if she were the one who'd been seconds from a brawl. "We can use this," she said quietly, not looking at the Sun Prince as she did. It skirted too close to what he'd said in the tunnel, all these questions about using and being used. "There's a good chance August is framing Bastian."

The Presque Mort gave her a withering look. "Did he tell you that?"

"Does it matter?" Lore didn't know how to explain that she knew Bastian was telling the truth, at least about this.

"You don't know him." Gabe shook his head. "Lore, Bastian is—"

"Has it occurred to you," Bastian interrupted casually, "that you are basing all of your assumptions on me as a child? Seems unfair, to be honest. Especially considering how it went for you when people did the same."

Gabe's fingers turned to slow fists by his sides.

A moment, then Gabe straightened, his one eye flinty. "If you want to believe him," he said to Lore, ignoring the prince completely, "we won't go immediately to August. We'll go tell Anton first and see—"

"No." It came from Lore and Bastian at the same time.

Gabe's brows rose.

Bastian pushed off the wall. "My father wants me gone," he said, as if he were commenting on the weather. "I'm not eager to see what he'll do if his plan to get rid of me legitimately—at least in the eyes of Auverraine—is upset." He gathered up his long hair, wet with sweat and water from the culvert, and tied it into a knot at the back of his neck. "And there's still the issue of villages dying overnight. I'd very much like to get to the bottom of that, personally."

"You've still given me no reason to trust you," Gabe said through his teeth. "You may have fooled Lore, but I'll take more work."

He said her name like an admonishment. Like he'd expected better from her. Lore tightened her arms over her chest, shame and anger kindling to an ash-taste in the back of her mouth.

"How about this for a reason, then." Bastian drew himself up, somehow managing to look regal despite his bare chest and bedraggled hair. "If you involve my father and my uncle in any way I don't want you to, I'll have you both sent to the Burnt Isles."

Lore couldn't swallow her harsh intake of breath.

Gabe's eyes darted her way, the stiffness with which he'd held himself slowly uncoiling. Finger by finger, he unclenched his hands.

"Fine," he growled.

"Perfect. That's settled." Bastian grinned. "I suppose you two work for me now."

But just because Gabe had given in didn't meant he was going quietly. "So when exactly did you decide to take an interest in your subjects dying?"

"Gabriel." Lore's voice was sharp, but they were off again, though thankfully without violence this time.

"I've taken an interest since the beginning, Remaut." Bastian dug in his pocket and pulled out another cigarette. Lore didn't know how he'd managed to keep it dry enough to light, but it did without issue. He breathed out a cloud of smoke. "As much of one as I've been able to, since both Anton and August tried their hardest to keep me in the dark about the details."

"Do you really need the details when you're probably involved?"

"There's an easy way for you to find out, Gabe." Bastian stuck his hands in his pockets and grinned. "Why not just ask the corpse when we go to the vaults? That's what Lore is supposed to be doing anyway, isn't it?"

She thought of what happened this afternoon, when August had admonished her for asking questions of the corpse she'd raised instead of telling it to obey his orders. She hadn't thought much of it then, but now she wondered why August and Anton hadn't wanted her around when the dead started answering questions.

"I'll ask again," she said. "When we go, I'll ask again."

"Excellent." Bastian ambled forward, casually strolling back into the manicured woods. The sky already looked lighter, the threat of dawn lurking around its edges. "If we have any further childhood traumas to work out after that, we can do it over breakfast."

⚘

Inside the Citadel, the hallways were empty. Even the most dedicated of the debauched had finally retired to private rooms. Their steps echoed on the marble floor as Bastian led them back through the tangled warren of gold sconces and oil paintings and bejeweled statues to the narrow, unmarked door of the vaults once again.

The guard Gabe had incapacitated earlier was awake now. He stood at sleepy attention, the sharp end of his bayonet sagging slowly to the floor before he roused every few seconds and pulled it back up. His brow furrowed when he saw them coming, but when he recognized Bastian, he stood up pin-straight and inclined his head, apparently not discomfited in the slightest by the prince's half nakedness. "Majesty."

"Hail." It was the most regal Lore had ever heard Bastian sound, not at all like he'd spent the last few hours getting beaten up on a dock. "I and my friends have business here. Lady Eldelore's mother is in poor health and recently purchased a vault, with specific instructions that her daughter inspect its views at all different times of the day and night."

Horseshit, but in that measured, princely voice, it sounded convincing. The guard's face didn't betray whether he bought it or not, but he nodded, opening the door behind him. "The Sacred Guard is still at his post."

"He won't be expecting us, but I'll explain." Bastian flicked his hand in obvious dismissal, and the guard stepped aside.

The three of them walked silently down the hallway beyond, still dark—no one had relit the candles after Bastian pinched them out. It made him a vague shape in the shadows, all dark hair and bare skin and bloody knuckles. He pushed open the door to the tunnel and waved Lore through with a bow.

Behind her, Gabriel snorted.

The Sacred Guard stationed at the end of the short tunnel said nothing as he watched them approach, but his grip on his bayonet eased when he saw the Sun Prince. Bastian didn't wait for him to speak. "We have business here," he said shortly.

The Sacred Guard nodded, though his eyes lingered curiously on Lore. He undoubtedly recognized her from earlier.

Fantastic.

But her mind didn't have much room for worrying over the Arceneaux brothers and what they'd think about her going to the vaults with Bastian, or what they'd think about Horse's reanimation when they inevitably heard. Lore could come up with something, lie enough to explain it away in a manner that would satisfy. Right now, she was too busy fighting down nausea at the prospect of seeing the child's body again. At the possibility that he'd come back to some awful semblance of half-life, too.

"Lore?" Gabriel, soft and worried.

She shook her head, straightened. "I'm fine." She set off toward the vault August had taken her to, trying her best to keep the tremble from her fingers. Above them, stars wheeled through the glass dome of the ceiling, the indigo sky streaked with fingers of lavender.

The opening in the side of the stone tower yawned like a toothless mouth. Bastian crossed his arms, cocked his head. "This the one?"

Lore nodded. She was pathetically thankful when Bastian entered first, ducking into the circular opening and disappearing into the dark beyond.

With one more look at her and a heavy sigh, Gabe ducked into the vault. Lore tipped up her head to the night sky through the glass, took a deep breath. Then she followed.

Her eyes adjusted slowly. Bastian stood between the stone Apollius's outstretched hands, the cavity of the god's chest positioned right behind him, like he was its missing heart. Gabe stood across from him, pressed into the opposite corner.

The child's body on the slab was still. Relief made Lore weak-kneed. What happened with Horse must have been a mistake, maybe she hadn't severed their connection fully—

But then, as if scenting her on the air, the body sat up.

The movement was unnatural. The corpse's arms swung loosely as it bent at the waist, as if a string were attached to the head, pulling him up. The eyes opened slowly, black pits in the pale face, as the corpse slowly turned toward Lore. Like he'd been waiting for her to arrive, to give orders.

The weakness in her knees wasn't relief anymore.

"Shit," Bastian breathed. "Shit on the Citadel Wall."

Gabe said nothing, but the very air behind her felt tense and cold, as if shock seeped out of him to infect the atmosphere.

It took her a moment to remember what she was here to do

when faced with those black eyes. She needed to ask the corpse what had happened. She needed to ask it to tell the truth.

"What killed you?" she breathed.

The small mouth unhinged, a circle of black. It spoke without moving. "The night," the child said, in a voice like a rockslide. "The night killed me."

The four of them—Lore, Gabe, Bastian, the corpse—stayed still and silent. Then Bastian gestured to the slab. "See, Gabe? Told you it wasn't me."

Gabe shifted on his feet and ignored him entirely. "*The night* doesn't help us much."

Lore's brows drew together, her concentration completely focused on the child in front of her. The mouth opened again, wider this time.

She expected an echo of the same message. But this felt different. The lips still didn't move, the dead vocal cords still didn't work. But there was a sense of *effort* this time. The corpse's words before had seemed rote, a trained bird repeating what it'd been taught to say. This was...intelligent. Purposeful.

Like something else was using its mouth.

"Find the others," the corpse said, the words rough and crawling from that dead throat, that dead and unmoving tongue. "They are not destroyed."

She half expected the body to fall backward after the message was delivered, the purpose served. Instead, those black eyes still stared at her, mouth still opened, and Lore remembered why she was really here.

Whatever she'd done to reanimate this corpse, she had to undo it.

Half a heartbeat, then she reached out her hands, closed her eyes. All she could think to do was walk back through the steps she'd taken before, see if maybe she could reverse the flow of death. Send it in, rather than pull it out.

Around the slab, Gabe and Bastian didn't move.

Instinct was all she had to follow here. Lore thinned that forest in her mind, loosening its protection. She took a breath, then held it until her vision began to white out, until everything faded to the muted gray of dead matter or the blazing white of something living. Gabe and Bastian were smudges of light, the body on the slab the color of charcoal—something between, something that should be dead, but with the death spooled out of it.

Mortem was easy to find—it lived in the rock, in the glass solarium above, slowly turning pink with incoming dawn. But it was hard for her to grasp, hard to get a handle on.

Bastian. Bastian was here.

Lore opened her eyes, fixed them on him. "Bastian. You have to go."

Incredulity crossed his face first, then a blaze of rage. "Absolutely not. I thought we established that—"

"I can't get a grip on Mortem while you're here." She was too tired to argue. Gods, how long had it been since she'd slept? "I don't know why, but if I'm going to do this, I need you to leave the vault."

To his credit, Gabe didn't look smug. He didn't look at Bastian at all, only at Lore, his brow furrowed. Channelers could see Mortem, but non-channelers couldn't—they could only see the effects it left on a person. Gabe had seen her reach for Mortem, seen her fail to grasp it.

She watched him a moment, saw him hold his breath, his fingers go white and cold. Testing to see if he could grab hold of Mortem when she couldn't. No dark threads attached to his fingers—he couldn't grasp the magic of death when Bastian was around, either.

Lore couldn't decide if that was comforting or alarming.

Bastian stared at her, not quite a glare, his arms crossed over his still-bare chest, his full mouth pressed into a white line. He nodded, just once, and stalked from the vault.

Gabe didn't ask questions. Didn't do anything but wait.

She was thankful for that. Lore closed her eyes, held her breath, lowered her mental defenses until she could sense Mortem again. She reached for it, twirled a thread of it around her necrotic fingers, her veins sludgy and blackened as her blood just barely moved.

The Mortem worked its way through her, death crowding her cells but not taking over. Slowly, it gathered in her palms, and slowly, Lore raised her hands and pushed it out.

It trailed across the vault, a viscous, dark line. It entered the corpse's slack mouth, the gaping nostrils, the open black eyes. And as it did, the body slowly sank back down, the unnatural bend of the waist lessening by incremental degrees.

She fed death to the corpse and laid it slowly to rest again.

Lore slumped on the floor, pins and needles sweeping down her whole body as her blood quickened again, itchy and uncomfortable. Her breath heaved, her heart working overtime after tithing its beat.

Gabe came to her. Knelt before her, pulled her up by the shoulders, stared into her face.

"I'm fine," Lore rasped, an answer to the question Gabe hadn't asked. Not quite true, but there wasn't anything he could do about it. "It worked, and I'm fine."

The vault door opened, like Bastian somehow knew it was done. He walked in, stopped when he saw Lore and Gabe on the floor. He didn't ask her if she was fine. Didn't show any kind of concern.

Because he knows exactly what you are. He knew channeling Mortem was as familiar to her hands as their heartlines.

Light filtered in through the now-open door, dawn blushing the sky beyond the glass-domed roof. They needed to get out of here. She'd done what she had to do.

But Gabe didn't move, still holding her shoulders, eyes moving from her face to the body on the slab. "What did he mean?" he asked quietly. "When he said find the others, that they weren't destroyed?"

"He had to be talking about the other bodies from the villages," she murmured, voice hoarse. She knew she was right, knew it with the same cell-deep awareness that pulled her to Gabe, pulled her to Bastian. "They weren't burned. August and Anton are keeping them somewhere."

CHAPTER TWENTY-TWO

Catastrophes come in waves.

                                    —Auverrani proverb

Sleep clawed at the corners of Lore's eyes, but she didn't let them droop. At least she tried not to; every few moments, her view of the sitting room in her and Gabe's apartments would dim, and she had to remind herself to stay awake.

They'd parted ways with Bastian after the vaults; even he was yawning by then. The Sun Prince hadn't said anything to them, just split off in the opposite direction as they turned toward the southeast turret. Both of them had been too tired to comment then, but apparently the climb up to the apartment had reinvigorated Gabe.

"It doesn't make sense." Gabe ran his hands over his shorn hair, elbows on his knees. He was too large for their couch, really, and angry confusion only made him seem larger. "There's no reason for Anton or August to lie about what they're doing with the bodies."

Lore shrugged, seated cross-legged in front of the fire, slumped over and propping her chin on her hand. "So you think I'm wrong?"

"I didn't say that." Gabe looked up, flames reflecting in his one visible eye. She watched him toss words back and forth in his mind, trying to find a combination that didn't sound like an accusation. "I just...how do you *know*?"

That was the question, wasn't it? The only logical one to follow, and of course she didn't have an answer. She could try starting at the beginning, explaining her origins, her strange connection to Mortem and Nyxara and the remains of the Buried Watch. She could tell Gabe the same story she'd told Bastian, the full truth as closely as she could remember it, and hope that it would make him trust her. She could tell him how something in her middle seemed to tug her toward the two of them, him and Bastian both, like they were raindrops running down the same gutter, always destined to meet.

But then she thought of what Bastian said. *I don't think you can compete with a god.*

She was already asking Gabe to keep secrets from Anton. It wasn't wise to push her luck.

So she shifted on the floor, knit her fingers together in her lap, and prepared to lie. "I think it has to do with the Mortem inside the corpse. With me being the necromancer that raised him."

It was as good an explanation as any.

Gabe shook his head. "Say you're right, and the bodies from the villages have been kept. Surely that means August and Anton have a good reason—"

"They lied to us." She turned completely around, now, facing him fully. "They lied to us about what was happening with the corpses. They said that they're disposed of after being checked over for clues. Between that and their insistence that Bastian is an informant when we know he isn't—"

"And it all comes back to trusting Bastian," Gabe sneered under his breath.

"I'm not asking you to trust Bastian." It was a struggle not to say it through her teeth. "I'm asking you to trust me."

"No, technically, you're asking me to trust Mortem. The power of death that has corrupted our city and had implications for the entire continent. The power that made people afraid of being buried underground, flowing from the corpse of a manipulative goddess." He stood, then, his shadow eclipsing her, stretched long on the floor. "Forgive me, Lore, but *the Mortem told me* isn't the most convincing argument."

Her face flushed hot, and she stood to match him, glaring up into his one blue eye. "What about *Anton doesn't care about you beyond what you can do for him* or *August is a liar who wants to kill his own son?* Are those convincing enough?"

His lip lifted. "Back to Bastian, again."

"At least Bastian isn't so far up someone else's ass that he can only see out of their eyes."

"No, he's too far up his own, and he's not doing anything but trying to get you in his bed."

"Even if that were true, why would you care?"

"Because I thought you were too smart to fall for a handsome face that tells you what you want to hear. Because I thought you made decisions with your mind instead of your—"

Her teeth ground, almost audibly, and her hands moved before her brain told them to. Lore shoved at Gabe's shoulders, forcing him back toward the couch—his knees hit the cushion and folded, making him sit down hard, cutting off what was sure to be something inappropriate for a monk.

Lore planted her hands on either side of Gabe's head, gripping the back of the couch. It put them almost at eye level, but the Mort didn't lean back. He kept his head steady, his almost-snarling mouth only inches from hers.

"His face has nothing to do with it." It was a whisper, hissing into the scant air between them. "It has everything to do with being used by the King, the Priest Exalted, the Presque Mort. I came here through manipulation and it's all I've known since. It's all Bastian has known, and it's all you've known, too. But at least the Sun Prince and I are smart enough to admit it."

Are you so accustomed to being used that you don't realize when it's happening, as long as it's done kindly? Bastian's words echoed in her skull. Gabe hadn't been used kindly, but he didn't think he deserved kindness. Maybe that was the root of it. All he accepted was constant penance for a crime he'd never committed.

When Gabe breathed, she felt it. And he was so close. So close, and all of him so warm, and there was a cold deep in Lore she was always trying to thaw.

"That's the thing about the manipulated," Gabe said softly. "They become the best manipulators. There's no teacher like experience."

They stayed there, too close and too heated, anger and something else crackling between them. And even as Lore wanted to lean forward, kiss him, wrap all of this up in something she understood, it strengthened her resolve.

Gabe couldn't know the truth about her.

He wanted her to kiss him. She could see it reflected in his one visible eye, almost a plea. Want was a palpable thing, vibrating in the air, but Gabriel was one of the Presque Mort through and through, and even in the haze of it, he couldn't be the one to lean forward and break his vow.

Slowly, deliberately, Lore released the back of the couch. Slowly, deliberately, she stood up, staring down at the monk as he gazed up at her like he was fire and she was fuel.

"I'm looking for the bodies," she murmured. "With or without you."

"Just you and Bastian, huh?" It came out like he'd wanted it to be flippant; instead, it sounded half breathless. "Good luck with that."

"Oh, I don't think getting lucky will be a problem."

Gabe made a low noise, then sat forward, wiping his hand over his face. A heartbeat, then he looked at her. "If the bodies *are* being hidden somewhere, what does that even prove?"

The tension of the previous moments dissipated; words no longer seemed to have double, heat-filled meanings. "Lots of things, probably, that we won't really know until we see where the bodies are and what they've done to them. But for now, it just means we can't trust August or Anton. It means everything they've told us about the bodies, about Kirythea—we can't trust any of it."

At the sound of Anton's name, Gabe closed his eye, and she felt a pang of sympathy. It hurt, carving out trust from places it had lived so long. Even if it had been manipulated into you.

Gabe stared at the carpet between his boots. "What about what happened when you tried to call Mortem with Bastian in the room?" He glanced at her, morning light reflecting off his reddish-gold hair. "Are we going to talk about that, Lore?"

He said it almost like an accusation.

"We can. But I don't know what it means." She sighed, rubbed at her tired eyes. "I tried to call Mortem when he first pulled me away from the ring. It was impossible. When he was touching me, I could barely sense it at all."

His brows drew low. "I couldn't sense it in the vault, either. Maybe something about him being an Arceneaux repels it, somehow."

"But I've never had that problem around August or Anton." Just Bastian, who didn't want to be an Arceneaux at all.

Gabe's expression darkened. "He could be using some kind of stolen elemental power to—"

But Lore was already shaking her head. "No one has had that kind of power in generations. And if Bastian had any means of consciously repelling Mortem, he'd be using it to help Auverraine."

Here was one more thing she just knew, one more place where she needed his trust but had no means to explain why she deserved it. Gabe angled his head so she couldn't see his eye, just the patch over the empty socket, the harsh line of his jaw. His stubble had grown in.

"We can look in the Church library," he said finally. "Anything about the Arceneaux line and their effect on Mortem should be in there. And if we find nothing, we'll know it's something Bastian is doing on his own."

It seemed to comfort him, this idea that they might be able to find some blame to pin on the prince. A concrete plan that would tell him whether he could trust his childhood friend.

Lore nodded. "We'll go look."

"And we'll look for the bodies, too." Gabe said it like a concession. "But give it a couple of days. More than one person saw us leaving with Bastian last night; August will undoubtedly be summoning us soon."

Lore nodded. She didn't like the idea of waiting, but she couldn't deny it was wise, especially if there was an audience with August in their immediate future.

Gabe stood, stretched. "I'm going to get some sleep." When Lore looked pointedly to the morning-bright window, he shrugged. "Everyone else in this gods-damned court sleeps in. We might as well, too."

He went to the threshold, stripped off his shirt, started making his pallet before the door. Lore stood in the doorway of her own room with its too-soft bed, shifting her weight from foot to foot. Then, decision a crackle of lightning, she marched across the room and flung herself down on the couch.

"Bed's too soft," she muttered, leaving out the part about wanting to trust him despite his words about manipulation, about feeling cast adrift, about not wanting to be alone and having only him to keep her from it. All that feeling was strained into those three words, though, and the quick look he gave her said he heard them.

Lore thought of that moment when he'd wanted her to kiss

him. When she'd thought about it, when she'd decided not to. She thought about her decision to keep her true origins from him, and how nothing about the want coursing through her made her question that decision.

She thought of vows.

Gabriel sighed, then she heard the telltale signs of him bedding down against the door. Lore turned her face into the couch cushions, inhaled their scent of dust, and imagined her forest, grounding herself in her own mind so death couldn't slip past.

Green-and-brown branches, azure sky. Black smoke curled against the blue, and distantly, she thought it looked thicker than before.

It took a whole day for Lore to feel like a human again. Gabe kept to the study off the main room, reading musty manuscripts and snippets of the Compendium, occasionally going down to the front hall to get them some food. Lore mostly napped on the couch, falling into the rest her body had been denied while traipsing around after the Sun Prince.

Gabe finally bedded down next to the door when night fell. It was a comfort to know he was there, close enough for her to reach in two steps if she wanted. Not that she would.

They slept late the next day, too, so when the knock came on the door, it took Lore a minute to wake.

She sat up, chemise twisted around her stomach, hair in tangles. "Gabe," she muttered from a sleep-hoarsened throat, not wanting him to get bashed if the knocker happened to have a key.

She needn't have worried. Gabe flinched, rubbing at his back, turning over to stare at whatever had been poked through the gap between door and floor as outside, footsteps receded down the hall. Pressing the heel of his hand to his still-whole eye, Gabe moved to sit cross-legged, a stiff white envelope in his lap.

"I do not recommend awakening by paper cut," he mumbled as Lore crossed the room and sat in front of him. It was the same position they'd taken that first night, when he taught her how to ground herself. She shifted uncomfortably and wondered if he noticed.

Remaut swirled over the creamy back of the envelope in Gabe's lap. A small flower was drawn next to the *t*.

"Alie," he said quietly.

Lore took the envelope from him and ripped it open. A simple white page, with words written in the same flourishing hand as Gabe's surname.

A laugh tickled at the back of Lore's throat. "A reminder about that croquet game. It's today, after lunch." She glanced at the window, lit with midday glow. "Which is probably right about now."

Gabe was already shaking his head, but Lore straightened her spine with new resolve. "We're going."

"Do you even know how to play croquet?"

"No, but you can teach me, can't you?" Her eyes felt gummy, her stomach sour from days of no rest followed by too much of it. Lore needed out of these apartments.

It also sounded nice to pretend at normality for a while, and a croquet game was probably as close as she was going to get.

Grimacing, Gabe rubbed at his eye. "I was rather good at it, once." He stood, offered her his hand.

She took it and let him haul her up. He let go as soon as she was upright, too quick to be casual. Things between them seemed mostly steady, now that they'd decided on a course of action, but all that heat still shimmered right out of reach, embers waiting for the right breath of air.

Lore dressed quickly, in a lavender gown with a high waist and sleeves that covered only her shoulders. The skirt was long and full, but not as much as some she'd seen the courtiers wear—she was in no danger of taking up the entire width of a hallway. She had no idea what appropriate clothing was for a croquet game, but this would have to do.

Her hair she frowned at for a moment before partially braiding it in a crown around her head, leaving the rest of it down. Its color wavered between brown and gold, most days, but the gentle shade of her dress made it look darker. A pause, then she pinched at her cheeks, bit her lips to coax some color into them. She told herself it had nothing to do with Gabe, and *absolutely* nothing to do with the chance of seeing Bastian.

Gabe was dressed when she came out of her room. Wordlessly, he offered her his arm. She took it.

They marched down the hall like they were headed to a sentencing.

Lore had grown used to the crosshatched iron bars set into the floors, so much so that she barely noticed them anymore. But after last night, the bars stood out again, incongruous and dark. A reminder that things like her did not belong here.

The lunch spread was in the same place as the day before, on a massive table groaning beneath the weight of pastries and hundreds of tiny sandwiches. Alie lingered with a knot of other courtiers, her cloud-pale hair making her easy to spot.

Just as easy to spot was Bastian standing next to her, sipping from a glass of wine and eyeing Lore and Gabe like a hunter peering into a set trap.

"Oh, excellent!" Alie clapped her hands. Delicate bracelets of pale-blue gems caught the light. "Now we'll have even teams!"

"Splendid," Bastian murmured. "Alie, dear, I think it's only fair that you be on Gabe and Lore's team. You and I on the same side wouldn't make for much competition."

The woman standing beside Alie—Cecelia, Lore recognized now, though she looked clear-eyed and poison-free this afternoon—gave Bastian a mock pout. "Are you saying you're better than me, Bastian? As I recall, I beat you last time we played."

He chucked her under the chin. "Yes, but I was very distracted."

Cecelia blushed prettily and cast her eyes away.

The man next to Cecelia glanced at Lore with a long-suffering expression. "You're always distracted, Bastian."

"You wound me, Olivier." Bastian put a hand to his heart. "Don't be cross; you distract me just as much as your lovely sister."

Olivier rolled his eyes, but high flags of color rose in his cheeks. The blush made him and Cecelia look obviously related, high-lighting bright-blue eyes and dark hair.

"Save your flirting for after the game." Alie marched forward, headed for the doors that led to the green. "I am focused on a different kind of conquest."

"Gods spare us all," Gabe muttered.

CHAPTER TWENTY-THREE

What's the difference between a poison runner and
a god?
If you pray, the poison runner might hear you.
    —Overheard in an Caldienan tavern, 306 AGF

An hour into their game, Gabe had fortunately managed to
refrain from hitting Bastian with a mallet. Lore had, too.
However, she'd also managed to refrain from hitting the ball
through the wicket.

"It's your right arm, I think," Alie said. She'd made Lore stand
still, bent over and ready to take a whack at the black ball on the
grass, so she could inspect her form. "You're holding it too stiffly,
so when you swing, you're hitting the ball with the side of the
mallet instead of the front."

"So I should bend it?" In the past hour, Lore had discovered
that while she held no real love for croquet, she especially didn't
hold any love for losing. She stuck out her elbow, taking it from
straight to nearly a right angle.

"Not *that* much." Alie pushed her arm in slightly. "There. Now
give it a go."

Lore did. The ball missed the nearest arch, but curved enough to inch through another.

"Finally!" She straightened, beaming, and resisted pumping the mallet over her head in victory.

Bastian, leaning on his own mallet at the edge of the playing field, gave her a gleaming grin. "Wrong wicket, dearest."

Well, shit.

"That makes the score ten for us and four for you." When Cecelia had first started keeping score, she'd sounded excited that she, Bastian, and Olivier were winning so handily. Now she almost sounded embarrassed.

Olivier, however, smothered a laugh in his palm. Cecelia smacked her brother's shoulder. She really wasn't that bad, when she wasn't sipping belladonna tea.

Next to Lore, Gabe sighed and hefted his own mallet. It seemed he hated losing just as much as Lore did.

Alie watched him line up his shot, her lip between her teeth. Lore picked up her mallet and came to stand next to her. "Sorry I'm making you lose."

"Oh, don't be silly." Alie waved a hand. "Last week, I beat Olivier in all three rounds we played on singles, so now he's just trying to save face and show off for Bastian."

Her words were light, but her eyes still tracked Gabe. Lore couldn't quite read the other woman's expression. It was too complicated to be longing, too soft to really be regret.

Gabe, for his part, had hardly spoken to his former betrothed beyond what was courteous. Lore had seen Alie try more than once to strike up a conversation, and while Gabe wasn't rude, he didn't do much more than nod. When Alie was near him, he itched at his eye patch, as if her presence reminded him it was there.

"Well," Lore said, "maybe you and I and Gabe can have a few practice rounds before next time."

A sunny smile broke over the other woman's face. "That sounds lovely. And it reminds me: I sent you that tea invitation for later this week, but I wanted you to know it was a standing invite—my friends and I meet every Sixth Day, and we'd love to have you join us whenever you're able."

Unfamiliar warmth suffused Lore's chest. This offer of friendship was probably more about Gabe than it was about her—the way Alie watched him made it clear she wanted to know the man her former betrothed had become—but she'd take it. She hadn't had friends in a while.

And being friends with Alie might help her find more information about who in the court could be working with Kirythea.

"Thank you," Lore said.

Alie took her hand and squeezed.

On the field, Cecelia took her turn—an easy point—and then sauntered over to Alie and Lore. As she walked, she pulled a thin flask from a pocket within her skirt and took a quick nip. The herbal scent of belladonna knifed at Lore's nose.

"Where do you get that?" she asked.

She expected Cecelia's eyes to widen, expected her to act like the caught criminal she technically was. But Cecelia just gave her a coquettish smile and took another sip. "The same place everyone here gets their poison," she said, primly capping the flask and tucking it away. "The storage rooms where the bloodcoats put it once it's confiscated."

Every muscle in Lore's body stiffened. Next to her, Alie pulled her bottom lip worriedly between her teeth.

Apparently, Cecelia didn't notice. "I can show you where it is, if you want," she said breezily. "It's not hard to find—"

"Cecelia." Though her friend didn't notice Lore's discomfort, Alie did. She shook her head, slightly, near-white curls ruffling.

The other woman gave a showy shrug. "Suit yourself." She wandered over to the rest of her team, offering both Bastian and

Olivier a sip of her flask. Olivier accepted, but Bastian declined, the dark glitter of his eyes arcing to Lore across the green.

The game ended quickly, with Bastian taking the winning hoop. Cecelia and Olivier excused themselves quickly, saying they had a dinner to attend. As they were leaving, Cecelia glanced over her shoulder at Lore. "If you change your mind," she said with a wave, "let me know! We can make a party of it!"

Lore's hand pulled into a fist at her side, hidden in the billowing lavender skirts of her gown.

Bastian walked over with his mallet swung across his shoulders, frowning after Cecelia and her brother. "What would you be changing your mind about, Lore?"

"It doesn't matter." She focused on releasing her fists. On taking in deep breaths and letting them out. "I won't be changing my mind."

He arched a dark brow. "It wouldn't be about poison, would it?"

Lore said nothing.

"I wish she wouldn't," Alie said softly. She'd crossed her arms over her chest, her fingers picking anxiously at the embroidery on her sleeves. "I know she has a good reason—as much as one can—but I still wish she wouldn't."

"There's no good reason to poison yourself." Gabe stood dour and looming at the edge of the group, mallet held in his hand like a cudgel. "Intentionally altering the balance of Spiritum and Mortem within a human body goes against the Tracts."

"There's more to right and wrong than what's in the Tracts, Gabe." Alie didn't snap, not really, but her voice had an edge in it that Lore hadn't heard before.

Gabe noticed. Surprise flickered across his face.

"I was unaware Cecelia was partial to poisoning until the night of the masque," Bastian said, taking hold of the conversation and steering it back in the direction he wanted.

"She just started." Alie sighed. "And she has her reasons."

"The high being first among them, I assume," Bastian said drily.

"It's not that. Or not *just* that, anyway." Alie shook her head. "She's sick. It's not hugely aggressive, the physicians say, but enough that her life expectancy is...lessened. Cecelia started taking the belladonna in the hope it would add some years." She rubbed at her forehead. "Now, she certainly shouldn't be taking as much as she did the night of your masquerade, Bastian, but she's scared."

Angry heat raised color in Lore's cheeks; she glanced away so none of them would see. Regardless of Cecelia's reasons, it was still true that her noble privilege kept her from facing the same consequences as someone outside the Citadel. Lore had known more than one person who'd taken poison because of illness, needing it to extend their lives so they could take care of loved ones. There were some deathdealers who only served such clients—Val and Mari did their running for free, charging the other deathdealers more to make up for it.

But when those clients were caught, no one cared about their reasons. It was the Burnt Isles for them all.

And apparently, the poison they paid so dearly for went into noble cups instead.

The hard shine in Gabe's eye said he followed Lore's thoughts. He dropped his mallet and crossed his arms. "There's many people outside the Citadel who are scared for the same reason," he said. "But they certainly can't walk around with a flask of belladonna tea."

"I'm not saying it's right," Alie said softly. "How she gets it *certainly* isn't right. But I understand why she takes it. I understand being afraid of death, wanting to do whatever you can to make sure it doesn't find you before you're ready."

Bastian said nothing, leaning on his mallet, a thoughtful crease to his brow.

"I should go, too," Alie said after a moment. She pointed at Lore as she walked backward, toward the Citadel. "You promised to practice, don't forget! I'll see you at tea, if not before!"

"See you then." Lore waved and managed a smile.

Then it was her, and Gabe, and Bastian, all alone on the quiet green. Silence settled between them like mortar between bricks, more impossible to break the longer they left it.

They didn't have to. A servant walked timidly up to them, holding an envelope between thin white fingers. His eyes flicked nervously to Bastian, then away, as if deliberating whether he could complete his given task with the Sun Prince around. He decided he could, and handed the envelope to Lore, apparently the least intimidating of the three of them, and hurriedly walked away.

Remaut, the envelope said. In thick calligraphy, this time, not Alie's swirling lettering.

She looked up at Gabe, shook the envelope between two fingers. "Three guesses."

"I only need one," Bastian said brightly.

Gabe ignored him as he took the envelope, tore it open. His one eye scanned the paper quickly before darting to Lore. "August. In the throne room, at our earliest convenience."

"Any chance *our earliest convenience* can be after a nap?"

"In my experience with my father, *earliest convenience* means 'get your ass here as soon as possible.'" Bastian flipped the mallet over his shoulder and ambled away. "Have a good time, can't wait to hear all about it!"

The bloodcoats at the throne room's golden double doors pushed them inward—more were present than there had been previously, to make sure no one walked in on this conversation. Lore and Gabriel strode in to stand before the Sainted King and hoped he didn't ask too many hard questions.

August looked as ill rested as they did. His customary dark clothes, while still fine, were rumpled, as if he'd worn them all night. His dark eyes were glassy, his face haggard, and he didn't wear his crown. He sat forward on the iron throne, the bars on the floor crashing up against its base like waves to a ship's hull, elbows on his knees and hands clasped before his mouth. He didn't look up when they came in.

Next to the throne, Anton stood, white robes similarly rumpled. The Priest Exalted inclined his head as Gabe and Lore approached the throne. Tired lines etched around his unscarred eye.

Neither Arceneaux brother looked like they'd slept much. It made unease drift ghostly fingers over the back of Lore's neck.

"You accompanied my son out of the walls the other night." August looked up, sighed. "I'm impressed. You managed to weasel your way into Bastian's good graces with ruthless efficiency."

The side of Anton's mouth twitched up, a quick, pleased smile that he immediately dropped.

Beside her, Gabe stood rock-still, tension coiling him into a monk-shaped knot. She stood on the side of his missing eye, so she couldn't see where he was looking, but his chin kept slightly angling in Anton's direction.

Lore swallowed.

Bastian had it wrong. Gabe's loyalty wasn't really to the Church, or to Apollius. It was to Anton, the man who'd stepped in when his father died, the man who'd given him a purpose and a means to earn back his honor. Who'd taken the worst moment of Gabe's life and made it seem like a blessing.

And Lore was asking him to lie.

She thought of that connection she felt to him, the instant familiarity that made it seem as if they'd known each other far longer than they had. He'd given no indication that he felt the same thing, but gods dead and dying, she hoped he did, and hoped it was enough for him to follow her lead.

"Did you learn anything?" August asked, sitting back in his throne. "Did he let anything slip?"

"Nothing of consequence," Lore said smoothly. "He took us to the docks, to a boxing ring. He lost."

"A disappointment in every way," August muttered.

"People rise to the heights that are expected of them," Anton said. "And you have never made a secret of how little you think of your son."

The King stared at the Priest Exalted, nearly identical stern expressions on their faces, the same muscle feathering in two jaws. Neither of them moved, but violence hung close in the vast room, as if Lore and Gabe had entered in the middle of an argument only stopped by formality.

Lore shifted back and forth on her feet.

Anton turned to her, dismissing his brother. "And did Bastian do anything...strange?"

Lore managed to wrestle her surprised expression into something that might pass for confused, even as the memory of trying to channel Mortem and failing raced to the forefront of her mind. "I'm not sure what you mean."

The Priest Exalted sighed. "In the boxing ring," he said slowly, "did he do anything that seemed odd to you?"

"No," Lore said, shaking her head. "He just got thrashed."

A shadow passed over August's face. He glanced at his brother, but the Priest Exalted didn't match the look. He just nodded thoughtfully.

Silence fell.

"You're doing well," Anton said after a length of uncomfortable quiet. "You've managed to work your way into Bastian's circle, which is exactly what we asked you to do." He slid a glance toward the throne. "We are confident that we will see the necessary results in time."

Next to her, Gabe was still and silent, his face pale, his mouth a flat line. The only sign that the praise discomfited him was a slight tremble in his hand, and he quelled it by pressing his candle-inked palm flat against his leg.

Their tableau was interrupted by the throne room doors slamming open. Malcolm rushed in, breathing ragged, dark eyes wide, a sheen of sweat on his brow.

"Leak," he gasped, hands on his knees. "Mortem leak. Southeast Ward. A big one."

CHAPTER TWENTY-FOUR

Mortem is invisible to all but those who can channel it–those who have come close enough to death to harness its power. No one else can see its threat until it is atop them, and that is why we cannot simply pray and hope it goes away.

–Phillipe Deschain, Auverrani scientist, presenting notes to the Church, 1 AGF (just before Apollius's disappearance)

I'm coming."

"You're *not*."

There'd been a moment of frozen silence after Malcolm ran into the throne room, but it'd been just that. A moment, a heartbeat, a split second of change when the atmosphere turned from familial dispute to clinical action. Anton had strode from the room, moving as fast as he could without running. Malcolm, still gulping lungfuls of air, followed behind. August stood from his throne and yelled for guards, giving instructions on closing down the Citadel, not letting anyone in or out of the walls, locking everything that could be locked. Lore thought about telling him that a locked door meant nothing to raw Mortem—it'd seep through the cracks in the stone, the wood and iron, death wasn't something you could hide from—but before she could, she saw Gabe turning on his heel to follow Anton and Malcolm, and hurrying after him seemed more important than telling off August.

So now she scampered down the halls, his too-long stride forcing her to jog. "I can help."

"Or you could die." Gabe shook his head once, sharp. "Not odds I'm keen on playing."

"This is the first true Mortem leak in...in...I don't know, exactly, but a *long* damn time, and you need me, Gabe."

His teeth ground in his jaw. He said nothing, just kept moving ahead at that punishing pace.

Anton and Malcolm were a few feet ahead of them, too focused on making their way to the Church to hear their hissed exchange. Just as well, since Lore couldn't be sure they'd side with her—her plan was simply to follow along behind the Presque Mort like a shadow and hope they didn't notice until it was too late.

"And the odds of dying aren't only mine," she whisper-yelled at Gabe's back. Bloodcoats ran down the halls; distantly, she heard surprised cries as courtiers were startled by their flight. "The Presque Mort may not be able to channel it all."

Real leaks—not just the little wisps of Mortem that sometimes escaped into the stone garden when the well was opened, but *leaks*, waves of power seeping out of the catacombs—were exceedingly rare. Not counting the first few years after the Godsfall, when magic had flowed from the Buried Goddess's tomb like opened floodgates, there'd only been three Mortem leaks on record. All of them had claimed significant casualties. All of them had made it beyond the borders of Dellaire before they petered out, the Presque Mort unable to channel it all safely into stone flowers and trees.

Gabe ignored her. The door that led to the front gardens and the bulk of the Church and South Sanctuary loomed ahead, all gilt and garnet in afternoon light. Bloodcoats stood on either side, ready to close and lock it as soon as the Presque Mort had left the building.

"I don't want you to get hurt," Lore said, voice a low rasp, out of breath. "All right, Gabe? I don't want you to get hurt, so let me go and help you, because otherwise you are *absolutely* going to get hurt."

He stopped. Turned. Stared down at her with that one blazing blue eye.

"Fine," Gabe said, and then he was stalking toward the open door, and she was running after him, and it was closed and locked behind her before her foot fully left the threshold. The door wouldn't open again until the Mortem leak was taken care of.

Either Anton would lock her in the Church instead, or he'd let her come. And Lore didn't think he'd turn down another set of Mortem-channeling hands.

Her assumption was proven correct as they all rushed to the Church door on the other side of the gardens. Anton looked behind him, did a double take when he saw Lore. "What—"

"You know you don't have enough channelers to handle a leak of any significant size," she said, brushing past him and through the second interior door that Malcolm held open. "I'm coming."

The Priest Exalted didn't try to argue. He stared after her, the scarred side of his face in shadow, dark eyes glittering. "Yes," he murmured, after a moment. "I think that might be a good plan."

Lore didn't pay attention to the Priest Exalted. She walked past Malcolm and into the cool darkness of the Church. It smelled like polished wood and incense, a scent that reminded her of Gabe's.

"You're sure you want to do this?" Malcolm murmured, falling into step beside her. Anton passed them both and led them away from the double doors of the South Sanctuary, down a gray stone hall toward what looked like cloister rooms. "To say it's not pretty is an understatement."

Lore nodded, resolutely ignoring the flip of fear in her middle. "You need me."

"I won't argue there," Malcolm replied.

Anton led them at a brisk pace, winding through hallways that felt nearly as labyrinthine as the ones in the Citadel, finally stopping at a wide, doorless room full of other scarred people—the Presque Mort. There were only around a dozen, all of them in varying states of undress, changing out of white robes that mirrored Anton's for dark, close-fitting shirts and leather harnesses. The harnesses held daggers, but only two, on the off chance they needed to defend against a human element rather than a magic one. The Presque Mort stayed armed, but that wasn't their purpose. Inked candles flashed in all their palms.

Every eye in the room locked on Lore, some in curiosity, others in outright suspicion. She tipped up her chin and stared right back.

Anton waved a hand as he descended the short set of stairs. "Another Mortem channeler," he said dismissively, as if Lore were of no consequence. "We'll need all the help we can get."

🦋

They didn't run to the Southeast Ward—they rode. A phalanx of black horses, cantering over the cobblestones, rushing around corners so close that Lore was afraid she'd gash her head. Everyone moved out of the way with a quickness, the news of the Mortem leak having spread through the city at a blessedly faster pace than the magic itself. Most civilians wouldn't be able to see the Mortem, and that added an extra edge of panic. The closer they drew to the Ward, the emptier the streets became, everyone who was able fleeing to the opposite side of the city.

Lore pressed her chest against Gabe's back and held on to his waist for all she was worth. She'd never been very comfortable riding horses. Her own feet or a cart were infinitely preferable.

But there was no denying the speed. They were in the Ward within half an hour.

And the very air tasted wrong.

Gabe dismounted, then reached up and grasped her waist, swinging her down behind him. Lore nearly stumbled. The ground felt unsteady, almost, a thin membrane over something decayed, ready to break at any moment. A sour, fetid smell permeated the air and made her stomach twist in on itself.

"Do you feel that?" Lore's voice sounded as shaky as her legs. "Smell it?"

"What is it?" Gabe narrowed his eye as he handed off the horse's reins to a waiting clergyman—not one of the Presque Mort, just a plain acolyte, who looked like he'd rather be anywhere else. "I don't smell anything."

Gabe's face looked blurry. The edges of him weren't clearly defined, as if he might morph into something else at any moment. His tattooed hands were slightly outstretched, like he thought he might have to catch her, steady her.

"Nothing." Probably just nerves. Lore shook her head and started walking, following Anton.

Nothing else looked blurred, she noticed as she walked, concentrating on keeping her gait steady. Only Gabe seemed like something in flux, caught in a state of unbecoming.

Just nerves.

The Southeast Ward was the part of Dellaire closest to the countryside, where farmers came to sell their crops. Farmland was visible past the houses lining the square, rolling green hills dotted with small barns and the faraway specks of livestock. It was the least-populated Ward in the city, but now it was completely barren, everyone either fled to western Wards or locked in their homes.

The only sound was boots on empty streets as the Presque Mort followed Anton toward the leak. He'd changed, too, swapping out the white robe of the Priest Exalted for dark clothes and a leather harness like the rest of them. It looked strange on Anton, like someone playing dress-up. He still wore his huge Bleeding God's Heart pendant, though, glinting gold and garnet in the falling evening light.

Lore felt the leak before she saw it. Her middle curdled, her steps faltering into a near-stumble as the sour smell in the air grew stronger. She caught herself before she could fall, though the sharp look Gabe shot her way said he still noticed.

The awareness of death pressed around her, like smoke searching for a crack to seep through. She tried to think of forests, of trees and blue sky. It kept the awful feeling at bay, but only just.

Up head, Anton stopped. "There."

The leak came from an abandoned storefront, similar to the decrepit building by the harbor where Lore had met the revenant nearly a week ago, when she raised Horse and got herself into this mess. Darkness rolled from the gaping, uneven doorway, seeped down the stairs and out into the street. It looked, somehow, like smoke and water at once—cohesive and flowing, yet with an insubstantial, eddying quality that made it hard to focus on. Small bones littered the edges of the strange black river, mice and other tiny creatures the Mortem had already eaten down to nothing.

Lore's stomach dipped.

The Presque Mort all did an admirable job of trying to hide their fear, but it was palpable in their nervous stances, their widened eyes. None of them had seen a leak like this before.

Malcolm stepped up first, standing next to Anton. He took a deep breath and held out his hands, the candles inked on his palms facing the river of Mortem. "Put as much as you can in the rock, first, but not too much, or it will break. If there's still some left, direct it there." Malcolm inclined his head toward the center of the square, where a garden had been planted in the midst of the cobblestones, shaded by thick trees and wild with summer blooms. "Once that's used up, go for the farmland. Don't use the horses unless you have to."

Lore looked behind her, where the terrified younger clergyman stood with all the placid horses. Why did it always come back to horses?

The rest of the Presque Mort fell into formation, making three lines on the left side of the leak. Gabe went to stand next to Malcolm and Anton, and Lore followed, the four of them forming the first line while the rest of the monks filed in behind. All of them raised their palms to the seeping pool of death magic, hands inked with symbols of the Bleeding God's light.

And almost completely useless.

It took Lore a moment to even realize they were channeling. Tiny licks of Mortem drifted up from the stream like smoke, dissipating into the air, never getting strong enough to actually connect with anyone and become the long threads Lore dealt with. The larger mass didn't shrink at all, despite the fact that every person behind her had necrotic, pale fingers, opaque eyes. One of them stumbled, tithing a heartbeat, but it didn't make a difference. None of them could channel this volume of Mortem.

This felt wrong, in a way she couldn't quite nail down. The bones littered on the cobblestones reminded her of mousetraps, of stepping into spring-loaded death with no idea an end was waiting.

Only Anton wasn't holding his hands toward the mass, wasn't looking at the river of Mortem at all. His one dark eye was fixed on Lore, narrow and unreadable, staring her down as death flowed before them.

He stared at her a moment longer. Then he turned to the leak, raised his hands.

The difference was night and day. Mortem rose from the dark river, coalesced in the air. It looked like the threads Lore could spin from death, but instead of going straight to Anton's hands, they knitted together in the air, twisting into an intricate, spiking knot. She'd never seen anything like it before. Surely, tying Mortem up like that would make it harder to channel into plants or stone—

"Lore."

Her name came like a wheeze of dying breath; she whipped her head around to Gabriel. He looked at her with a completely whited-out eye, no color at all where blue had been. His lips pulled back from his teeth, his cheeks sunken in, skin molded to the skull below. "You said you wanted to help," he rasped, "so *help*."

The air still smelled sour. Her feet still felt wobbly. Anton was still knitting Mortem into some unfathomable tangle, shaping it in a way Lore didn't understand. But Gabe was right, and it was clear from the pathetic wisps of Mortem curling up from the leak that the Presque Mort wouldn't be able to channel all of this away on their own.

So Lore raised her hands, closed her eyes. Held her breath, let the world go black-and-white, and called death into her.

Her vision grayed out, but something was different. She could see the knot Anton had made, pulsing in the air above the leak. Lore tried to avoid it as she reeled in threads of death, but she wasn't sophisticated enough for that, hadn't learned how to be careful.

As she pulled in Mortem, Anton's knot unraveled, the dark threads curling free into the stagnant air.

She anticipated him shouting at her, doing something to stop her, trying to gather up that magic into its tangle again. But the Priest Exalted merely stepped aside, the corona of white light around him turning to face her.

Lore tried to stop, but the instinct was too strong now, and she was caught in its current like sand in the tide. The threads of

Mortem that Anton had altered flowed to her hands, breached her skin, found her heart.

It felt different. Stronger, somehow, slithering through her veins in a torrent. And it didn't come back *out*.

Panicking, Lore planted her feet and flexed her fingers, trying to hold up against the onslaught—

That's when the screaming started.

Her body wouldn't obey when Lore tried to close her hands, frozen like the corpse she undoubtedly resembled. Everything in her was cold, a deep, numbing wave coursing from her out-stretched fingers and all the way down her spine, her heart stopped and stilled as if a giant fist had closed around it.

And still, the screaming. The screaming that, somehow, was her fault.

But it was hard to hear over the voice in her head.

This isn't something you can escape. Haven't you figured that out by now?

It echoed in every one of her bones, danced on every icy nerve. The voice was alien and familiar at once, and sounded strange, like two throats twined together and speaking as one, harmoniz-ing with itself.

One of those voices sounded like Lore's.

Every day, it grows stronger. Growing in you like rot as you come nearer to ascension. The voice felt like oil poured over the grooves of her brain, slipping into every empty surface. It reminded her of the voice that had told her to use her power, that day in the square with Horse, but stronger, more sure. *You can't flee from what you are, daughter of the dark. Death is the one thing that will always find you, and you are its heir. The seed of the apocalypse, end-times walking. You are the wildfire necessary for the forest to grow, the destruction that brings rebirth.*

Lore felt death clenching at her lungs, her heart, every organ that was ripe and vital turning shriveled and dry. She hadn't been

able to channel any Mortem out, only draw it in. It wasn't killing her—that'd be too simple—but it was doing *something*.

Changing her. Taking her capacity for power and burrowing
into it, making it wider, so it might swallow her up. Hollowing
her out to be filled again by something vast, something dark.

Her eyes wouldn't open, as if her lids had been sutured
together. Lore bared her teeth, pulling up strength she didn't
know she had. With a roar, she forced the Mortem out of her,
through veins that felt like they might burst, through bones that
wanted to break against the pressure.

The rock beneath her feet was too brittle already, but Lore
could feel the life surrounding her the same way she could feel
death—the two of them inverted, different streams from the
same source. She felt the heaving bodies of the terrified horses,
the fear-curdled heartbeats of the other Presque Mort. The
placid, unthinking life of the garden, still green and blooming,
and beyond that, the farmland.

There was too much Mortem to direct it with any kind of
finesse. So Lore let it loose into both, funneling death into living
roots both close by and far away, the death in her veins guiding
her to life.

Law of Opposites, she thought distantly. Death and life
strengthening each other, death and life entwined.

Spiritum fled every bloom and leaf in the garden, replaced not
by death, but by stasis, freezing them in time. Mortem wove into
the aura of every scrap of life both seen and unseen—cocooning
tiny bugs, larvae, the aphids invisible to the naked eye. Then it
went deeper, spearing through the cobblestones of the road, turning to rock the tiny shoots of grass that tried to find cracks of sun,
the earthworms waiting for rain, the bulbs of fall-blooming flowers that hadn't yet broken the surface. Then the farmlands: wheat
turning to spears of thin rock, roots becoming intricate statues
beneath the earth. She managed to spare the livestock, but only

just; the panicked lowing of cattle came loud enough to hear, a deeper counterpoint to the human screams.

Everything, stone, their lives frozen as Lore let herself be death's causeway, let Mortem flow through her like water in a mill wheel. Gabe had told her this kind of channeling required care, but it came through her like chaos.

Lore didn't realize her own screams had joined the rest until all the magic was gone.

They want your power, the voice said quietly, fading along with the Mortem as her body slowly clawed its way back to living, dwindling to nothing but the barest whisper. *They'll force you to be stronger, and then break you down. Reduce you to nothing but a womb for magic they can't make. But only if you let them. Even when you ascend, you must remember that you are wholly your own.*

Lore opened her eyes.

The leak was gone. That was good. But it hadn't gone quietly. One of the Presque Mort, a man whose name she didn't know, was now on the ground, staring at his foot. What had been his foot. Now it was only bone, the flesh eaten away, the muscle gone, and even the bones weren't in the right shape—just a pile, a discarded jumble. They gleamed wet ivory in the sunlight, and he stared, and screamed and screamed and screamed.

Lore whipped around, searching for more casualties, but it appeared only the one man had been caught in the Mortem leak. So preoccupied was she with looking for more bony limbs that she didn't notice at first the way all the other Presque Mort were looking at her.

With shock. With horror. With revulsion.

Anton stood at the front of the company, his face still blank. The knot of Mortem he'd made was gone. He watched her like someone might look at an animal they didn't recognize, curious and wary, seeing what they might do.

Next to her, Gabe stood still, his one blue eye wide and staring at the fallen Presque Mort. He hadn't moved away from her, but when Lore reached for him, desperate for something to hold on to, he flinched.

Her hand crumpled in on itself like a dying spider.

"Did I do that?" It came out small and fragile, almost child-like. Immediately, she wanted to swallow it back down, but she had to have an answer.

Gabe didn't give her one.

The Mort on the ground had stopped screaming, and that was somehow worse. He just stared at the place where his foot had been, now only that mess of picked bones.

Her legs were unsteady. Her vision blurred—on everything, now, not just Gabe. The sour-empty smell of Mortem lay thick in the air, even though the leak was gone, and it drowned her with every gulping breath she took.

"Did I do it, Gabe?" she asked again, but the words were slurred, and she fell into the dark before she heard him try to answer.

CHAPTER TWENTY-FIVE

The body always knows.

—Eroccan proverb

Her mind felt sludgy, her mouth sour, her limbs leadened. Neither awake nor really asleep, but caught somewhere in between, where the air tasted stale and mineral, where there was nothing soft.

Lore knew she was dreaming—or something like it—but it didn't stop the kick of fear against her ribs when she saw the tomb. It looked larger than she remembered, a block of obsidian gleaming night-sky dark. Looming like a slice of the earth itself, prepared to bury her beneath it, to crush her into itself and make her part of whatever waited inside.

She moved with the thick slowness of dreams, the float that didn't acknowledge arms or legs, made her a mass of thought and weightless matter. Lore tried to back away from Nyxara's tomb, thinking that she crawled crablike, but she felt no bite of shale into her palms, no rasp of fabric over floor. No matter how far she moved, though, the tomb stayed the same distance from her, as if it were a dog and she the leash. As if they were shackled together, her and the tomb, her and the goddess buried inside it.

Surfacing, just for a moment, her mouth breaking through black water long enough to breathe.

"She's alive." A voice she knew in her bones, one that made her think inexplicably of fire, of incense, of rage held tight and trees burning. "She's alive, but she isn't waking up."

"She will." The other voice she didn't know, not like she knew the first. Low, muffled, speaking from far distance while the first had been chime-clear. "Give her time."

"It's been three days—"

"You saw what she did." There was no real accusation in the tone, but the words still hung ax-bladed. "Something like that takes time to recover from."

Silence from the other voice, the one she knew.

Lore went back under.

❦

Time passed. She didn't know how much. She was suspended in inky darkness and saw nothing, felt nothing.

Then, sand. Ocean. Sun and blue sky.

She knew this dream, at least.

The same figure sat next to her as always. Lore turned her head, wondering if this time she'd be able to see them clearly. For a brief moment, there was a spark of recognition, the smoky effluence solidifying into a shape she should know. But then it was gone, only shadows again.

Something tugged at her chest. Lore didn't like it, so she crossed her arms, hiding her heart away. The tug hurt, felt like it wanted to pluck the organ from her chest, but Lore kept it all to herself, something wholly her own.

No smoke spilled into the sky. It was nothing but clear, shining blue.

The figure seemed startled; at least, as startled as something essentially noncorporeal could be. "Curious," murmured the empty voice, void of any emotion or texture. "It seems more power begets more control. But we have time. We'll try again."

Lore wasn't listening. She was drifting again.

❦

Surfacing. A sheen against her eyes, unbearably bright after so much darkness, the vague impression of a room that should be familiar. The sensation of her limbs, heavy and limp but present. This was the closest to alive she'd felt in what seemed like ages.

It was because of the person next to her. The person whose hand she could feel on her arm, a sun-blaze of heat. The darkness and death that had settled in her fled from him, repelled. The vast cavern her center had become, a hollow vessel for something else to fill, seemed to churn itself inward and knit itself whole.

"How long has she been like this?" She knew this voice, too, coming from whoever touched her. Warmth and life, honey tinged bitter. It twisted up her insides with mingled love and hatred and fear and hope.

"Nearly a week." The first voice she remembered, the one that burned and crackled. "Anton says it's to be expected, but—"

"Fuck Anton." The grip on her arm tightened. Lore wished she could say it hurt, but she couldn't move her mouth. "You should've let me in the first time I came, instead of making me go tell on you to your priest like a petulant child."

"You'd know all about that, wouldn't you?" Coals and embers, low smoldering.

Silence. Lore wished she could open her eyes and see if they were about to kill each other. It felt like something that had come close to happening before.

"I let you in now," the fire-voice said, finally. "Though it's not like you can do anything to help her."

But he was. Something about the hand on her arm was chasing out darkness and death, repelling both in a way that felt simultaneously wonderful and horrible, but Lore couldn't tell them, because her mouth still wouldn't open, because this moment of lucidity was fading, because she was drifting again.

🖤

Unpleasant didn't begin to cover the way Lore felt when she woke.

Her mouth tasted rank, like she'd gulped a glass of storm-drain water. Her fingers ached as if she'd kept them bent for hours. When she looked down at her hands, they were knotted into tight fists, so perhaps she had.

Not hours. Days.

And all of that unpleasantness was merely a precursor to the memories of the Presque Mort whose foot had turned to bone, all living tissue eaten away by stray Mortem.

Lore concentrated on loosening her fists, one finger at a time, bending them back and forth. It was painful, enough so that her mouth bit around an animal noise, but she didn't let it out.

The voices she'd heard—Gabe. Bastian. She hadn't been able to conjure their names, in that in-between state where she floated with her mind and body barely tethered, but they'd been here. Now her room was empty. Bowls with traces of leftover broth she didn't remember drinking were stacked on her vanity, and a half-empty glass of water stood on the bedside table. Lore took it, drained it. The taste in her mouth slightly improved.

The look on Gabe's face before she'd passed out was stark in her mind as Lore forced herself out of bed, nearly stumbling on numb legs, putting a hand on the bedpost to steady herself. He'd looked horrified. Horrified of her, horrified of what she'd done.

But he'd been here. Despite what she'd done, he'd been here.

What *had* she done? There'd been no straight answer, though the looks on the other Presque Mort's faces, that mingled fear and disgust, said it was her fault. But if the other man had gotten in the Mortem's path, somehow, gotten tangled in the strands that tied her to the leak, she couldn't have stopped it. *That* part wasn't her fault, and she didn't care if the Presque Mort thought otherwise.

But if Gabe thought it...

That felt like a spear through the gut.

Her mind kept spinning up that last image of Anton, looking at her with placid curiosity. Anton, who'd shaped Mortem in a way she'd never seen before her untrained fingers channeled it through her veins. Had he done something to it? To her?

She wanted to believe that, but it felt like an excuse. And she knew Gabe would think the same thing.

The burning in her chest wasn't quite sadness, and it wasn't quite anger, and it had more shame in it than she'd care to admit. But at least it gave her something to concentrate on as she hobbled toward her bedroom door, something other than the voice she'd heard as all that Mortem coursed through her hands, into her heart.

They'll force you to be stronger, and then break you down.

Lore shook her head and pushed open the door.

Someone sat on the dusty couch, the fire before them teased to roaring. Not Gabe.

Bastian.

She stood silent and confused in the doorway as the Sun Prince looked over his shoulder, golden-brown eyes reflecting flames. He stood, stretched casually, the hem of his pristine white shirt riding up to reveal an abdomen still bruised from boxing. "Morning," he said. "Or, evening, as it were. You slept through dinner, which I suppose isn't a shock, since you slept through a whole week, too. I brought you something to eat."

His voice sparked in her, like the connection she'd always felt in his presence had sunk deeper, insinuated itself into muscle and marrow. An image flashed across her mind, roses and sunlight in a mountaintop garden, but then it was gone.

A tray stood on the small table behind the couch, covered with a gleaming silver cloche, wafting a rich scent Lore didn't immediately recognize. She pulled off the cloche, barely registering what the dish was before shoving a forkful in her mouth. A bird of some kind, roasted with vegetables.

"Peahen," Bastian offered with a flip of his hand, settling on the arm of the couch to watch her eat. "I hate it, but it seems you don't."

"I'd eat anything right about now," Lore said around a full mouth.

"See, had you not just gone through something rather traumatic, I'd be making an off-color joke about that. As it is, I will let it lie. Please admire my restraint."

Something rather traumatic, indeed. Suddenly the roasted peahen tasted like ash. Lore chewed and swallowed what was still in her mouth, then set down the fork, crossing her arms, staring at a charred ring of onion instead of Bastian. "Did Gabe tell you what happened?"

"Of course Gabe didn't tell me," Bastian scoffed. "Malcolm did, and only because I was in the South Sanctuary when he carried you inside." He paused. "Gabe wouldn't let me come see you, but when I brought it to Anton, he insisted."

The fact that he'd willingly gone to his uncle made her blink. "Why?"

"Why wouldn't Gabe let me in, or why did I want to come in the first place?" But his face said he knew which question she was asking. Bastian crossed his arms, looked at a place on the carpet as he considered his answer. "Would you believe it's because I care about you?"

It hung in the air, a firmly drawn line that Lore didn't know how to cross. She stayed on the safe side of it. "I suppose that tracks. You've conscripted me into being your employee on threat of the Burnt Isles; it's natural you'd want to protect your investment."

"You know that's not what I mean."

She refused to do this right now, not when she was sore and trembling from a week spent in bed. "So you *won't* send me to the Burnt Isles if I tell your father or your uncle you know their plans?"

Bastian was silent, and the silence was the answer. That felt right, too, felt familiar and expected. He cared. But not enough to loosen his hold.

Lore nodded as if he'd spoken.

"I don't want you hurt," Bastian murmured, sidestepping a true answer. "Believe what you want about me, but I don't want you hurt. And not because you're working for me. Just because it's you."

"We haven't known each other long," she said finally, barely a whisper.

The prince snorted. "No, we haven't. But it sure feels like we have, Lore."

She had no argument for that, but it wasn't a conversation she wanted to wade through; it wasn't one she knew *how*. A glass of watered wine stood beside the tray; Lore picked it up and took a sip before she tried speaking again, changing the subject. "Why were you in the South Sanctuary in the first place?"

He let the conversation bend in the direction she twisted it, as if he, too, was eager to leave questions of care and knowing. "Some of the people I like kissing live in the cloisters."

"Bleeding God."

"Not *Him*." But jocularity faded quickly from Bastian's face, his arms crossing over his chest. "I was there because I tried to follow you to the leak," he said, after a moment of quiet. "I didn't make it out before the Church doors were locked."

"Why did you want to come? You couldn't have done anything."

His eyes raised from the floor, one dark curl falling from his forehead to brush his cheek. "To keep an eye on you." A scoff. "And Remaut, too. Neither of you excel at self-preservation."

Lore didn't have the energy to bristle at that. She just sighed and ate another forkful of Bastian's hated peahen.

"Did Malcolm tell you what *exactly* happened?" she asked after she'd swallowed. "With the other Presque Mort? I was there...it was my fault, I mean, but I don't know—"

"It was not your fault." It was the fiercest she'd heard him sound, barring that night in the alley, and it made her look up from the remains of her dinner. Bastian still sat on the arm of the couch, the lines of his body nonchalant, but there was a tenseness to him that belied anything casual. "You did what you could."

You can't flee from what you are.

She considered telling him about the voice. But the moment the thought came, it was dismissed, instinct telling her to keep that to herself. She had to have *some* secrets.

A moment of quiet, where she stared at her food and the Sun Prince stared at her, then Bastian sighed. "He told me," he said. "But before I tell you, you should know that the Presque Mort whose foot was...injured...is recovering just fine, and the Church will pay for a prosthetic. He'll be well taken care of."

Lore nodded numbly.

"Apparently," Bastian continued, "when you started channeling Mortem, it...surged. Like a wave. It ignored all the other Presque Mort and came only to you."

Like it'd been waiting for her. Or directed toward her. "All of it?" she asked. "Or just the Mortem that Anton shaped?"

Bastian's brow rose. "No one mentioned anything about Anton."

Maybe she'd imagined it, both the knot and the voice. Maybe the Mortem flowing through her had made her see and hear things that weren't there.

"Anyway, the Mort—his name is Jean—stepped up to you, presumably to help." Bastian shrugged. "But he came too close. The Mortem was still seeping over the ground, and his foot got caught in it. Malcolm pulled him out before it could eat any further, and then they left you to it."

They'd tried to help. A man who didn't know her at all had stepped forward, and lost a limb for it.

"It's honestly remarkable you're standing," Bastian continued, softer now. "You were unconscious for a week. There were more than a few times where we wondered if you'd wake up."

She'd wondered, too, floating in that in-between, caught in dream and memory. Lore took another mindless bite of food.

"Gabe is recovering fine, too." Bastian pushed a curl out of his eyes. "If you were worried."

A flurry of panic swam through her stomach. "Recovering?"

"He reached for you and lost the tip of his finger." A wicked smile twisted his mouth, but the look in Bastian's eyes was almost... resigned. "Not that he was using it to any great effect, if you get my meaning. Not with those vows."

Gabe had reached for her. It didn't make up for the fact that he wasn't here, but it was something.

They stood there, the only sound the merry crackling of the fire. A moment, then Bastian stood, brushing dust of the back of his dark pants and scowling at the mess of clothes and blankets Gabe had left on the floor. "No one has been allowed in here to clean since you've been ill, but I'm sending around a maid. Remaut is apparently unable to keep up with his own housekeeping."

The sight of the blankets was a balm, another small proof that Gabriel had cared even after seeing what she'd done.

"Thank you, Bastian," Lore murmured.

"Of course." Bastian stood, headed toward the door. "You should rest. At this point, you might as well go back to sleep. Morning is in eight hours or so."

Lore nodded listlessly but didn't rouse herself to go back to her bedroom. Bastian was almost to the door when she managed to speak again. "Do you think Gabe is coming back?"

His blankets were on the floor, but she needed the reassurance. Needed someone to say they thought he'd still choose her, someone who knew what she was.

Someone who knew what she was, and cared anyway.

Bastian's hand paused in the air a moment before settling on the wood of the door. "Of course he will. You're here."

Then he slipped out into the hall.

Lore took a few more halfhearted bites of peahen before lying down on the couch, the upholstery holding on to Bastian's heat. She wondered how long he'd been here before she roused. It was hard to imagine Bastian sitting still for long, but the warmth of the cushion under her cheek was proof he'd stayed awhile.

She closed her eyes, heaved a sigh. But the image behind her eyelids was Gabe's face, blank and terrified and looking at her like some kind of monster. So she opened her eyes and stared into the fire instead, thinking back over the little she could recall from her dreams.

The only concrete thing she could remember were the voices. Gabe's, Bastian's. Their voices, and the fact that Bastian's presence—Bastian's touch—had chased away the heavy Mortem holding her under, brought life into death. It reminded her of the alleyway, how she couldn't call her magic when Bastian was near.

Did it have something to do with being an Arceneaux, being Apollius's chosen? No one in the Arceneaux line had ever used Spiritum before, as far as anyone knew, but maybe they were looking at it wrong. Maybe Spiritum was just as changeable and mysterious as Mortem, and wielding it was something subtle.

Those would be questions for Gabe, when he showed up again.

The rich dinner Bastian brought sat heavy in her stomach as Lore worked at her fingers, bending them back and forth, still slightly numb from all the Mortem she'd channeled. She checked her mental barriers on the off chance she went to sleep, closing her eyes again long enough to visualize the forest, the interlocking branches, the blue sky beyond. One more thing to remind her of Gabe and the tangled web they'd strung between them, heat and friendship and suspicion and divided loyalties.

Not that she could really blame him for the divided loyalties. Not after hearing that voice.

You can't flee from what you are.

"Watch me," she snarled into the flame-glow of her gloomy room, fierce even as her eyelids grew heavy.

❦

The creaking of the door hinges woke her.

Lore sat up quick, a fight-or-flight urge punching at her chest, her hair tangled and her gown twisted uncomfortably.

But the discomfort didn't matter, because Gabe was standing in the doorway. A bandage was wrapped around the end of his pointer finger, shorter than it should be.

He looked at her. She looked at him. Neither of them knew what to say.

Eventually, the silence weighed Lore's gaze down from his one blue eye, bringing it instead to the package in his hand. A cloth bag, bundled up. She vaguely recognized it as being from one of the local apothecaries.

Gabe followed her eyes, then held the bag out. "Medicine." It came quiet and almost hoarse, like he hadn't anticipated using his voice, and he was surprised to hear it issue from his throat. "For your hands."

Lore stood, crossed the room. Took the bag without touching his skin. Inside was a small bottle of salve with a strongly medicinal smell that seeped through the cork stopper. She recognized the scent. Clove and cinnamon, warming things.

"We use it when we have to channel," Gabe continued, somewhat less hoarse now. He straightened, and she had the sense of a mask wedged back into place. "It stings like a bitch, but brings the feeling back into your fingers faster."

"Like a bitch, huh?" She looked up and gave him the edge of a smile, but maintaining eye contact felt too difficult, so she focused on the slight freckles across his nose. "Two weeks out from under Anton's thumb, and you start swearing like you were born to it."

The mention of Anton made him flinch, just a bit. But Gabe just shrugged. "I blame you."

Said lightly, but those three words could carry so many meanings between them, be the foundation for so many stones. They both seemed to realize that at the same time, and though neither moved, it suddenly felt like there was more space between them.

"Thanks," she said, tucking the bag with its bottle under her arm. She was cold, after stepping away from the fire. She hadn't realized just *how* cold until now, and gooseflesh rippled across her skin almost painfully, as if making up for lost time. She shivered, turned back to her room. "I'm going back to bed, I think. I know I slept for a week, but it wasn't *good* sleep."

"Who was here?"

Lore's brows knit as she glanced back at Gabe. His eye was on the tray full of half-eaten peahen. The twitch of his fingers—curled like a fist, then forced straight—said he already knew the answer.

"Bastian," Lore said, and refused to make it sound regretful. "He was here when I woke up."

She didn't mean for it to seem like an admonition, but the way Gabe turned his face toward the fire said he took it as one. It was nearly a flinch.

Orange flame-light bathed his features, made the shadows of them stark. The sight plucked at something almost like a memory in Lore's still-tired mind. She shook it away.

"Do you think Malcolm would let us into the Church library?" she asked.

"If we had a good reason. Do we?"

Lore bit the inside of her cheek, working out how she wanted to phrase it. "You know Bastian's presence makes it hard to call Mortem," she said finally. "Like that night at the boxing ring, and then later, in the vaults. You felt it, too. But while I was...out...I felt it when he came in the room. Felt his presence, again."

The Presque Mort's face was expressionless beneath his eye patch, his shoulders held tense.

She shrugged. "It helped." Weak words for something so strange. "And I think it might have something to do with Spiritum. With the Arceneaux line."

"I wouldn't jump to that conclusion," Gabe said quickly. "I understand it was strange—and somewhat alarming, in the vaults—but even though the Tracts say Apollius gave them the gift, there's disputes about the literal interpretation—"

"That's why I want to take a look at what's in the library," Lore interrupted. "Just to see if there's more information. And not just about Spiritum and the Arceneaux line, about all of this." Her hand waved in the air, encompassing them and Bastian, the villages, a Mortem leak after so long without. "It's all connected, somehow. Maybe there's something in the Church library that can help us make sense of it."

A moment of stillness, then Gabe nodded, perfunctory and business-like. "We'll ask Malcolm tomorrow." His eye flicked to her, finally. "Did you tell Bastian of your suspicions?"

He kept his tone even, but there was something dark behind it. They might be bought and bound by Bastian's threat of the Isles—a threat Lore knew wasn't idle—but Gabe's loyalty was free, and it wasn't for the Sun Prince. It never would be.

"No." Lore shook her head. "No, I didn't."

Relief softened Gabe's shoulders. He nodded.

For a moment, they stood there, and they could've filled the space between them with so many things. But Lore turned on her heel and left it empty.

Behind her shut door, Lore put the salve on her vanity before changing into a woolen chemise she found in the bottom of the wardrobe. Still shivering, she dug out a thick robe, wrapped it around herself. She felt the chill of death down her to bones, as if seeing Gabe had somehow made her body remember.

Her fingers felt numb as she fumbled the cork off the bottle of salve, poured the medicine into her palms. Gabe was right; it did sting like a bitch, and she hissed curses through her teeth as she rubbed her hands together, spreading it over her fingers and up her wrists. Eventually, the sting gave way to warmth, and she crossed her arms, making herself small as she burrowed under her covers.

But sleep wouldn't come. She was so exhausted, but she was so cold, and rest hovered just beyond her grasp.

Getting up wasn't really a conscious thought. Neither was padding to the door and pushing it open, looking out into the dim glow of the banked fire, out to where Gabe huddled next to the door, bare chest gilded in ember-light, staring up at the ceiling with one blue eye and one leather-covered wound.

He turned to her as she made her slow way across the dusty carpet, arms still crossed, still huddled as if she stood in a blizzard instead of a courtier's apartment. He watched her come and didn't say a word.

"I'm so cold," Lore murmured.

And he still didn't speak as he took hold of his blanket and held it out, an invitation.

Lore lay down next to Gabe, and he let the blanket fall over her, turned so his back was to the door and his chest pressed against her spine. He was warm, and it seeped into her slowly, blotting out the numbness, reminders of life in a body that knew so much death.

Gabe's arm settled over her waist, pulled her close. The bandage over the missing tip of his finger was stark against the dark blanket. His breath stirred her hair. And Lore closed her eyes and fell into deep, thankfully dreamless sleep.

CHAPTER TWENTY-SIX

The significance of natural phenomena in fluctuations of divine power cannot be overstated. Apollius was the god of the sun, and Nyxara the goddess of the moon. Their union proved to be a volatile one, and one that spelled destruction for the world as we knew it before the Godsfall; however, when their symbols come together in the sky, it can be a time of great power for those who know how to use it. An eclipse signifies change, change to the very nature of magic. It is a time when opposites can come together.

–Solenne Bacque, lecturer in Cosmological Theology at Ularha College in Kadmar (pre-Kirythean conquest)

O*uch.*"
Gabe's voice startled Lore awake, much closer to her ear than it should be. Her eyes flew open, registering the world at an odd angle—sideways, and from below. Every muscle in her body felt like it was on the verge of cramping, and something behind her back pressed her forward uncomfortably.

It was Gabe, arching away from the door. Gabe, lying next to her with his chest bare. Gabe, whom she'd slept with the night before, chasing warmth and not thinking about how it'd leave them in the morning.

Lore scrambled up, taking the blanket with her, clutching it around her shoulders. She'd slept with plenty of people, in both senses of the word, and didn't much care about modesty besides. But something about it being Gabe, pious, vow-bound *Gabe*, made her cheeks heat furiously and an uncomfortable vulnerability crawl through her chest.

The flush across Gabe's cheekbones said he was having his own uncomfortably vulnerable moment. She saw the decision flash across his face as he chose not to address what had happened last night, and she was absurdly grateful for it.

Gabe reached behind him, picking up whatever had come through the door. She wondered how long he'd been awake, if he'd just lain there with his arm around her as she slept.

It was another envelope, pushed under the door, *Remaut* once again scrawled in elegant script over the front. A seal covered the envelope's closure, deep-purple wax impressed with an image of the Bleeding God's Heart. The Arceneaux seal.

"Is it a summons?" Lore asked as Gabe sat up and ripped the envelope open.

His eye tracked over the paper, then he handed it to her. "Not quite."

An invitation to a dinner and a ball, to celebrate the coming eclipse. The ball was a large event, but the formal dinner afterward was only open to a select few, and she and Gabe counted among the chosen.

The date on the paper stared back at her. Midsummer. She hadn't realized her birthday was so close.

A solar eclipse on her birthday, and a ball to celebrate.

A tremble in Lore's fingers made the paper quiver, just a bit. Surely it had to be a coincidence. Anton had said they would plan a Consecration for her, but a ball was not a Consecration—

"Lore?"

Gabe looked up at her from where he still sat on the floor, face twisted in concern. There was stubble on his jaw—she'd felt it last night, rough against her hair. "Are you all right?"

She forced a smile. Waved the invitation limply in the air. "It's on my birthday. My twenty-fourth."

His brow climbed up his forehead.

"It doesn't say anything about a Consecration, though. Hopefully I can avoid an embarrassing ceremony. I assume there's no getting out of the dinner?"

"Not if August purposefully invited us." With a groan, Gabe stood, stretching out his back. Lore looked away. "It'd be obvious if we didn't attend."

Lore nodded again, lip between her teeth. She went to go place the invitation on the table with the others—next to the remains of last night's dinner; she'd have to find someone to take care of that before it got too disgusting—and another envelope stared up at her, one inscribed with just *Lore*, not her false surname.

Alie's invitation to tea. At the croquet game, she'd said it was standing, that she and some friends got together every Sixth Day. "What day is it?"

"Seventh," Gabe answered, headed to the door of his unused bedroom to find clothes.

So she'd just missed the tea. She should probably try to make it to the next one. It'd seem strange if she didn't go at least once, and she might find out something valuable.

Even if she didn't, it'd be nice to pretend to have friends for a couple of hours.

Lore changed quickly, once again opting for whatever dress was easiest to get on by herself. This one was a deep gold, with a flowy skirt made of layered chiffon that swished around her legs. The sleeves were chiffon, too, long and gathered at the wrists.

Part of her wanted to dig further in the closet and find the winter gowns she was sure were waiting. She was still chilled.

The thought came that she could ask Gabe to hold her again, but she shook her head, physically pushing it away.

When she emerged from her room, Gabe was dressed, morosely rolling his voluminous sleeves to the elbows in an attempt to make them more manageable. He gave her a wry look. "I suppose you're wanting to go straight to the Church library?"

She gestured grandly. "Lead the way, Mort."

After a moment of consideration, Lore placed the dinner tray Bastian had brought her beneath the Bleeding God's Heart candelabra across the hall. He'd said he'd send around a maid—hopefully they wouldn't mind picking this up, too.

Lore scowled down at her dirty dishes. She'd successfully avoided thinking about the Sun Prince for at least an hour while she and Gabe got ready, but now she'd have to reset her internal counter. It felt strange to think about Bastian when she could still recall the press of Gabe's chest against her back.

None of them had time for silly romance games—were this any other situation, she'd just sleep with them both and have done with it, so they could concentrate on the important things like finding a stash of dead bodies, figuring out why August and Anton had hidden them, and learning what made them dead in the first place.

But one was the Sun Prince, and one was a celibate monk, and thus the circumstances were a bit more complicated.

One had chased Mortem away from her with nothing but the touch of his hand, and thus the circumstances were *extremely* more complicated.

When Gabe arced a pointed glance from her to the dishes, Lore shrugged. "Bastian said he'd make sure a maid came up here sometime soon. He was less than impressed with your housekeeping."

Gabe rolled his eye, then reached up and itched at his patch. He'd removed the bandage on the tip of his finger, and Lore was relieved to see that the damage wasn't all that bad—part of the appendage was simply gone, as if someone had amputated it right below the nailbed. Dark stitches still showed in the skin, but it looked like it was healing cleanly.

He followed her gaze, but didn't comment. Apparently, they weren't going to talk about his wound or how he'd gotten it. That suited Lore fine.

They took the back staircase without needing a discussion first, both of them wanting to avoid running into anyone who might ask what they were doing. Especially Bastian.

Despite the connection she felt—despite that he cared—Lore didn't want Bastian to know about her suspicions regarding Spiritum. Something about the knowledge felt volatile, as if it could tip a perfectly balanced scale.

No one was on the narrow stairs, and no one but two blood-coats were at the southern double doors leading out of the Citadel. The guards let them through with no comment, expressions bored. It made Lore think of the guards who'd seen her enter two weeks ago in a borrowed dress flanked by Presque Mort, made her think of what Gabe said about them being sent to the Burnt Isles.

"The Church library is in the south wing?" she asked as they stepped out onto the green. "That's unexpected. I thought it'd be near the North Sanctuary."

Gabe shrugged. "The nobles don't have much use for a bunch of old manuscripts and Compendiums."

"But they're extremely valuable, right? That seems like the kind of thing the Church would want to keep away from the common rabble."

"Malcolm gets far more requests to view manuscripts from commoners than from nobles, actually."

Surprise nearly made her foot get caught in her skirt. "That's allowed?"

"Honestly, I'm not sure what the protocol is," Gabe answered. "But ever since Malcolm was promoted to head librarian, he's tried to make sure everyone who wants to view a manuscript has the opportunity. At least, all the manuscripts that don't need special dispensation. No one can waltz in and ask to look at prophecies without Anton's permission."

Lore thought of Anton, of his scarred face and how he'd gotten it. She frowned.

"Malcolm told me a story, once," Gabe continued thoughtfully. "From when he was a kid, before he had the accident that scarred up his arms and led to him joining the Presque Mort. He was fascinated by books, but his family only had a few, and he heard there were more in the Church. He walked right up to a clergy member and asked to see the books. It didn't even occur to him that it might not be possible. Books are for everyone, he thought."

"Did the clergyman think the same?"

"He did, fortunately. He took Malcolm to the library, and the head librarian at the time let him look at whatever book he pleased." Gabe's voice was quiet, contemplative. "After, when Malcolm got the ability to channel Mortem and joined up with the Mort, he insisted on being able to work in the library. Eventually, he took over from the other clergyman."

"Seems like he stays busy."

Gabe huffed a brief laugh.

She peered at him from the corner of her eye as they made their quiet way across the green, the walls of the Church looming up ahead to block the thin morning light. Gabe held his lips pursed, contemplative. Lore wondered if talking about his friend's life before he joined the Presque Mort made Gabe think of his own, of the boy who had a father and a home and two working eyes.

The Church door opened on soundless hinges, and they stepped into the quiet darkness inside. Gabe went in the opposite direction he'd taken on the day of the Mortem leak. The highly polished wooden rafters reflected the light of the stained-glass windows.

Six such windows lined the hall they walked down. The first was Apollius, in shades of white and gold, dark hair flowing around His shoulders and blood on His hands. The second was Hestraon, god of fire, pictured bent over a forge and engulfed in orange flame. Lereal of the air was third, Their face upturned to the drifts of iridescent wind carved into the glass above Their head. Then Caeliar of the sea, Her arms outstretched in a spar-kling blue wave, followed by Braxtos of the earth, flowers sprout-ing from His hands. At the end of the hall was a window made of nothing but panels of dark glass, deep blues and purples and shimmering black.

Lore frowned as they passed, the light dappling her skirt. "It's strange that you have depictions of the other gods. I thought Apollius was the only one you were allowed to revere?"

"Depiction isn't reverence," Gabe said quietly. His eye swung to the dark window, then away.

The hallway ended in a short wooden staircase; Gabe jogged up and turned to an arched doorway on the right, rapping a knock.

Lore came up the stairs much more slowly. The walk from the Citadel had left her winded; that week abed was doing her no favors.

The door creaked open. Malcolm cocked his head curiously. "Gabe? Didn't expect to see you here."

"We have some questions," Lore said, trying not to sound as out of breath as she felt.

"Questions that will probably involve a lot of religious theory and other technically heretical pursuits," Gabe grumbled.

The head librarian grinned. "Then you, my friends, have come to the right place."

He pushed the door wider and beckoned them inside.

The Church library rivaled the one within the Citadel, as far as sheer volume went. It was just as beautiful, too, though in a different way. Where the Citadel library was bright and airy, the Church library was austere, everything made of dark, gleaming wood and lit with the golden glow of gas lamps. The room was at least four stories high, though the upper floors were reached by a sliding ladder rather than clever staircases. Long tables ran the length of the room, and down the center of each was a domed glass lane with small hinges placed at equidistant points. A few ancient-looking books rested beneath the glass, where they could be read but not touched. A small door set into the shelves opened on what looked like a reading room, with another glass-covered table. The shelves in that room were full of much thinner books, with covers embossed in gold lettering too ornate for Lore to make out from a distance. Small potted plants had been placed along the bookcases, green tendrils snaking over shelves. There were no windows to provide sunlight, so Lore didn't know how they grew, but they all appeared to be in perfect health.

"Religious theory, you say?" Malcolm walked to one of the books on the long tables and opened a small door in the glass above it. He slipped his hands into a pair of pale gloves before gingerly reaching in to close the cover, then picked the book up with the care of a father to an infant. "That's a rather broad topic. Narrow it down for me."

"Information on Spiritum," Gabe said. "Mostly theories on how it might manifest."

"Easy enough." Malcolm opened one of a series of drawers on the back wall and gently placed the book inside before soundlessly sliding it closed again. "That's the same thing Anton's been researching."

Chapter Twenty-Seven

Answers mean nothing without the right questions.
                                         –Kirythean proverb

The next week fell into an easy routine. Gabe and Lore would wake up, eat breakfast, and go to the Church library. Then they'd spend hours poring over old manuscripts and bound copies of notes from the years after the Godsfall, Compendiums translated from Eroccan and Kirythean and even old Myroshan, from before Myrosh was subsumed by the Kirythean Empire and the language was outlawed. The mentions of Spiritum, when they found them, were brief. Still, they came every day, looking at the books Malcolm had already procured for Anton, trying to find something to make everything—Bastian, the bodies from the villages, what August and Anton were planning—coalesce into sense.

Their studies included more obscure subjects, too. Namely, texts on the strange things accomplished by channeling elemental power leaked from the minor gods. Someone had made a ship sail faster by using the power of Caeliar; another had managed to make events from dreams mirror in the waking world with the power of Lereal. It made sense that Anton would've researched such things, if he suspected that the sudden deaths were due to leftover elemental magic. But nothing in the books resembled what had happened to the villages.

For six days, Malcolm let them work in relative silence, keeping his curious looks to a minimum. When the questions finally came, Lore was surprised it'd taken so long.

"You know," Malcolm said slowly, "you could just ask Anton what he's found out."

Lore froze. Across the library, bent over a book, Gabe did, too.

They'd both known that at some point, they'd either have to come clean to Malcolm or come up with a plausible lie. On that first day, Gabe had conferred with his fellow Presque Mort while Lore looked at the books and told him that they'd rather the Priest Exalted not know of their current project. Lore had tensed, but after a brief moment of silence, Malcolm agreed. He and Gabe were old friends, and from what Lore understood, the librarian wasn't quite as devoted to Anton as Gabe was. If Gabe was asking him to be discreet, Malcolm knew it was for good reason.

But now, Gabe didn't move, so Lore made a quick decision. She stood from the bench and stretched out her back, feigning nonchalance. "What exactly is Anton researching, again?"

"He didn't give me specifics," Malcolm said, sliding another book from its shelf and giving it a cursory study. He'd given Lore and Gabe a pair of the gloves he always wore, but neither of them were allowed to touch the rarest books even with them on. "He wanted everything with a mention of Spiritum's practical application brought to him. I assumed he had an idea for how it might be used to counteract the Mortem issue, but since it's been a couple of months and he hasn't broached the subject, *helping* doesn't seem to be his objective."

There was something brittle in Malcolm's voice. Lore slid a look to Gabe; the Presque Mort was looking at his friend with his lips pressed together, a line drawn between his brows.

Malcolm didn't notice, attention absorbed by his books. He carefully opened the one he'd just retrieved to a certain page and slid it beneath the glass in front of Gabe. Then, removing his gloves so as not to soil them, he retrieved a small watering can from the corner and began carefully tending to the incongruous plants growing along the shelves. "All the references to Apollius granting Spiritum-channeling abilities to the Arceneaux line seem to be metaphor for them being His chosen rulers of Auverraine. No Arceneaux has ever actually channeled Spiritum. It's all around us, just like Mortem is, but it's not something that can be *grasped*."

"Neither was Mortem, until Nyxara died," Lore said.

Malcolm pointed at her. "Precisely." Clearly, he didn't get many opportunities to debate theories of magic; he seemed nearly giddy at the prospect, his dour manner from earlier forgotten as he finished his plant tending and retrieved his gloves. "So if you subscribe to the idea that Apollius isn't dead, just waiting in the Shining Realm, it makes sense why no one can use Spiritum. There isn't a body for it to leak from."

"*If* you subscribe to the idea?" Gabe looked up incredulously from the book he'd been reading through the glass.

"You did say your research would be heretical." Malcolm shrugged, pulling his gloves back on. "I'm just living up to your example." He gestured with one hand, then the other, indicating one thing following another. "Whoever has the power has to die—or, for the sake of pious sensibilities, we'll just say *experience a change of state*—in order for someone else to use it."

Even with the concession, Gabe didn't seem terribly pleased by the direction the conversation had taken. With a furrow of his brow so deep it shifted his eye patch, he looked back at his book.

"Now," Malcolm said, still addressing Lore, "theoretically, you could pull Spiritum from a living thing, much like taking Mortem from a rock or deadwood. But living things cling fiercely to life; they don't give it up easily."

Lore wandered over to one of the shelves of books Malcolm actually let her touch, bound copies of lecture notes from the university in Grantere, a smaller city farther north. "I would imagine taking Spiritum from a living thing would leave it dead."

"That does logically follow, yes," Gabe said drily.

She ignored him. "And you'd have to pull from something large, like a person or a big animal or a shit-ton of flowers to get enough Spiritum to *do* anything." She hadn't the foggiest what someone might attempt to do with Spiritum, but Mortem wasn't exactly the most useful thing, either.

"If we follow the theory that it works similarly to Mortem, yes." Malcolm leaned back against the table, crossed his arms. "But note: No human has ever actually channeled Spiritum, so we don't really know if it works the same way. This is all conjecture."

"Then why is it mentioned in the first place?" Lore moved on from the lecture notes and instead grabbed one of the non-rare copies of the Book of Holy Law. She flipped to the notation, memorized now. "The Book of Holy Law, Tract Two Hundred Fourteen. 'To my chosen, I bequeath my power—Spiritum, the magic of life.'"

Malcolm grinned.

Lore eyed him over the edge of the book's cover. "You have some fiddly little scholarly fact about this passage, don't you?"

"Not *fiddly*, thank you very much, just a translation dispute." His grin widened. "Tell me; is *chosen* singular or plural?"

Her mouth opened to answer, then shut with a click of teeth. Lore looked to Gabe; he looked just as confused by the seemingly simple question as she was.

"It can be either, depending on the context. And therein lies the problem." Malcolm went to the bookshelf, pulling out another copy of the Book of Holy Law. This one was written in Rouskan; he flipped to the same page and pointed out Tract 214. "I don't suppose you read Rouskan, but they have slightly different variations on the spelling for their equivalent of *chosen*, one sin-gular and one plural. This copy was translated just after Apollius disappeared—the translator would've gotten the dictated pas-sages from Gerard Arceneaux himself." He tapped the word on the page. "And he used the singular spelling for *chosen*."

Gabe got up from the bench, came around to look at the Rous-kan translation. "Was the singular translation only in Rouskan?"

"All languages that have separate spellings of *chosen* to denote singular and plural went for the singular option until about 16 AGF—so fifteen years after Apollius disappeared, right in the middle of Gerard Arceneaux's reign." Malcolm was off and run-ning, now, pulling other copies of the Book of Holy Law from the shelves and turning to Tract 214 in all of them, littering the table. "At that point, all translations swapped over to the plural spelling."

"It's a sin to change the words of Apollius." Gabe leaned over and braced his hands on the table, peering at the books like he could make them confess something.

"Sounds like Apollius should've chosen His words a bit more carefully, then," Lore muttered.

Gabe straightened. "Hmm."

"So if it was meant to be singular," Lore said, "that would mean that instead of *all* the Arceneaux line having the ability to channel Spiritum, it'd be only one of them."

Malcolm nodded. "That's the same conclusion Anton came to."

The mention of the Priest Exalted made the air heavier.

The librarian stared at them a moment, dark eyes glinting with curiosity. When he spoke, it was quiet, and with the air of something decided. "Do you want to see the most recent book we acquired? I had to send for it from Grantere, after August specifi-cally requested that Anton find it."

"Malcolm—" Gabe started, but the other man held up a gloved hand.

"Things have been rotten for a while, Gabe." The teasing

excitement he'd had while talking about translations was gone now; Malcolm sounded resigned. Sad, like someone coming to terms with a fact they'd long suspected but tried to ignore. "Anton and August are clearly keeping secrets, and Anton trapped you in the Citadel when he knew it was the last place you wanted to be. Between that and the research he's doing—not just about Spiritum, but about Mortem and how it can be manipulated—I'm not convinced he's who I want to be following."

Gabe was stricken silent. They'd all skirted close to heresy in here, but Malcolm's words came the closest of them all.

"Not that I necessarily want to be following you two on whatever harebrained quest you're on, either," Malcolm said wryly, "but I have a . . . a feeling, I guess. Something is changing, and I want to be part of changing it."

Neither Lore nor Gabe knew what to say to that. But after a moment, Gabe reached out and clapped the other man on the shoulder. He kept silent, and looked troubled, almost afraid.

Malcolm returned the gesture, then turned to the cabinet where the rarest volumes were kept. "Let me find that book. It might shed some light."

Next to Lore, Gabe crossed his arms, face drawn and pensive. Lore tapped her fingers on the tabletop. "You said Anton was looking into Mortem, too? What about it?"

"Awful stuff," Malcolm said softly. "Reports on the necromancers, back in the first years after the Godsfall. Apparently, the ability to raise the dead wasn't about how much Mortem they could channel, but how they manipulated the Mortem that they *could*. And others worked in pairs—one to raise the dead, the other to control them, through some complicated channeling ritual."

Lore frowned and twisted at one of the ribbons on her sleeve. She'd worn a new gown today, a powder-blue number with short puffs of fabric covering her shoulders, the ribbons that gathered the sleeve trailing down the backs of her arms. They itched.

Malcolm frowned, opening and closing another drawer. "Dammit," he muttered under his breath. "It's on transubstantiation, so I would definitely have put it in this drawer, not the one up top..."

"Would you happen to be looking for *Theories on the Physical Practice of Transubstantiation* by Etienne D'Arcy?" Bastian asked. "Because I have it right here."

Lore's head whipped around so fast her neck creaked.

The Sun Prince of Auverraine stood just inside the door to the library, one shoulder leaning against the jamb. He held a large leather-bound book in his hands, absently riffling the pages back and forth, mindless of their age and value. A guileless half smile lit one corner of his mouth, but his eyes glittered darkly in the dim light.

Malcolm recovered first, the sight of a book being manhandled taking precedence over everything else. "Careful!" He rushed to Bastian and took the book from his hands, too delicately to be snatching, but close. "This thing is at least two hundred years old."

"Explains the smell." Bastian relinquished the book without protest, tucking his hands in his pockets and strolling casually to the table where Gabe and Lore sat. Lore eyed him like a mouse would a cat, but Gabe just tensed up, rigid as the glass in front of them.

"Normally, I would be upset that you two didn't invite me along," Bastian said, apparently unconcerned with Malcolm's presence. "But as it stands, I had my own research to conduct. Thus the book."

"How did you get in here to take it?" The rush of saving the book from the prince's flippant hands was wearing off; Malcolm didn't look nervous, exactly, but his face had drawn into wary lines. "The door is always locked—"

"Ignoring the fact that I can get any key I please," Bastian interrupted, "I wasn't the one who took the book from the library.

I found it in my father's study." He cocked his head toward Malcolm. "And if you think I was mistreating it, you should've seen what *he* was doing. He'd left it open and weighted down the pages with a wineglass to keep it that way."

"Bleeding *God*." Malcolm hurriedly flipped the book over in his hands to inspect the spine.

Bastian turned back to Gabe and Lore, his eyes sliding from one of them to the other. "Now," he murmured, "do either of you know why my father was studying transubstantiation? I doubt he could even spell it, so I assume Anton gave him the book, which means it probably has something to do with the villages, and possibly with trying to frame me."

"Are you sure you want to do this here?" Lore kept her voice low and jerked her chin toward Malcolm, currently preoccupied with cataloging book damage.

"Oh, right." Bastian straightened, turned to the librarian. "Hate to do this, Malcolm, but needs must: Gabe and Lore are working for me, now, because it seems my father and my uncle want to blame me for the deaths of the villages and frame me as a Kirythean spy. Congratulations, you're part of it now. Breathe a word and all three of you can catch the next ship to the Burnt Isles."

Malcolm froze, the book at an awkward angle in his hands. Blinked. "Well," he said after a moment. "Thanks for telling me."

"Anytime." Bastian planted his hands on the table again, leaned over the glass. "Back to my question."

"We have no idea," Gabe gritted out through his teeth. "We've been in here for a week, researching Spiritum, because—"

Lore's eyes darted his way, quick and panicked.

"Because we thought it might hold some kind of clue about the villages," he continued smoothly. "We hadn't even discussed transubstantiation—whatever it is—until right before you showed up."

"It was my idea." Malcolm walked over to them, holding the

book gingerly in his gloved hands. He eyed Bastian's bare palms, made a face, pulled another pair of gloves from his pocket and thrust them at the prince. "My library, my rules. Put on some damn gloves."

Arching a brow, Bastian obeyed. "Elaborate, please," he said as he worked his fingers into too-small white cotton.

There was only a flicker of hesitation in Malcolm's eyes before he sighed, opening the glass and sliding the book beneath it, flipping to a certain page. "We were discussing how in some earlier translations of the Compendium, the verses about the Arceneaux line channeling Spiritum use the singular *chosen*. As in, only one chosen Arceneaux could actually do it."

"That'd explain why none of us ever have," Bastian said. "But not what transubstantiation has to do with anything. Or even what it is, really." He tapped the glass over the book. "This thing was not written with a layperson in mind."

"Transubstantiation is essentially having one thing stand in for another." Malcolm leaned forward, peering at the book. "Or, as D'Arcy puts it, 'the spiritual overcoming the physical to the point where the physical is changed.'"

"What does that have to do with Spiritum?" Lore mimicked Malcolm, leaning over the glass and squinting at the tiny words on the page. They all seemed to have more syllables than they should, and the flourishing hand dissolved into squiggles before she could make sense of it.

"By definition alone, nothing," Malcolm answered. "And scientifically, no one gives the idea much credence. It's not meant to be taken literally. But Anton desperately wanted me to find this book, and since everything else he's been looking into lately has to do with Spiritum, I assume he's found a connection between the two."

Gabe frowned, crinkling his brow above his eye patch. Every mention of the Priest Exalted's name seemed to set him on edge.

"So what we have so far," Lore said, holding up a finger for each point, "is that the ability to channel Spiritum might be held by only one Arceneaux—we have no idea who—and the fact that Anton is looking into bunk science that says you can physically change something if you...what? Believe it hard enough?"

"That about sums it up," Malcolm agreed.

They fell into silence. Then Bastian straightened, crossing his arms. "It makes perfect sense to me."

Lore crossed her arms, too, like it was a challenge. "How so?"

"One Arceneaux can control Spiritum. The power of life. My father was looking into how he could make himself into that one Arceneaux." Bastian shrugged. "The last desperate attempt of a dying man to save himself."

They stared at the Sun Prince. The Sun Prince stared back.

Gabe was the one who managed to speak. "You mean..."

"Oh, right, I forgot to tell you." Bastian pushed his hair away from his face. "August is dying."

CHAPTER TWENTY-EIGHT

Remember this: No gods are ever gone. They simply change.

—The Book of Holy Law, Tract 713*

Quiet, so complete it seemed to ring in Lore's ears. August was dying. That explained the poison he'd been drinking, the desire to get rid of Bastian so he could name a different heir if it didn't work. It didn't tell them anything about what was really happening in the villages, at least not directly, but she couldn't shake the feeling that all of it was connected.

"Wait." Gabe raised his hand as if asking for more silence, though it was all any of them had offered for minutes. "How long has he been ill? And why didn't you tell us before?"

"I didn't know until today, actually." Bastian propped one hip on the table and gave Gabe a weary glare. "I'd seen him drinking from that flask more than usual, and knew by the smell it wasn't just spirits. When Alie told us about Cecelia's predicament, it gave

---

*Stricken from the Compendium after Margot D'Laney, Second Night Priestess of the Buried Watch, attempted to open Nyxara's tomb in 200 AGF.

me the idea to ask August's physicians. A hefty bribe made the doctor's assistant happy enough to give up the records. I received them about two hours ago, after they were all compiled neatly for my reading pleasure." He leaned an elbow on the glass. Malcolm made a choked sound, and with an almost-chagrined look at the librarian, Bastian backed away from it again. "I sneaked into August's study to see if I could find anything pertaining to the villages, but all I found was that transubstantiation book."

The fact that he'd gone to look—that he must feel everything was connected, too—only solidified the idea in her mind. Lore chewed the inside of her cheek, considering her next question. There was no way to phrase it that wasn't treason, and though no one here had a leg to stand on in that regard, it still made her nervous to voice. "Bastian, do you think...could it be possible that August is killing the villages, somehow?"

No sounds of surprise, no raised brows. They'd all arrived at the same awful conclusion.

"I think he's involved," Bastian said. "But that still doesn't tell us anything about *how*. It's far too convenient that all of this starts happening right when he gets sick and wants to choose a new heir. But I can't come up with any plausible theory for how he'd manage to kill so many people from so far away, and leave no marks at all. Or what he'd gain from it. There has to be an easier way to frame someone."

Malcolm reached out and tapped the glass gently. "This could have something to do with it, maybe. Using transubstantiation to...I don't know, give his sickness to other people?"

"I thought you said it doesn't work," Lore said.

The librarian threw up his hands. "I don't *know*. It's all theoretical. Mortem and Spiritum are both the powers of gods; they weren't made for human use. That's why all the gods had to ascend from human forms, become something different. It's entirely possible—likely, even—that there are aspects of both we have no context for, that we're fundamentally incapable of understanding."

"We have to tell Anton."

Gabe's voice was low, but it cut through the room like a knife. He stared straight ahead, into the glass and the book beneath it.

"We can't, Gabe." Lore tried to sound soft, but she couldn't sand down the edge of irritation. "Anton is the one who got the book in the first place."

"That doesn't mean he's involved." The Presque Mort stood from the table, glowering down at her. "He could be trying to research what August is doing, or fix it, somehow."

"But we can't risk—"

"Why would he bring you here if he didn't want to find out what's happening? If he didn't want to stop it? Think, Lore. Why would Anton—or August, for that matter—bring in a necromancer to ask the bodies how they died if they already knew? If they were fucking *involved*?"

"Language, Your Grace," Bastian said softly.

One blue eye burned rage as Gabe flicked it to the prince, then back to Lore. "It doesn't make sense," he said finally. "The simplest answer is usually the right one, and the simplest answer is that Kirythea is doing this, somehow. Trying to start a war so they can finally take over Auverraine, too."

"Everything is always going to come back to Kirythea with you." Bastian tapped his fingers on the glass. "Perhaps you're not the most impartial party to evaluate this, Remaut."

The Presque Mort's hands tightened into fists. He took a step closer to the table.

"Gabe," Malcolm cautioned.

The sound of his name from his old friend was enough to make Gabe's shoulders soften, just slightly. He looked away from Bastian, ran a weary hand over his face.

"I haven't been able to raise a body other than the one Anton and August chose," Lore said quietly. "And they didn't want me to be present when they started asking questions. Maybe the point wasn't the questions, but the raising. Maybe they tampered with it somehow. *How*, I don't know." She cut her hand toward the book under the glass. "But it seems there's a lot we don't know."

"Then the solution is to find a body they haven't chosen for you." Bastian looked at the floor, lips twisted thoughtfully. "One of the ones they've hidden away somewhere."

"Exactly." Lore slid a glance to Gabe, still quiet, still looming. "So, essentially, we're back at where we started."

"With the added bonus of a slowly dying King, it seems," Malcolm added. With a sigh, he sat at the table. "Apparently I'm in this now, and seeing as I have no desire for an extended stay on the Isles, I'm going to make myself useful and read this damn book." He raised a brow at Gabe. "You cross-reference the Compendiums on the table over there. It'll keep you occupied, and it might turn up something new. I've stared at them until the words run together."

"What should I do?" Bastian asked brightly.

"I wouldn't dare give orders to a prince."

"Come on, Malcolm, are you salty about the Burnt Isles threat? I understand, but my hands are tied, here. Pardon the poor choice of words."

Malcolm's dark eyes rolled to the ceiling, as if beseeching Apollius for a moment of peace. "You look through the lecture notes. See if you can find anything."

Everyone fell to their tasks with quiet focus. Lore hadn't been given a job, and didn't necessarily want to ask for one, so she drifted over to Gabe, taking a seat next to him at the other long table.

"I'm sorry," she said, because she didn't know what else to say.

"For what?" He didn't look at her, eye fixed to a glass-protected page, but he wasn't reading. Just staring.

"I don't know." A sigh, and she folded her hands on the table, rested her head on them. "You're right that August and Anton wouldn't bring me here to find out the truth if they already knew it, and I can't think of another reason why they'd want me in the Citadel—like Bastian said, there's certainly easier ways to frame someone. This could be a huge conspiracy, or it could just be a series of misunderstandings. But we have to know."

Gabe was silent for a moment. Then: "There's another option."

"What?"

"Maybe they don't want you here to find out about the villages." He shifted on the bench. "Maybe Anton is planning something that will save us all—save us from Kirythea, save the villages, even save Bastian from August. And maybe you're part of it."

"That sounds extremely far-fetched."

He shrugged uncomfortably. "I just want…" It trailed off into a sigh. "I just want this to end in a way that I can live with."

And Anton being a villain wasn't something he could live with.

Lore didn't know what to say. So she kept silent, kept her head pillowed on her arms, lulled by the flip of pages and the dim lights of the library, her eyes slowly falling closed.

White sand. Blue water. Blue sky.

Lore could sense the same insubstantial figure next to her as always. Something about them felt more *solid*, though, as if she'd drawn closer, though the distance between them appeared to be the same.

She turned her eyes, the movement taking far more effort than it should. But though there was a brief moment of corporeality, when the shape almost took a form she could recognize, it was gone in a heartbeat.

"Now," the textureless voice murmured, slithering across her dream. "Let's try this again, since you've had some time."

A tug at her heart, painful this time, as if a hand had reached behind her ribs and plucked the organ like fruit. A soundless scream wrenched her mouth as smoke poured from her chest, twining into the sky, twisting across the blue.

"Lore."

Something at her shoulder. A hand, shaking her. "*Lore.*"

With conscious effort, she opened her eyes.

Gabe frowned down at her from his place on the bench, but the hand on her shoulder was Bastian's. He tapped her on the forehead, then straightened, making a show of looking at the clock on the wall. "If we hurry, we'll still make it."

Make it? She counted back the days, trying to think of what he might be speaking of—

"Shit." She shot up from the table, running a hand over her mussed hair. "I have to go to a tea party."

❧

Bastian escorted her out. Lore could feel the needle-points of Gabe's eyes on the back of her neck, but he didn't make any excuses to try to accompany them. He and Malcolm kept poring over Compendiums and lecture texts to see if there was any scrap of helpful information, and he told her he'd try to be back in their apartments by the time she was done with Alie's tea.

"Such a conscientious cousin," Bastian said as they swept from the library.

Lore elbowed him lightly in the ribs, feigning a trip over her hem so it looked like an accident. The bend of his mouth said he didn't buy it.

The transubstantiation book was tucked beneath Bastian's arm, held close so as not to attract attention. When they entered the Citadel, Bastian unhooked his opposite arm from Lore's grasp, then slipped a piece of paper into her hand. "A map to my rooms."

"Not exactly the most opportune time for a proposition, but I respect the effort."

"Get your mind out of the gutter, Lore." Bastian chucked her under the chin. "Alie is hosting her tea in my apartments today. Her own are being deep-cleaned. I have to go return this book before my father notices it's gone; I'll meet you there." He sauntered down the hallway, his stride giving no indication that he held contraband beneath his arm. In another life, Bastian Arceneaux would've made a good poison runner.

Lore studied the map, and started in what she thought was the right direction, toward the northwest turret—Bastian had helpfully drawn a winking face over what she presumed to be his apartments. After a hallway full of marble statues and another made entirely of windows, she reached a large, grand staircase, carpeted in lush crimson.

"Much nicer than the southeast," she muttered as she mounted the stairs. "And no creepy statues."

Though nicer, the turret was constructed in the same way, with stairs that ended on short landings leading to longer residential halls. According to Bastian's map, his apartments were at the very top, up at least ten flights.

Where the hallways leading to Gabe and Lore's quarters were kept dim, here everything was bright and clean, the hallways wider, illuminated by both gas lamps and natural light through crystalline windows. Vibrantly woven tapestries hung next to oil paintings in bright colors—clearly made with more care than the shabbier ones in her own turret. Lore found herself not minding the climb to the top as much as she'd anticipated; it was almost like being in a museum.

Somewhere on the third landing, Lore's foot got tangled in her lavender skirt, sending her sprawling up the last few steps before she caught her footing again. "Shit on the Citadel Wall," she hissed.

But the near-trip was serendipitous, because it made her look up from Bastian's map, and it made her see the figure in the hall before he saw her.

It was easy to recognize Severin Bellegarde. His dark hair gleamed in an orderly queue, his clothing sleekly fitted to his tall, thin body in muted colors. He walked down the hallway in the opposite direction of the stairs with his hands behind his back, as if the tapestries he passed were prisoners trotted out for inspection. Each one, he stopped to peer at through narrowed eyes, examining it like he was reading the weave before moving on. One of the hands behind his back held a small, folded piece of paper.

He'd been holding a similar one that night she and Gabe ran into him on the stairs, Lore remembered. When they were running to the vaults.

She didn't have time to puzzle over it right now, though. Lore straightened and turned toward the next set of stairs, hoping Bellegarde didn't notice her.

"Eldelore Remaut."

No such luck.

Lore arranged her face into pleasant nonchalance, spun to dip a clumsy curtsy as she returned his greeting in kind. "Severin Bellegarde."

The other man had stopped in front of a tapestry near the stairs; apparently, he'd changed direction while her back was turned. A line formed between his brows, and he didn't speak. But he did back up, slightly, the tapestry shuddering as his shoulder brushed against it. He stared at her with an expression Lore couldn't place as admonishing or thoughtful.

She was almost ready to turn and walk away, dismissing herself if he wouldn't do it, when Severin finally spoke. "Will you and Gabriel be attending the ball on the solar eclipse?"

Her brow furrowed. Bellegarde didn't seem the type to be concerned with others' social plans. "I assume so," she answered, fighting down an involuntary shiver. The ball on her birthday, her twenty-fourth. The day she'd be Consecrated, if she'd been raised by people who believed in such things.

The involuntary shiver became an involuntary lump in her throat. Thinking of Val and Mari still hurt.

Bellegarde's green eyes pinned her in place. "It is a great honor to be chosen."

The word made her think of the Compendium, of everything she and Malcolm and Gabe—and Bastian, now—had been studying in the Church library. Wariness made her spine straighten. "Yes. It seems only a few were invited to the dinner after the ball, correct? Gabe and I plan to do our best to attend."

"You plan to do your best?" One dark brow lifted. "What could possibly be more important than attending an event the Sainted King himself invited you to, on such a spiritually auspicious occasion? Total eclipses are rare, especially during waking hours. They are phenomena of great import."

Lore tried to smile, but knew it looked more like a grimace. "Nothing is more important, of course," she murmured, a miasmic, unformed dread beginning to uncurl in her middle. "We'll be there."

"Good." Bellegarde gave one terse nod. "I'm sure it will be a time of great reflection for us all. Which is something we will need, as Kirythea draws closer. As the death toll of our outer villages rises."

The false, pleasant smile fell off Lore's face. "What do you mean?"

"Have you not heard?" The man's face was a mask, as unable to be read as a carving rubbed clean. "Another village was struck this afternoon. A few hours ago."

Another village.

She'd failed to find out what was happening, and while she wasted time spinning in circles, another whole village had died.

"How did they find out so fast?" Her voice felt like it issued from a different body.

A muscle jumped in Bellegarde's cheek, like he'd said something he hadn't meant to. "The Church and Crown have informants all over Auverraine," he said, not really an answer at all.

Lore wanted to crumple, her eyes finding the floor before they blurred. She thought of the little boy in the vaults, framed between Apollius's garnet-bleeding hands. "I hate to hear that," she whispered.

"A tragedy, to be sure." Bellegarde watched her closely, though his expression still gave nothing away. "And all the more reason for us to come together at the eclipse. A time for new beginnings."

She was too numb to nod.

"Severin?"

August, coming down the hall toward them. The King looked remarkably ordinary, with his gray hair and his deep-red clothing, his station denoted only by the golden circlet on his brow. He stepped between Lore and Bellegarde gracefully, but in a way clearly meant to sever conversation, and though his smile was bright, it didn't mask the wariness in his eyes. "And what would you two be discussing so ardently?"

"The eclipse event." Bellegarde's voice was cold. "I was making sure Eldelore and Gabriel will be attending."

If the other man's strange fixation on Lore's social calendar puzzled the King, he didn't show it. Instead, he looked almost relieved. "Excellent news. We'll be thrilled to have you."

She managed a nod.

"It's sure to be a splendid time," August said, "and Gabriel will doubtless enjoy an eclipse not spent shackled to the Church's doings. The Presque Mort typically spend all eclipses in prayer, but for this one, my brother made an exception." He clapped Bellegarde on the shoulder, a succinct dismissal. "Go on, Severin. Let us leave the lady to her social responsibilities. She's dressed for a party."

Bellegarde's face cramped, but he nodded. Then the two of them watched Lore.

It took her a moment to realize they expected her to leave first. With another clumsily dipped curtsy, she did. Right before the turn of the stairs blocked them from view, she ducked to look at Bellegarde and August again. They'd started down the steps below together, speaking quietly. Bellegarde's hands, she noticed, were empty, the paper he'd held now gone.

Lore crouched on the landing above, hidden from view.

"Everything is coming together nicely," Bellegarde murmured. "The next group is set to be processed by this evening."

"And the bindings?" August sounded impatient.

"Seem to be in working order."

"But we won't know until I try."

A heartbeat. "Correct, Your Majesty," Bellegarde said.

Then silence, but for the sound of boots on plush-carpeted stairs.

When the tread was gone, Lore counted to fifty. Then, moving as quietly as possible, she stood and crept back down the stairs.

The hall was empty. Lore didn't waste the moment. She ran straight to the tapestry where Bellegarde had stood, the one right before the stairs.

It didn't look any different than the others lining the sumptuous corridor. White thread picked out a rearing unicorn, hooves slashing at the air, surrounded by silver-helmed knights and blobby wildflowers in spring pastels. Lore frowned at it, tracing the thread pattern with her eyes until they went blurry.

He'd been looking for something in the tapestries. Lore was familiar with how people acted when they didn't want to seem suspicious; the overly casual stride, the rapid movement of eyes. Severin Bellegarde had ticked all the boxes.

And there'd been that paper in his hand. A paper that had disappeared when he left with August, either disposed of or slipped into a pocket. Maybe he'd been looking for a hiding place, somewhere to put it?

With a quick glance up and down the hall to make sure she was still alone, Lore shoved her hand behind the tapestry, between the fabric and the wall. Nothing but smooth wood, at first, but as she ran her fingers along the thread-nubbed back, they caught on something sharp.

A pin, holding in place a tiny slip of paper. She'd bet money it was the same one that had been in Bellegarde's hand.

Lore only stuck herself once as she carefully pulled the paper off the sharp end of the pin, leaving her thumb in its place so she could put it back exactly where she'd found it. Keeping her hand beneath the heavy fabric required crouching strangely next to the wall, so she unfolded the note and read it as quickly as she could.

But the note didn't have words. Just a number.

75.

She frowned at it a moment before hurriedly thrusting the note back behind the tapestry, pricking her finger again and hissing a curse. She was already hopelessly late, and there were seemingly endless stairs between her and Bastian's apartments.

After making sure the note showed no sign of meddling, Lore went back to the stairs, doing her best not to run. A blister was forming on the arch of her foot, helped along by her thin slippers, and it gave her a counterpoint of discomfort to concentrate on as she thought over what she'd found.

75.

Seventy-five *what*? Maybe it wasn't for anything important after all. Maybe Bellegarde was cataloging the tapestries—she didn't know how many were in the corridor, but seventy-five didn't seem outside the realm of possibility. Maybe he wanted to make sure the turret he lived in during the season had more tapestries than any of the others. It seemed like something a Citadel courtier would do.

She couldn't quite buy that, though. Bellegarde had acted strangely when he saw her. He'd stood in front of the tapestry like he was trying to hide it, and conversely brought it to her attention instead.

Lore stuck her finger in her mouth, sucking at the tiny bead of blood the pin had brought up. She hoped the note meant something, or she'd just impaled herself for nothing but discovering how many gaudy tapestries August hung in a hallway.

A tactical mind for the ages, Gabe had called her. Gods dead and dying.

Bastian's directions kept her heading up the stairs, until she reached their end at a corridor wider than any of the others she'd passed. She glanced down at the crude map, at the words written in a surprisingly graceful hand beneath the badly drawn winking face. *Between the palms.*

The landmark was unneeded. There was only one door at the end of the long, wide hallway, painted white with a swirling pattern of golden suns, two leafy palms on either side. The sounds of laugher drifted from within.

"Here goes." Lore strode down the hall, raising her hand to knock.

A maidservant opened the door before she could, and to her credit didn't give Lore the appraising once-over she surely deserved, out of breath and limping due to her rapidly growing blister. Instead the maid only inclined her head, stepping aside to let her into the most beautiful room Lore had ever encountered.

It was breathtaking in its simplicity. The walls were pale marble, veined in delicate traceries of gold, left bare of art in favor of showing off their simple beauty. Tiles in blushed, subdued colors made up the floor, turning the whole expanse to a disorienting whirl of swirls and arabesques, like standing in a cloud. In the center of the room, a stone fountain shot jets of water up toward the domed glass roof, disturbingly similar to the one covering the vaults, and arched windows in the walls were nearly blocked by a green profusion of plants. Beyond the open foyer, a staircase led to what Lore assumed were more rooms, a mansion in its own right sitting on top of the Citadel.

She might've stood there gaping for hours if Alienor hadn't called to her. "Lore!"

Alie, grinning brightly and dressed in pale yellow that made her copper skin glow, hurried over to clasp her arm. "I'm so glad you could come!" She waved a hand to indicate the room. "Isn't it gorgeous? Bastian usually keeps it a mess in here, but apparently his apartments were deep-cleaned before ours were."

"It's beautiful." It was easy to imagine Bastian here, in the glow of the light through the clear windows, surrounded by lush plants in the prime of health. Alie looked at home here, too. They both had some inner, shimmering quality that made them fit in with light and air, with easy luxury.

Lore wondered just how out of place she looked.

"Ridiculously beautiful, much like the man himself." Alie arched a pale brow. "At least he put the peacocks in the garden for the afternoon. I hate those things. They're so loud, I don't understand how he ever sleeps."

"I don't think he sleeps in here much," said a new voice. In an alcove walled completely in sparkling glass and stuffed with emerald ferns, a woman with jet-colored hair and eyes to match took a sip from a delicate teacup, its pale gleam complementary to her golden-brown skin. "Just hosts parties and carouses."

"He has to sleep sometime," the courtier next to her said. Her hair was golden, pin-straight, and worn loose to frame her pale white face and full lips. "Lucien told me his bed is nearly the size of his whole room."

"Lucien would know." The other woman smirked and raised her teacup in a salute.

"Let's please discuss literally anything other than Bastian's conquests," Alie said as she tugged Lore over to the others. "It seems rude while we're in his apartments. Like discussing the quality of the beef while the butcher is right there."

"Lucien would also know about the quality of the beef," the dark-haired one said, and it sent them into peals of laughter, even Alie, who playfully swatted at her. She put down her teacup to grab Alie's hand out of the air and gave it an exaggerated kiss.

Lore managed to smile, though nerves crept in a noose around her neck. These women moved like old friends, like people who had grown up around each other the way old trees grew around fence posts. Their laughter seemed good-natured, and the curious looks the other two gave her weren't in any way malicious. But such groups had difficulty changing shape to accommodate newcomers.

There was no whiff of belladonna in the tea. That was something, at least.

Delicate china met delicate lips, delicate pastries were sampled by delicate hands. Lore felt like a horse let loose in a jewelry shop.

"Everyone," Alie said, keeping firm grip on Lore's arm as if she could feel the urge to run seeping from her pores, "this is Eldelore Remaut, Gabriel's cousin. Though I'm sure you already know."

"Lovely to finally meet you, Eldelore. I'm Danielle." The golden-haired courtier smiled brightly. Her gown was a pale green and cut similarly to Lore's, though the ribbons trailing from Danielle's sleeves were wrapped around her upper arms and tied into bows, so they didn't dangle.

So *that's* how you were supposed to wear them. Not hanging so low they made you think you had ants crawling all over you. Lore felt the sudden urge to fix her own, but stilled her hands and nodded instead, returning Danielle's smile.

"Brigitte," offered the dark-haired woman who'd kissed Alie's hand. Her gown was different, peach-colored with fitted sleeves that went to the elbow and ended in a ruffle of lace. Lore vaguely recognized her from the masquerade that first night. She'd been dressed as a mermaid, shimmering green painted into her hair. It still looked siren-like, even now, half of it twisted into a black crown around her head, the rest worn in long locs down her back.

"It's wonderful to meet you," Lore said, taking one of the other seats at the wrought-iron table. "Thank you for letting me crash your party."

"No crashing needed." Brigitte took a macaron from the pile in the center of the table. "We were thrilled to finally have the chance. You and Gabriel have been the talk of the Citadel for nearly a month."

The tingle of nerves traveled from the back of her neck to trail the length of her spine. Lore forced a smile. "Well," she said, and wasn't sure how to continue, so she just didn't.

"Bri and Dani are my dearest friends," Alienor said, finally taking a seat and pulling over a plate of pastries. "We've been close since we were learning our letters. Bri and I took piano together, and Dani's father is an associate of Lord Bellegarde's." No one seemed to find it strange that Alie referred to her father by his title.

Dani shifted in her seat. Lore wondered if her relationship with her father was as apparently frosty as Alie's was with her own.

"I didn't want to overwhelm you with a huge party," Alie continued, selecting something covered in powdered sugar and spearing it with a tiny fork. "Though since one of Bastian's fetes was your first social engagement, anything will seem small afterward."

Lore laughed politely, fighting her anxiety's urging to shove pastries in her mouth one after the other. "It was certainly enlightening."

Danielle's smile was genuine, if nakedly curious. "We've barely seen you since your dramatic entrance at Bastian's masquerade, other than your introduction at First Day prayers." Her tone was still friendly, but something sharp flashed in her eyes. Curiosity, and not a small bit of wariness.

"I've been ill," Lore said, searching for a way to explain her long absence that wasn't *I channeled too much Mortem and then looked for proof of treason in the Church library.* In a flash of inspiration, she gestured to her middle. "Cramps."

"Ah." Brigitte nodded knowingly. She pushed a cup of tea across the table; it smelled just as bright and delicate as everything looked in this room. "That should help. I have terrible pains when my time comes, too, and so does my brother. It's awful."

The sympathy in her voice made Lore almost sorry she was lying. Well, only technically—she might not be bleeding now, but when she did, it felt like someone kicking her repeatedly in the organs. She took a sip of the offered tea. It was surprisingly tasty. "I should be fully recovered in a few days. Then I'll hopefully be able to look through my stack of invitations. And get in that croquet practice I promised Alie."

"I'm sure you've been invited to *everything.* It's not often we have a newcomer." Danielle picked up a chocolate and popped it in her mouth, speaking around caramel. "Most of us started coming to the Citadel in the summers as children; we've known each other for ages."

"So I've heard." Lore traced threads in her mind, recalling the backstory she and Gabriel had come up with. A country home in . . . shit, Gabriel had told her a name to use, and she'd completely forgotten it . . . a childhood sickness that kept her confined . . .

But the questions, when they came, weren't about her at all. "So," Danielle said, leaning forward, eyes darting mischievously between Lore and Alie. "Why is Gabriel really back in court? Is it truly just to escort you?"

Lore nearly choked on her tea. That odd glitter was still in Danielle's eyes, almost like this was a test.

"Dani." Alienor sounded halfway between laughing and screaming, with the kind of nervous strain that came from both desperately wanting and not wanting a conversation to happen. "We don't need to talk about Gabriel. There's no need to go excavating ancient history." Though Alie's blush was the color of the cherry jam in Lore's pastry, there was a still a hopeful light in her eyes. Lore recognized it. A torch long held. And it made her think of Gabe's bare chest and how it'd felt pressed warm against her back a week ago and Bleeding *God* nothing could be simple, could it?

"Poor Bastian." Brigitte shook her head, face solemn, though the words were teasing. "Went to all this trouble, let Alie use his suite and everything, just for her to ask about Gabriel."

"You know it's not like that with Bastian," Alie said. "He's like a brother."

"Unfortunate, honestly," Brigitte countered. "I mean, I *don't* think being an Arceneaux Queen would be a grand time, but he is unconscionably handsome."

"Unconscionably handsome, yes," Dani said, "but he'd make an awful husband, if you wanted anything like loyalty. Bastian has someone new in that huge bed three times a week."

"Sounds like fun to me," Brigitte said with a wicked grin. "It's really just the queendom that doesn't suit." She picked out another macaron. "Don't tell my father I said that, though. He has half a mind to try and get us betrothed before the end of the season."

Now Lore's face was nearing the color of Alienor's.

"*Gods*, betrothals." Dani rubbed at her temple, as if the very thought sparked a headache. "I don't want to think about them."

There was genuine exhaustion in Dani's voice. Alie and Brigitte shared a quick, sympathetic look.

"Has your family come around at all, Dani?" Alie asked tentatively. "To the idea of you and Luc?"

"Of course not." Dani sat back with a sigh, crossing her arms and staring at her tea. Her eyes flicked up to Lore, then away. "He's a commoner. It doesn't matter that he's the son of a well-regarded shipbuilder; they only care about lineage."

"And Hugo didn't put in a good word for you?"

"No," Dani said miserably. "I did what we talked about—I made Hugo take me on a night Luc was fighting, acted like we'd never met. Luc won the match, of course, and Hugo won a pile of money on the bet—Luc did, too. But when I brought up that I might want to marry a well-off commoner...it didn't go well." Her mouth twisted. "In the words of my dear brother, it'd be like throwing money into the ocean."

Lore stayed quiet. She wondered if Luc was someone she might know if she saw him.

"But we're thinking of a new plan," Dani said quietly, hopefully. "Luc and I. Amelia is the oldest; she's the daughter who will need to marry for status."

"Maybe she can have a crack at Bastian," Brigitte said.

Dani rolled her eyes. "You sound just like her. She's convinced she would make an excellent queen, but my parents are playing it safe. They're currently in negotiations with Viscount Demonde. Amelia is less than thrilled."

"Gods, I bet." Bri scowled. "If I had my sights on Bastian Arceneaux and got ancient Demonde instead, I'd be furious."

Lore's smile felt very brittle.

"He's ancient, but the Demonde line is, too. And he's rich as sin, *and* much easier to secure than an Arceneaux heir. If Amelia makes a prestigious match, then my marriage can be just about money." Dani shrugged. "Luc is the heir to a modest fortune, and making more money on his own, besides."

Again, a slant of her eyes to Lore, so quick it could've been imagined.

"Is he building ships, too?" Alie asked.

"Not quite," Dani answered. "Apparently, a new company has been hiring men off the docks to do transfer work. Carrying cargo from one place to another, things like that. They pay ridiculously well, and it's usually only a night or two of labor." She took a contemplative sip of tea. "It's not exactly aboveboard, I assume, but if they're paying the cargo carriers that well, their budget for bribes is probably quite healthy. Not that anyone would dare arrest Luc, once they found out who his father was."

After hearing from Cecelia where the courtiers got their poison and how thin the rules held when you introduced money, Lore was sure that was true. "What's the cargo?"

"I don't know," Dani said. "And I don't care, really—it's a *lot* of money, enough that Luc could buy a town house in one of the nicer Wards and pay my dowry even before his father dies and leaves him the business."

Something tugged in Lore's gut, not sitting quite right. As if this conversation was somehow a continuation of the one she'd been having all week in the Church library.

"Anyway, enough about all that." Danielle waved a hand, dismissing talk of betrothals. "I believe we were discussing the handsome Duke Remaut and his presence in court, yes?"

"Apollius's wounds," Alie muttered, burying her face in her hands.

Lore took another drink of her tea, too quickly, burning the roof of her mouth. Brigitte and Danielle's eyes fastened on her—clearly, she was supposed to speak next.

"It really is just to escort me," she said finally. "My parents wanted a relative to help me through the season, and Gabriel was the only option. He wasn't pleased about it."

Alie made a small sound from behind her hands.

"I mean," Lore said quickly, "there were parts he was looking forward to." She turned to Alie. "I know he was excited to see you again."

Technically a lie—Gabe had told her no such thing—but it didn't feel like one.

"Truly?" Alie dropped her hands with a sigh. "Because I feel I made a mess of it all. It's just been such a shock, seeing him again. Seeing him so... so grown up."

Bare chest in firelight, the shadow of an eye patch made darker by the brilliant blue staring down at her. Lore swallowed more too-hot tea. Grown-up indeed.

Memories closer at hand were less pleasant. The clench of his jaw as he read another seemingly useless book. The way he'd drawn inward in the past few days, always preoccupied by something he wouldn't talk to her about.

"He was taken aback, too," Lore said. "It's been . . . complicated for him, I think."

"More complicated than it would be for anyone else, probably." Dani shook her head in sympathy. "Some of us thought he was coming back to court for good, at first. But it seems like he's holding fast to those vows."

Alie's cheeks went pinker. "Being one of the Presque Mort is a lifelong appointment. Once you gain the ability to channel Mortem, it's not like you can give it back."

"But he could stop, couldn't he? Stop channeling, leave the Presque Mort. I know they don't allow such a thing, technically, but he *is* a duke." Brigitte looked excitedly to Alienor. "He could get a dispensation from the Priest Exalted—"

"No." Alie shook her head, firm and final. "No."

And that was enough to make her friends stop, make them nod like the word carried far more meaning than a syllable should be able to shoulder.

Brigitte took a sip of tea and grimaced. "I wonder if Bastian has any wine stashed around here."

"It's Bastian, of course he does." Danielle stood, holding out a hand for Brigitte. "Let's look."

"Searching through the Sun Prince's rooms might be a bit too forward," Brigitte said, brow arched.

"Not if we tell him it was for Alie and Eldelore." Danielle gave them an exaggerated wink, to which Alie rolled her eyes.

"True." Brigitte took Danielle's proffered hand. "White or red, ladies?"

"Anything, as long as it's sparkling," Alie responded.

Brigitte bowed deeply, then she and Dani sauntered away, giggling over something.

"I apologize," Alie murmured once the other two women were out of earshot. "I don't know how many different ways I can tell them there's nothing between Gabriel and me."

"Because of what his father did?" Lore couldn't quite make her voice sound neutral. It still made her heart twist, the way everyone here seemed so determined to nail the father's sins to the son's back.

Alie shook her head, then snorted a rueful, un-lady-like laugh. "Well, that's part of it," she said. "But honestly, I think perhaps that could've been salvaged. The thing that made it impossible was when he joined the Presque Mort."

Gabe had said something similar. "Your father has always disliked the Church, then?" Lore tried to sound nonchalant, speaking from behind the rim of her china cup. She thought of what Gabe had told her when she asked the same question—complicated tangles of religion and politics, the belief that it should all be consolidated into one ruling body.

"I think my father dislikes almost everything." Alie picked up a pastry, tore off the corner, and put both pieces down without eating one.

"It sounds like his beliefs have strained your relationship," Lore said. "You and your father's, I mean."

"What relationship?" Alie asked darkly. She picked the pastry on her plate into smaller, still uneaten pieces. "Honestly, we don't do much at home but pass each other in the halls, and barely even that when we're at court. My mother died long ago, and I'm the only child."

"That sounds lonely." Lore knew loneliness. It covered everything she did, a spiderweb that couldn't be seen but was impossible to free yourself from. It clung.

"Yes," Alie murmured. "Yes, it is."

"No pastries left, then?"

The voice was deep, familiar. Lore spun around to face Bastian's easy grin. He braced his hands on the back of her chair, leaning over her, his shadow darkening her teacup.

The tension locking her shoulders leaked out, just a bit. Returning the book to his father's study must've gone smoothly. Part of her had been worried he'd get caught and send all of this crashing down around their ears.

Bastian dropped a quick, reassuring wink, like he could read the pattern of Lore's thoughts on her face. "There's more where this came from," he said to Alie, keeping his eyes on Lore. "If my sweets haven't had enough sweets."

Alie groaned. "Please, not the puns."

"Give me a moment, let me workshop something with *buns*."

"I would truly rather perish." Alie grinned, dark-green eyes sparkling. "Besides, you've treated us enough, I think."

"Never." He spun one of the empty chairs around and sat in it backward, propping his chin on his crossed arms and peering at Alie through the dark fringe of his hair with mock lovesickness. "Is there anything else I could get you to prove my undying affection, Alienor Bellegarde? Would you like the chocolates in swan shapes next time? Bare-chested attendants to feed you grapes?"

Alie lifted a wry eyebrow. "I imagine you'd be the bare-chested attendant?"

"Of course." Sly eyes slid toward Lore, a nearly imperceptible flicker. "Though I could probably get Remaut to come, too."

Her playful smile fell only a fraction, pink staining Alie's cheeks. "Actually," she said, "Bri and Dani just went to pilfer through your rooms in search of wine."

"I truly can't think of a corner where I haven't hidden some, but if you want to be sure they'll find it, go tell them to look behind the mirror next to the bed on the top floor."

"Of course that's where it is." Alie stood, wagging her finger between Bastian and Lore. "Behave yourselves."

"Oh, *never*," Bastian replied. He watched until Alie was out of sight. Then he turned to Lore, all playfulness gone. "It happened again."

The village. Lore nodded. "I know. I ran into Bellegarde on my way here."

He grimaced. "My condolences."

"He was acting like he was looking for something," Lore said. "Or looking for somewhere to *hide* something—he had a piece of paper in his hand. When he left, I looked behind one of the tapestries, and found the paper there, pinned to the back. But it just said *seventy-five*, so I don't know whether it was actually a note or something else."

Bastian's face went pale. "It had to be a note."

"Why?"

"Because that's how many people died in the last village," Bastian said. "Seventy-five exactly."

Chapter Twenty-Nine

It takes more than one cloud to make a storm.
                                        –Kirythean proverb

That..." Lore's head spun, fitting the information together. "If it was the number of bodies—"

"It means Bellegarde is in on it," Bastian finished, low and dark.

"We met August in the hallway." Lore's mind twisted in a thousand different directions, taking pieces and filling them in where they fit. "He didn't look at the tapestry where Bellegarde hid the note, but they were talking when I left. Something about groups being processed, about bindings—"

Danielle's bright voice cut her off. "Bastian! We found the wine. It isn't sparkling, but I suppose it will suffice."

"Well, I didn't know you wanted *sparkling*." The Sun Prince flipped from serious to jovial in an instant. Even the way he held himself changed, rigid tension softening into lazy lines as he settled into his still-backward chair. "That's in one of the second-floor guest rooms."

"This will do." Dani wagged the bottle in the air, a slight frown drawing a line between her brows when she looked at Lore. "Are you all right, Lore? You look pale."

"Just my stomach," she said, picking up her now-cold tea and taking a long sip.

"I'll have some of that sent to your rooms," Brigitte said, nodding to the teacup as she wrapped the cork of the wine bottle in her skirt and tugged. It came off with a pop, and Alie offered quiet applause. Brigitte bowed and poured the wine into the now-empty cups. "It's the only way I get through the cramps."

"Thank you," Lore murmured. Lying to Brigitte felt rotten. Repaying kindness with dishonesty always did.

Bastian stood so the four women could have the chairs—"I will lean fetchingly against the wall instead, and if any of you feel the sudden inspiration to paint me, I won't even charge a modeling fee"—while Alie and the others sipped their wine and idly gossiped.

Lore sipped her wine and thought about how in the myriad hells she was going to find where August, Anton, and now Bellegarde were hiding seventy-five-plus bodies.

"I'm hoping to see Luc again next week," Danielle said. Her eyes darted from her teacup to Lore. "He's on a business trip with his father for a few days."

Luc. The docks. Lore frowned, putting something together. "You said someone was hiring people from the docks to move cargo?"

For the second time, curious eyes turned Lore's way, not quite sure what to make of her question. Lore forced a grin, hoping they thought her strangeness was due to social ineptitude bred in country isolation. "I...ah...have an interest in transportation," she stuttered. "The...the mechanics of it. What are they moving? And how?"

Well done, Lore. Not only will they think you're socially deficient, they'll also think you have the most boring interests in all of human history.

An unreadable look flickered over Dani's face. "Like I said before, I don't know what it is they're moving. Just that they're being paid quite a lot to do it."

"I'm telling you, it has to be poison." Brigitte settled back in her chair, holding the slender stem of her wineglass. "What else would someone pay good coin to haul from one place to another?"

Dani waved a dismissive hand. "Luc said it's far too heavy to be plants. It takes at least three men to push the carts to the drop-off point. That's the only detail he'd give me." She grinned. "It's all very cloak-and-dagger."

Poison could be pretty damn heavy if you had enough of it, but Lore thought Luc was probably right—poison runners were a secretive bunch, not prone to hiring random help off the docks. "Did he say where that drop-off point was?"

Behind Dani, Bastian leaned against the wall with one booted foot propped up and his arms crossed. His face betrayed nothing, but his eyes were sharp and calculating on hers. He knew what she was thinking.

Dani shook her head. "They're all sworn to secrecy on the locations. And apparently whoever made them swear was scary enough that no one will think about crossing them."

Lore glanced up at Bastian, wondering if that meant more to him than it did to her. But the Sun Prince was implacable.

"Interesting," Lore finished weakly. She took another long drink of wine.

Conversation faltered back into more mundane directions for a few minutes more, until finally Brigitte stood and excused herself, saying she had to meet her parents for dinner. Danielle followed, wanting to take a nap before a party she was to attend that night.

"It was lovely to meet you," she said to Lore as she stood. "Be on the lookout for me in your mountain of invitations—I'll host next time, Bastian, unless you want to have us in your rooms every week?"

"Hosting a group of beautiful women is really no hardship," Bastian said, kissing Dani's proffered hand. "Invite a wider selection of beautiful people, next time, and I'll truly be in paradise."

Brigitte smiled and rolled her eyes. "I'll send the tea," she assured Lore as she followed Danielle out of the room.

"I'll be off, too." Alie rose from the table. She smiled at Lore. "Thank you for coming, truly. I know being in the Citadel can be overwhelming, but it's easier with friends in your corner." She arched a brow at Bastian. "Am I safe to leave her in your care, or will you require a chaperone?"

"I probably always require a chaperone, but never fear." Bastian tugged Lore up by the hand and then tucked her fingers into his elbow. "I'll take Lady Remaut back to her rooms, and I'm sure her pet Presque Mort is there, so we'll have all the chaperoning we need."

Alie colored a bit at the mention of Gabe, but Bastian didn't comment on it. The three of them drifted out of the prince's palatial apartments and down the stairs. Alie gave Lore's hand a squeeze before turning down the hallway below Bastian's, apparently toward her own rooms.

Lore waited a couple more flights before speaking, pitching her voice low. "I think the people being hired at the docks are moving the bodies."

"Obviously." A courtier came up the stairs; Lore tensed, but Bastian didn't, giving them a lazy smile and waiting for them to disappear before speaking again. "So we need to go down there again. Preferably tonight."

"Tonight? But it was only two weeks ago that—"

"While I'm touched by your concern, I will be just fine." He looked at her, then, and his smile was so warm she could almost forgive the chill it left in his eyes. "I think I scared the ruffians who found us out last time enough to keep them quiet."

"Whoever is hiring the dockworkers apparently scares them

enough to keep quiet, too." She didn't have to draw the parallel. Whoever was hiring had to be someone with considerable power, if they could intimidate a whole crew of cargo haulers into silence.

Maybe someone as powerful as another Arceneaux.

Bastian's jaw tightened, highlighting the dark stubble on his chin. "I've considered that," he murmured.

Hiding the bodies didn't necessarily mean that August had something to do with the deaths. But hiding the bodies coupled with his insistence on implicating Kirythea—implicating Bastian, and thus clearing the way to choose another heir—didn't paint a pretty picture.

Especially now that they knew August was ill. That he was desperately searching for a way to cheat death, whether through poison or through manipulating Spiritum.

And how did Anton fit into it? Clearly, he was looking for ways August could heal himself with Spiritum, too. And he and August had worked together closely to bring her here; they both had to be involved in tampering with the corpses. But did that mean they were complicit in killing the villages, or just being dishonest with what happened afterward?

Either way, they couldn't trust Anton any more than they could trust August.

Though she knew Gabe would think differently.

Bastian kept quiet as he led her through the front hall, past the great doors that led out of the Citadel, into the shabbier corridors of the southeast turret and up to her and Gabe's rooms. Lore was glad of it. They were both deep in thought, and the silence was comfortable. Probably more so than it should've been.

"Midnight," Bastian said as they approached the door, rapping smartly on the wood. "Same place as last time. Wear something inconspicuous."

The door burst open. Gabe looked rumpled, like he'd been trying to catch up on sleep. The hours they'd spent in the library had grown longer and longer as the week wore on, and neither of them counted as well rested.

"Gabriel!" Bastian grinned, putting his hands on Lore's shoulders to thrust her forward. "See you this evening. Lore will tell you everything."

Then he was gone, leaving the two of them staring at each other.

The silence grew too heavy to hold without slipping. "Are you all right?" Lore asked quietly.

Gabe rubbed at his eye patch, turned away from her. His shirt had rucked up in sleep, and he did his best to straighten it, though it was hopelessly creased. "Just tired. The last night I remember sleeping well was when you woke up after the Mortem leak."

As soon as it left his mouth, Gabe froze, and it took Lore a moment to realize why.

The night she woke up, she'd come in here. Slept next to Gabe on the floor. So cold, and seeking warmth, something to cling to.

They'd never talked about it. They'd let it fade into the chaos of everything else, the edges rubbed away until they didn't catch their thoughts. But now Gabe had brought it forward, pulled it into the light again.

They could talk about it now. Or they could continue pretending it never happened.

Gabe opened his mouth, and she couldn't tell which path he was going to take. Which one she wanted him to.

So she didn't let him speak. "Someone is hiring people from the docks to move cargo," she said, brushing past him and into the room. "We're going down there tonight to see if we can find out what the cargo is, and who's doing the hiring."

"*We?*" Gabe turned with her, closing the door as he did. The latch caught with a sharp, final sound. "So Bastian is coming, then."

"Yes, Gabe, Bastian is coming."

"I don't think that's wise."

"Not this again." Lore rubbed at her eyes. The lack of sleep was catching up with her, making her head heavy and her temper short. "Why do you hate him so much?"

Gabe was silent for so long, Lore thought he might ignore the question entirely. He stood by the door, still, head craned to watch the dying fire. "I don't hate him," he finally murmured.

Numerous acid-tongued retorts went through her head, but Lore remained silent. She knew that whatever lay between the Presque Mort and the Sun Prince, it wasn't as simple as hatred. Lore sank onto the couch and waited for Gabe to grasp the thread of his thoughts.

"Bastian is careless," Gabe said. "He always has been, ever since we were children. Careless with his power. Careless with his authority." He paused, jaw working beneath gingery stubble. "Careless with people."

There was enough ice in that last statement to make her eyes find her clasped hands, even though Gabriel still wasn't looking at her.

A minute, hanging. Then Gabe sighed. "I wasn't supposed to be in Balgia that day. I was supposed to be here."

That day. The day his father turned the duchy over to Jax and the Kirythean Empire. The day his father died, and Jax pulled out Gabriel's eye.

"Bastian and I fought. It was over something stupid—I think he cheated at cards. But I was incensed, the way only a ten-year-old child can be. We fought, and I beat the shit out of him." A wry smile twisted his mouth. "It wasn't much worse than what we usually did to each other, but for whatever reason, that was the only time he went to his father about it. Ivanna had just died the year before. I think Bastian had exhausted every other way of trying to make August care about him. This was a last resort." Gabe shrugged. "Didn't work for getting August's attention, but it got me banished back to Balgia for the rest of the season, sent there with all the attendants who were supposed to be my surrogate parents. The week after I arrived, my father surrendered to Jax." His hand rose, rubbed at his eye patch. "My presence wasn't enough to change his plans."

Lore knotted her hands in her skirt. "Gabe...I'm..."

But he cut her off, like he was afraid of hearing anything that might be pity. "I'm not stupid enough to think what happened to me is Bastian's fault. We were children. But I'll admit that I'm jealous." He huffed a rueful laugh. "I'm jealous that his actions never seem to have consequences, when I'm carrying the consequences of an entire family. I'm jealous that it would take a miracle for him to be left all alone and with nothing, when everything was taken from me in an instant."

She'd seen it, all the things he listed, though she'd classify it differently. Bastian's carelessness was artificial, a façade built to keep anyone from knowing just how *much* he cared. She still remembered the lightning-quick way he'd changed that night in the alley, how the lazy air of entitlement had fallen away like a discarded cloak. So many layers, so much crafted, careful nonchalance. Bastian was drowning in it, but he didn't fool her, though the weak points she'd seen were only hairline cracks in the armor he'd forged over years.

It reminded her of herself. How she'd been Night-Sister-Lore and then poison-runner-Lore and now spy-Lore, each a persona she'd eased into, a different shell to wear. When she thought about what might be left when all that artifice was stripped away, she came up blank. Like all the things that made her were window dressings on an empty house.

And though Bastian had never had to run, had been born into his cage instead of molting into different ones over and over, she thought he'd feel the same. That all his careful personas might hide an emptiness the same shape as hers.

He'd weathered Gabe's anger with what she'd thought was grace, let the other man's barely leashed rage roll off his back. But maybe it wasn't grace. Maybe Bastian held this memory just as closely as Gabe did, and maybe he felt like he deserved that anger.

Lore didn't know how to articulate any of that, though. Not in a way Gabriel would understand. Where Bastian struggled against his cage, Gabe clung to his own, wanting the walls to shape him, shoving himself inside to make boundaries he knew. He'd built himself into something he thought the world wanted, and though it chafed at him, Lore still envied it, just a bit. There was a reassurance in knowing exactly how you were going to be let down.

Gabe mistook her silence for condemnation. "I know it isn't fair of me," he said, almost accusingly, like he could turn the finger he imagined she pointed. "I blamed him, before. I don't now, at least not in the same way. But that jealousy is still there."

"I understand," Lore said. And she did.

That was all. They sat in silence, the only sound the hiss of the fire in the grate.

Finally, Gabe sighed, itching at his eye patch, straightening his shoulders. "Right," he said decisively. "What harebrained plan are we following now?"

🦋

No moon, weak stars, and the gardens were dark as pitch. Lore crept along behind Gabriel, keeping close enough to his back that she felt the heat of him through his shirt. It was distracting, to say the least.

"I don't like this," he said, for the third time in ten minutes. Probably the fifteenth time overall. He'd started the litany when she told him the plan, there in that lull of vulnerability after talking about Bastian, and had kept it up intermittently since. If Lore hadn't been so insistent that the two of them at least try to get some sleep before night fell, it would probably be the thirtieth time she'd heard the sentiment.

"Noted," she muttered at his back. "Again."

He huffed, the breath of it visible in the cool air. "It's not safe. This could have nothing to do with the villages; we might be inserting ourselves into some poison runner feud for no reason."

"We don't know that, though, and this is the only lead we have." Lore glared at his back. "Again."

No retort but a low growl. They clattered over the cobblestones of the garden in their boots, slipped between the trees of the manicured forest. When they exited the woods, Bastian was alone at the culvert. Dressed dark, like they were, leaning against the stone and having a smoke, hair tied back and booted foot on the wall. He butted out the cigarette before tossing it into the culvert—it still hadn't rained, and the grass was dry; the last thing they needed was to start a fire—and pushed off when they approached, beckoning them into the shadows. He didn't speak until they were ensconced in stone walls and the roar of dirty water.

Bastian passed out the same plain black masks they'd worn before, sloshing through the storm drain as he tied his own over his eyes. "The primary plan is to lie low. We're there to spectate. See if we can spot someone talking to people, recruiting. But if all else fails, we start asking around, like we're looking to get hired."

"What about those men who saw us a few nights ago?" Lore asked. "If they spilled about who you are, and you start acting like you want work moving mysterious cargo, whoever is doing the hiring will know immediately that they're caught."

"That's why I'm not asking." Bastian glanced over his shoulder. "You are."

Next to her, Gabe stiffened.

"I can't," Lore stuttered, steps faltering until she stood still in the shallow rush. "People there might know me—"

"Which works out in our favor." Bastian continued forward, waving a hand as if her protestations were just so much noise. "If they ask why you're looking for a new job, you can say something went south with the team you were running for. You switched jobs quite a lot, didn't you? That's how a spy does their spying."

Lore pressed her lips together and didn't protest further.

They splashed through to the end of the tunnel, to the slick stone platform jutting from the wall and the crossbars of the culvert, replaced since they last used this route. Bastian climbed up and loosened the screws, then offered a hand to Lore.

She reached for him, and at the moment his fingers closed around her arms, Gabe's hands gripped her waist. The two of them hauled her over, and being caught between their bodies made heat flame across her cheekbones.

Lore scrambled through the open culvert and onto the street beyond, not turning around as she listened to Gabe and Bastian make their way out behind her. Bastian grunted; Gabe made a sound like a swallowed snort. When they walked into her field of vision, Bastian was shaking out his fingers like they'd been stepped on.

They walked in silence down the nearly deserted street, the orange glow of the harbor lights and the distant sounds of shouting heralding when they grew close to the boxing ring. "Eyes peeled," Bastian said, then they were in the crowd.

It was thicker tonight than it had been before, far more bodies pressed together around the hay bales, and they all seemed more intent on getting closer. The night Bastian fought Michal, the boxing ring had seemed more like a convenient meeting place than a draw in and of itself, with spectators lurking on the fringes in groups, talking and laughing and barely paying attention. Not so tonight. Tonight every eye was fixed on the fighters, and the stares were intense.

When the crowd parted, Lore saw why.

Two femme-appearing figures fought viciously in the center of the hay ring, hair braided back and breasts tightly bound. Blood dyed one's pale hair nearly pink, and the other wiped at a split lip with the back of one linen-wrapped hand.

"Lightweight Night!" bellowed a man who saw her watching, clearly on the fast dip toward drunk. "Fancy a spar? You've a bit too much curve to be a lightweight, but we could find someone about the same size to make it a fair match."

"I'm fine, thank you." Lore backed up until she hit another warm form—Bastian. She could recognize the hand that came to rest on her shoulder.

The drunk man shrugged and turned back to the ring. The blond fighter launched at the bruised one, fist curving through the air to connect with a kidney. The other fighter fell to the hay-covered cobblestones.

Lore whirled on Bastian. "Did you know it was *Lightweight Night?*"

"Truthfully, I didn't know such a thing existed." Bastian grinned beneath his mask, craning his neck to see over the crowd. "How marvelous."

She cursed under her breath and turned away from the ring to scan the masses of people who'd gathered to watch. It was harder to get a feel for the crowd when there were so many of them, but most were focused enough on the match that it should be easy to spot someone slipping off for a whispered conversation. Gabe slumped a few feet away from her and Bastian, facing the fight, but with his one blue eye scanning back and forth through his mask.

The boxer with the bruised lip feinted to the side. The blond one stumbled, a punch overthrown.

"There," Bastian said.

He didn't point, but angled his chin toward the shadows on the far edge of the ring, a place between streetlights where the dark was deepest. Three figures huddled, angled away from the match. The one whose face Lore could see looked like he was listening intently to whatever was being said. The figure speaking had their back turned.

Bastian and Gabe exchanged a look. Gabe nodded, then started moving toward the group, pushing through the crowd like a shark through a school of fish.

"Come on." Bastian took Lore's arm and tugged her after him. "I don't think our pet monk will need any backup, but we should stick close, just in case."

A roar went up from the ring. When Lore looked back, the blond boxer was on the ground.

The group in the shadows broke apart before Gabe could reach them, the figure who'd been speaking fading into the crowd without Lore getting a good look at them.

Gabe approached one of the men who'd been listening, struck up a casual conversation. Bastian and Lore stopped a few feet away; from what she could hear, it sounded like Gabe was talking about sailing weather.

"Bleeding God," she muttered, and Bastian snorted.

A few more inane words about northwesterly winds, and Gabe nodded in the direction of the now-disappeared speaker. "You all wouldn't know about any job opportunities opening up around here, would you? I'm looking to make some extra coin." A pause. "Something that could be done in one night would be ideal."

"Laying it on a bit thick," Bastian whispered. Lore dug her elbow into his ribs.

The man Gabe spoke to—very small and slight, if it weren't for the thick stubble on his jaw, Lore would think his voice still hadn't cracked—glanced at his companion, then rubbed at his neck. A constellation of bruises bloomed there, deep purple and new. "I might," he said slowly. "But the details aren't mine to share."

Gabe's jaw tightened, and the slight man stepped back, eyes

widening in brief alarm. Lore didn't blame him. Gabe didn't look like the kind of person you'd want to anger.

"How could one find someone willing to impart details?" Gabe asked.

The man's companion—larger than he, but still young looking—let out a harsh laugh. "Lose," he said, cutting a hand toward the ring.

Lore looked back. The blond fighter was up again, but blood trickled steadily from a cut across her forehead, dripping into her eyes.

"Lose?" Gabe's confusion drew his brows together, wrinkled the black domino mask.

"Lose a fight," the slight man mumbled, rubbing at his fresh bruises again. "They only approach people who lose a fight."

"Why?"

"Gods damn me if I know," he replied snappishly. "I guess because you have to buy in to fight a match, and those of us who just lost money are more likely not to ask questions."

Another roar from the crowd. The blond fighter was down, this time for good. A huge man with a tangled black beard stepped over the hay bales, laughing, and lifted the other fighter's arms over her head. Her eye was blackened, her smile viciously triumphant.

Gabe looked back at Lore and Bastian, then sighed. "Who do I talk to about getting in the ring?"

"You can't." The bruised man looked Gabe up and down, then shook his head. "Not tonight, anyway. It's Lightweight Night."

Three eyes turned to Lore—Gabe's one, Bastian's two, a question in them all.

"Fuck," Lore muttered.

CHAPTER THIRTY

The past will always have its last word.

—Eroccan proverb

Ten minutes and a handful of Bastian's gold later, Lore, the Presque Mort, and the Sun Prince stood right at the outside edge of the hay-bale ring and waited for her opponent to arrive.

"I know the point is to lose," Bastian said, wrapping white linen around her knuckles. "But do at least try to give them a show. I doubt anyone will approach you about cargo running if you go down at the first punch."

"I'll do my best." She was too nervous for wit.

Next to her, Gabe stood glowering, jaw set tight enough to bristle his reddish beard stubble. "I don't like this."

"I'm not exactly thrilled myself." Lore bounced on her knees, nervous energy imploring her to move. "Shockingly, I'm not very good at fistfights."

Bastian stopped wrapping and arched a brow. "You were a poison runner, yet you weren't good at fistfights? What *were* you good at?"

She bared her teeth. "Running."

"Brawling doesn't take much skill," Gabe said. "Survival instinct takes over. And you have that in spades."

"Debatable," Bastian muttered. Gabe and Lore both pretended not to hear him.

A moment, then Gabe sighed, as if finally resigning himself to what was about to happen. "Aim for the kneecaps."

"Ah, yes." Bastian tied off the linen on her hands. "The kneecaps are the eyes of the legs."

They both stared at him. Then Gabe shrugged. "That's actually pretty good advice."

"Excellent help, the both of you." Lore worked her fingers back and forth, fighting down the numbing anxiety tingling along her spine.

On the other side of the ring, the crowd parted. A girl with coppery hair in long braids and an expression like she'd smelled spoiled milk hopped over the hay bales and stood on the other side, hip cocked, arms crossed. She came in an inch or two shorter than Lore, but had a similar rounded, muscular frame.

"Well, that's terrible form," Bastian muttered. "Her knuckles aren't even wrapped."

"I don't think she needs them." Lore eyed the other girl's hands—a mess of bruises and swollen joints, the signs of a seasoned fighter.

She clenched her own into tight fists. Her pulse beat through them, as if they were external hearts.

The bearded referee stepped into the center of the ring. "Last call for bets!"

"If they find out I lost on purpose, we'll be chased out of the city with pitchforks," Lore said.

"Then you'd better make it look like you didn't lose on purpose," Gabe replied.

At the crook of the bearded man's finger, Lore stepped forward, Gabe and Bastian's last words of tentative encouragement drowned out by the rush of blood in her ears. Her opponent approached, giving Lore an up-and-down glance that finished in a sneer.

It made Lore very irritated that she had to lose.

"Bets are in," the referee called. "Let's see which one of you can send the other to your own personal hell first, ladies!"

Hoots and catcalls echoed through the harbor street. Lore paused, waiting for the official sign they were supposed to start.

It came with a fist in her gut.

The red-haired girl swept out her foot while Lore was still hunched over her aching stomach, but Lore saw it coming and jumped out of the way. Her opponent, disturbingly unperturbed, smacked an open palm across Lore's ear with her opposite hand, and Lore stumbled to her knees, ears ringing.

"At least get one hit in!" Bastian's voice, yelling from the sidelines.

"I'm trying," Lore gritted out. She looked up—the other girl stalked slowly across the ring, a feral smile on her face, the cheers of the crowd encouraging her to take her time with an obviously weaker opponent. Lore heaved in deep breaths as she drew closer, willing her stomach to expand, pushing the pain in her head to the edges. She shifted her aching body—ass on the ground, legs bent before her, hands braced behind. A halfhearted struggle made it look like she was trying to get up and failing, which only sharpened the redhead's smile.

The girl finally came close enough to touch, though Lore didn't lash out, not yet. She cocked her head and looked down at Lore the way one might look at a petulant child. "I would offer you the chance to yield, but I need the practice." Her fist closed, pulled back.

Lore's seated position put her at eye level with the other girl's stomach. Perfect.

Leg rising, leaning back on her hands, a quick look to make

sure she aimed correctly, all in the span of a second. Lore kicked at the other girl's kneecap, and it sent her sprawling backward with a hoarse cry of pain.

"The eyes of the legs," Lore muttered, and heaved herself up from the ground.

The crowd cheered, their loyalties changeable as the weather. Bastian whooped, but Gabe looked worried. He wanted her to yield, she could see it in his eyes, but she didn't think her opponent would give her the opportunity, especially not now.

Losing big it was, then. Lore winced preemptively.

"You'll pay for that." The other girl shook her leg out, barely limping, though agony shone in the rictus of her mouth as she ran forward.

"Yes, I suppose I will," Lore sighed.

"Break it up!"

The shouts came from the streets back toward the city, accompanied by the sounds of boots on cobblestones. The cheers of the crowd turned to shouts of surprise.

"Bloodcoats! Clear out!"

The hay ring was abandoned; spectators and waiting fighters alike turned tail and hauled ass, disappearing into alleyways as a group of bloodcoats surged into the street, bayonets catching the orange glow of the streetlights. It made them look like spears of flame.

The girl Lore had been fighting cursed, turning to run on her sore leg. She didn't give Lore a second glance. Revenge came long down the list of priorities when escaping the Burnt Isles was number one.

A hand on her arm, steering her forward. Gabe. "Let's go. This was a dead end."

They ran with the crowd up the streets, the sounds of capture and occasional gunfire spurring them on from behind, until Bastian darted out of an alley's narrow mouth. "Over here!"

Gabe didn't break his stride as he turned, steering them both into the relative safety of the dark. Lore leaned against the wall, arms crossed over her stomach. It still hurt from getting punched, and the impromptu run hadn't helped.

"We need to go back to the Citadel before this gets out of hand." Bastian stood right inside the lip of the alley, shadow cutting across his face as he peered out into the street. A group of bloodcoats ran by, and he pressed against the wall, disappearing into dark. "We'll come back tomorrow—"

"Absolutely not." Gabriel loomed in the center of the dank alleyway, voice stony, expression stonier. "This was a stupid plan from the start."

Bastian looked back over his shoulder, the streetlights catching the gleam of his teeth. Lore recalled the last time she was in an alley with the Sun Prince, how he'd changed so quickly from layabout royal to something sharp-edged and angry.

"Do you have a better plan?" he asked, his voice a match for Gabriel's blade-tones.

"There has to be one," Gabe replied. "We can talk to—"

"That's not going to work," Lore said softly. "You know it's not, Gabe. The only way we can find out who's doing the hiring is to find them ourselves." She gestured to the mouth of the alley. "A raid happening tonight is a sign. We're on the right track, and someone knew we were coming."

Gabe turned on her, one blue eye blazing through his domino mask. "You don't know how dangerous it is to keep doing this. To keep coming here—"

"I'm *from* here." She managed to straighten, despite the pain in her middle, and glare up at him. "Has it occurred to you that you might be taking your role as protector a bit too far?"

She hadn't planned to say it, didn't know what shape her anger and fear and irritation would take until the words were forged and thrown. All three of them froze, staring, knowing that this was a door opening onto something much bigger than they had time to deal with right now.

Gabe took a step forward, blue eye glittering. "Would you rather I throw you to the wolves over and over to further my own plans?" He didn't look at Bastian, but he didn't have to. The accusation was an arrow, and its target was obvious.

Bastian's gaze weighed heavy on Lore's shoulders. He knew what she was, where she'd come from, that she could survive a few wolves. He knew that if she were made of glass, she'd have shattered long ago.

Gabe didn't know all those details like Bastian did.

Maybe it was time to fix that.

Lore took a deep breath. "Gabe, there's something—"

But she was interrupted by a shape flying from the shadows and knocking her backward.

Her already-aching stomach felt like it was catching fire as her skull cracked against the dirty wall. Through the high-pitched ring in her ears, she heard Gabe shout, heard the sound of fists meeting flesh, a snarl that could only be Bastian.

The blow to the head made her vision blurry, but Lore pried her eyes open.

"You didn't learn your lesson, huh?" There was something familiar about the voice; she'd heard it before. But there was an almost desiccated quality to it, now, as if the throat she'd heard it from the first time had been scoured out. "Doesn't matter you're a prince. Doesn't matter you're a lady. I need more money, and I know you fuckers have it."

Lore's vision stopped swimming gradually, making sense of the figure blocking the gas lamp's light. He looked far worse than he had before—his large frame sagged, like he lacked the strength to hold it up, and lines of gray rock crisscrossed where his veins should be—but she recognized him. Milo, the bruiser who'd tried to shake Bastian down for more than his bet the last time they'd come to the ring.

Gabe was crumpled against the dirty brick, conscious but dazed, dark purple spreading over his temple. The handle of Bastian's dagger stuck out of Milo's shoulder, but the man didn't seem to feel it at all. His veins were so full of stone, it was a miracle the blade struck through his skin at all. The man had dosed himself halfway to a revenant.

Bastian slumped in the center of the alley, arms crossed over his middle. Milo had landed a knife-blow, too. Crimson seeped through Bastian's shirt, night-black in the dim light, pattering softly to the trash-strewn ground.

Milo turned the bloody knife in his hand. "Don't care who you are," he murmured in that stony, graveled voice. An unsound smile lifted his lips, slowly, his eyes unfocused and glassy with a euphoric poison high. "This time, you die."

Time slowed. Something crystallized in Lore's mind, fully formed, instinct she knew how to follow.

"Move," she said to Bastian, her voice somehow strong despite her aching stomach and ringing head.

Whatever deep knowledge she followed, it seemed he knew it, too. Bastian pressed his hand harder against his middle and stumbled down the alley in the opposite direction, as far away from Lore and Milo as he could get, much faster than he should be able to run with a stomach wound.

Milo moved to follow, but Lore was faster. With Bastian farther away, Mortem was simple to call. It came easily, flowing from the stone walls, the trash piled in the corners, the cold steel of the dagger that was even now slicing through the air toward her.

It was stronger than it ever had been, a wave that should've overwhelmed her senses. But Lore took the power, and took it with ease.

Hands stretching out, vision graying as she held her breath and dropped into the place where death was visible, death was a tool. Lore channeled Mortem through her body, veins blackening and eyes going opaque, heart going still in her chest for one beat.

Almost without thinking, she took all that death and pushed it out toward Milo.

Weaving death felt like taking in air, like an intrinsic part of her that had just been waiting to bloom. Before, she'd done this without thinking, her born ability making such a careful thing easy. But now, she paid attention and reveled in just what she could do.

Lore spun the Mortem like thread, knitting it around the man like a shroud. Like the roses in the garden, merely cased in stone, merely frozen. Just enough for stasis, just enough to stop him, because she didn't have any other choice.

See how easily you take to it, daughter of the dark?

The voice was faint, but it was enough to break Lore's concentration. She shook her head and opened her eyes.

Milo was stone. The tip of the knife glinted mere inches from her throat. She expected his face to be frozen in a snarl, but instead, the expression he wore was open-mouthed terror.

"You..." Gabe gaped, his daze shaken off, hands opening and closing on empty air as he pushed himself up from the ground. "You shouldn't have..."

"What else would you propose she have done, Remaut?" Bastian, striding up from the end of the alley. His shirt was bloodstained, but he didn't clutch at it anymore, and he didn't walk like a wounded man. "Waltz with him?"

Gabe didn't respond. He leaned against the wall and stared at the statue Lore had made of a living, breathing human being.

Milo. He'd been a person, with a name and a job, even if that job was extorting bets on illegal boxing matches. A person she'd turned to stone. Was he still aware, somewhere in all that? Did it hurt?

She shook her head. She didn't want to know.

Lore didn't look at Gabe. She knew his expression now would

be so much worse than it had been the day of the Mortem leak, and she couldn't take it, couldn't face it, not when there was so much else to do.

"How's your gut?" she asked Bastian, her voice thin and shaking.

He glanced down like he'd forgotten, frowned at his bloody shirt. "Fine," he said. "Must've just been a scratch."

It'd been more than that. At least, Lore thought it had been. But when he raised his shirt, the skin was unblemished, marred only by a scrim of dried blood.

A hand on her shoulder—Bastian, gently moving her away from the outstretched knife in Milo's stone hand. His fingers slid to the back of her neck, into her hair; his thumb brushed her cheek, then dropped, and he stepped away.

"Right," he said, with a decisive nod. "Well. We can't leave him here, and I assume you aren't up to changing him back just yet?"

"If we can." Gabe's voice was quiet, hoarse. "If we can change him back."

"Either way, we'll have to move him." A rickety cart slouched against the wall on the other end of the alley; Bastian went and tugged on one of the handles. The cart moved, though the squeaking was awful. "But to *where*, I have no idea."

"I do," Lore said. Her lips felt numb. "I know where we can take him."

❦

There was a moment of slight panic as Bastian and Gabe conferred on how to tip the stone man over into the cart—and whether the cart could even hold the weight, decrepit as it was; Milo wasn't a small man even when he was flesh—but in the end, the Mortem-made statue was easier to move than it looked.

Gabe and Bastian heaved together on a count of three, and the man fell into the cart, the bottom of it cushioned with trash that

Lore gathered from the alleyway. Bastian stood back, eyes wide. "That was much easier than I anticipated."

"It's not solid stone," Gabe said. Then, with a shake of his head, "*He* isn't, I mean."

Not solid stone, just a living person knit into a shroud of death. Lore felt sick. Gabe didn't look at her.

Gabe covered the stone figure with more trash, then he and Bastian manned the cart while Lore crept to the mouth of the alley, looking both ways. "Clear," she murmured, "but we have to move fast."

"Yes, I imagine this would be difficult to explain away." Bastian hauled the front of the cart up behind her. Gabe stayed at the back, keeping it steady. She wondered if he'd chosen that position because it was farthest away from her.

Slowly, Lore moved out of the alley, Bastian and Gabe and their uncanny cargo following. She remembered the route, rounding the turns and taking the shortcuts without any conscious thought needed. For ten years, Val's crew had worked out of the same warehouse, and she remembered how to get there even though part of her wished she could forget.

She hadn't wanted to get them involved. Even today, when it'd become clear that answers might be found nearer to her poison-running past than her falsely noble present, Lore hadn't wanted to go to Val and Mari, had wanted to keep them as far from all this as possible. Both to keep them safe, and because the idea of seeing them pried at a very precise wound in her heart, like pushing on a bruise.

But there was really no choice now.

Fog hung low over the street, thickening the closer they drew to the harbor. The full moon reflected on the black water, visible in the distance as a glimmering expanse not unlike the sky above it.

Looking at the moon made her think of the upcoming eclipse, the ball on her twenty-fourth birthday.

The warehouse was a long, dark block of a building, with virtually nothing to distinguish it from the other long, dark blocks of buildings around it, and intentionally left to look abandoned. The roof sagged in the middle. The gutters were full of dried gull shit. Water marks bloomed over the rough wooden paneling of the outer walls.

Most of the other buildings were actually empty, a haven for revenants looking for someplace to sleep off their latest fix, or for a quiet place to finally die after ossifying themselves into too-long lives. Val never kicked anyone out of the empty warehouses, but she'd send in people to look for bodies occasionally. Especially in the warmer months, when the little flesh they had left started to stink. They burned the corpses they found, didn't bother trying to figure out next of kin to contact. If someone was crawling down to die in the empty warehouses by the harbor, they didn't have anyone looking for them, and probably didn't care much about reaching the Shining Realm. Not many people out here did.

"Where, exactly, are we going?" Bastian barely sounded out of breath. When she looked back at him, the muscles of his shoulders were tense against the blood-stiff fabric of his shirt. It only drew attention to his corded arms, the well-formed plane of his chest.

She looked away. "Poison runner den." No sense dithering over it.

"Oh, excellent," Bastian said. "I've never been to one."

Behind him, Gabe was still silent.

The streets around the warehouse were empty, which was typical. Val made her crew stagger times they were seen near the headquarters so as not to draw attention. It must just be force of habit now. Val had her papers, she was officially sanctioned by Church and Crown. Turning Lore over to Anton had bought her a veil of legitimacy.

Streetlights were far behind them, now, and the only illumination was the round moon, the scattering of stars. It made the building loom like an executioner's block.

Lore paused before the door, nerves writhing around her middle. But she had a mostly stone man to hide until she figured out how to change him back, and this was the only place she could think to do it.

So she knocked. A familiar pattern, ingrained in her since she was thirteen. Two sharp raps, then two more with a four-second pause between them, and a final drag of her knuckles.

It opened immediately. "Gods dead and dying, what took—" Mari's rich alto voice faltered as her willowy form filled the door. Her eyes widened. "Lore?"

Her lip wobbled, despite herself. "Hi, Mari."

CHAPTER THIRTY-ONE

The bonds of family are sacred, but they are not
always bound in blood.

—Myroshan proverb

The inside of the warehouse completely belied the shabbiness of the outside. The floors were well swept, the ceilings high and built up with multiple layers of wood and tin to keep the deliberate disrepair of the roof from affecting the interior. Cots lined the walls, some made and some not—most of the crew didn't live here, and Val and Mari had a small apartment above their office, but they kept beds just in case someone needed a place to stay. To the right, the open office door spilled golden light into the dim, cast from a gas lamp at the edge of the desk. The lamp was Mari's prized possession. It'd been a gift from Val for their anniversary, when Mari couldn't stand to do their accounting by candlelight anymore.

A few boxes were stacked in the shadows at the back of the space, proof that a drop would happen in the next few days. Val didn't keep poison here unless she had to.

Mari stood in front of the office door, arms crossed, staring at

Gabe and Bastian and the cart behind them with an unreadable expression as Lore rattled off their story. Lore kept to the truth, mostly, though she didn't tell Mari why they were at the docks in the first place. She wanted to, though. Seeing one of her mothers had made the pain of Val's betrayal fall away; Lore felt like a child again, eager to spill everything to one of her surrogate parents and let them fix it.

She also kept Gabe and Bastian's identities out of the story. Telling Mari that the Sun Prince of Auverraine and one of the Presque Mort were in her warehouse was sure to fly like a dead bird.

When Lore finally dropped into silence, Mari nodded slowly, mulling the story over with her lips pressed to a thin line. "So," she said, dark eyes wary, "you want us to keep a dead person—"

"Not dead." It was the first time Gabe had spoken since the alley, and it startled Lore nearly as much as it did Mari. Next to him, Bastian stayed quiet, arms crossed and eyes thoughtful. They both still wore their masks, though Lore had taken hers off, and it had the disconcerting effect of making them look nearly like the same person from the corner of her eye.

"A *not dead* person," Mari conceded, "in our warehouse until you can figure out how to fix them."

"It won't be long," Lore said. Her voice had the same almost wheedling edge it'd carried when she was a child, begging for something she wanted. "In fact, I'm going to try in just a minute or two."

She felt Gabe's gaze snap to the back of her neck, raising gooseflesh. Lore bristled. Leaving Milo in this state was bad, trying to fix him was bad—she wasn't going to please Gabe, no matter what she did, and she wished she didn't care.

"We just needed a place to bring him," she finished quietly. "We couldn't leave him in the alley."

"No, I suppose you couldn't." Mari sighed, reaching up to

tighten the knot holding her silky scarf in place over her the twisted lengths of her hair, making the sea-glass beads at the ends clink. They must've caught her right before she went to bed. "Fine. He can stay."

"Hopefully not for long." Lore turned and looked at the stone man in the cart. The trash they'd piled on top of him had shifted, uncovering Milo's terror-stricken face.

Mari glanced at the cart. She arched a brow at Lore.

"Give me just a second, and I'll fix him," Lore said. "I just needed...I just needed privacy."

Privacy, and a place she felt comfortable. Lore hadn't realized just how tightly she'd held herself until the tension bled out, a drop at a time. Despite everything, this warehouse still felt like home, and *gods* she missed it. Being here filled a hollow in her chest she wasn't aware of carving out.

"You can have it." Mari glanced toward the door. "Val should be here soon."

The hollow emptied again. Lore gnawed on her lip. "Will that be a problem?"

"I don't think so, to be honest." Mari looked her in the eye, something softening in her face. Sadness and resignation shaped her mouth. "She was between a rock and a hard place, Lore. The Priest Exalted didn't give her any choice. It was you, or the whole crew swung."

Behind her, Gabe stiffened.

"Swung?" she repeated quietly. Val said it'd been a choice between her or the crew, but Lore thought that meant prison time, fines, maybe the Burnt Isles...

"Death for us all," Mari whispered. She chewed the corner of her lip. "He wanted you, mouse. Badly."

She thought of that first day after Horse, when Anton told her the Church had been watching since she was thirteen, since she first raised Cedric from the dead. Watching, keeping tabs, letting her live a life she thought was free until the rope finally pulled taut.

They'd waited until she got older. Until her power over Mortem had matured, grown. Because it had—the stone man in the cart was proof. She wouldn't have been capable of something like this weeks ago, as if her time in the Citadel had somehow strengthened her ability.

Her time in the Citadel, and the slow march toward her twenty-fourth birthday.

Instinctually, her eyes darted to Bastian, seeking some kind of strength from the Sun Prince. She didn't realize Gabe had stepped away, far enough into the warehouse to be out of earshot, until he crossed behind Bastian, pacing like a caged animal. The Presque Mort looked back once, his gaze cutting between her and the other man, before turning away again.

A knock at the door. The same pattern Lore had used. Mari went to open it.

Val stood on the other side.

"Sorry, love, I was..." Val trailed off, mouth staying open and no words coming out, eyes round as she stared at Lore.

"Mouse," she said, and then she rushed forward.

Lore didn't know what to expect. By the wall, Bastian looked ready for a fight—shoulders loose, fists curled.

But Val threw her arms around Lore and hugged her tight.

Of the hugs they'd shared, it was the longest. Though there'd only been three before this, all carefully cataloged in Lore's mind, so maybe that wasn't a fair metric—Mari was the softer one, the mother more likely to give comfort. Still, after the initial moment of being frozen in shock, Lore returned the embrace just as tightly, her anger forgotten in the familiar scent of Val's hair, the familiar rasp of her shirt against her cheek.

"Oh, mouse." Val's voice was choked and hoarse. "I'm so glad you're all right."

Lore didn't respond. She tucked her chin, burying her face in Val's shoulder, and hoped the older woman didn't feel the warm salt seeping through her work shirt.

Lore didn't let herself really cry, though. That was a dam she couldn't strike just yet; there wasn't time.

She had a better hold on herself when they broke apart, tears drained away, chin steady. "I understand why you did it," Lore said softly. "I know he'd been watching since... since Cedric. And Mari said he threatened to hang the whole crew."

Val's eyes were tired. She nodded and ran a hand over the scarf holding her pale hair in place. "He made it sound like it'd be good for you, too. Living in the Citadel, where your... your condition could be better understood. He made it sound like they'd teach you about it."

Lore shifted uncomfortably. It pained her, to hear that Anton had used the promise of teaching her to make Val agree. It made her wonder how often Val had wanted to help and just not known how.

The old poison runner's sinewy arms shook as she placed her hands on Lore's shoulders. "If I'd known they were tracking you, I would've protected you," she murmured. "I hope you can believe that."

"I believe you," Lore murmured. And it was true. "I'm sorry I brought this all down on you, Val."

"Don't." Her mother gave her an impatient little shake. "This isn't your fault. None of it. I'm just glad you're here, and you're fine."

"Not *that* fine," Mari said. "What with the man in the cart turned to stone, and all."

Val's eyes widened. "Pardon?"

"It's a long story," Lore sighed.

"Save it, if you want." Val had finally noticed Gabe and Bastian. The grizzled poison runner eyed them both warily, one hand dropping from Lore's shoulder to hover over the leather holster on her hip. Val always had a pistol. "I'm more interested in the not-stone men currently in my warehouse."

Lore opened her mouth, trying to run together cover stories, but she needn't have bothered. Of course Bastian beat her to the punch.

"Blaise," Bastian lied, with a bow. "And my surly friend is Jean-Baptiste."

Gabe's jaw flexed at the flowery false name Bastian had given him. It was almost a relief to see annoyance spike across his face, something different from cold detachment and simmering anger.

"And the two of you know Lore how?"

Bastian didn't falter at all beneath Val's shrewd eye. "We've been helping her in the Citadel," he said, skirting close to the truth without revealing it. Then, with a wry smile, "Us outsiders have to stick together, my lady."

"Don't *my lady* me." Val's eyes swung from Bastian to Lore, calculating. "If Lore trusts you, so will I. But something easily given is easily taken away, and if you put so much as a toe out of line, I will cut it off."

"We wouldn't dream of it," Bastian replied. "All appendages will stay exactly where you want them."

Val gave him a curt nod, apparently placated. "Now," she said, crossing her arms. "What are you planning to do about the stone fellow?"

❦

The complete lack of a plan shook out something like this: Bastian, ever the charmer, chattered mindlessly as he and Gabe lifted the strangely light stone man from the cart and propped him against the wall. Lore caught snatches of shipping talk, questions about whether Mari and Val ever frequented the boxing ring—the answer was a resounding no—and comments on the excellent camouflage they'd constructed for the warehouse, but she was only half listening. All her concentration was on Milo, the human being she'd knit death around, and how she could unravel it.

If she could unravel it.

"Will he remember?" she asked Gabe quietly. "When he's... un-stoned?"

His answer came low, and chilly as the wind soughing off the sea. "In the few times this has happened before," he said, with a deliberate tone that said he highly disapproved of every single time, "the victim hasn't remembered much from the last few hours before they were attacked. He likely won't recall seeing us at all."

Victim. Attack. Deliberate choices of language. Lore's shoulders hunched.

Gabe's fingers flexed in and out of fists, an unreadable look in his one visible eye. "So how do you want to do this?"

She'd hoped he would have an idea, but that must've been a bridge too far. Lore swallowed, bending her hands back and forth in preparation for pins and needles. "I guess the same way I fixed the corpse in the vaults," she said finally. "Just try to...reverse it."

He nodded, one hard jerk of his chin. "I'll help."

It didn't sound like an offer of assistance, though. It sounded more like an order. Like he didn't trust her to do it on her own. And even though Lore didn't really trust herself, either, it still felt like salt in a cut.

Bastian noticed the tension hovering between them, so thick it was nearly visible, and herded Val and Mari back toward the office, still talking. Val looked irritated, Mari bemused. Still, both of them seemed to sense that this was something done better without an audience, and let Bastian lead them away.

Good. She didn't want them to watch this.

Banishing thoughts of her childhood and her surrogate mothers, Lore turned to Milo and his terrified stone eyes. "All right," she murmured. "Here we go."

Tentatively, she stretched out her hands. She felt the air displace next to her as Gabe did the same. A breath into two sets of lungs, taken and held, dropping them into the space where Mortem and Spiritum became tangible.

Lore's senses flooded with death immediately. This wasn't like with Horse, a natural expansion of Mortem as the body died, a widening corona of darkness. The entropy surrounding Milo was thick as tar, a conundrum of nothingness made nearly solid by its sheer mass. The contradiction of it made Lore's mind slippery.

She gritted her teeth. This wasn't about thinking—the two times she'd done this, it'd been on pure instinct. It was about feeling.

Her eyes stayed open, her vision graying out into the black-and-white that showed life and death in stark contrasts. The man before her was all in black, a nimbus of blazing dark outlining his form. Dark threads spun from her fingers, thin filaments like spiderwebs, connecting her to the Mortem she'd channeled into his body, the shell of it she'd spun.

But at his center was colorless light, a kernel of life untouched. He could be saved.

To turn living matter to stone, she'd knit death into the cells, like a cocoon around a butterfly. Lore could sense the places where that death waited now, delicately entwined with life, separated by the thinnest membrane. Two sides of one coin, unable to exist without the other. Strengthening one strengthened them both.

She thought of the Law of Opposites.

"Can you see where the Mortem starts?" She looked at Gabe. His one eye was opaque, his veins tarry, his extremities necrotic. The skin of his lips had shrunk, revealing more of his teeth, making it look like he snarled.

Monstrous, just like her.

"I can," he said, quiet and matter-of-fact.

"Let's unravel it, then. Slowly."

Deft work, careful work. Hands still outstretched, Lore twitched her finger, and the dark filament attached to it quivered. Slowly, she swiveled her finger as if she were winding thread back onto a spool. The Mortem spun away from the assassin, back toward her. Her lungs felt emptied, her heart growing still and dull as she channeled it through herself, then directed the threads toward the stone floor, funneling death back into already-dead matter. The floor here was thick enough to take it without getting too brittle.

Gabe did the same beside her, silently, and with markedly fewer threads. Together they unspooled death from the man before them, unraveling Mortem to free the kernel of light still within.

The whole time, Lore expected the disembodied voice, the murmurings that sounded both like her and wholly different. But none came.

It should've been reassuring. It wasn't.

When all the death was gone and the light in Milo's center sluggishly radiated outward to the rest of him, Lore dropped her hands, gasping in air. Her heart tithed its beat; more painful than usual, a lurching thump that rattled her rib cage. She grimaced, pressed still-necrotic fingers to her chest. Slowly, her monotone vision faded to normal colors, and she faced what they'd done.

Milo looked normal again. Markedly healthier than before, even. His skin glowed pinkish; veins that had been solid charcoal faded to a smoky gray, all the way back to blue in some places. His limbs were limp, and the dagger fell from his hand with a soft *clink*.

His eyes had closed, at some point. His mouth, too. He looked like he was asleep.

Gabe stepped forward, licked the side of his finger, held it beneath the still man's nostrils. "He's breathing."

Relief made her knees go watery. "So we fixed him?"

Gabe turned, not meeting her eyes, and started toward the office. Bastian's arms cut swaths of shadow through the lampglow, telling some story or other, and Mari's tinkling laughter seeped from the crack beneath the door. He didn't answer.

Milo showed no signs of waking up, not even when Gabe and Bastian heaved him up by his arms and legs and carried him out of the warehouse. Mari had suggested letting him stay in one of the cots, but Val refused. "He's poison-addled, and there's plenty here to steal," she retorted, and said that there was a warehouse down the alley where people often went to sleep off too much drink. "If he remembers anything, hopefully he'll think it's a hallucination. Gods know he's familiar with them."

Grumbling, Gabe and Bastian lugged the man's deadweight over the rough cobblestones, their breaths pluming in the air. Their boots on the street and the huff of exertion harmonized with the gentle sound of the tide coming in, distant bells on ship prows.

Val led them down the narrow lanes, approaching a dark warehouse and gently pushing open the door. It creaked, but if the sound woke anyone inside, they didn't protest. Bastian and Gabe settled Milo on the floor, then left quickly, soundlessly. He didn't stir.

"You're a sneaky lot," Val commented once they were all outside. "Have either of you considered poison running?"

Gabe looked stricken, but Bastian shrugged. "Not as such, no, but never say never. Although my current schedule wouldn't allow for it."

"That's a shame." Mari shook her head. "Our crew is dwindling rapidly these days."

"Arrests?" Lore asked quietly. Val's operation might be newly legal, but bloodcoats had been known to arrest anyone they didn't like the look of.

"If only it were that simple." A laugh huffed from Mari's mouth, twisting into the air like smoke. "Our most loyal are still around—everyone you'd know, mouse, don't worry—but the newer folks keep getting lured away." She tightened the knot on her headscarf again, lips twisting wryly. "I guess getting paid enough to cover your rent for a year with one night of work is a hard bargain to pass up."

The words registered with all three of them at the same time. Bastian's eyes widened. Gabe's lips went flat. Lore's pulse thumped in her wrists. "You know about the cargo movements?"

"*Cargo*," Val said derisively. "It's contraband, has to be. No one pays that amount of money to move anything legal."

"Oh, it's absolutely not legal." Mari snorted. "Phillip let some of the details slip when he came by to quit, and you'd think he'd signed his own execution warrant when he realized. I had to promise up and down for nearly an hour that I wouldn't tell anyone before he'd go."

"Do you have any information about where they move it to?" Gabe sounded like he was conducting an interrogation. Lore scowled at him. He paid no mind. "Or anything about who is actually doing the hiring?"

Val gave him an icy glance. "I believe Mari just said she promised a friend not to disclose anything."

The skin on Lore's shoulders prickled. The last thing she needed was for Gabe to goad Val into a fight. She was certain Gabe would lose.

Bastian apparently thought the same thing. "Of course we would never want someone to go back on a promise," he interjected with a smile. "I apologize for my friend's impertinence."

If looks could light someone on fire, the glance Gabe shot Bastian would've left him in cinders.

Mari crossed her arms, thoughtfully chewed her lip. "This is information you need, though, isn't it?" she asked Lore softly.

"For whatever they're having you do up at the Citadel. Which means it's more than just hauling contraband."

"Yes," Lore said. She'd never been able to lie to Mari. She saw through to the core of things, even when you tried to hide them.

Her mothers' eyes flickered toward each other. "Can you tell us anything, Lore?" Mari asked softly.

She wanted to. She wanted to let all of it go—the bodies, the lies, the esoteric mysteries she knew had to fit in somewhere, and the specter of war hanging over it all—but knowledge could be a noose.

They could stop it. She and Bastian, and Gabe, if he'd still work with them after this. No need to make Val and Mari panic. No need to get them mixed up in this any more than she had to, at least until there was no other choice.

"No," Lore murmured. "I'm sorry, but no."

Beside her, Bastian's hand tensed, rose the slightest bit into the air. Like he'd lay it on her arm. But he didn't.

"That's fine, mouse," Val said. "We understand."

Mari nodded, a determined bob of her chin. "I don't know much," she said. "But just the little bit that Phillip told me was enough to make him nearly wet his pants, so I need to know you'll be careful. All of you."

"Of course," Bastian murmured. Gabe nodded. Lore did, too.

"All I know," Mari said with a sigh, "is that whatever they're moving, they're taking it to the catacombs. *Deep* in the catacombs. All the way under the Citadel."

CHAPTER THIRTY-TWO

Every shape of affection can maim
but a triangle's formed most like a blade.
—Bar song lyric

Tomorrow night." Bastian affected no nonchalance, not any-more. He stood with his hands braced on the back of Lore and Gabe's couch, his hair falling over his brow and shadowing his face. "It has to be tomorrow night. We can't wait longer; it could mean another village if we did."

"Won't the guards get suspicious?" Lore stirred the embers in the fireplace with the gleaming silver poker, then blew a thin stream of air to make them ignite. Her skin was still goose-bumped from channeling Mortem, a cold worked bone-deep. "It's one thing to sneak into the city; it's entirely another to sneak into the Presque Mort's supposedly secret garden with its supposedly secret catacombs entrance."

Gabe's hand, hanging close to her face as he leaned the oppo-site elbow against the mantel, twitched toward a fist. He'd been silent ever since Mari told them about the catacombs, for the entire walk back to the Citadel and into their apartments. She glanced up at him; his eye patch faced her, and the line of his mouth told her nothing.

"Not if we bring one of the Presque Mort." The Sun Prince's expression she could read just fine—anger, and the expectation of a fight. "And not if we're careful. The real question is how we'll find the bodies once we're inside the catacombs. *Under the Citadel* doesn't narrow it down much."

Lore looked at him, chewing her cheek and willing him to read the answer to that in her eyes. She'd been so close to telling Gabe the truth of what she was in the alley, but that was before she turned Milo to stone, before Gabe started looking at her as if she were sin incarnate. She didn't want to tell him the truth now. Didn't *ever* want to tell him.

Bastian caught her eye. Understood. He dipped his chin in her direction. "We'll find a way, though."

"How do you suppose?" Gabe didn't look at either of them, still facing the fire Lore had coaxed to life. His hand had given up the fight against a fist and curled inward, the points of his knuckles casting sharp shadows on the floor. "The catacombs are vast."

"I'll find a map," Bastian said, as if it were the easiest thing in the world. "There has to be one somewhere."

Lore expected Gabe to call him out on the asinine answer, but instead the Presque Mort clenched his teeth to match his fist.

"And once we find these bodies?" he asked the flames. "What then? What do we do with them?"

"Then," Lore said softly, "I ask them how they died. Again."

A frown pulled down Gabe's mouth. He didn't have to say what bothered him; they all remembered what happened to the first corpse she'd raised. The one that told her to find the others. *The night killed me.*

Lore shifted so she could pull her knees to her chest, a makeshift shield. "I know how to fix it now," she murmured, a rebuttal to the thing Gabe didn't say. "If I…accidentally make it last, again."

Gabe flinched. She pretended not to notice. Icy silence blanketed the room, distrust crystallizing in the corners.

It ached, but part of her wondered what had taken it so long. Gabe was never meant to trust her. They might have the same monstrousness, but it wasn't an equal share, and his was taken as a kind of honor.

Hers was just a curse.

"On that subject," Bastian said, "it's probably time to let Claude rest, too. After all this is finished, of course. We can give him a proper burial. I'll talk to the florist."

Her eyes slid to his. He gave her a tiny smile, rueful. Trying to warm the ice in here, but even Bastian's sun couldn't thaw the dead of winter.

Silence reigned a few minutes longer, the kind that held you in thrall, dreading what would come after but unable to escape it. Finally, Gabe straightened, looking first to Bastian, then to Lore. "All of this is assuming that Mari isn't lying."

His tone made it clear—he was starting a fight, and he didn't care.

Lore could've stopped it. She could've let the words lie, not allowed them to be the catalyst Gabe apparently wanted. But she didn't have the patience for that.

Slowly, she stood, spine straight, head angled so she could match the glare he leveled at her. "Are you calling Mari a liar?"

"I have no reason to believe she's not," Gabe said. The fight was gone from his voice now; it'd just been there to strike the flint. Now there was a blaze, and he kept himself expressionless, as if he was above it. "She's a poison runner."

"So was I," Lore snarled.

Gabe cocked his head. "And see how loyal you've been to the crown that rescued you from your life of crime?"

She slapped him.

The sound cracked through the room like a gunshot, just as jarring. Gabe's head wrenched to the side, the impression of her fingers blooming scarlet across his cheek, but he stayed silent, turning back to face her as soon as inertia allowed.

Behind the couch, Bastian did nothing. His eyes stayed on Lore, narrowed and calculating.

"It could be a trap." Still in that low, expressionless voice, even as Gabe's face burned a stinging red from the impact. "Your old friends could be trying to lure you into the catacombs."

"Why would they do that?" He didn't know about what was down there. *Who.* If someone wanted her back in the catacombs, it wouldn't be Val or Mari. "They have papers from August. They're privateers now. Does that change your estimation? Make them seem more *loyal*?"

"No," Gabe said. "Just more easily bought."

"And you'd know *all* about that, wouldn't you, Duke Remaut?"

His one eye blazed, as if some deep ember within him had finally sparked.

Bastian spoke up, voice quiet but carrying. "I think this is about more than a desire to protect our latent necromancer, isn't it, Gabriel?"

Gabe glanced at him, and then away. It would've been dismissive if not for the fury clear on his face.

"The Church forbids entering the catacombs without special dispensation," Bastian continued. "Which I doubt we're going to get. I understand, friend. You feel as though you have plenty of sins already, and don't want to stack another on top of your hoard." Something like contempt bled through his casual tone. "What would Anton say to that?"

A muscle feathered in Gabe's jaw. He said nothing.

"Lore and I will go," Bastian said, with the air of a conversation decidedly closed. "I know the way to the stone garden; we're both smart enough to make it there without being caught. We'll figure out what's going on, and the tatters of your honor won't be further shredded. I know how dearly you hold them."

Gabe was silent, still as the man Lore had turned to stone. He stared at the fire like it could tell him something as Bastian straightened and made to leave.

"Tomorrow night," Bastian called over his shoulder at Lore as he pulled the door open. "I'll meet you here."

Then he was gone, slipping into the shadows of the hallway. The Bleeding God's Heart sconce on the opposite wall had gone out completely, candle wax dripping over the golden arms like melting bone.

When Bastian was gone, Gabe looked at her. Just looked, didn't speak, didn't move. His face was blank, scrubbed clean of any emotion, though that smoldering heat in his eye still burned.

He'd watched her channel Mortem, watched her raise the dead. Those things he'd forgiven, moved on from; he still saw her as a person despite them. But turning a human being to stone—sending him to a place between life and death—was the last straw on his already-beleaguered back.

Gabe believed in the afterlife. Believed in the myriad hells, the Shining Realm. When they'd spoken of it in the garden, it'd been all in abstracts, an intellectual exercise. But he believed she'd sent Milo to his eternal reward, only to rip him back out again. And that made her the kind of monster he'd sworn not to be.

Lore swallowed. Her eyes pricked, and that mortified her, welled up anger that made her vision even blurrier. Damn her feelings. Damn her heart, still wanting to be seen as *good*, when that had never, ever been an option.

"Really?" It came out small and hoarse. "You're going to stand there and not say anything? You're going to leave it like that?"

He stood there. He didn't say anything. He left it like that.

Lore fled into her room and slammed the door behind her.

❦

Sleep was hard to come by, but when it did, it washed over her like a black wave. No dreams, thankfully. Just rest, a vast and blank well of it.

Still, when the door clicked open, Lore woke immediately.

She sat up, sleep broken like a brittle board, completely awake in the time it took for her head to rise from her pillow. Someone stood at the threshold, silhouetted by firelight, tall and broad-shouldered and short-haired.

Gabe.

He didn't speak, still. Neither did she. Nor did he move, but Lore slowly swung her legs around and put her feet on the floor, walked toward him until there was barely a handspan between her chest and his. He was warm; it radiated from him as if from a fire, calling to her cold.

This didn't feel real. Not in the ditch of night, when the light was gone and thoughts were blurry, unreal hours meant for sleep. It didn't feel real, and that was why both their hands raised at almost the exact same time. Hers settled on his bare chest; his rested on the back of her neck, fingers threading through the tangle of her brown-gold hair.

No words, no sound but their breathing. Then he bent forward, and she raised her chin to meet him, mouths colliding in warmth and need.

Gabe didn't kiss like seduction. He kissed like starving, a hunger born from ill-fitting vows and anger and want. She could feel his teeth against her lips, his tongue sliding against hers insistently, and the moan that hummed in his throat was no artifice. Heat pooled between her legs; Lore's mouth opened, wanting more, relishing the nearly animal intensity of him.

He pushed her farther into the room; she felt the windowsill dig into the small of her back, a sharp pain that Gabe alleviated by lifting her to sit on it instead. She wrapped her legs around his waist; he trailed openmouthed kisses down her neck. "Bleeding God," he cursed against her collarbone, hoarse and rough. "Gods dead and *dying*."

She could feel him pressed against her center, and it made her gasp as he pulled the shoulder of her nightgown aside, kissing the bared skin while his hand molded her breast. His thumb found the peak of it, drawn tight; he circled it lightly, and Lore gasped again, pressing closer, conscious thought fading into a hazy ache and a fire that burned everything else away.

When his mouth found hers again, Lore reached for Gabe's belt.

He stilled, one hand on her breast, the other tangled in her hair. His lips wrenched away from hers, then his hands fell, bracing on either side of her hips on the windowsill.

It was so cold, with him gone. The glass pressed against her back, chilling her through.

Gabe's forehead tipped against hers. Neither one of them said anything, just sitting like that for a moment, sharing the same breath and the knowledge that whatever had been about to happen wasn't going to happen anymore.

Then he was gone, disappearing into the dark. Her door opened, his body blocking the sliver of light, then closed again.

Lore leaned back against the window and let the cold seep down to her bones.

CHAPTER THIRTY-THREE

Hold tight the rein of your body, for it will lead you
into ruin.

—The Book of Mortal Law, Tract 67

She woke late the next morning, achy and tired, her eyes
gummed with sleep. Last night felt like a dream, and she
might've convinced herself it was, were it not for the slight bruise
on her shoulder. A place where Gabe's control slipped, lavender
proof of near-sin.

Lore scowled at it and hiked up her nightgown. His control had
won out, in the end. And as frustrating as it had been in the moment,
part of her was glad for it now. Daylight through the windows chased
out idle fantasies, limned everything stark and real and simple.

Things were complicated enough without all *that*.

Embarrassment made her middle a writhing knot, but Lore
kept her chin high as she pushed open her door. Gabe would act
like nothing happened; she'd let him. It was easier.

But when the sitting room lay before her, it was empty. Gabe's
nest had been reassembled into carefully folded blankets and left
on the corner of the couch.

He'd left before she got up, then. Good. Simple, easy. Gods-dead-and-dying-damned easy.

A breakfast tray gleamed on the table behind the couch. A note was stuck under the tray's lip, short words in a familiar elegant hand.

Last night made me hungry. I assume it did the same for you. Rest up. —Bastian

He surely hadn't delivered breakfast himself, so the double entendre of the note must've been for the benefit of possible prying eyes. Lore's lips twisted. The whole Citadel thought she was sleeping with the Sun Prince already; might as well lean into it.

Especially if they were going to be traveling to the stone garden tonight on their own. A lovers' tryst would be a convenient excuse if they were caught.

Thoughts of lovers and the stone garden naturally led to Gabe. Lore opened the tray with a clang and set to the fruit and pastries inside, staunchly refusing to think of him, to think of last night and what they'd almost done. What it might mean.

Nothing, she told herself, shoving a cherry tart between her teeth. *It doesn't mean anything at all.*

When the tray was nearly empty and she'd poured herself a cup of coffee to wash it down, Lore sat on the couch with a sigh. *Rest up*, Bastian's note said, and she took it as code for *stay in your room*. Probably a good idea. If she kept far from courtiers, there was little chance she'd be questioned by Bellegarde or anyone else who might have some connection to the bodies in the catacombs.

She'd have to raise one of those bodies tonight. The back of her neck prickled at the thought.

At least now she knew what to expect. The open, unmoving mouth, the whispering. She could only hope that this time, the corpse said something helpful.

Lore dropped her head into her hands with a frustrated growl.

She was stuck in her room, and there was nothing here to do.

Nothing but those books of erotic poetry she'd taken from the gilded library. Exploring the halls with Gabe, laughing at the ridiculousness of the Citadel, felt like lifetimes ago.

With another long sigh, theatrical as if someone could hear it, Lore got up and retrieved the books from her bedside table, then took them into the tiny study to the right of the door. She sat down in the single chair at the desk, hooked one leg over the arm, and opened the book to a random page. The poem seemed to be about a priest forsaking his vows for the favors of a deep-bosomed lover.

"Ironic," Lore mumbled.

🦋

When her stomach was rumbling insistently enough that more pastries wouldn't satisfy, Lore disobeyed the Sun Prince. Throwing on clothes, she left the room, nearly slamming the door behind her, and started the winding trek down to the main hall.

The long table was set with just as many delicacies as it had been before. A wine fountain burbled in the center, surrounded by vegetables and bread and meat, including Bastian's hated peahen. Lore served herself a heaping plateful, and it felt like spite as much as hunger.

"Lore!"

Alie. Her gown was a pale orange today, matching the jeweled pins holding back the white curls of her hair. She looked like a butterfly, something meant for air and flight.

Lore allowed herself to be hugged. An affectionate touch that didn't require something of her in return made a mortifying lump rise in her throat; Lore swallowed it down.

Alie kept her hands on Lore's shoulders when they parted, eyebrow cocked. "Please tell me you were invited to the eclipse ball and the dinner afterward? It will be dreadfully boring, otherwise. At least, I assume so. It's not like I've gone to one before." She giggled. "My father has always insisted that we attend all-night vigils in the sanctuary during eclipses. This is the first time he's allowed us to do something livelier."

It would be rude to shove bread in her mouth to keep from answering. Still, Lore contemplated it for a moment. "We were," she said finally.

The mistake of using *we* wasn't clear to her until Alie's eyes brightened. We, meaning she and Gabe. Gabe, for whom Alie still held a guttering candle. Gabe, who'd come to Lore's room and kissed her like a dying man before disappearing.

Her smile was very hard to hold.

"Oh, thank all the gods." Alie's hands fell; she half turned to pick up an apple and polished it on her gown before taking a bite. "If I had to spend all night with the King and my father, I'd go raving mad."

"Are those the only people attending?" Lore's hands clawed around her plate, her taste for peahen suddenly gone. "Just August and your family?"

If so, that would obliterate any chance of coincidence.

Alie took a moment to swallow, unwilling to speak around a mouthful of apple. Courtly manners. "Not quite," she said, after a sip of wine to wash it down. "There were quite a few people invited to the ball. As for the dinner: Anton will be there, of course. And a few others. But it's going to be a quiet affair, apparently. Very exclusive." She leaned in a bit closer, like she didn't want to be overheard. "Bri didn't get invited to the dinner portion, though Dani and her family did. Not that Bri is complaining; there's a huge party happening at Fabian Beauchamp's estate outside of the city, so she's taking a carriage over there after the ball." The wistfulness in her voice said she'd much rather be at that party than August's. Lore couldn't blame her.

"But we'll have a good time, if you and me and Gabe and Bastian are all there." Alie's smile widened when she said Gabe's name, just a bit. "Bastian can liven up even the most boring court functions. He'll make sure it isn't dull." She took another sip of wine and moved away. "I have to go to my piano lesson, but send me a note when you have a free afternoon! We still need a croquet rematch, I hope you've been practicing!"

Then she was gone, weaving between the courtiers in their afternoon finery, leaving Lore with a plate full of food she didn't really want anymore but couldn't bear to waste. With a sigh, she started back toward her room.

Whatever the eclipse ball would be, she was sure *dull* wouldn't qualify.

Lore walked quickly to the carpeted steps leading back up to her turret, head down. So she didn't see August until the Sainted King cleared his throat.

She froze, hands full of china plate and heaped vegetables. Panic spasmed through her chest; she dipped her head and bent her knees in a truncated curtsy, hiding her face in case it spasmed through her expression, too. "Your Majesty."

He looked...awful. Deep shadows stood out around his eyes, his skin pale and almost clammy looking, as if a fever had recently broken. There was a slight, tired stoop in his shoulders, but it didn't diminish his presence, and she still felt herself standing up straighter as he narrowed his eyes.

August didn't waste time with pleasantries. "You've been spending time with my son?"

His mouth wrenched on the word *son*, like it was something disgusting he had to spit out.

"Of course, Your Majesty." Lore nodded, brows drawing together. "We're following your orders to the letter."

Considering that the orders had never gotten more specific, she wasn't even lying.

"Good." The King fumbled at his waist, pulling that thin flask from within his doublet and taking a hearty drink. "There will be a resolution soon. The whelp will finally get what he deserves."

Then the Sainted King pushed past her, breath reeking of belladonna. He didn't say goodbye.

Lore stared after him for a moment before wearily mounting the steps to her room.

᭟

Lore sat at her window and waited for the sky to darken. There was a smear across the glass, one that hadn't been there yesterday; either from sweat-rumpled fabric or a grasping hand. She scrubbed it away as the clock on the wall ticked by the time, inching ever closer to midnight.

Gabe was still gone. She'd stopped listening for him in the halls. She wondered if he'd moved back into his cloister. Back to walls that would keep him safe from himself, from all the things he wanted that he'd been taught were sin. Surely Anton would relent after he confessed that he'd nearly broken his vows for a poison-running necromancer.

It set an ache in her gut sharp as a bayonet's end. Lore tried to reason it away. It wasn't like she hadn't done the same thing before—played hot and cold, ultimately decided on cold. It didn't have to mean anything.

Still.

She shook her head like she could knock him out of it, closed her eyes. It'd be better to spend this time actually preparing for what would happen at midnight, rather than worrying over a monk who'd seemingly decided she wasn't worth his questionable salvation.

Instead, she concentrated on her forest, the wall she'd built around her mind to keep out the awareness of death. She concentrated on close trunks and interlaced branches and the subtle weave of smoke beyond her trees, black against an azure sky, thick as if something was always burning.

The minute hand of the clock ticked toward twelve. As soon as it reached its zenith, a knock came on the door.

Lore stood up. Tried not to think about what waited for her down in the stone garden, where the catacombs seethed their darkness.

Bastian stood in the corridor, dressed all in black. The Bleeding God's Heart sconce was full of candles on the wall at his back, outlining him in hellish light and hiding the vagaries of his expression. She could see his eyes, though, a dark glitter, and there was nothing playful in them. Tonight's Bastian was all business. "Ready for a chat with the dead?"

"Ready as I'm going to be." Lore stepped out into the hall and closed the door softly. Beyond the sconce's glow, the corridor swam back into shadow.

"Gabriel decided not to join us, I take it?" Bastian fell into step beside her.

"No." Lore stared down the hallway; the dark was preferable to talking about Gabe. "I haven't seen him since last night."

"Hmm." Bastian didn't ask any further questions.

He overtook her as they reached the branch in the hall, weaving in front of her to lead. The route they'd taken to sneak out into the back compound and through the culvert to Dellaire would be too obvious tonight.

She thought of August earlier, drinking poison and looking half a corpse. *The whelp will finally get what he deserves.*

In abstract, she'd known that August hated Bastian. But actually seeing it—naked hatred, not disdain veiled behind false concern—made pity coil at the base of her throat, pity she knew Bastian wouldn't want. Still, it stayed there. She'd taken it hard when Val turned her over to Anton; she couldn't imagine how one lived with the knowledge that your true-born parent wanted you gone.

"Are you all right?" she murmured to Bastian's back as they turned down an unfamiliar corridor. Thick tapestries lined the walls, muffling her voice. Sculpted suns and stars wheeled over the ceiling in three-dimensional gilt.

He glanced over his shoulder, brow arched high. "Yes, sneaking through the halls is not an act that engenders in me much turmoil."

"I mean..." She waved her hand, pursed her lips. "With... everything."

He would not want her pity, but she wanted to give him *something*. A place that offered softness, if he wanted it. Tenderness didn't come easily to her, but she'd try.

A gleam in his eye; he understood despite her fumbling. Bastian shrugged, turning back around. "I," he said decisively, "am coping." He pulled something gleaming from his pocket—a flask, tipped quickly into his mouth, then passed back to her without looking.

Lore took it. Sniffed just enough to make sure there was no whiff of poison, then sipped. Whiskey, strong enough to make her nearly cough. "That's quite the method of coping."

"Better than it could be." Bastian took the flask back. The corridor branched; he took the left one, gleaming marble. "Stay close to the wall. There's a long pool in the middle of the floor all the way down this hall."

"Who thought *that* was a good idea?"

"Some ancestor of mine with too much money and too little taste. So really, it could've been any of them."

The questionable corridor ended, widening into an atrium filled with night-blooming flowers beneath a domed glass ceiling. It was beautiful, and Bastian slowed his pace. Lore allowed it. She was in no rush.

A few of the flowers she recognized—hellebore, the color of dried blood. Datura, climbing up a wooden trellis to open twisting blooms to the moon. Poisons she knew, poisons that anyone outside of the Citadel would be arrested for growing, and here they were just decoration.

"My father is a bad man."

She turned away from the hellebore—Bastian wasn't looking at her, instead standing with his hands in his pockets and his head tilted up to the moon, like he was some night-blooming poison himself. "That makes it easier," he said quietly. "Easier to deal with the fact that he wants me dead. Maybe it makes me *good*, even." A snort, his eyes closing as his head tipped back further. "The Law of Opposites, right? If a bad man wants me dead, that makes me good. In the most technical sense."

It didn't seem like a conversation that wanted another participant. Lore just watched him, smelling sweet poison and tracing the lines of his face with her eyes. Far too handsome, she'd thought before, but in the moonlight, Bastian was the kind of beautiful that rent hearts in half.

The air around him almost seemed to glimmer, gold dust in the dark. Moonlight made him more beautiful, yes, but in the same way that darkness emphasized a flame. He didn't belong in it; Bastian Arceneaux was antithetical to night.

"My mother wasn't good, either," she murmured.

His eyes slid her way, a subtle invitation to continue, but Bastian kept his face toward the sky.

"After I was born—after all the Night Sisters realized what I could do—she stayed distant. I don't remember her ever touching me with any kind of affection." The razored lump in her throat that Alie's embrace had risen tried to return. She swallowed, again, rubbed at her neck like she could physically force it away. "By that point, she was totally devoted to the Sisters. To their mission, to keeping the Buried Goddess from ever rising again."

Go, she'd said, pushing Lore out into stabbing daylight while her palm still ached from her branding, a bird shoving a fledgling from a nest. Maybe not totally devoted, then. But enough.

"Something about me..." Here, Lore's voice broke, and she paused until it mended itself. "Something about me was wrong.

Something about me went against everything she'd dedicated her life to."

She didn't realize she was staring at her moon-scarred hand until it was covered by Bastian's. He'd crossed to her, shadow-silent, and closed his fingers around hers. She could feel the lines of his scar against her own, the now-healed runnels of half a sun.

"I get it," Lore murmured, staring at their hands. "People are different, and just because you're related to someone doesn't mean you're good for each other. But she was all I had, and she looked at me like I was a monster." Lore closed her eyes, briefly, took a breath. Looked up at him. "But even she didn't want me dead. She saved me. Took me to the mouth of the catacombs when the rest of the Sisters wanted to send me into the Buried Goddess's tomb."

The corner of his mouth lifted, a shaky smile. "That's something."

They stood in the atrium for a handful of heartbeats, hands entwined, her scar against his. In the corner of Lore's eye, something like fog twisted around them, a dance of darkness and gold, glitter blown into smoke. But maybe it was just lurking tears she wouldn't let fall; when she tried to focus on the strange shimmering, it disappeared.

"Well," Bastian said finally. "We aren't dead yet." He dropped her hand and started forward, toward the door of the atrium.

Wordlessly, Lore followed.

Past the atrium, Bastian led her down a flight of narrow stairs, and after that, the corridors slowly became more familiar. They'd wound their way to the main floor, headed toward the front of the Citadel rather than the back. Lore heard courtiers, giggles and soft voices and lovers' moans, but they didn't see anyone.

Not until the bloodcoat appeared at the end of the hallway.

Bastian was quick; he grabbed her arm and pulled her toward a recessed alcove framing a window. There wasn't a curtain to draw over it, nor were there any on the other alcoves close by.

"Shit," Lore hissed. "Shit shit shit."

"Hold your smuggler's tongue." Bastian's back pressed against the alcove's arch; he looked around, measuring the distance between them and the guard. His eyes swung back to her, dark and serious. "We *will* get by him, but you have to follow my lead."

"Fine, lead on."

"Kiss me."

Her eyes widened. The booted steps of the guard drew closer.

"Oh, come *on*," Bastian muttered, rolling his eyes even as he grabbed her arm, tugged her forward, and sealed his lips to hers.

Lore made a small noise in her throat before she realized Bastian wasn't really kissing her. Sure, their mouths were pressed together, but he didn't move, didn't try to deepen this light and technical embrace. His hand curled around her hip, the other bracketing her wrist, still held in the air from where he'd pulled her.

Slowly, Lore let her hand settle on his shoulder, realizing what this was, what he was doing. Two courtiers trysting in the hall at midnight would be a common sight, nothing to raise hackles. The guard would walk right by them.

Bastian angled his head so their faces were hidden from the hall, the curls of his dark hair falling against her cheek. His lips broke from hers, though they were still close enough to brush when he spoke. "There's our poison runner," he said softly. "Thinking on her feet."

His breath tasted like mint leaves. His every exhale became her inhale. He was too much, too close, inescapable, and the damn guard was walking so *slow*.

Boots approached. Passed. Not even a pause. Lore and Bastian waited in the alcove, pressed together edge-to-hollow, breathing the same air until she felt light-headed. Their faces were too close for her to see his expression in anything but pieces, but she could see the bend of his grin, and it was near-feral.

When the boots didn't echo anymore, Bastian leaned away, head lolling against the wall. His hands stayed on her hips. "Ready?"

Lore nodded. Stepped back. Bastian led her into the shadows again, and neither one of them spoke.

But she thought of that not-kiss, and how there'd been a moment when she felt a twitch in his control, like he would've really kissed her if he'd thought she would let him.

And she didn't know whether she would have or not.

Finally, a narrow and nondescript door, set between naves presided over by small statues of the Bleeding God, chest empty and hands full of garnets. Bastian twisted the wrought-iron handle; it moved soundlessly, and the door glided open into night air. "After you."

Lore stepped out onto the soft grass. To her right, the walls of the stone garden butted up from the manicured lawn, rough blocks of darkness in the moonlight. No one was around, the only sound the wind soughing through the rock flowers, rushing against the edges of granite petals.

They approached the gate. Bastian fiddled with the lock for only a moment before it glided open in his hands, then nodded her inside.

The garden had been strange but pretty the first time Gabe brought her here—in the moonlight, it was eerily beautiful. The stone roses cast solid shadows on the cobblestones, the dark leaching everything of color so it all looked gray, even the plants that hadn't yet been turned by Mortem's careful application.

And beyond, in the center of the garden—the well, cold and dark, leading to the catacombs.

Bastian approached it cautiously. The circular lid rested on top of it, held in place with the statue of Apollius. He grasped it, pulled, grimaced. "It's damn heavy."

"That's by design," came a familiar voice from the gate.

Lore turned.

Gabe.

At the sight of him, Lore froze, but Bastian barely reacted at all. He straightened from where he'd been hauling at the statue, ever graceful. "Gabriel," he said conversationally. "And here I thought you'd decided against joining us. Whatever changed your mind?"

Mouths and hands and fumblings in the dark. Blood rushed to Lore's face.

Gabe didn't look at her. His arms crossed over his chest, the black leather of his eyepatch eating the light, making that side of his face look lost in a void. "What changed my mind," he said, "is the certainty that if I wasn't here, you'd invariably fuck it all up somehow."

"Listen to the Mort now." Bastian rolled his neck, shook out his shoulders. "We'll have you renouncing your vows in no time."

She was glad of the dark. The heat in her cheeks could light a damn candle.

Bastian inclined his head to the well. "Some help, then?" He went back to pushing at the statue, apparently much heavier than it looked, inching it along the wooden platform toward the wall of the well.

With a rumbling sigh, Gabe stepped forward, his shoulder brushing Lore's as he passed her. She didn't move, and that was meant as a challenge. The way his eyes flickered to her said he took it as one.

"Where have you been?" Lore asked.

"Thinking." The line of his jaw was harsh, casting a deep shadow over his neck.

"And did you come to any interesting conclusions?"

He finally looked at her, then. Turned so that one blue eye blazed down at her like a lighthouse at a rocky shore, danger and safety at once. "I came to the conclusion that I couldn't let you do this by yourself."

"I have Bastian." Truth and a weapon and a memory of breath shared in an alcove. "I was never going to be doing this by myself, Gabriel. Just not with you."

A muscle in his jaw twitched.

"What you should've been thinking about," she said, "is what you're going to do when it's finally proven to you that Anton is a liar." Then she turned around to go help Bastian move the statue.

After a moment, Gabe followed.

CHAPTER THIRTY-FOUR

In our observation of the captured necromancers who worked in pairs, the more powerful necromancer would channel the Mortem, while the less powerful one would direct it. In this way, they were able to raise more of the dead using less energy by binding them together. Some necromancers were also able to shape raw Mortem before channeling it through themselves, causing things like increased strength or stamina once this shaped Mortem was finally taken in. Theoretically, this practice could be harnessed for military purposes, but so few are capable of it that further research into the possibility is impractical.

–Notes from Thierry LeMan, researcher
working in the Burnt Isles circa 10 AGF

With all three of them working, moving the statue was fairly easy. Gabe directed them—the statue was on a track, barely visible against the wood grain in the dark—and they inched the statue forward until it slotted into a notch carved into the top of the well wall.

"Upon reflection," Bastian said, hooking his hands on his hips and scowling at the statue, "moving it toward the notch seems obvious."

"What an auspicious start we're off to," Gabe muttered.

Lore was too out of breath to say anything. Even sliding along a track, the damn statue was heavy.

Bastian moved the wooden piece covering the top of the well, now unencumbered by stone gods. Inside, a perfect ring of pitch-black, so thick it looked almost liquid. Cold emanated from the depths of the well, and all three of them took a tiny, instinctual step back.

"Do you have a key?" Gabe's voice was low and dark, still suspicious. He arched a brow at Bastian, who looked utterly confused.

"A key for what?"

"The chambers," Gabe said. "The chambers within the catacombs. They aren't just left open."

"Well." Bastian pushed back his hair. "Fuck."

"I can get in."

Lore didn't look at either of them. She looked at that vast well of darkness, an entry to deep parts of the earth where the living weren't meant to go. "I can get in," she repeated.

Gabe's brows knit. "How?"

Behind him, Bastian said nothing.

A swallow worked down her dry throat. "I can get into any chamber we find. Just trust me."

She knew it like she knew the shape of the catacombs, like she knew her name and the crescent edges of the scar on her palm. No part of that world beneath the earth would remain closed to her.

The war in Gabe's mind played out on his face, cut through in silver moonlight. They circled trust, but never quite landed, carrion birds with a body dying slowly.

"She was a poison runner," Bastian said, cast in darkness

beneath the lip of the well's roof. His arms were crossed, his voice low. "She knows how to pick a lock."

Gabe could tell there was more to it, and could tell she wasn't going to share. Lore could read it in the line of his mouth, hard and unyielding and shaped like well-hidden hurt.

Gabriel Remaut had lived a lifetime of subtle wounds, and she just kept giving him more.

But he shook it off. Nodded. "Fine."

Bastian's eyes never left Lore. The moment she felt steadier, tamped down the guilt in her gut, he seemed to know. A tiny inclination of his head, then he stepped up to the well. "Right. Lore and I will go in and search. I don't know how long it will take to find the bodies, but I would imagine we'll be back before dawn. Remaut, you stay here and—"

"Absolutely not." It was near a growl. "You think I'll let you take her down there alone?"

"I think you're going to have to," Bastian said, his voice smooth and courtly and more weapon-like for it. "Someone has to keep watch, and you make the most sense."

"Why do I feel like you planned this?"

"I can assure you I didn't, Mort, seeing as neither of us knew until five minutes ago that you were even coming. You left Lore alone all day."

"I'm sure *you* didn't."

Bleeding God and His absent heart, these two were going to drive her mad.

"Bastian is right. Someone has to stand watch." Lore said it quick and firm. Whatever territory Gabe and Bastian were edging into, she wanted them out of it. "And people will question you being here a lot less than they'll question him, Gabe."

The moon reflected off the gilded roof of the Citadel, gleamed in Gabe's blue eye. He stared at her a moment, then rubbed at his patch. "Think, Lore," he murmured. "If I have to stand watch, so be it, but I'd honestly feel better if you went on your own instead of with him."

"You left." The words recalled the wordless—her dark room, bodies fitting together before coming decidedly apart. "I know you prefer me alone, Gabriel, but I don't."

He shifted back, away from her. The gleam of moonlight left his eye; shadow fell over him like a cloak.

Bastian hopped up onto the lip of the well, then crouched down to peer into the dark. A *click*, his pearl-handled lighter flaring to life in his fist. The tiny flame didn't do much, but it did illuminate a short, narrow staircase, spiraling down the side of the well. "Any idea how far this goes before you reach the bottom?"

"The well is about ten yards deep." No emotion in Gabe's voice. It was flat as placid water.

"Excellent." Carefully, Bastian stepped onto the first stair. "See you at dawn."

Lore could feel Gabe's eyes burning into the back of her neck, scrutinizing, knowing there was something she hadn't told him.

Something she wouldn't. Even if his silence, his unwillingness to ask, made her conversely feel like maybe she should.

The top of Bastian's head slowly disappeared as he wound around the stairs. Lore climbed up on the well's lip.

"Lore."

She half turned. Gabe stood with his arms crossed, a handful of inches shorter than her from this new vantage.

"I didn't want to leave," he said finally. "Last night. I didn't want to stop."

Her fingers twitched, half a reach. She clenched them tight. "Then why did you?"

His eye flickered away. "Because it didn't feel...*right*, being with you. It felt dangerous. Something I should get away from while I had the strength to do it." He worried the corner of his lip with his teeth, as if he wasn't sure how to phrase it. "It felt like a mistake, but one I'd made before. One I knew would end badly."

And he was trying to tell her something, here, something that skirted the edges of what she'd felt since she met him—the instant connection, the ways it felt like she knew him and Bastian both on some cell-deep level that couldn't be explained. But only one word stuck out to her, and that one word made her recoil.

"A mistake," she repeated softly.

Gabe flinched, as if he hadn't realized how it sounded until he heard it in her voice. "Lore, I didn't mean—"

"You made it very clear what you mean." She put her foot on the first step and climbed down, chased by the sound of Gabe's sigh.

🌿

Every part of the catacombs looked the same. The walls, stone-built and old-bone-dry, narrowing and expanding with no rhyme or reason, as if someone had marked them out to the pattern of sick lungs breathing. The dirt floor, ground up with bits of rock. The scent. Empty and ozonic and stinging her nose.

She could feel Mortem, sense it phantom-limb-close; death in all this stone, death from the bones of revenants who'd crawled here to die. People with no one who cared enough to burn their bodies.

It surprised her, to sense so much Mortem with Bastian close by. But whatever dampening effect he'd had on her ability seemed to have lessened in recent days, until it was barely a concern at all. Instead, his presence seemed almost to clarify her senses, make Mortem seem sharper, like he was a whetstone to its blade.

Her mind turned, inexplicably, to her birthday. Consecration. The darkness of the moon covering the sun. She glanced at Bastian; there, in the corner of her eye, a glimmer of gold that slid away from her gaze when she tried to concentrate on it.

Lore shook her head.

A haphazard pile of old wood, dried-out plant stalks, and twine waited at the end of the narrow stairs. Bastian lashed the material together into a torch and held the pearl lighter to its end, catching flame. He passed it to her wordlessly.

Lore took the proffered torch. Panic bubbled just beneath her breastbone, oil in a too-hot pan, leaping up to burn her. Now that she was here, in the dark, every sense screamed for her to turn around, clamber back up the stairs to open sky and clear air—

"Lore." Hands on her shoulders, warmth and the scent of wine. "Breathe."

She did, slowly. In and out, keeping her eyes on his, whiskey-brown and very close.

When she had herself under control, she stepped back. His hands fell.

Bastian nodded, picking up material to make his own torch. "So. Which way?"

Lore closed her eyes and let her interior map of the catacombs fall into place. It was like a grid laid over the inside of her eyelids, a dark spiderwebbing tangle. One spot in the map throbbed, a darkened heart of Mortem concentrated in a single place. That'd be where the bodies were. Close to that knot, two sparks of white light—she and Bastian. So all she had to do was find a path in all those jagged lines that connected them.

Looking at her map was like looking at a maze from above, gazing down into a pit of tangled string or exposed vein. Far below, barely a glimmer, she saw another handful of white lights, so few of them now. Another knotted, throbbing storm of Mortem.

The Night Sisters. Nyxara's corpse. There in the strange subterranean cathedral at the bottom of the catacombs, there next to that obsidian tomb. Lore could see it, now that she had it fixed in her mind, see it as if she stood beneath the crystalline stalactites herself, the walls flecked in constellations of mica, the gleaming block of the tomb, a deeper dark than even the cata-combs themselves...

But that's not why she was here. Lore pulled back, rearranging her mind's eye, tracing a path between her and Bastian and the bodies.

"This way." She started forward. Behind her, Bastian quickly lit his own torch and followed.

It didn't take them long to come across the first piles of bones, old and dry and wrapped in a ratty cloak of indeterminate color. Bastian frowned, toeing aside what looked like a femur. "Foul," he murmured. "I've already had quite enough of corpses, and we haven't even found the stash yet."

"Imagine how I feel," Lore replied.

They lapsed into silence. When she glanced over her shoulder, Bastian's brows were knit, the flames of his torch casting his face in wavering shadow. "You haven't told Gabe, have you? About growing up down here?"

"Does it matter?" The question came out sharper than she intended.

"No. It's your business, you tell whoever you want." He shrugged, but it didn't quite mask the pointed look in his eye, a spade delving into dirt for answers buried. "It's just interesting, is all. Since you two are so clearly pining after each other."

"I am not pining after Gabriel Remaut."

"Well, he's certainly pining after you."

"No." Her laugh was short and harsh. "He isn't."

"Could've fooled me."

"Fooling you is not a difficult task."

Now it was his turn to bark a harsh laugh. "Not for you, maybe." A pause. Then, softer, "Why'd you tell me, then?"

"Because you threatened to send me to the Burnt Isles if I didn't." The path ahead forked, split into uneven halls. Lore stopped, breathed. Hung left.

"That isn't all of it," Bastian said behind her. There was a quality to his voice she hadn't heard before, though. Doubt. "You trust me, Lore. Despite everything, despite yourself, you trust me."

"You haven't given me much choice." But it didn't come out like an accusation.

"I didn't feel like I had much choice, either." The doubt in Bastian's tone grew a harder edge. "I keep trying to figure out why I wanted to know about your childhood, about who you were. Why I *needed* to know. To protect myself from August, sure, but it was more than that. It was like...like something pushed me. Like it had happened before, it would happen again, and I was part of it whether I wanted to be or not."

They weren't the same words Gabe had used by the well, but they were an echo all the same. The sense of things falling into place around them, the sense of being moved into position by forces so much bigger than themselves, bigger even than kings and wars. She and Bastian and Gabe, comets that couldn't help colliding.

Lore turned around. Bastian's eyes glittered, angry and lost.

"I know you." Bastian said it like a sentencing. "And you know me. Why is that, Lore? Why does it seem like I've always known you?"

It could've sounded romantic, in any other context. But here, it just sounded like pain and confusion, one more unquantifiable thing. Lore stared at him and said nothing.

"Tell me I'm not alone in that." The Sun Prince wasn't one to beg, she knew; Lore thought this was probably the closest he'd ever gotten. It splintered in her, a wound that had been healed and reopened time and time again. "Lore, tell me I'm not alone here."

And wasn't that all she'd ever wanted? Not to be alone?

She stared at him across the dark and the torchlight, the rocks and bones. "You aren't." It came out hoarse; she swallowed. "You aren't alone, Bastian. I feel it, too."

Then she turned and started forward again. Behind her, Bastian pulled in a ragged sigh, and followed.

CHAPTER THIRTY-FIVE

Nothing is new.

–The Book of Mortal Law, Tract 135

Lore could tell the first chamber they came to wasn't the one they were searching for. The map in her head told her to walk straight past it, to keep winding farther into the dark.

But Bastian paused, raising his flickering torch to the splintered wooden door. "Should we check this one out?"

"It isn't the right one," Lore said, pushing ahead. It was cold this deep beneath the earth, and numbness tingled in her fingertips. "And we need to keep moving if we want to be back by sunrise."

"How can you tell?" Bastian gave the door one more glance before ambling after her. "I don't think we'll be able to see when the sun rises down here. Bleeding God, I don't think we'd be able to tell if the whole world ended."

Hyperbole, but Lore's shoulders still inched toward her ears. "I can tell." Her intuition was a spark in her chest, a torch that didn't lead her wrong. Part of her was at home in the catacombs in a way she never was anywhere else.

All she'd ever wanted was to find somewhere she fit that wasn't in the dark. But shadows and death were the only things that held space for her.

"You never did tell me exactly how this navigation thing works." Bastian stepped up so they were level, adjusted his longer stride to keep it that way. "I assume it has something to do with being born here?"

Lore shrugged, studying the dark before her rather than the Sun Prince beside. "I assume so."

"Then you're the only one who knows the catacombs like this, because you were the only one born in the catacombs."

"No, I wasn't."

His brow cocked.

Lore sighed, rubbed at her eyes. It was a good thing Bastian was the one to come down here with her; she didn't have the energy to keep secrets. "There were other babies born to the Night Sisters," she said. "More than one unmarried pregnant person thought hiding in the catacombs was preferable to dealing with their families on the surface."

"Doesn't say much for their families."

"Or society in general. It takes more than one person to make a baby, but the onus always falls on the one who bodily carries the proof."

"True." Bastian dipped his chin in acquiescence. "But I assume children born here aren't all able to use Mortem?"

"Nope." Lore gave a halfhearted attempt at a laugh. "I just got lucky, I guess."

He snorted, then inclined his head to her moon-marked hand, swinging by her side as the other held her torch. "Did all children born to Night Sisters get marked?"

Her hand curled closed. "No. Only those chosen to go into the tomb on the eclipse and see if Nyxara's body has stirred."

His eyes darkened at the word *eclipse*, knitting it together with the planned ball, synchronicities that itched.

A few steps of silence. Then Bastian swallowed. "You shouldn't go to the ball on the eclipse, Lore."

"I have to. If I don't, it will be obvious that we—"

"No, you fucking don't." The words shredded in his teeth, vehement and bladed. "You don't have to jump when August or Anton says jump. Remaut and I can come up with cover if we have to. Pretend you're sick, lock yourself in your room, *hells*, run through the storm drain and go find a tavern to get raging drunk in, but I don't think you should come."

She stopped. "Do you know something?"

"Of course I don't *know something*." Bastian looked irritated. "But I don't have a good feeling about it, and when it comes to you, that's enough for me."

"Why do you care so much about protecting me?" She planted her feet in dry dirt and bone dust, faced him like an oncoming cavalry. "Why do I care so much about protecting you?"

"I don't know." Rounding the bend to what they'd said before, this feeling of knowing each other, of being pulled along by strings they didn't tie. "I don't know."

Lore sighed, looked away. "Fine. I will try to get out of going to the eclipse ball." But even as she gave the promise, it sat heavy on the back of her throat, and tasted like a lie. Her thoughts turned to Gabe, to how he'd take it if she suddenly decided to completely defy Anton. He'd gone along with all this so far because of the threat of the Burnt Isles—the threat to her, specifically, since his connections and title could probably get him out of it. But after last night, she didn't want to test how far he'd go for her, whether that line had finally been crossed.

Bastian nodded. "Thank you."

"You shouldn't go, either," Lore said, ripping her mind away from Gabe. "What with your father trying to get rid of you, and all."

"I've been bringing in my own food," Bastian said. "And I won't drink or eat anything at the ball, so that rules out overdosing me with one of his poisons. If I were someone who partook in such things, it would make his job easier, but I've always had a distaste for it." The corner of his mouth lifted, his bared teeth gleaming in the light of his torch. "And if he tries to kill me in a less subtle way, who can blame me for returning the favor?"

Disquiet thrummed in her temples. "Let's hope he behaves, then."

The look in Bastian's eyes said part of him didn't hope for that at all. Part of him wanted a bloodbath.

Up ahead, the catacombs branched again, a *T* of tunnels leaving no option other than left or right. The path she'd traced in her head said to go right, but as she turned, the light of her torch flickered over something on the wall. Words.

She stopped, frowned.

Bastian came up beside her, the light of his torch illuminating the words further. The lettering was shaky, deep in some places and barely there in others. "Looks like gibberish," he said. "Maybe a revenant got loquacious right before they died."

"I don't think a revenant is going to go this deep." It'd been half an hour at least since they'd passed remains. Lore held her torch closer to the wall.

She squinted, puzzling through the inscription aloud. At least it was in Auverrani. *"Divinity is never destroyed,"* she murmured. *"Only echoed."*

"My vote is still on gibberish." But there was a ribbon of disquiet in Bastian's voice that said the words felt just as heavy to him as they did to her. "Revenant or not, how did someone manage to write on a stone wall?"

Something pale was half hidden in the dirt. Lore nudged it with her toe—a bone, the end sharp. The surface was pockmarked and pitted, as if it'd been here a long time. "Maybe you were right about the revenant."

Bastian's nose wrinkled. "Good for me." He nodded down the branching tunnels. "Which way?"

She jerked her head to the right and continued on, a little quicker than before. She kicked the bone into the dark.

They kept up the faster pace, torches sputtering. Lore thought it'd been a little over two hours since they descended through the well—still plenty of time before sunrise, but Gabe would be worried. He'd be pacing, she was nearly sure of it. Pacing and pulling at his eye patch.

"Do you think he's all right?" It pushed past her lips without her conscious thought to voice it.

"Remaut?" Beside her, Bastian stiffened, but his voice was even. "I'm sure he's just fine. Maybe he's taking the opportunity to get some sleep. He's looking less than well rested these days."

"He sleeps in front of our door," Lore said. "To guard it."

"Always one for dramatic shows of chivalry."

"Maybe you could learn something from him."

A stretch of silence. Then, "Would you like me to, Lore?"

It could've been flirtatious, easily said in his usual flippant tone. But it wasn't. It was earnest, and Lore didn't answer.

Her mental map guided them through a handful of turns, torches flickering against the damp stone. In her mind, the white lights of her and Bastian drew closer to the knot of Mortem, until the two were on top of each other. They'd reached their destination.

Which was, apparently, a solid wall.

"Dammit." Lore slammed her hand against the rough stone. "Fuck!"

"There has to be a door somewhere." Bastian waved his torch, casting shuddering light in either direction. "Maybe there's a trick latch or something?"

"There's not." The hall was narrow; Lore could lean backward and hit the opposite wall. She slid down it, pressing the heel of her hand against her forehead. "There's nothing here."

"There has to be. You led us—"

"I led us *wrong*, Bastian." She dropped her hand, looked up at him with daggers in her eyes. "I was wrong. Maybe we're wrong about this whole damn thing. Maybe we should just leave it."

"Leave it," he repeated, cold. He stared down at her, the fire-light making him look as regal and distant as a statue of Apollius. "Just let my father and my uncle collect bodies for who-knows-what purpose and march us into war?"

Lore didn't drop her gaze from his, but neither did she respond. She was tired. Tired of trying to fix something she didn't fully understand. Tired of being yanked along in one direction or another, used from every angle. Maybe some of those angles were justified, but they still stung.

Bastian cursed, pushing his torch into a small pile of rocks to keep it upright, then slowly ran his hands over the wall. Still searching for that hidden latch.

She watched him for a moment, unable to make herself stand. Then, with a sigh, she pushed up and did the same.

He glanced at her sideways but stayed quiet. Smart man.

As predicted, there was no hidden latch. But as Lore's hand passed over one section of rough stone wall, her palm . . . stopped.

She frowned. She could move her hand if she tried, but her skin seemed drawn back to that one spot—smoother than the rest of the rock, and colder, too. At first Lore thought that was the reason her hand strayed there, a simple matter of texture. But as she pressed her palm to the stone, she felt something *thrum*. A swirl of winter, slow-clotted blood.

Mortem. Mortem, calling to her. Gathered here and knotted.

"I think I figured it out," she murmured.

Bastian stopped running his hands over the wall, his dark hair gilded with dust. He stepped back, palms open before him as if in surrender. "What do we have to do?"

"It's a lock," she said, hand still pressed to the stone. "But with no key. A mechanism that has to be tripped with magic, not something physical."

"Magic is all you, unfortunately." He swallowed, narrowing his eyes at the wall. "Is it safe?"

"Absolutely not."

"Well, then." Bastian stepped behind her, like he could offer some support. "I've got your back. Try not to die."

Lore closed her eyes and tipped up her chin, probing her senses forward into the wall as she took down her mental barrier, the forest that would always make her think of Gabe. She tried to gather Mortem from the surrounding stone, but the way it'd already been worked into this hidden door kept her from pulling it forward.

She took a deep breath, held it until stars spun behind her eyes. When they opened, her vision had gone grayscale—the wall before her was a writhing tangle of black, her hand against it the dim-glowing gray of a channeler at work. More Mortem lurked in the wall behind her, in the dirt; Lore pulled it up, thin threads of darkness winding around her fingers. Lore channeled it through herself, quick with practice. Then, gently, she pushed it into the wall.

The Mortem in the wall had been fashioned into a puzzle box, a knot in the center, other strands outlining the shape of a door. To open it, she'd have to solve the puzzle box.

This had to be Anton's work. It reminded her too much of what he'd done at the leak, twisting threads of Mortem into an intricate knot, working it in ways she'd never seen. But whatever Anton had done at the leak was simple compared with this. She'd never known Mortem *could* be used this way, twisted and fashioned rather than run quickly through a channeler and into dead matter. Made into a tool. It must've taken intense concentration to channel and shape it at the same time.

But had he channeled, at the leak? Now that she was thinking of it, Lore wasn't sure. Anton had shaped the Mortem, but she didn't recall seeing the opaque eyes and necrotic fingers that meant he was moving the power of death through his body.

Had he just shaped raw Mortem? Made a tangle of it, then sent it to her to channel inward? Such things had been done before, but it'd been centuries ago.

No time to wonder over it now. Lore sipped air through her lips as she probed at the puzzle box, the strands of Mortem she channeled picking at the ones from the Priest Exalted, thin fingers on violin strings.

The goal of the puzzle was clear—unravel the knot in the center, and it'd be a straight shot through the box and around the outline of the door, an easy thing to trace her own threads along and open. The untangling would take ages, probably. A series of tiny movements, one after the other, executed in exactly the right way and exactly the right order—

One of her threads slipped, the effort of pushing through stone making it go sideways. Something in the puzzle box slid into place.

The tangled knot smoothed.

For just a moment, Lore stood still, not quite able to believe she'd solved the intricate puzzle box by accident. Then, with one last push, she sent the Mortem she'd made down the line.

A *crack*. The wall before her swung open.

Lore stepped back, the threads of Mortem falling away as she gasped in air, color returning to her vision and blood coursing into her fingers. Cold emanated from the now-open door, and the dark beyond was tar-thick. She picked up her torch with shaky hands; even the flame-light didn't penetrate more than a foot or two into the chamber.

"I'll go first." Bastian rolled his shoulders, set his jaw. He stepped through the door before she could stop him.

A short, startled yelp. Lore lurched over the chamber's

threshold, apprehension forgotten, and nearly collided with Bastian's back.

"Got you," he chuckled.

Lore shoved a hand between his shoulder blades. "Fuck you."

"I thought we talked about asking nicely."

There was a current of nerves running beneath the banter, one no jokes could hide. The darkness was thick, pressing around them, but there was also a sense of space here she hadn't felt in the tunnels, a *vastness*.

It was somehow worse.

"What's this?" Bastian stepped to the side—more steps than Lore anticipated, and she scrambled to keep up—until he reached the wall. He groped along the stone, pulling down something that looked like a leafless vine. A fuse.

"Do *not* light that," Lore said, at the very moment Bastian put his torch to the fuse's end.

Flame shot down the line, but rather than leading to a stack of explosives, the fuse took the fire to another torch set into the wall. Then another, and another, light traveling around the room until the whole cavern was illuminated in flickering orange.

It was huge, as large as three of the throne room. Stone plinths were set at equal distances, reminding Lore eerily of the iron crosshatching on the floors miles above their heads.

And on every stone slab, a corpse.

All different sizes, different genders, but in death they appeared uniform. All of them were covered in dark fabric. All of them looked like they were merely sleeping, as long as you didn't get close enough to notice their pallor, the waxy texture of their skin.

And all of them looked nearly the same age. No children, no elderly. These corpses would be in the primes of their lives, if they weren't dead.

Bastian moved first. Tentatively, still holding the lit torch, though now they didn't really need it. "Where are the rest of them?"

No children. No elders. It itched at the back of her neck, some formless apprehension she wasn't sure how to parse. "They could be in another chamber, couldn't they? Kept apart?"

"I guess." Bastian's brows slashed down. "But why?"

Slowly, Lore approached the nearest slab. Femme, muscular, maybe a handful of years older than her. Reddish hair, a smooth, unlined face. And not a hint of rot.

The last attack had been two days ago. Two days, with seventy-five victims. But there were far more than seventy-five bodies in this room, so these had to be corpses from all four attacked villages.

But why were they divided by age? And how had they been so well preserved?

"Lore." Bastian's voice was quiet, like he was afraid to disturb the dead. "Their palm."

One of the corpse's hands had fallen from the plinth. Lore didn't want to touch it; instead, she crouched and craned her neck to look.

An eclipse was carved into the meat of the corpse's palm. A sun across the top, its curve running beneath the fingers, rays stretching to where they began. A crescent moon across the bottom, completing the sun's arc.

"I don't understand," she murmured, straightening, closing her own scarred hand into a fist. "What does that mean?"

"Only one way to find out," Bastian said.

Lore placed her fingers lightly on the stone plinth before her. She closed her eyes and found the death hiding deep in the body, tugged on it gently.

The breath she took and held tasted of emptiness and mineral cold. Her fingertips grew cold and pale as strands of darkness eased from the corpse and into her, the world losing its color again.

Something didn't look right. She could see her own body, white light and gray and the mass of dark in her center. Bastian next to her, a light so bright it nearly throbbed. But right above the heart of every corpse, there was a knot of darkness, thickly tangled, the color of a sky devoid of moon or stars. It reminded her of the leak, of the door. Anton, again.

What had the Priest Exalted *done*?

Her heartbeat came slow, slower. Her limbs felt heavy. She'd taken in nearly as much Mortem as she could, and she slammed her palms down on the plinth, channeling it into the rock, feeling it grow porous and brittle.

Her veins were sluggish; her lungs couldn't pull in enough air to satisfy. She'd taken in more death than she should've been able to, in the short while she'd channeled. It was . . . was *thicker* than it should be, denser.

Her knees wobbled, and Bastian rushed to her, a warm arm over her shoulders holding her up and keeping her steady.

"What happened to you?" Lore murmured to the dead, her voice thin and reedy. "Who did this, and why?"

But the corpse in front of her was still and silent.

"I don't understand." Bastian's eyes narrowed. "What did—"

A creaking sound cut him off as every corpse in the cavern sat up. As every corpse in the cavern twisted to look at them with dead, blank eyes.

Understanding crashed into Lore like a wave: When she'd pulled the death out of one of them, it'd somehow pulled death from them all. Those writhing knots of dark she'd seen over their hearts must connect them, somehow.

Bastian shouldered in front of Lore as if on instinct. His hand fell to his side, to a dagger hidden in his dark clothes. What he would do with it, she didn't know—it wasn't like he could kill them all again.

But none of the dead moved to attack. Instead, as one, their mouths dropped open, wider than human jaws should allow.

"They awaken." It came from the first, the corpse closest to them. Blue lips didn't move, just like the child in the vaults. "They awaken as do the new vessels." The words became a chant, sonorous and echoing. "They awaken. They awaken as do the new vessels."

Lore felt as cold as the corpses, as still as death.

"They awaken." The corpses near the woman took up the chant. "They awaken as do the new vessels."

The chant spread like a drop of ink in a pool of water, rippling out until it reached every corpse in the cavern. They spoke at different speeds, picked up the chant at different times, a symphony of voices that filled the vast space of the cavern and came upon her like a tide.

Then the words cut off, and the dead began to scream.

CHAPTER THIRTY-SIX

Wounded dogs always go back to their masters.
                                        –Kirythean proverb

Gods, it was loud. A screeching cacophony echoing around the too-vast chamber, bouncing off stone walls, shaken into discordancy that stabbed at Lore's ears. She stumbled back from the plinth with its screaming corpse, tripped over a loose stone, landed on her ass with her hands clapped over her ears and her teeth gritted.

Thin threads of Mortem still clung to her fingers, strung between her and the stone-like residue from a spider's web, brushing cold against her face. An anomaly, something she'd never encountered before—once you stopped channeling, the threads should disappear. But something about this place, deep beneath the earth and inundated with death, seemed to make Mortem linger.

Next to her, Bastian knelt on the ground, the heels of his palms pressed so tightly to his ears they might leave a bruise. Neither of them tried to get to the door. It was too much; both of them focused only on staying together through the awful noise.

At least, until the bodies started moving.

Jerky at first, dead limbs waking, and all of it synchronized as if it'd been rehearsed. The right arm rising, fingers flexing. Then the left leg, swinging over the side of the plinths. All the while still screaming, mouths still hanging open.

"Shit," Lore breathed, and scrambled up from the ground. "Shit, this shouldn't be possible, *shit*—"

Bastian's eyes were closed; he didn't see, still hunched over his knees. Lore grabbed his shoulder and pulled him toward the door. His eyes opened as she did, widened, a curse inaudible below the din of the screaming corpses.

The door was, thankfully, still open. Lore dragged him out behind her just as the bodies in the chamber stood up. Every dead face turned to them at once, eyes black, mouths made maws, dark and opened wider than they ever should be.

Slowly, they started forward.

"Close it!" Bastian yelled, all thoughts of secrecy forgotten. Surely, all this screaming could be heard from miles away.

"I don't know how!" Lore thrust her hands at the stone, but the trailing threads of Mortem brushed against it listlessly, useless. "The magic is...it's *clinging*, I don't understand—"

Gods, there was so much she didn't understand. This power had lived in her for nearly twenty-four years, and it was still a mystery, unknowable, a curse diamond-faceted.

Bastian shouldn't be able to see the strands of Mortem on her fingers—he couldn't channel—but somehow, he did. The widening of his eyes and the way his mouth opened said he did.

One more mystery.

He rushed forward, pulled her hands away from the door. Shimmers of gold wavered in the air around his fingers, too much to be imagined, too corporeal to be a hallucination. She could see them clearly now, wrapping his palms, trailing from him the way Mortem trailed from her.

The Sun Prince gathered up the strands of death in his gold-shrouded fist and *yanked*.

The Mortem let go, tugging out of her like a thread through a needle's eye. Lore gasped, her vision flaring bright. Life itself seemed to spill from where Bastian touched her, blushing her skin and rushing her pulse, every nerve alive and tingling. Mortem fled from him, but she could still feel it, still grasp it if she wanted.

There was something else, too, a sense of duality: holding a rope made of shadow and one of light at once, like she was two things pressed into one form. Just a flicker of awareness, an answer to a question she hadn't known to ask—

The bodies in the chamber collapsed. The screaming stopped, leaving ringing silence behind.

They stood in the doorway, her hands cradled in his, breathing hard. His forehead tipped down, rested on hers; she let it. The heady feeling that had rushed through her when he pulled out the strands—*life*, glowing and vibrant, anathema to the magic she carried—slowly faded. And with it, that flash of knowledge, of something clicking into place. Answer and question falling away.

Lore pulled her hands out of Bastian's. "How did..." Her throat felt like she'd choked down a handful of gravel; Lore cleared it, tried again. "How did you do that, Bastian?"

He stared at his hands. The shimmer in the air around him had dimmed, but just barely, and it flared again when he raised his hand in her direction. Lore flinched, acting on instinct, and he let his hand drop.

"I don't know." He shook his head. "It must be something about being in the catacombs..."

Dawn was soon. Lore knew it, felt the certainty in her bones, just like she felt everything down here. They had to move; they didn't have time for this.

"What about you?" he asked, his voice still thin with nerves. "Has Mortem ever done that before?"

"Clung to me like that, or made a bunch of corpses start to chase me?" Her rueful laugh came out shaky. "No, on both counts."

"Rude of them not to answer your questions before they started screaming," Bastian said. "What was it they were muttering? Something about awakening?"

"*They awaken.* Nearly the same thing the first one told me." Lore frowned. "It'd be helpful if we had any idea who *they* is referring to."

"You mean it's not just nonsense?"

"The dead don't lie. It's an answer to the question I asked, if an oblique one." She rubbed at her forehead, leaving behind a streak of dust and torch ash. "But we have no idea what it fucking *means*."

Bastian turned to study the door. The sconces inside the chamber still burned, illuminating the mess of bodies littered over the floor; neither of them moved to douse the flames. The increased light revealed what their torches hadn't—an *X* on the stone door, barely visible against the pockmarked gray. "Think whoever made this also wrote that charming passage a few tunnels back?"

"Possible, but I doubt it." Lore ran her fingers over the *X*, then held them up, black with charcoal. "This was meant as a temporary marking, easy to remove."

"So hopefully not made with a bone."

"But it was locked with Mortem. Mortem used in a way I've only seen once." Lore wiped the charcoal off on her thigh. "At the leak a couple of days ago."

"Anton." Bastian's jaw was a tight line, his arms crossed as he stared at the door.

"Anton," she agreed.

This entire expedition had been about proving Anton a liar. But now that they'd done it, found incontrovertible proof, it weighed heavy on Lore's shoulders. And the blank, lost look on Bastian's face said he felt that weight, too.

My father is a bad man, he'd said in the atrium, limned in moonlight and poison flowers. It had to sting, to know your entire legacy was corrupt.

He sighed, looked to Lore. "So my uncle and my father are killing their own citizens to provoke a war?"

"Seems likely." Lore reached inside the chamber without actually stepping over the threshold and took one of the torches from the wall to replace the one she'd dropped. "But I don't understand *why*. Kirythea is at our doorstep anyway; an eventual war is nigh inevitable. Why exacerbate it?"

"There has to be some advantage we don't know about." Bastian walked beside her, frowning, his hair falling over his forehead. "Something that would make a war profitable, rather than a drain on resources."

"Not that a drain would ever be felt in the Citadel, anyway."

He inclined his head in agreement.

Their journey back to the well was silent. Lore led them by the map in her head, retracing their steps through the tangle of tunnels. When they passed the words etched into the wall, she only allowed herself one glance.

Divinity is never destroyed.

Up ahead, a thin ray of light shone, too bright to be the moon. Dawn had sneaked up on them, and the strength of its glow after hours in the catacombs made Lore's head ache.

Bastian stopped at the bottom of the stairs, scowling up into the sliver of sun. "He left it open," he muttered. "Barely."

"He'll be there to pull it off."

"Such faith you have in our monk." Bastian mounted the stairs and started climbing, carefully, the muscles of his shoulders moving beneath his dusty shirt as he kept his balance with one hand on the wall. "He's such a fickle thing; I wouldn't be surprised if he turned tail as soon as we came down here."

"You should have more faith in him," Lore said to the broad

expanse of Bastian's back. Realizing she was staring, she dropped her eyes to her own feet making their careful way up the narrow stairs. "He showed up, didn't he?"

Her answer was the lid of the well opening, sending down piercing light. Not full morning, but edged enough into dawn that the brightness made her look away.

When she turned back, Bastian was gone, the round opening ahead showing nothing but pink-washed sky. Lore rolled her eyes. Of course he would just hop out of the well once she was proven right. He and Gabe were probably spitting curses at each other right now.

But when Lore reached the top of the stairs, Bastian was on his knees between two of the Presque Mort, his head wrenched back, the tip of a bayonet denting the skin of his throat. Behind him stood Malcolm, his expression pensive, but the line of his mouth set in determination.

Before the well, Anton, his Bleeding God's Heart pendant glinting in the thin light.

And next to Anton, Gabe.

Bastian laughed, a terrible, rueful sound, all teeth. "What was it you were saying about having faith in him, Lore?"

But Lore didn't speak. She knew when she was caught.

A pause, the only sound the flap of Anton's robes against his legs in the morning breeze. Then Gabe stepped up to the well, offering a hand to help her down.

She didn't take it. She didn't look at him. She stepped down to the cobblestones on her own, even though her legs were shaking.

Anton waved a weary hand. "Take them to the Church. Our colleagues are waiting."

"Your *colleagues*?" Bastian spat. The Presque Mort hauled him up; she vaguely recognized both the guards holding Bastian from the day of the Mortem leak, and they both seemed a bit too eager to manhandle the Sun Prince. The bayonet tip never left his throat, but Bastian didn't stop snarling. "That's an interesting way to say *fellow traitors*."

Next to her, Gabe flinched. Bastian noticed, and turned his blazing eyes toward him, mouth twisted in an ugly mess of anger and betrayal. "I guess it's true what they say, huh, Remaut? When someone shows who they are, you'd better believe them. I thought to give you the benefit of the doubt. More fool me."

Gabe wasn't close enough to touch, but the very air around him seemed to vibrate with the force of keeping himself still. His fist curled by his side, white-knuckled.

"He's right."

All eyes snapped to Lore. She stared straight ahead, not looking at any of them, keeping her gaze locked on the thin flaring line of the sun emerging over the garden wall. "It seems like betrayal comes easily to you, Duke Remaut."

She'd wounded him. She'd meant to. Still, the subtle deflation of his shoulders, the way his face turned so all she could see was that infernal eye patch, made all her organs tie themselves in knots.

"I'm afraid it's a bit more complicated than you and my nephew think." Anton peered at her, the rising sun behind him making the scarred side of his face a mass of runneled shadow. "Questions of betrayal and treason often are. But we're getting ahead of ourselves." He turned sharply, headed toward the door cut into the wall of the garden that led back into the Church. "Come. We have much to discuss."

❦

The Presque Mort deposited Lore and Bastian in a large antechamber, empty other than a long table and a handful of chairs, hung with one simple tapestry of Apollius clutching His bleeding chest. It reminded Lore of the room she'd been taken to after accidentally raising Horse.

Her bonds were a bit more intricate this time. So were Bastian's. Instead of ropes, their hands were manacled, and those manacles attached to thick iron rings in the floor. A slanted echo of the iron bars crossing the floor in the Citadel.

She supposed no one needed that particular reminder of their holy purpose in the Church. There were reminders everywhere.

It was Malcolm who locked the manacles around her wrists. "Why?" she asked as he worked, not bothering to whisper. "I thought you wanted things to change, Malcolm? I thought you were on our side?"

She didn't mean to sound so wounded.

The head librarian took a moment to answer. When he did, it was with a sigh. "Anton will explain," he said. "Gabe came to him, then they both came to me, and what they told me let me know that we have to work together."

Lore scowled. Next to her, another Presque Mort shackled Bastian, but the Sun Prince stayed silent, staring at the floor.

An hour later, and that silence still held. In that hour, she'd observed that they both handled betrayal differently. Lore iced over, letting no emotion cross her face. Bastian, by contrast, cycled between looking like he might attempt to pull the iron ring out of the floor with his bare hands, and looking like he'd just lost a friend.

She supposed he had, in a way. The thing between her and Gabe and Bastian wasn't friendship, not really—it was both deeper and less complicated than that, somehow, a primal knot none of them could untie. Gabe's betrayal stung, but in a way, it also felt inevitable.

"I'm sorry, Lore," Bastian murmured.

Her brows knit. "Sorry for what?"

"If Gabe betraying me feels this bad," he said to his bound hands, "then I can't imagine how it feels for you, when you care for him the way you do."

"I don't care for him like... like anything." It came out breathy, not enough power behind the words to make them a truth or a lie. They just hung there.

The door opened. Both of them looked up.

Anton and Gabe, as expected, and Malcolm with them. The librarian darted a quick, furtive look at Lore, apprehension coiled in his expression.

The Presque Mort parted, revealing another figure behind them.

Severin Bellegarde.

"Well then," Bastian said, sitting back in his chair with a clanking of chain. "It seems like everything we theorized is true. But what do you get out of war, Severin? Money? You've already got more houses than family members, and your style of dress makes it clear you care nothing for current fashion—"

"No one wants a war, Bastian." Anton had changed out of his robes and into the close, dark clothing he'd worn the day of the leak, matching Gabe and Malcolm. He sat down at the table and crossed his arms, looking suddenly like a much younger man despite the gray shock of his hair. "That is, in fact, precisely what we're trying to prevent."

We. Apparently meaning him and Bellegarde.

Bastian's eyes slid to Lore's, the same realization hitting them both—the door to the chamber was closed. No one else was coming.

And August wasn't here.

Bellegarde watched the thought spark on their faces, a thin smile creasing his dour face. "The only person trying to start a war is August," he said. "And we are not in accord."

"My brother believes we are on the same side, but we haven't been. Not for a long time." Anton shifted on the table, rested his elbows on his knees, and looked to Bastian. "I'm sorry, nephew."

"Sorry for what?" Bastian had wiped all emotion from his face, donned the mask of careless prince. He tipped up his chin, dark hair falling down his back. "Bit late for regrets, isn't it?"

"I'm sorry," Anton said slowly, ignoring him, "that sickness and jealousy have made your father a bad man. I am sorry that you have borne the brunt." A pause. "I'm sorry he wants you dead, when you, of all people, do not deserve his ire."

A muscle twitched in Bastian's jaw. His manacled hands tensed, just enough to make his chains click together, and something sorrowful flickered across his face. His father was dying; his father wanted him dead. Both things that sat heavy.

The half-tender and half-unsettling moment ended when Anton turned Lore's way. "What happened when you tried to raise the body in the chamber?"

Her mouth opened to lie on instinct, to claim no knowledge of a chamber or a body in it. But they were long past that. Lore slumped in her seat, manacles clanking.

By the door, Gabe winced, just a bit. She thought of him that first day, loosening her restraints, trying to make her as comfortable as she could be, and pushed the memory viciously away.

"We know that's why you went there," Anton said wearily, taking her silence as reluctance. "And that's why we didn't stop you. Why we left the note, why Danielle was instructed to tell you about the docks—her family also realizes what kind of threat August has become, and is loyal to Church over Crown, to gods over humans. We need to know what happened, Lore."

The note Bellegarde had planted, Dani at Alie's tea. Lore had been led along like a child holding a parent's hand; they'd been brought here so easily.

Beyond Anton, Gabe closed his eye, tilted his chin away. Had he known? Had he been part of Anton's plan from the start?

The rest of them looked at her, the Presque Mort and Bellegarde and even Bastian, with varying levels of confusion and expectation. Lore shrank in on herself, suddenly self-conscious of her failure once again. "It didn't work. They didn't say anything new."

"Nothing new," Anton repeated. "So the same thing as last time."

She nodded.

A quick look slid between Anton and Bellegarde, so fast she might've imagined it. "And what else happened, Lore?"

"I had to get past your lock, first," she said petulantly. If he was going to talk to her like a child, she could play the damn part.

A slight smile bent the Priest Exalted's thin mouth. "Yes. That was quite a feat. It took much practice to bend Mortem in such a way. Practice, and research." He nodded briefly to Malcolm. "It is fortunate that we've kept such a wealth of knowledge in the library."

Malcolm's lips pressed flat. He said nothing.

"And after that?" Anton prompted.

"I raised one of them." She didn't mention the markings on the corpse's hand. "But all of them got up. Every single one in the chamber."

"Got up?" Bellegarde asked excitedly. Behind him, a slightly repulsed look spasmed across Malcolm's face before he schooled it into neutrality again. "They were ambulatory?"

She nodded, though the nobleman's excitement at a bunch of moving corpses made her mouth twist in the same disgusted way Malcolm's had. "They all moved at the same time. Got up off their slabs and started coming toward us."

"While screaming," Bastian added. "Don't forget the screaming."

But the screaming aspect didn't seem to matter to Bellegarde. He turned to Anton with barely leashed excitement. "That means the binding works. All that's needed is—"

Anton held up a hand, and the nobleman went immediately silent.

"What binding?" Lore snapped. "What are you talking about?"

The Priest Exalted sighed. "We bound the corpses," he said

quietly. "I tied the knot yesterday, but Gabriel and Malcolm channeled the Mortem. Putting all those years of study on the properties of magic to use."

Her eyes darted to Gabe, instinct overriding the desire not to look at him, a renewed sense of betrayal making her stomach feel hollow. Gabe's shoulders were crooked, his head tilted so she couldn't see his expression.

Anton noticed. A calculating look flashed in his eye. "We connected the corpses," he continued, "so that what happened to one would happen to the others, once the Mortem in them was channeled out again. As an experiment, you understand, to see if waking one of the dead could wake them all." He gestured to Lore. "But the waking must be done by a powerful necromancer. The most powerful we could find, and only after their power had been honed, both by nearing the age of Consecration and by proximity to Spiritum." His gesturing hand went to Bastian. "We needed the two of you to be close together, so your powers would sharpen each other. The Law of Opposites in action."

"I don't have any fucking Spiritum," Bastian hissed. "None of us do; it's a fairy tale."

"Apollius gives the gift to his chosen," Anton said softly. "And that's you, Bastian." His fingers rose, touched the scarred side of his face. There were scars on his hand, too, Lore noticed. They looked new, still red and angry.

"I was told so by the god himself," Anton continued. "Told that you were the Arceneaux to whom he'd bestow his power. Told that Gabriel Remaut and a child from the catacombs must stay close by you after your Consecration, and that it would pave the way for Apollius's return."

"What?"

Gabe's voice, thin and quiet. His blue eye was wide, his mouth opening, then closing again.

"This has all been in motion for years," Anton murmured.

"Echoing through time. Apollius reaching down to commune with us. An Arceneaux prince, a child of treason, and the child of a Night Sister, born able to channel Mortem." He spread his hands, smiled gently with the side of his mouth that could do such a thing. "The clearest anyone has ever heard His voice since Gerard Arceneaux himself."

Shock made Gabe's face taut and pale. He shook his head, slightly, like he could make Anton's words connect in a different way, one that made sense.

Of course the thing he latched onto was her. This proof that she was something unholy. "The daughter of a Night Sister..." Gabe turned to Lore, shock transmuting to horror. "What is he talking about?"

She didn't know what to say. All the reasons she hadn't told him came into sharp focus: the sickened expression, the way he took a short, instinctual step back from her, though they were yards apart already. Anton had just said they'd all been used this entire time, made to play out a vision he hadn't shared with them wholly. But the part that hit Gabe hardest was Lore the Night Sister, Lore holding death in her hands since birth.

Bastian noticed. His eyes narrowed, a cruel curve bending his mouth. "See why she didn't tell you, Remaut?"

Gabe swallowed. "You told *Bastian*?"

She still couldn't make herself speak. The Sun Prince did it for her. "Yes," he said, leaning back in his chair, its legs creaking and his chains clanging. "She told Bastian."

Malcolm, Bellegarde, and Anton said nothing, letting the silence drop around them like a shroud around a body. Anton's expression was blank. He'd just dealt a blow to Gabe, and he didn't give a single shit. He'd just completely torn apart everything they thought they knew about each other, about *themselves*, and not one emotion crossed his face.

Visions and prophecies and coups and wars, but all of those

things paled for Lore in the face of the death they'd wrought. The justice she'd apparently never been working toward, that she hadn't known until this moment she wanted so, so badly.

"So you killed them, then?" Lore asked. All those bodies, that child—all killed for an experiment, to see what could be done with the awful magic leaking from a buried goddess and a girl who'd been cursed with it. To the Citadel and the Church, they were all expendable, and Lore hated that more than she'd ever hated anything in her life. "You murdered all those villages?"

"No," Anton said, almost pityingly. "No, Lore, I did not murder the villages."

All this, and they still didn't know. All this, and they were no closer to answers.

"But what's killing them pales in comparison with what August is planning to do with them," Anton continued. "He plans to use them as an army. An army that cannot be defeated." He looked to Lore. "But it's an army that you now control, Lore. That's why we led you to the catacombs tonight, before the eclipse ball. So that you could take control of the armies of the dead before August could."

CHAPTER THIRTY-SEVEN

Curdled love is the most bitter medicine.

—Caldienan proverb

"No," Lore said.

Even Gabe, still stricken with the revelation of her past and Anton's vision, looked almost proud of her for that. Almost.

"No?" Anton said mildly.

"I won't do it. I won't raise them." Her eyes swung from Anton to Bellegarde to Malcolm, looking for a sign that this would work, that her refusal would mean something. "I won't raise them, I won't control them. I won't do anything for August, or for you."

Anton sighed. "My dear," he murmured, "I'm afraid it's too late for that."

The sun rising in the window beat heat onto the back of her neck, a burn mirrored by the moon-shaped scar on her palm. "What do you mean?"

The Priest Exalted sighed again, as if this pained him. He raised a brow, a teacher urging along a particularly reluctant student.

But Lore didn't want his gentle prodding. She wanted fucking answers. "What do you *mean*, dammit, tell me what—"

"Lore." Gabe's voice was hoarse. Still, it made her own vanish.

Bastian lifted his head, staring daggers at the other man.

Gabe didn't pay him any attention. He looked only at Lore. "Do you remember what happened with Horse? Why we had to go check on the body in the vaults, that night Bastian found us?"

Her brows drew together, unsure what to make of the sudden swerve in conversation. "Of course," she said slowly. "I raised him, and then he—"

And he stayed raised. She raised him, and he stayed raised, just like the body of the child in the vault.

Anton said that the corpses from the villages were bound together—what happened to one, happened to all of them.

Lore lurched from her seat, the weight of the iron manacles pulling painfully at her shoulders. "I can fix it. I did once before."

"You can't this time," Anton said gently. "It's hundreds of bodies. Lore—even for you, channeling that much Mortem would be nearly impossible."

"You have to let me try!" She didn't want to cry here, not in front of them, but she was so angry and overwhelmed and crying was always hardest to fight off when she was overwhelmed, thinking of the catacombs beneath them, full of screaming corpses who'd been people, just people—

"So this is why you led us down there." Bastian's voice, calm and cold and cutting through her panic. His gaze was squared on Gabe. "This is why you came back and helped us. So that Lore would raise the dead, and there'd be no way to undo it."

Gabe didn't say anything. He didn't have to. The look on his face proved the accusation true.

Bastian sat back, casual as if the chair and chains were a gilded throne. "Why are we supposed to believe you aren't working with my father, again? After you just made us start up his undead army?"

"Because August doesn't control the army," Anton said. "And if we're successful, he never will."

"August wouldn't be able to control it, anyway," she said. "He can't channel Mortem."

"Not yet," Anton murmured.

In the distance, bells began to toll. First Day. Somewhere, sunrise prayers were beginning.

Gabe stood still as a statue in his place by the door, face stony, revealing nothing. Lore closed her eyes, turned her head. She didn't want to look at him, but her eyes kept sliding his way, consistently drawn back into his gravity.

"And what, exactly, made you both decide you couldn't let this happen?" Bastian asked. "My father has been a tyrant for years. He's sucked this country dry, let nobles—let *you*—grow richer while everyone outside the Citadel walls has less and less every year. So you only care when his mind turns to war? When it becomes something that might affect *you*?"

"August cares nothing for Apollius." Bellegarde's expression wasn't quite a sneer, but it was close. "He would attempt to change his role in history. To take a place that is not his, to try and avoid his own destiny. The Priest Exalted's vision was clear. August cannot go to war with Kirythea. It would undermine everything."

It wasn't an answer, not really, but it gave closure just the same. This wasn't about protecting Auverraine. This was about power, and about using religion to secure it.

Bastian's sneer was much more obvious than Bellegarde's. "None of this changes the fact that I don't have any magic. I'm not the *chosen*."

"It clings to you like ink on paper." There was a note of reverence in Anton's voice; he looked at his nephew with a peaceful expression, as if the sight of him soothed some ache in his heart. "Whether you believe it or not, Bastian, you are the one we've been waiting for. The one Apollius has blessed. I'm sorry I didn't realize it from the beginning."

Bastian twitched against his chair, like he would've tried to move away from his uncle if his chains hadn't prevented it.

Lore's head hurt. She thought of last night, when they'd stood in that atrium full of poison flowers, of the gold that wreathed his hands.

Bastian's eyes flickered her way, like he was reliving the same memory. He took a shaky breath, steeled the line of his jaw. "Who knows about this?"

"Everyone, if they believe the Tracts."

"You know what I mean, old man." Something poison seethed beneath Bastian's voice. Something right at the edge of violence.

Anton noticed, eyeing his nephew thoughtfully. "Only your father, and those of us in this room." His peaceful expression darkened. "It's another reason August wants you dead. He thinks he can substitute himself as Apollius's chosen when you're out of the way."

"Transubstantiation," Malcolm murmured quietly. "Overcoming the physical with the spiritual."

The Priest Exalted nodded. "And once he has Spiritum, he can take Lore's power and channel them both. Wield life and death like a sword in each hand."

"You can't have both." Lore shook her head. "Mortem and Spiritum cancel each other out."

"On the contrary," Anton answered. "One strengthens the presence of the other. They can only be held simultaneously in certain circumstances"—his one seeing eye flickered between Bastian and Lore, unreadable—"but it can be done. On an eclipse, for example."

Bastian in the catacombs, making her promise not to go to the eclipse ball, all because of a feeling. All of them knowing things they shouldn't, knowledge slotting into place with no reasoning behind it.

"So it's been you from the beginning." Lore's vision blurred, the iron ring that held her chains becoming a splash of gray against the floor. "You watching me since I came up from the catacombs, you organizing the raid so I would show myself. You bringing me here and planting clues that would lead me to raising the army, all to make the pieces of your vision fall into place. Stringing August along, too, until he decided he wanted a war."

Anton nodded, smooth and unruffled.

So used to being used, all of them.

"And you?" Tears blurred her vision still; when she looked at Gabe, all she saw was a tall shadow, a shock of red-gold. "Staying with me, being with—being my friend?" She caught herself before she said something else, something more heated. "Was it all an act?"

"Gabriel was as unaware as you were," Anton said. "When he came to me yesterday and told me your plan, he expected me to stop you. He was very reluctant to let you roam the catacombs."

Lore dropped her eyes and concentrated very, very hard on the floor between her feet.

"I told him, then, what we needed to happen. What we'd been working toward. Our necromancer raising the dead, and my nephew's powers being sharpened by yours, so he could step into his rightful place. Now, unfortunately, there is still the matter of the eclipse. Of your Consecration, Lore."

"My Consecration?"

"Your power over Mortem will reach its height on your twenty-fourth birthday. Which happens to coincide with the eclipse." Anton crossed his arms. "August plans to kill you both and take your power at the ball."

"But how would he do that?" She directed her question to the floor; her head felt too heavy to lift. "Steal our power?"

The Priest Exalted's scarred face was nearly pitying. "Killing you at the moment of totality, when the moon fully covers the sun. When the powers of life and death can be wielded together." His eye glinted. "When chosen vessels are made manifest."

"No." Bastian and Gabe said it at the same time, their voices harmonizing against the marble walls. Lore's head came up; the two men looked at each other with naked hatred, all that complicated feeling finally alchemized into something blade-sharp.

"He won't kill Lore." Gabe tore his gaze away from Bastian to look at Anton instead. "You said—"

"Peace, son." Calm words, but Anton's voice snapped. Gabe flinched. "Lore will be perfectly safe."

"It still seems like the best course of action would be to hide her until the eclipse is over." Gabe stepped up, a determined tilt to his chin; he expected another reason to flinch, and wanted to keep it from happening this time. He said nothing about Bastian's safety. "Keep her here, or send her to her mothers."

Mari and Val. Calling them her mothers, even now that he knew her true origins, felt like some kind of absolution.

But Anton shook his head before Gabe finished speaking. "It won't work. We need things to continue as if we have no idea what August is planning, to keep him from getting suspicious."

"So we go to this damn ball as if nothing has happened," Bastian said, looking at Lore, "and we trust that you'll keep my father from killing us and starting a war."

Skepticism ran deep furrows in the words.

"You," Anton murmured, "have no idea of all the things I've stopped your father from doing, Bastian. All the things I've shielded you from."

It was enough to break his gaze away from Lore's. The Sun Prince looked, for the first time since she'd met him, completely at a loss.

"Now then." Anton turned to Gabe, as if the matter was concluded. "The ball is in two days. I suggest you all get plenty of rest before then, as it's bound to be a long night. Lore, you stay in your rooms. Gabriel will take you there and keep guard."

Keep her prisoner. Make sure she didn't escape. Lore wished

she had the energy to attempt it anyway, but she didn't. The last few days had reached inside her and clawed everything out.

"Bastian," Anton said, turning back around. "I think it best if you stay here."

A bark of harsh laughter. "There it is." Bastian sat back in his chair, shook his wrists so his chains clanked. "So I'm a prisoner now?"

"Think of it as being a guest," Anton said.

Bastian didn't respond, but his eyes glittered a cold, violent promise.

"I will keep you safe, nephew," Anton murmured, almost reverently. "Everything will be revealed in time."

Lore didn't know what that meant. It looked like Bastian didn't, either. She let Gabe unlock her chains, let him lead her silently to the door.

When she looked back, day had fully broken in the window behind Bastian, casting his features in shadow, limning their edges gold. It illuminated him like rays around a sun, like a halo.

Chapter Thirty-Eight

Sometimes, you can see love coming. And when it takes a different path, you should be thankful.

—Fragment from the work of Marya Addou, Malfouran poet

The walk back to their apartments was silent. Gabe stayed behind her, a one-eyed shadow dogging her steps and making sure she went where she was supposed to. She no longer wore chains, but it was the first time Lore had truly felt like a prisoner in the Citadel.

Their room was locked. Lore had the key half fitted in the door before Gabe stepped up beside her. "It won't work." His voice was low. "Anton had the lock changed."

She looked at him and said nothing. There was nothing to say.

Gabe swallowed. He unlocked the door with a key he produced from his pocket, then stepped aside to let her in first.

The apartments felt strange now—foreign and ill fitting, where before they'd been as close to comfortable as she could find here. Especially knowing Anton had changed the lock sometime after she left last night. Myriad hells, he'd probably had someone waiting in the halls, watching for her to leave so they could immediately set to work.

Because Gabe told him. Gabe told him everything.

Her wrists felt raw. The iron had made them itch. Lore rubbed and rubbed at them, trying to force the feeling out of her skin, trying to make it stop—

Gentle pressure, Gabe's fingers interposed where hers had been. "Lore, you're going to hurt yourself—"

It'd been the truth when she told Gabe and Bastian that she was no good at brawling, but instinct made do. Lore snatched her wrist from Gabe's hand and struck out with the heel of her opposite palm, smacking him in the shoulder, pushing him off balance and away.

"Don't touch me," she snarled. "Don't fucking touch me."

He stared at her, one blue eye wide. His jaw clenched beneath the reddish stubble on his chin. "I was trying to keep you safe."

"By going to the *very person* we knew was lying?"

"He's on our side! You heard everything I just did, you know that Anton is working against August!"

"But *you* didn't." Her fingers went back to her wrist again, itching, itching. "You had no idea what Anton was involved in, and it's pure stupid luck you didn't get all three of us murdered!"

"It was either that or watch you go to a far more likely murder in the damn catacombs!" Gabe ran his hands over his close-shorn hair, turned away. "I wanted him to stop you from going down there at all. *Both* of you. That seemed like a much more pressing matter than playing politics—"

"It's more than *playing politics*! If we'd been right, if Anton and August were still on the same side, Bastian might've—"

"Forgive me," Gabe cut in, nearly a snarl. "I forgot that one must always be thinking of Bastian first."

"Save it," Lore hissed. "We both know what happened here. You got overwhelmed with the thought that maybe, just once, you were wrong about something. You got *scared*."

Gabe's hands twitched back and forth to almost-fists. Instinct had ahold of him, too, and it told him to defend the man who'd stepped in when his father bled out. "Whatever side Anton was on," he said, "I knew that would be the right one."

She laughed, high and harsh. "Gods, Gabe, you're like a kicked dog going back to the damn boot. Anton took you in because he hallucinated that a vanished god told him to. He doesn't love you. He never has. He's not your father, no matter what the Church wants you to call him."

The Presque Mort took a step toward her, and she was reminded, against her will, of that night in her room, his mouth on her neck, his roaming hands. She wondered if he'd kiss her like that again now. It seemed to be what they defaulted to, the only way they could communicate when everything else piled up in jagged mountains, unable to be climbed.

"I wanted to keep you safe." It rumbled from him, low and dark, but he stopped paces away and held himself there, not allowing his body one inch closer to hers. "And if that meant Bastian got hurt, so be it."

Lore bared her teeth. "I am gods-damned tired of being the rope in your and Bastian's tug-of-war."

"Especially since you've already chosen the winner of the match, right?" He laughed just like she had: no joy in it, none at all. "You did the moment you told him where you came from."

There it was.

"You didn't know that until an hour ago," Lore said. "Don't act like it's an excuse."

"How long?" Gabe growled. "How long has he known? I asked you, that first day. I asked you how you came to channel Mortem, and you lied to me. Did you ever lie to him, or was he worthy of the truth from the beginning?"

He stood straight and unbowed as ever, but there was a crookedness to the line of his shoulders. Gabe worked so hard not to show hurt on his face; it came out in other places.

"I told him the night he took us to the boxing ring," Lore answered. "The first time."

His eye fluttered closed, then open. "That long, huh?"

She said nothing.

Gabe nodded, his lips twisted in a bitter smile. "You two have been laughing at me for a while, then."

"It wasn't like that, Gabe. The only reason I told him was because he threatened—"

"Maybe you weren't laughing, but he certainly was. And maybe he did threaten you, Lore, but we both know you would've told him eventually. You trusted him enough to follow him into the damn catacombs." He shook his head with a sharp laugh. "One more way he's beaten me. One more way he's better."

"Bleeding God, not everything is about you and your guilt!" Lore shook her head. "You want to know why I didn't tell you where I came from? Because I knew how you'd react. I knew you'd think I was some kind of monster."

"You don't know me at all," Gabe said, and it was true. Him and her and Bastian were somehow bound, yes, but it didn't truly make them known, not in all their intricacies. Their odd connections emphasized that point, rather than obscuring it.

"No. I don't," Lore said wearily. "And maybe it's best if I keep it that way."

As if she had a choice in the matter. As if she didn't feel the walls of *something* closing in, trapping the three of them in its center.

There was no flicker of emotion on Gabe's face—no hurt, no anger. He'd scrubbed it all out, left blankness in its wake.

"Get some rest." Flat, cold. "I'll be outside." He skirted around her, opened the door.

Lore turned to follow him with her eyes. "And when can I leave?"

"Eclipse ball is two nights from now, at eight," Gabe answered. "So about ten minutes before that."

The door closed. The lock clicked.

🦋

She didn't mean to fall asleep.

It almost seemed out of her control. One moment, she was sitting in the tiny study, curled up on the one chair, and the next she was by the vast blue ocean, white sand crumbling beneath her feet, the tide gently rolling in to slide against her bare ankles.

"Huh," Lore said, and then realized it was the first time she'd been able to speak in one of these dreams. That felt important.

The figure beside her seemed to think so, too. Lore didn't turn her head to look at them, but she felt them stiffen, as if they'd grown more corporeal. "Your time grows near." Smooth, textureless, a voice that didn't seem to go with a throat. "And I don't know how the process will change, so we might as well get as much out of this as we can."

The voice seemed to be convincing itself.

A tug at her heart, as if it was being pulled through her ribs. The stream of black smoke, spilling from her and across the sky.

It was an effort to turn her head. But Lore did.

The figure turned, too. And it was Cedric. Cedric's perfect, unblemished face above the ruin of his body, his bloodstained teeth spreading in a wide smile.

But the figure shifted. The child from the vaults, mouth hanging open. Another blur, and it was her mother's face staring back at her.

Her hair was long and straight and pale, her eyes the same bright hazel as Lore's. With a gentle smile Lore had never actually seen her wear, she leaned forward, pressing a hand to her daughter's cheek.

"She just never stops trying," she murmured as her thumb

brushed Lore's skin, though the voice wasn't right. It was unnaturally smooth, the same voice from before, everything human stripped out of it. "She doesn't understand that He cannot allow Them to return." The facsimile of her mother sighed, smoothed her hair. "It's not your fault. At least we can use what She gives, this time. It will all be over soon."

The tugging feeling in Lore's chest became unbearable, as if her body was trying to turn itself inside out. She screamed as smoke plumed gracefully across the sky.

❦

"Shit."

Lore sat up, pushing tangled, sweaty hair from her eyes. Her neck felt like it was on fire—she'd fallen asleep with it angled on the chair arm. Cursing again, she rubbed at the ache and stumbled into the main sitting room, squinting at the clock.

After a day of isolation, the darkness outside the window told her it was the very early morning of her birthday.

Tonight was the eclipse.

Food was on the table behind the couch. Easy things, apples and bread and cheese, things that could be set out and forgotten.

She read it like it was a code. No one would be opening that door, not until they were ready to escort her to the eclipse ball.

Escort her to her Consecration, and whatever ritual August had planned around it to make her magic his own. A ritual she had to trust Anton to stop, or she and Bastian would both be dead.

It was almost funny, how easily she accepted that Bastian was magic. That he was born to channel life the same way she was born to channel death, that she was his dark reflection. Down there in the catacombs, with the unquiet dead making their slow way to the door and threads of Mortem tangled in her fingers, she'd felt it when Bastian pulled the clinging threads away. *Life*, rushing, her veins flooded with too much blood, her lungs full of too much air. In that moment, he'd commanded both life and death, he'd held them both in his hands.

She'd been his lightning rod, the darkness that made the light shine brighter after his Consecration. And now, hers approached. She'd felt her power growing stronger as she spent more time with Bastian, as time marched her down to twenty-four years. A moment that, for others, meant holy celebration.

For her, it meant possible murder.

That figured. Lore grabbed a piece of cheese and flopped back on the couch.

A tear rolled down her temple and wet her hair. She didn't realize she'd shed one until it dripped into her ear, warm and wet and distinctly unpleasant.

"*Fuck* you, Gabe," she murmured into the air, hoping he was still outside the door, hoping he heard. Half of her wanted to try to open it, see if he was on the other side. See what he would do if she tried to walk out. Would he tie her up? Knock her out? Kiss her?

All of those options seemed possible.

Thinking of Gabe made her mind turn to Bastian yet again. Where he was, whether Anton was being cruel. She didn't think so—the strange conversation they'd had while chained made it seem like Anton had been keeping Bastian safe for longer than they realized; she couldn't shake the memory of his near-reverent voice. Still, leaving him at the mercy of his uncle made her nervous.

None of them were safe here. None of them could leave.

Her mind drifted, but she didn't let herself sleep again. The light through the window brightened to morning, deepened to midday, began the slow, golden melt of a midsummer afternoon.

She ate a little more, mostly to settle her sloshing stomach. She opened a bottle of wine from the sideboard below the window, and briefly thought of the first night she and Gabe had pilfered through it before giving a violent shake of her aching head, like the memory was a fly she could slap.

Lore drank half the bottle and swam pleasantly in the warm buzz of it as another hour ticked past and the window dimmed. It still hadn't rained, and the dryness of the air gave the sunlight a brittle quality, like just-polished glass.

When the clock noted half an hour to eight, the door opened. Gabe. He looked at her wild hair and her flushed face and didn't comment on either of them. He held a garment bag in his hands and thrust it at her.

"Get dressed." He sounded like he hadn't spoken in days, like the last words he'd said were to her and in anger. "We'll leave in twenty minutes."

"Such a man of his word."

His jaw twitched. Gabe laid down the bag and backed out the door, clicking the lock behind him again.

Carefully, still feeling some aftereffects from the wine, Lore made her way over and picked up the bag, pulling out a gown. It wasn't heavy—panels of sheer dark lace made up the skirt, with a simple black bodice that dipped low in the front and back and left her arms bare. No appliques, no embroidery. Just black lace and black silk.

"Showtime," Lore muttered.

CHAPTER THIRTY-NINE

To hold both darkness and light–to hold everything the world is made of–should be the burden of only one god. All powers will come into My hand, and then the world will know the hour of My return.

–The Book of Holy Law, Tract 856 (green text, spoken directly by Apollius to Gerard Arceneaux)

Twenty minutes later and ten until eight, Gabe opened the door again, just as Lore was dragging a comb through her hair. "Give me a second," she said, twisting it into a messy braid and winding it around her head. The bag had held a handful of jet hairpins; she stuck them in the braid to hold it in place and only stabbed her scalp once.

He didn't say anything, didn't relax his pose. Gabe's shoulders nearly took up the width of the doorframe, solid and straight. He'd evened out whatever apprehension had made them crooked before. A harsh sound; his throat clearing. "You look..."

She looked *good*, and she knew it. The gown fit perfectly, as if it'd been made for her, and the lack of ornamentation or jewelry suited it just fine. Lore resisted the urge to twirl. She'd done it a couple times before he opened the door, but as satisfying as the swirl of skirts had been, it felt somewhat morbid, what with an impending doom ritual. Instead, she ignored Gabe, nodded at her reflection in the spotted mirror, and approached the door. "Let's get this over with."

But he didn't move. Gabe blocked the door, looking down at her with an expression that seemed to hover somewhere between determination and pain. She met his gaze, tried to keep her own expression from saying anything at all.

"I'm going to keep you safe," he murmured. "You can trust that."

"I can't trust anything," she said lightly, and there was no waver in it; she wouldn't give him wavering. Lore nodded to the door. "We're going to be late."

He stood there a moment longer, looking for words and not finding them. Finally, Gabe turned and offered her his elbow, the same way he'd done when they were newly arrived and dressed like foxgloves, headed to Bastian's masquerade with no idea what to expect.

They walked into the hall. They were silent.

❦

In a twist of dark irony, the eclipse ball was taking place in the same atrium that Bastian and Lore had crossed through on their way to the catacombs. A long table stood at one end of the glass room, nearly covered by the leaves of poisonous flowers, though the plants stood far enough away so as not to be a danger to the wine fountain burbling in the table's center. Silver chairs were placed next to the gleaming windows, clustered for ease of gossip. A string band was stationed in the corner, playing a lively song for the spinning dancers in the center of the floor. There were far more guests than Lore had expected, enough to make the large atrium feel crowded.

She recognized Cecelia in the corner, though she didn't appear to have any poison tea at this particular party. Next to her, Dani, along with another blond woman who had to be her sister. Amelia, Lore remembered. The blond woman's eyes tracked to Lore as soon as she entered the room, then darted away, but Dani didn't avert her gaze even when Lore met it.

It hurt more than it should, to know that she'd been working for Anton from the beginning, that all her overtures of companionship had an ulterior motive. Unfair of Lore to judge for that, all things considered, but the hurt remained as she tore her eyes from the other woman. Briefly, she wondered if Alie was in on it, too, if all the tentative friendships she'd made here were predicated on eventual betrayal, an even shakier foundation than she'd assumed.

Lore made herself stop thinking of that. She didn't have the time or the energy for it now.

August's throne wasn't helping the crowding issue. It wasn't the huge one from downstairs—instead, a travel throne stood on a wooden dais at the front end of the atrium, wrought in woven strands of gold and silver. At the top, a sun and moon hovered over each other, held up by threads of precious metals so thin they were nearly invisible.

The Sainted King himself looked oddly stoic for a party. Stoic, and even worse than the last time Lore had seen him—his face gaunt, his eyes set back in darkened hollows, the skin beneath them bruised. He watched Gabe escort Lore inside but didn't acknowledge them, his face drawn in thought.

He appeared to be the only major player here so far. There were no Presque Mort, no Anton, no Bellegarde, though Alie was among the spinning dancers. This seemed like any other party, and the normalcy made Lore's dread go from a slink through her middle to a slow spiral in her chest.

Lore looked for Bastian, hoping he was here even if his captors weren't. She didn't see him. Nerves made her hand twitch—Gabe tightened his elbow around it, as good as a vise.

"You make a good jailer," she murmured from the side of her mouth.

Something in him collapsed, just by a fraction, the steel in his frame buckling. "Lore, please—"

"Finally!"

On the floor, Alie broke away from her dance partner—Brigitte, who tipped Lore a wave before heading toward the wine table— and nearly ran to them, grinning widely. "I was wondering when you'd get here! The dancing is almost over!"

Even with the way Anton's reveals had twisted everything, having Alie close still felt like a comfort. "I thought it didn't start until eight?" Lore asked.

"The *dinner* starts at eight," Alie corrected. "Or a bit after, I guess—I think the idea is to time it with the point of total eclipse."

The reminder of totality—of what August planned to do when the moon covered the sun and dipped the world in darkness—made the dread in Lore's gut go from a slow spiral to a sharp knot.

Alie fanned herself with her hand, drying the glowy sheen of sweat on her brow. "Why August is so adamant about making his select few guests eat in the dark, I have no idea."

A select few guests. So those August thought were on his side, who either wouldn't interfere with the ritual or, like Bellegarde, planned to betray their King and stop it.

Lore wasn't sure which faction unsettled her more, really.

The band struck up again, this time at a slower pace—a waltz. "The last dance of the night." Alie swallowed, then firmed her chin and looked up at Gabe, who'd been silent since she approached. "Would you dance with me, Gabe?"

He flinched; Lore felt it, her hand still imprisoned in the crook of his arm. "I'm afraid I..."

"He'd love to," came a voice from behind them, low and familiar.

Bastian, thank the gods.

The Sun Prince looked none the worse for wear, other than a clinging tiredness around his golden-brown eyes. His clothing was dark and unadorned, a match for Lore's gown, his only ornament the golden circlet on his head, this one devoid of garnets. He wore a smile, but his face was pale beneath it. The smile went bladed as he clapped a hand on Gabe's shoulder, a little too hard to be companionable. "Duke Remaut is never one to leave ladies waiting."

Something dark slithered over Gabe's face, but he nodded. "I'd love to, Alie."

It sounded genuine, even. Lore thought it probably was, despite everything.

His elbow unbent; her hand was free. Bastian took it immediately, his callused fingers closing around hers like a door against a cold night.

Alie pulled Gabe toward the dance floor; he looked back over his shoulder, brows drawn low over one blue eye, one leather patch. "Careful," he murmured.

Neither Bastian nor Lore responded. Gabe melted into the crowd after Alie.

The music struck, and Bastian turned her into the dance, leading as effortlessly as he had the night of his masquerade. The smile had disappeared from his face the moment he no longer had to hold it for Alie's benefit. "We have to run."

She'd expected it. What she hadn't expected was the swoop it put into her middle, the feeling of vertigo that the thought of running away brought her. Leaving would be as futile as trying to catch the ocean in your hands. Not just physically, but *spiritually*, like something anchored her here.

"We can't," she murmured. "As much as I don't want to trust him, Anton is our only—"

"You don't understand, Lore." There was something desperate in Bastian's tone, something that told her he felt the same pull to this night as she did and was desperately fighting against it. "It happened again. Another village."

Only Bastian's hand on her waist kept her from tripping over her hem. Lore's fingers went cold. "When?"

"Last night." He kept her close, spoke in her ear—to anyone watching, they'd look two minutes away from sneaking off to a secluded corner, but their faces were twin masks of fear. "A few of the Presque Mort went to collect the bodies—Anton put Malcolm in charge."

Another village. She thought of her uncomfortable sleep, dark dreams she could only recall fragments of.

Lore shook her head, banishing the half-formed speculations. "Where is Anton, then?"

"I don't know." Bastian led her through a spin. "Preparing to stop August, I guess. It doesn't matter. I'm not going to let my uncle be the only thing that stands between you and death. I can get you money. Food. Get you on a ship—"

"I can't leave Dellaire. Mortem won't let me."

"Damn this." He hissed it through his teeth, his grip on her waist so tight it almost hurt. "*Damn* this. Fine. I can find a place for you in the city—"

"Bastian." She shook her head again, her nose grazing his neck. They didn't have to stand this close, but it was a comfort, and neither of them moved away. "They'd just find me. You know that."

Her road ended here, in the Citadel. Either dead from August's ritual, or kept in a gilded cage, a tool to aid in controlling a mad and dying King. Lore knew it. Gabe knew it. Bastian did, too. Of the three of them, he was the most likely to try to change the unchangeable, the one most predisposed to thinking he could shift the world to suit him. But even Bastian had to realize it was pointless this time. Lore was caught.

But just because she was caught didn't have to mean all of them were.

"I can't leave," Lore repeated, a murmur against his ear. "But you can."

For the first time, Bastian stuttered in their dance; other courtiers swirled around them as if she and the Sun Prince were rocks in a stream, but he and Lore just stood still, her hands on his shoulders, his on her waist, his eyes boring down into hers.

"And leave you." Gruff, not quite angry, but more than halfway there. "Leave you here."

"Anton said he'd stop the ritual." A thin defense, but it was all she had.

"Say he does. Then what?" People were starting to stare; Bastian swept her up into the dance again, the tight line of his jaw a stark contrast to fluid movement. "I leave, and you just stay a prisoner in the Citadel? You hope August doesn't try to kill you again, that Anton doesn't find a way to use you like a weapon? Those two will never come to any kind of peace, and you will always be in the middle of it."

"Notice all of that has to do with *me*, not you."

"Dammit, Lore, do you not get it?" He spun her with greater force than necessary, cinched his arm around her waist and jerked her close. "I told you in the catacombs. We're in this together, somehow, you and me and Remaut, too, even though I fucking hate that. I can't just abandon you here, even if I wanted to. Even if it'd save my hide."

"*If*?" Half a laugh bubbled in her throat, but when it came out, it was indistinguishable from the beginning of a sob. "Abandoning me would *absolutely* save your hide."

"And yet." The dance ended; they stood motionless, still locked together. "You're stuck with me. Whatever comes next."

Whatever comes next.

She looked up. The sun was low in the sky.

Movement at the front of the atrium, behind August's throne. Severin Bellegarde slipped through a small door, dressed just as dourly as usual. He stepped to the side, not attracting attention, and waited next to the potted poison flowers with his hands clasped behind his back.

August stood from his throne, as if Bellegarde's entrance had been a sign. He raised his hands, the picture of a benevolent ruler. "Thank you for joining us," he said, in tones clearly meant as a dismissal. "Tomorrow will mark the beginning of a triumphant new era for Auverraine. I can feel it." He smiled. "Even the darkness can be wielded to strengthen the light."

Polite applause from the gathered crowd. Then the courtiers gave their goodbyes, filtering out of the atrium in a bright parade. A few cast curious looks over their shoulders, eyeing those who remained, but none of them seemed to think it was anything strange. Lore resisted the urge to scream at them, to see if someone would turn and help, if they would notice something bad was happening and be inspired to stop it. But none of them would. The Sainted King had spoken, and his word was better than law.

Once they'd gone, only about twenty people were left. Lore recognized Bellegarde, Alie, and a few of the Presque Mort, who must've shown up at some point while she was arguing with Bastian. Not all of them. Some had been sent with Malcolm to inspect the village that had been wiped out yesterday. She couldn't help wondering what metrics Anton had used to decide who would stay and who would go.

Dani and Amelia stood near the wine fountain with a handful of people Lore took to be their family. Any trace of friendship that had been on Dani's face at that tea with Alie was gone; only the calculation was in place. She'd played her part admirably, sending Lore along to the next station in Anton's bizarre plan.

Where *was* Anton?

August stood in front of his silver-and-gold throne, hands still upheld, rubies winking on his fingers. Silence blanketed the room. Lore wanted to curl into herself—none of the gathered courtiers were staring at her, all these coconspirators of either the Sainted King or the Priest Exalted, but they were *aware* of her. It made her head hurt, her stomach unsteady, eerily similar to the comedown after channeling too much Mortem.

A presence at her back. Gabe. He didn't touch her, but his hand hovered over his dagger, and Bastian's arm still looped over her hips. The three of them standing close, drawn together again.

August's eyes narrowed at them, but only momentarily. Then his chin tilted up, addressing the sky through the window rather than his gathered faithful. "If you're here," he said, "you know the cusp on which we stand. Violence, yes, but for a purpose, and with an end—a war we are sure to win. For the glory of Auverraine. For the glory of Apollius, the Bleeding God. To pave the way for His return and make the world new, a rebirth from the ashes of the old."

"May He return," rose voices from around the room, among the scattered poison flowers. "May He return in blood and fire and His wounds be healed."

It echoed the call and response of First Day prayers, shaded sinister.

Next to her father, Alie's brow creased, confusion marring her slightly amused expression. At least *she* hadn't been in on it. At least Lore had one friend.

Bastian's arm lay heavy across her waist. Two friends.

And though Gabe had given them up to Anton, he still stood at her back. Maybe Lore had more people than she thought.

Cold comfort, while staring down a King who wanted her dead. While the man who was supposed to stop him was still nowhere to be seen.

August continued. "An eclipse is a time of great power, when the light and the dark join together. When the world becomes a portal of change, and things can be set on new paths." His dark eyes shone as he leveled them at his son. "The world is off balance, since Apollius disappeared. Things do not always turn out as they are meant to be. And when that happens, it is up to us to change it."

"Where the *fuck* is Anton?" Bastian hissed from the side of his mouth, the question directed at Gabe behind him. "This isn't the time to start running late."

"He's coming." But Gabe sounded just as scared as Bastian did. Lore's palms slicked with cold sweat.

Across the atrium, Alie's deep-green eyes flickered between August and her rapt father and Lore, trying to fit together the pieces of an unlikely puzzle. Worry carved lines in her brow; then determination smoothed them.

She made a tiny motion forward, as if to join Lore and Bastian and Gabe in the center of the room; Bellegarde's hand shot out, closed tightly around her wrist, fish-belly-white against copperbrown. Alie was too far away to hear, but Lore saw the tiny sound of pain steal from her mouth.

Gabe did, too. He stiffened, the lines of his body straining toward Alie, caught in between.

August ignored them all. An unsound smile lit his pale face, head still tipped toward the heavens. "In a god's hands, a curse can become a gift. In a god's hands—one god, the true god—darkness and light can come together. *Every* power can come together, housed in one holy body. One god, one crown. One empire that spans the world, heals all its ills and puts it back to rights."

As he spoke, more Presque Mort filed into the room, their dark clothes and scarred bodies scattering through poisonous blooms. They said nothing, just lined the edges of the atrium, blank-faced as soldiers sent to a battle's front. The Priest Exalted was still nowhere to be seen.

Finally, August lowered his head, facing the small crowd

instead of the sky. His expression was one of deep peace, deep fulfillment, someone seeing a plan come to fruition after years of careful coordination. Subtly, he nodded.

The Presque Mort moved, quick and silent. Bastian realized it first, turning with his teeth bared, a knife he'd hidden in his boot suddenly in his hand and catching a wicked gleam. Gabe took a moment longer, confusion writ large across his features—but when one of the Presque Mort put a rough hand on his shoulder, he spun, gripping his own dagger, though he didn't draw it yet.

Lore had no weapon, but when the Presque Mort grabbed her, she struggled anyway, lashing out with her feet, clawing with her nails. It was useless, but she tried.

Anton had deserted them. He wasn't here to stop the ritual.

Maybe he'd never planned on it in the first place. Maybe he'd only pretended, as a way to keep them docile, keep them from running. A gentle touch on the rabbit's neck before you broke it.

She caught a glimpse of Gabe's face. He hadn't quite been able to make himself draw his dagger on his fellows. Through his snarl, he looked lost, stricken.

Across the room, Bellegarde held on to Alie's hand, tight enough to leave a mark. The slighter woman had no chance of getting away, but still she strained forward, panic on her face. "Gabe!"

Something about his name in Alie's mouth shook Gabe from his stasis. With an anguished sound, he finally drew his knife, slashed at one of the Presque Mort. They were on him in an instant, overwhelming him, hauling him away. He gave a word-less shout, one that almost resolved into Alie's name but never quite made it there. A sickening *thunk* as a fist crashed into his temple; he slumped to the ground.

Someone grabbed Lore's braid, fallen from its jet pins, and jerked it backward. She snarled, but the Presque Mort's arms closed around her, kept her confined. It took two to do the same to Bastian; the Sun Prince thrashed, shouting curses that echoed through the slowly darkening atrium. One of the monks struck out with a dagger; the sharp edge sliced through Bastian's eyebrow, sheeting blood and shocking him into enough stillness to be subdued, arms twisted behind his back.

The shadow of the moon moved closer to the low-hanging sun.

The Presque Mort who held Lore steered her toward August's throne. The Sainted King stood motionless and aloof, hands behind his back. Another Presque Mort—the one from the leak, walking almost normally on a prosthetic foot—approached the dais and handed the King a dagger, cast in silver and scrolled over with gold. It matched his throne, a marriage of night and day, sun and moon.

"It was always meant to be this way," he said quietly, pitched so only Lore and Bastian could hear. "Mortem and Spiritum, bound together, held by the same person. The age of many gods is past; now, there's only room for one."

"So you decided it should be you?" Lore's voice was harsh, made hoarse by the way the Presque Mort held on to her hair, her neck stretched forward like an offering. She had to strain to see August, fingering his fine knife.

"Apollius decided it should be someone in our family." August shrugged. "He chose incorrectly, when deciding on the specific person, but that can be easily remedied. When we are one—when I become His avatar, His vessel—He will understand."

The Presque Mort hauled Bastian up on the platform as he spat and cursed, twisting in their grip like a cat. His flailing fists had connected with more than one of them—the Mort who held his arms had a rapidly blackening eye, and a bruise bloomed on another's cheek as his hand tangled in Bastian's hair and wrenched his head back, just like Lore's. Bastian squinted through the blood from his head wound, chest heaving, teeth bared.

August sighed as he looked at his son, always the disappointed father.

In return, Bastian laughed, quick and sharp. "How fitting," he snarled. "You always did have to do things as ostentatiously as possible."

The King shook his head. A streak of sorrow crossed his face, quick and bright as a passing comment, made more terrible for how genuine it was. "It never could've been you," he murmured. "No matter what Anton's vision said."

"Because I'm not *pious* enough?" There was no chance of escape; still, Bastian fought against the Mort holding him, muscles straining. "Would it be me if I'd killed my own people and farmed their bodies for an army?"

"I didn't kill them, Bastian." The sorrow on August's face turned cold. "That's one sin you can't lay at my feet."

His eyes turned to Lore, slow and deliberate.

Her throat closed. Her mind did, too, shuttering itself against some impossible realization. Mortem couldn't do something like that. Mortem couldn't kill an entire village and leave the bodies perfectly intact. No mere channeler could do such a thing.

No mere channeler.

"Now." August raised his knife as the room slid closer and closer to darkness, closer and closer to the eclipse's totality. "Let's begin."

Lore expected the knife to flash down to Bastian's exposed throat; the way he thrashed made it clear he did, too. But the Presque Mort holding the Sun Prince didn't pull his head back farther to make his neck an easier target. Instead he and the other monk wrestled one arm out from behind Bastian's back, thrust it forward to present his palm to his father.

The scarred lines of half a sun gleamed red in the fading light.

The Presque Mort holding Lore did the same—twisted her hand out from behind her, the hand the Night Sisters had burned the moon into eleven years ago today. Lore tried to curl it into a fist, but the monk forced her fingers backward, almost to the breaking point.

It was quick. August carved Bastian's hand first, fast and brutal, blood rushing from his son's palm to patter on the floor, joining what still leaked from his head wound. Then Lore; she gritted her teeth against a scream as the dagger point dug into her flesh, sheared through life and heart lines to add to an old scar.

Half a sun, arcing up from the points of her crescent moon. She knew without looking that Bastian's palm would match, a moon sliced beneath his sun, their two scars fit into one symbol. Life and death, light and dark.

Through the atrium window above, the sky slipped into totality, two celestial bodies momentarily mirroring their new scars before the moon covered the sun.

Dropping the bloody knife, August took their cut hands and pushed them together before him, palm-to-palm, wound-to-wound.

Lore felt like she'd been struck by lightning. Power arced from where her hand pressed against Bastian's, shooting down every limb, a magnification of what she'd felt when he pulled the strands of Mortem from her in the catacombs. *Life*, a rush of blood, a torrent of clean air in labored lungs.

And Bastian felt the opposite. She saw it, and felt it, too, the connection she'd sensed all along made manifest as a bridge between them. Cold and stillness, emptying, traveling through him in a storm of death. Opposites, brought together, strengthening each other.

August's mouth opened. He made a high, mad sound, not a laugh or a cry but something more animal than either. In the darkness of totality, the angles of his face were stark as a skull.

He dropped Lore and Bastian's hands. Both of them slumped, consciousness hard to hold. Lore's body felt like it was pulled in opposite directions, like it would shake itself apart at the seams. Dark and light and life and death, things that shouldn't live in the same space, both held in her now.

"That's quite enough."

Anton. Finally.

The Priest Exalted stood at the other end of the atrium, wearing his white robe and the gleaming pendant. It swung as he walked, slowly, up the center of the floor.

August impassively watched his brother approach, toying with his knife. A smear of blood marred his doublet. "You finally deign to show up," he said, hiding his wariness behind a haughty tone. "It's your turn, now. Their powers are bound together, but only a priest of Apollius can strike the last blow and redirect the magic into the proper vessel." The curve of his smile gleamed as merciless as his blade. "I know you've longed for this moment, when your power is needed instead of mine."

Anton gave his brother a gentle, almost pitying smile. "And you know I cannot put our earthly desires over those of Apollius."

Every courtier August had invited, everyone he'd thought was on his side, watched the Priest Exalted walk slowly toward him without raising a finger. The Presque Mort holding Lore and Bastian backed away as Anton came forward, bringing them off the throne's dais and down to the floor. Lore's knees buckled, so they dragged her. Bastian stepped in a pool of his own blood, tracking it in boot prints across the floor. Behind them, Gabe was still unconscious, sprawled against the wall in a boneless heap.

"But he isn't worthy." To August's credit, he didn't sound afraid. His voice remained clear and ringing, even as his illness-dulled eyes went wary. "We've discussed this, Anton. The boy cannot be the chosen, there has to have been some mistake. He isn't ready, and time grows short."

Anton climbed the stairs to stand before his brother. "But he will be," he said. "He can be, with the proper training. The leadership he needs."

"But he cannot hold this power." Even now, when things were so clearly going sideways, August looked stronger than he had, the promise of magic invigorating his sickened body. He stood straight, his head tipped upward to gaze at the eclipse-darkened sky, as if he could see Apollius Himself somewhere in it. "It would be too much for him."

They were of a height, the King and the Priest, near-perfect mirrors, differences marked only by their clothing and the scarred half of Anton's face. So when Anton stared at him, their gazes were perfectly level. "Then someone else will have to guide him. To show him the way."

"I can be that leadership." For a moment, a sly smile tugged at August's mouth; the sense of an opening, a way he could still spin this how he wanted. "I'm his father."

"But you never acted like it," Anton said.

When Anton plunged his own knife into August's side, he barely had to lift his hand to do it.

CHAPTER FORTY

Behold my return.
—The Book of Holy Law, Tract 896 (green text,
spoken directly by Apollius to Gerard Arceneaux)

L ore didn't know what she'd expected. Anton had said he'd
stop August from completing the ritual, and killing him
certainly did that. She considered this fact with aloof detachment, even as death and life still rushed through her in a heady
mix, making her vision blur from color to grayscale and back
again.

Bastian's eyes were wide, his face pale. His mouth hung open, but
no sound came out. At some point, he'd been forced to his knees,
and now he knelt in his own blood, like a supplicant at an altar.

No one else could see what had happened, not yet. The way the
brothers stood blocked the view of everyone behind them. Anton
dropped the knife, the blade streaking the white fabric in crimson
on the way down before landing in the folds of his robe by his
feet, keeping it hidden. His hands gripped his twin's shoulders,
holding him up so they stayed eye-to-eye even as the King's knees
went out from under him.

Pinkish fluid burbled on August's lips. He made a choked, gasping sound.

From the corner of her eye, Lore saw Bastian flinch.

"You never understood," Anton said, low and soothing, like one might talk to a scared horse. "Apollius does not make mistakes. Ever. About anything."

"You're right. I was wrong." August's words were broken things, tripping jaggedly from a failing mouth. A last bid to save himself. "I didn't know just how holy—"

"You didn't want to know," Anton snarled. "You didn't want to understand, because you wanted that power for yourself. A prophecy come to bear, and you closed your eyes against it." He shook his brother, spatters of blood flying from August's mouth, staining his cheek. "This is the price of treason."

"No," August said quietly, using the last of his strength to speak. "It's the price of jealousy. Who's sinning now, brother?"

Anton's blood-speckled face went cold. In one motion, he let go of his twin's shoulders, stepped back. The Sainted King crumpled to the ground.

August was still gulping in useless air, still twitching as Anton turned to the crowd. None of the gathered courtiers looked surprised. They'd expected this. Everyone August had trusted had turned their loyalty to Anton instead, the Church finally winning over the crown.

The only stricken face was Alie, still in Bellegarde's grip, hand clapped over her mouth. Alie, and Bastian. Bastian looked like he'd collapse at any moment, still kneeling in his own blood. His head had stopped bleeding, crusting the side of his face in rust, the lurid color making the whites of his widened eyes stand out.

Anton raised his hands, the exact same stance August had taken. "Faithful," he intoned. "We all knew that August wasn't the one to lead us into our new—"

A scream interrupted him. Lore didn't realize it was her own until she felt her jaw stretch.

Pain bloomed in her abdomen, white-hot and burning. The Presque Mort holding her let go, startled; she slid to her knees.

The knife. August's knife, silver and gold and sticking out of her side.

Behind Anton, the bloody heap of the King listed over, hand outstretched from where he'd thrown the blade. His palm hit the dais with a meaty thump, a smile revealing gore-streaked teeth.

"It won't be him," he said, the words slurred with blood and bile, with all the fluids a dying body releases when the balance finally tips. "Not if *I* kill her."

Lore's vision seeped to monotone, everything colored black or white or a gray in-between. Her own body was a chaos of black and white glow, Mortem and Spiritum tangled together, both from the ritual August had performed and from the wound in her gut.

Distantly, she heard someone calling her name. Bastian.

But Anton didn't seem fazed. He lifted his eyes to the sky, sighing like a parent with an unruly child, then turned around to the fallen King. "A gut wound takes time to kill someone," he said. "A fact I'm beginning to regret."

Anton lifted his foot, clad in heavy boots, and brought it down on August's head. The white light around the King billowed away like a breeze, a cloud of darkness taking its place.

Brain matter caked the sole of Anton's boot as he lifted it from the ruin of August's skull.

Lore heaved up wine. It puddled sticky in her lap, mixing with blood from her stomach.

More shouting, but it sounded like it was coming from underwater. She couldn't focus her eyes, couldn't organize her thoughts into straight lines. All was pain, and all was fading.

Bastian's voice cut through the din, the timbre recognizable even if the words weren't. Gabe's, the same, soundless roars, growls, clashes of steel and the meaty sound of fists in flesh. He must've woken up. That was good. Maybe they'd both live. Two out of three wasn't bad.

"Take her to the gardens," Anton said, and distantly, Lore felt hands beneath her knees, around her shoulders, lifting her like a fainted noblewoman. "She's waiting for us there."

Lore's eyes fluttered closed.

🦋

Hard ground. Cold seeping through her ruined clothes, making the wound in her side and her sliced-up hand ache. Wind through stone, curling around leaves turned to rock, granite petals.

Lore forced her eyes open.

The stone garden. Torches burned around the well, replacements for the light stolen by the eclipse. Her vision was still blurry, pain and blood loss making it hard to focus, but she could see Anton standing before the open pit of the well, the statue of Apollius that held it closed placed carefully to the side. Other muted shapes around him—the Presque Mort, all of them that hadn't been dispatched to the village to deal with the new corpses.

New corpses, after her dream...

There was another figure near Anton, standing on the other side of the well. Willowy, dressed in black, with a long river of pale hair.

Anton turned before her mind would let her comprehend what she was seeing. A small blessing. "Ah. Lore."

At the sound of her name, two of the Presque Mort approached, gingerly helping her up. Blood soaked the side of her gown; her head felt as heavy as the stone roses lining the path.

"You did so well," the Priest Exalted said as she stumbled toward him. "Really, Lore, you should be proud of yourself. To be part of this, to have Apollius speak of you *by name*. And more than once! The vision that brought me my scar is where I first heard of you, but He has spoken to me since—He told me to learn the art of dreamwalking, how to draw out your power to make our undead army."

He talked too fast, too excited, as if he'd been waiting for the chance to spill all these secrets. "Shut up," Lore said, but it came out nothing more than a croak, and Anton didn't hear.

"Gabe teaching you to guard your mind did present a bit of a problem," the Priest Exalted continued. "I paid dearly for showing him that trick." His whole hand stroked the other, the one with the new burn scars.

His non-scarred hand held a golden circlet, studded in garnets. August's crown, the simple one he'd been wearing when his brother cut him down. Lore wondered why Anton hadn't put it on yet.

"But all has worked out as it should now," the Priest Exalted continued. "When you finally die, when I strike you again—my apologies for that bit of unpleasantness, but needs must—your power will go to Bastian. He will have the magic of life and of death, Spiritum and Mortem. And then it will begin."

But Lore was barely listening, the words sliding off her like water to oil. Because her eyes had finally focused on the person across the well.

Smooth golden hair. Pale, fine features. A body long and thin, so different from Lore's own. But the bright hazel eyes, those were the same.

A Night Sister. The one who'd given her the moon-shaped scar, and then decided to save her instead, sending her to the surface rather than into that obsidian tomb to have her mind scooped out, her eyes made blank, something vital ripped away.

The woman smiled, and there was true sorrow in it. "Hello, daughter."

CHAPTER FORTY-ONE

Endings take time.

–Kirythean proverb

Lore had never known her mother's real name. The Sisters didn't use them. By the time Lore was born, her mother had been living with the remains of the Buried Watch for months, completely assimilated into their ranks, though the others watched her with apprehension.

Lore knew why. She'd been told the story. After she arrived, her mother had approached Nyxara's tomb, as every Sister must, and darkness had reached out. Darkness had caressed her middle, where Lore still slept, unaware of the world and the role she'd have in it.

So the first time Lore channeled Mortem, by accident—pulling a strand of it from the Buried Goddess's tomb and sending it into the rock that made their underground cathedral, nearly causing a collapse—it hadn't been a surprise. It'd been something they were waiting for.

The flashes of memory she retained from her first thirteen years were brief—she'd done her best to bury them—but they were filled with sidelong glances lit by the strange phosphorescence of the crystal on the walls, murmurs behind hands.

When the eclipse came, her mother had approached her with the crescent moon brand glowing orange, and that hadn't been a surprise, either. She'd wept as she burned Lore's palm, the sign that she would be the next one to enter the tomb. Lore remembered that it'd been a time of celebration for the other Sisters, how they'd congratulated her mother for her strength, for finally doing the right thing.

But that night, while Lore slept—a nudge in her side, her mother's terrified eyes. She'd led Lore up the tunnels, up to where the light of the last day before the eclipse was already coloring the sky.

"Run," her mother whispered.

And Lore had.

She'd run and run, and it'd all been in a circle. Because here she was again. Looking at her mother's face and seeing something like terror, something like deep sorrow.

"I've missed you." Oh, gods, the genuine note in her voice made it all so much worse. The Night Sister stood on the other side of the well, but her hands still stretched out, as if she could gather Lore into her embrace. "You're so grown up. So beautiful." She sighed, a hitch in her throat. "I wish it could be different. I thought maybe there was a chance She would change Her mind, that you wouldn't be one of the chosen..." Her eyes closed, a crystalline tear falling down her cheek, catching the light. "But the goddess is unchanging. I should've sent you into the tomb before, let Her power consume you, burn itself out before you reached the age of ascension. Now death is the only way."

Lore thrashed in the Presque Mort's grip despite the sting in her side, the stark words finally enough to snap her out of her haze. "No," she said, and it sounded like her mouth was full of cotton. "No no no no I don't want to—"

"We can't let it happen again, my love," her mother murmured. "The Night Witch was one of Nyxara's chosen, too; she was to become the goddess's avatar. And She would've laid waste to the world. I'm so sorry. You have to die, and I'm so sorry."

"But you'll wait." Anton's voice was different, the thin veneer of sense stripped away. Strange, to hear it gone and realize this was what waited beneath. "The deal was that you get your avatar back after six villages are added to the army, and that I get to strike the killing blow. The paperwork to make Buried Watch once again part of the Church is filed, but I can rescind it at any time if the terms aren't met."

"Of course," the Night Sister murmured. "A deal is a deal."

"Precisely. I see why the Sisters made you the Night Priestess." Anton's eyes shone with unsound light. "I hope you do better by the title than the last one."

Lore's mother—the Night Priestess—simply inclined her head.

Three mothers, two betrayals, all for some greater good that Lore couldn't bring herself to care about. She only cared about living. The greater good could hang.

"Please don't let him kill me." Lore knew she sounded pathetic. She *was* pathetic, limp between two Presque Mort, bleeding out and helpless to stop it. "I haven't done anything, I didn't choose it, please..."

"Oh, dear heart." The Night Priestess's hand came up, then fell, like if they'd been closer she would've cradled Lore's cheek. "It's the only thing we *can* do. The world wouldn't survive you."

"A deal *is* a deal," Anton said, turning to face Lore. "Now let's settle our accounts, and we can all be on our way."

The Night Priestess's lips flattened in distaste. She waved a hand. "Take what you're owed, then."

"I'm thankful for your cooperation," Anton said, though there was a sneer in his voice. "Thankful that you understand there is only room for one god, this time."

"There certainly isn't room for six again," the Night Priestess said softly. "Gods are not content to share power."

"That's the trouble with ascensions," Anton agreed. "When humans become gods, they bring their natures with them." The Priest Exalted bared his teeth, a triumphant rictus as he stepped toward Lore. One hand raised.

It was the same tugging feeling she'd felt in her dreams, but without the buffer of sleep, it was agonizing. Her heart stilled, just so much meat, and felt like it was being pulled slowly from behind her ribs. Strands of dark Mortem leaked from her chest, seeping out slowly like blood from a million tiny wounds.

The mad priest knotted raw death in the air, gnarling the strands together. "Apollius," he murmured, looking up at the sky as if he could find his god there. A rapturous tear slid down his cheek. "See what I do for You. How I manipulate the power of Your treasonous wife and turn it to Your glory."

He still pulled power from her as he spoke to the empty sky, weaving it between his fingers. It coalesced above their heads, a writhing, intricate knot, pulsing like an organ as it took shape. Tendrils reached from the central mass, curling into the eclipse-shrouded sky, seeping outward as if they were looking for something.

Looking for another village. More people to kill, more corpses for Anton's undead army. Using her to do it; Mortem channeled from her goddess-touched body, fashioned to do things no other channeler could do.

"You've given us Your sign," Anton murmured to the sky. "Your promise that a new world awaits, one You will shape for Your faithful. Remember, Bleeding God, how I helped usher it in, here when two opposite powers can be held in concert."

Opposite powers.

Even through the slow leak of her blood, the chill in her fingers and the cold creep of death, Lore could feel Spiritum, the comet-streak of life woven through her when her and Bastian's hands were carved, then thrust together at the moment of totality.

She had them both. Mortem and Spiritum, life and death. Both of them lived in her, both of them could be channeled.

There wasn't time to overthink it. Lore thrust out her hand and *pulled*.

Light flowed from Anton, a surge of it flashing across the garden to her waiting fingers, stolen from the corona around his living body. It didn't come together like a thread, a pliant thing to be braided; this was lightning, this was all crackling energy, and Lore's roar echoed Anton's own as she pulled it into herself, her veins running hot and full, her heart thumping hard enough to bruise her lungs.

White-hot pain in her side, an encroaching burn. She knew it was healed without looking, the power of life rushing through her and healing *everything*.

Lore couldn't hold on to it. It was too much, too bright. She relinquished her hold with a shout; the lightning-crackle left her hands, rebounded across the garden to Anton's kneeling form. The old man breathed like a bellows, his hands clutched over his heart, his lips pulled back from his teeth.

"Little deathwitch," Anton snarled. "You think you're in the right?"

"I think," Lore panted, forcing herself to stand, "that I'm not going to let you kill anyone else with *my* power."

"That's what you don't understand, Lore," her mother said, slender and sad and wreathed in flame-light. "It isn't yours. It's Hers. And the longer you live—the more powerful you grow—the more like Her you will become."

"We can't have another Godsfall." Anton got up, slowly, looking every inch the frail old man. Except for his eyes. Those glittered with a sheen of madness, a fervor that made her recoil. The knife he'd used to stab August twisted in his grip. "We can't let it happen again."

"So you kill people instead?" Even healed, her side still ached;

Lore pressed her fist against it. "You're addled, Anton. There won't be another Godsfall, because *there are no more gods!*"

"There is *one*, and you will cede your power to Him," Anton replied, spittle flying from the corner of his scarred mouth. "The world brought to heel beneath Apollius's merciful rule, through His blessed—"

A scream ripped the night, cutting off whatever Anton had been about to say. Torches toppled, rolling across the cobblestones; another torch swiped through the air. The living flowers growing on top of their stone counterparts were dry and brittle from a summer without rain; they licked into flame, surrounding the well in jumping tongues of fire.

And Bastian stepped through them.

His fine shirt was ripped, crusted with blood from the cut through his eyebrow. His teeth gleamed in the flickering light, bared and snarling.

Anton's face split in a beatific, unsound smile, one that made Lore's stomach twist uncomfortably. He had hidden all this… this *worship*, this devotion, keeping Bastian at arm's length even as he worked to keep him safe from August. But now that everything was coming to a close, he looked on his nephew with the same light in his eyes that he'd cast toward the sky as he prayed.

"Bastian, my boy!" the Priest Exalted called. "I'm sorry you were hurt; I told them that you weren't to be harmed, but when things get chaotic—"

"Your monks are all hurt far worse than I am." Bastian held a short sword he must've taken from someone; he turned it so the bloodied edge caught the firelight.

The Presque Mort scattered around the garden seemed uneasy; hands fell to the harnesses around their chests. They glanced at their Priest, waiting for instruction, ready for violence if it was called for.

"It's good that you're here," Anton continued, oblivious to the low, dangerous tone in Bastian's voice. "Things have gone a bit off schedule with the girl. But now that you've arrived, we can move forward. Perhaps you can convince her to see reason."

Bastian's eyes swung to Lore, panic flashing bare and jagged across his features. "Are you hurt?"

"She's fine," Anton said dismissively, waving his hand. "Better, even; she channeled Spiritum and used it to heal herself." A sharp laugh echoed over the stone roses, the hiss of flames. "If *her* magic has been heightened to such a level, imagine yours!"

Across the well, the Night Priestess stood still as a carved icon. Her expression wavered in the growing flames, but she didn't look at Bastian with fear. It was closer to resignation, as if his appearance here marked a sea change, diverted the flow of her plan. She turned her eyes to Lore. There was no pity to be found in her face.

Slowly, she made her way closer, close enough for her whisper to be heard. "You care for him," her mother whispered. "Don't you?"

Lore didn't answer.

"If you care for him," she murmured, hazel eyes sheened in tears, "if you care for *anyone* in this world, you will let this happen. Please don't make it harder than it has to be, Lore. You don't understand what hell you could bring on the world."

"I'm sorry for keeping you in the dark." Anton moved toward Bastian the way one would approach an altar, Lore and the Night Priestess cast completely from his mind. Bastian stood still. The fire gilded him, made him look cast in gold rather than flesh.

"There was much I didn't understand, not until recently," Anton continued. "And I know you were fond of the girl—for that, I'm sorry, but you must understand it's a weakness, an echo that cannot be allowed to continue for all our sakes. You must overcome it, must be ready to sacrifice old feelings and remake the world in Apollius's image." A tear broke from the line of his lashes and spilled down his cheek. "In *your*—"

"You won't be sacrificing anyone."

Gabe.

He appeared behind the Priest Exalted, flame-wreathed, his dagger in his hand. The blade pressed against Anton's throat, and his hand didn't shake as he took the Priest's wrist, twisted it to make him drop the knife still caked in August's blood. Gabe looked worse for wear than Bastian, his eye patch lost, bruises forming on nearly every inch of visible skin.

"Ah, Gabriel," Anton sighed. "Your loyalties are ever-shifting. I suppose I should expect that." A snarl lifted his mouth. "Part of you knows, I think. What you could become if this is allowed to continue. An abomination. Recurring sin."

Gabe's throat worked as he swallowed, as he shoved the blade close enough to pucker skin. "Be quiet," he said, the ghost of something broken in it. "Please, Father, be quiet."

"I'm not your father, boy," Anton hissed.

A flinch, Gabe's one blue eye fluttering closed, then open again.

"Lore." Her mother's hand was cold on her arm. "Lore, please, before this comes to a point we can't return from."

The sky was lightening, slowly. The moon edging away from the sun.

The knot of Mortem that Anton had been molding was still rotating in the air, a mass of death and darkness held in stasis. Annihilation, waiting for its target.

Anton's bright eyes tracked to Lore and the Night Priestess. "I'm still owed a village," he said, almost irritated, as if he didn't have a knife to his throat.

Lore reached up, eyes fixed on the Priest Exalted's, and called her Mortem back in.

It felt the same as before—the deadened limbs, the grayscale vision, the lurch of her heart in her chest. But as she unraveled the knot of Mortem and let it funnel back into herself, she realized what was different. What made this something more.

This death was hers, spooled from her own bones, the meat that made her up. Its *power* was hers. She wasn't just channeling it, she was *absorbing* it: sewing it between her vertebrae, braiding it into her veins.

The knot unspooled in the space of two heartbeats, tangled threads that slid into her fingers, settled alongside the current of light that was Spiritum. Both she could sense, both she could use.

The more powerful you grow, the more like Her you become.

Her mother let loose a sound that was somewhere between a sigh and a sob. "This is what I saw, in the reflections of the tomb." She whispered it almost to herself, broken-voiced. "It's what the goddess dreamed, but I thought I could prevent it. I thought you would choose the world over yourself."

"I'm far too selfish for that," Lore whispered.

The Presque Mort did nothing as their leader's carefully wrought twists of power unraveled, watching with wary eyes. It seemed like they were all looking to *Bastian*, not Anton, as if the Sun Prince held their loyalty.

"Bitch," Anton spat. "One way or another, Apollius will prevail. You only—"

"Shut up." But Gabe's voice was shaky. He looked around at the other Presque Mort; their passivity seemed to unsettle him as much as it did Lore. Gabe's one eye went to Bastian; the empty socket of the other made a pit of shadow. "He's a mad old man, Bastian." His tone was pleading. "Strip him of his title, and he can't hurt anyone."

Bastian didn't answer him. Instead, he turned to face Lore and her mother, and held out his hand.

"If you touch her," he said evenly, dark eyes trained on the Night Priestess, "I will go into the catacombs and haul all of you out myself."

"Lore," the Night Priestess said, a last-ditch effort. "Please."

Lore looked up at her mother. Then she walked forward and

took her place next to Bastian, kicking Anton's dagger away as she went, sending it skittering into the fire.

The Night Priestess loosed a shaking breath.

Lore tore her gaze from her mother, looked around them at the Presque Mort, ringed in flame. "Why aren't they doing anything? What are they waiting for?"

"I don't know," Bastian said. "I don't care." He took a step toward his uncle.

Gabe hauled the Priest Exalted back, away from the approaching prince. "*Bastian.*" Warring emotions twisted his face, fear and sorrow and anger. "We talked about this."

"*You* talked about this." Bastian was doing something strange with his hands. They flexed back and forth, fingers curling, as if he was trying to wind in an invisible rope. Gold light glimmered in the space around him.

"He's confused," Gabe said, backing up another step. Anton hung limp, eyes cast upward, as if in prayer. "He's just a man; take his position, give it to someone else, but don't *kill* him!"

"I'm the fucking Sainted King." It wasn't a scream. It was barely more than a whisper. Still, it reverberated against the hiss of the fire, and when Bastian tilted up his head, the flames seemed to make a halo around his head. "I will kill whoever I please."

"Then you're no better," Gabe snarled. Fire leapt behind him, as if his anger stoked it higher. "No better than him, no better than your father."

Beyond Gabe's shoulder, Lore could still see the silhouette of her mother, shimmering against the flames. "Listen," she murmured, stepping between him and Bastian, "everything that's happened tonight has been pointless violence, we don't have to—"

"Not pointless," Anton murmured. "Not unless you count stopping an apocalypse as pointless. Her power will keep growing, Bastian, especially now that she can channel Spiritum, too. It will infect her mind; *Nyxara* will infect her mind. Give the girl death now, or watch her beg for it later, when the world falls down around her as Apollius makes it His." A low, wheezing laugh hissed through Anton's teeth, his eyes arcing heavenward again. "The cycle has begun, and you are all caught in its weave, forced into a caring that has ruined you before and will ruin you again."

Tension ran through Lore's shoulders, echoed in Bastian's; the tip of Gabe's knife wavered.

"It's been prophesied, but none wanted to believe it," Anton rasped. "None except I. Hear me, Apollius! Hear how I warn them of the coming age, of what happens when new gods rise and try to stand against Your will!"

Gabe stumbled, trying to keep a grip on the mad old man who'd been a kind of father, the only kind he could keep. His eye darted to Bastian, pleading.

The Sun Prince—no, the Sainted King—watched on, implacable. His hands kept flexing, back and forth, working up more golden light. "You're going to give us another solution, old man," Bastian murmured. "Don't make me cut it out of you."

Gabe looked away, but his dagger didn't waver.

"There is one." Lore stepped forward, shaky; her wound was healed, but still sore. Her hair had fallen down, hung around her face in gold-brown strands made darker by blood. "I learned to guard my mind from Mortem before. Gabe taught me. It can't be that much different now. I can keep myself from sensing power, from growing stronger. Keep myself..."

She trailed off, not sure how to finish. Not sure if she needed to. It was a whole thought on its own.

Anton laughed again. "You always were willing to do anything to save your own skin."

"You don't know me," Lore said.

His one eye narrowed, glittering with the same cutting light as Gabe's blade. "Are you so sure?"

"What do you need to do?" Something had changed in

Bastian's manner, in his carriage. Gone was the languid prince; he'd fully stepped into being the King. It was the other side he'd shown her that night in the alley, the night she told him her history. A King had always been waiting. A brutal one.

Lore glanced at Gabe. He was trying so hard to keep his emotions off his face, trying and failing. Pain lived in the furrows of his brow, the fierce curve of his mouth around his bared teeth. But there was hope, sparking to life when their gazes met. Hope that he could yet save the wretched man he held so close, the man who'd only sought to use him.

"I can teach her," Gabe said. "Teach her to guard her mind even more fully. Make sure nothing like the villages happens ever again."

He'd done it once already, she suddenly realized. That night she woke him up, made him sit with her and concentrate, soothing the darkness until sleep could come peacefully, without those strange dreams. There'd been no death that night.

But Anton shook his head, mindless of the blade still against his neck. Gabe tried to move it; he didn't in time, and a thin line of crimson creased the old man's skin. "It won't last," he rasped. "These roles are fixed. To let the girl live is to invite oblivion, for the world, but for yourselves most of all."

"Spare us your religious bullshit," Bastian hissed.

Another braying laugh from the Priest Exalted. "Oh, nephew, that's the one thing you can't be spared. You'll learn."

"Lore."

The Night Priestess's voice was quiet; still, it echoed. Her face was emotionless, though something like resignation lurked at the corner of her mouth, in the shine of her eyes. "Things have progressed more than we thought," she said softly. "I see that now. I can't make you choose death."

"Damn right," Bastian snarled, shouldering in front of Lore.

"I was too weak before," the Night Priestess continued, ignoring Bastian. "And for that, I'm sorry."

"Sorry for letting me live?" Lore's voice came out ragged. "Sorry for saving me?"

Her mother lowered her chin, her long, pale hair almost covering her face. "But you can be strong now," she said, as if Lore hadn't spoken at all. "You can make the right choice."

"You're asking her to die, and you think you're in the right?" Gabe nearly spat it.

But the Night Priestess didn't respond. She looked only at Lore, only at her daughter.

"It all springs from this choice," she murmured. "You are the seed of the apocalypse."

And it was true. Lore didn't know how, not yet, didn't understand the intricacies. But she felt the truth.

But it was also true what she'd told her mother. Lore was selfish. If it came down to her or the world, Lore chose herself.

The Night Priestess sighed. Nodded, knowing Lore's answer though she didn't speak. Then, in a quick movement that the flickering flames bisected into strange jerks, she climbed up onto the lip of the well and descended the spinning stairs into the dark.

Bastian moved forward, as if he'd follow and extract some kind of revenge, but Lore put her hand on his chest. "No," she murmured, and had nothing else to add. "No."

He listened.

"You've chosen your path, the three of you," Anton murmured. "Woe betide us when the rest follow."

Bastian looked at Gabe. Flicked his hand. "The old man will live, Gabe."

Shoulders slumped in relief, Gabe finally took his dagger from Anton's throat. He stepped back, letting the Priest Exalted stand on his own.

Bastian's hand moved, twisting in a graceful motion that looked near impossible. Golden swirls carved through the air, coalescing around his fingers, threads spun from the sun itself.

Then Bastian thrust his handful of gold toward Anton.

The strands attached to the ground around the Priest Exalted, and it erupted. Thick green vines grew rapidly through the stone, thorn-studded, the ends opening in blood-red rose blooms identical to the ones burning near the path. They wound around his legs, his middle. They entered his mouth before he could so much as scream. His eye rolled as the empty socket of the other was filled with green, then red, a rose unfurling in the scarred orbital, petals brushing his flame-ravaged brow.

It was over in an instant. Anton Arceneaux was encased in roses and blood, one more statue in the garden.

And Bastian had done it so easily, as if it was second nature.

Gabe made a small, hoarse noise, stumbling back. "You said you wouldn't kill him." His voice went ragged at the end. "You said you wouldn't!"

"I said he would live." Bastian stepped forward to the remains of his uncle and wrenched the bloody crown from his hand. The Priest had held on to it all this time. "And he does."

The smallest rise and fall of Anton's chest. The thinnest whistle of breath. Bastian was right; in all those roses, Anton was still alive.

Gods, it was worse.

Gabe's eyes went from his Priest to his King, shock curdling to hatred, hot and vitriolic. "You're no better," he said again, an echo. The flames of the burning roses in the garden seemed to bend toward him, as if drawn to his rage. "Is this how it's going to be, then? You as a magic tyrant, worse than August could ever be?"

Bastian didn't answer. Instead, he placed the crown on his head. It crossed the bloodied line on his brow. "Long live the Sainted King."

EPILOGUE

H er chair was uncomfortable.

It wasn't just the chair itself—being here at all was uncomfortable, up on the dais in the throne room, seated next to Bastian. Her chair was silver, taken from one of the countless storage rooms in the Citadel when Bastian went through them for things to sell off, give away, or melt down. It was a haphazard way of trying to help those living outside the wall, but it was something. Centuries of hoarded wealth were hard to liquidate all at once.

But this chair he'd taken to put on the throne's dais. For her. So she could sit next to him in a show of equality.

Almost like a Queen.

Some of them called her that. She'd heard it whispered—the poison queen, the hemlock queen, the deathwitch queen. The court loved a nickname, apparently.

Lore didn't want to be here. She didn't want to be this visible, this vulnerable. But by now, the story of what she was—what August and Anton had been trying to do—had spread through the Citadel and beyond. Her anonymity was lost; the safety Bastian offered was all she had left.

Especially as news of her power trickled beyond Auverraine. To Kirythea.

It was only midmorning, but already there'd been a stream of business to take care of. Petitions to hear out, prisoners to pardon. All of them were courtiers who'd been at the eclipse ball.

The one that stuck in Lore's mind was Dani. Her whole family was sent to the Burnt Isles, other than Amelia, the older sister who'd been hastily wed a week before to Lord Demonde, who didn't care about the scandal attached to his new wife's old name. Dani had glared at Lore the entire time, even as the manacles were fastened around her wrists.

Bastian kept Lore beside him because it was safer for them to stick together, but she wished he'd let her hide behind the throne or something.

Now, on the marble floor before her, Mari and Val bowed, their new contract clutched in Val's hand. All pardons had to be reconsidered by the new King; Val and Mari's privateering had been high on Bastian's list of things to renew. He'd sweetened the pot for them, put them and all their crew on the Citadel's payroll. His next step, he'd told Lore, was legalizing poison's use for the terminally ill, those who might need to extend their lives a bit longer to make sure their families were taken care of, or to dull pain. He was pushing through pardons for arrested poison runners with no other charges as quickly as his pen could sign his name.

All things that were good for Dellaire. Still, Mari's dark eyes were apprehensive as they flickered to Lore. Worry lived in the line of her full mouth.

She and Val didn't speak as they left the throne room, their business concluded. But they both looked back at Lore one more time before the door closed.

Lore desperately wished she could follow them.

"One more." Bastian shifted in his throne, lifted up a hand to readjust his sun-rayed crown. It looked good on him, better than it had ever looked on August. "Then we can get something to eat, and we won't have to look at this fucking room for a few days."

"Who is it?" Lore asked. She hadn't studied the docket of pardons today. She'd been too tired.

Sleeping scared her, now. She did it as little as possible.

Bastian gave her an unreadable look. "It's—"

The door opened before he could answer.

Gabe.

The former Duke Remaut wasn't in irons. He'd spent the past two weeks since August's death imprisoned in the Church, locked in a cloister—a favor, really, keeping him out of the dungeons. Lore had asked for that, but she hadn't had to beg. Bastian agreed on the first mention, like he hadn't wanted to keep Gabe in the dungeons, either.

Still, he looked haggard. Thin, bruised. He'd found another eye patch after losing his first, but it didn't fit well, and his whole eye looked sunken.

Lore's chest twinged.

She didn't know what Gabe had been formally charged with. There were choices. Treason, accessory to murder. All things that could carry a person to the Burnt Isles or the gallows.

Myriad hells, *surely* Bastian wouldn't do that. She'd speak up if she had to.

But she didn't want to have to.

Gabe stopped in the middle of the floor. He took a deep breath, then looked up.

If he was surprised to see Lore there, he didn't show it. His blue eye tracked to her, then quickly away, with no sign of emotion.

"Gabriel Remaut," Bastian intoned, the same as he had for every penitent. "Do you know why you're here?"

"Skip this part." His voice was hoarse. "Can we just fucking skip this part? Your Majesty?"

Contempt dripped from his voice. Lore bit her lip.

But Bastian nodded. "We can." He sat back in his throne, knees canted wide, taking up all the room. Even the throne fit him better than it had his father. "Gabriel Remaut, do you promise your loyalty to the crown of the Sainted King and to the Church of Auverraine, to lead it in steadfast devotion and piety as we await the return of Apollius?"

He said it so quickly, so nonchalant, that it took both Lore and Gabe a moment to parse the words. Gabe's eye went wide. "I don't—"

"Just say yes, Remaut." Bastian tapped his fingers on his knee. "You know what it is. You've heard the annunciation before."

Lore's mind finally caught up with the pronouncement, with what it meant. Her mouth dropped open.

Gabe straightened. Nodded. "I will."

"Then I pronounce you as the Priest Exalted."

Silence. Neither she nor Gabe knew how to react, what to say. He'd gone from being a prisoner to being the second most powerful man in the country in a span of seconds.

And Bastian just looked bored.

"Now," said the Sainted King, flicking his fingers dismissively. "Get out of my sight. My deathwitch and I have much to discuss."

Acknowledgments

This book, and all of my books, wouldn't exist without the incredible work of my agent, Whitney Ross. Here's to tons more stories in the future, hopefully growing increasingly bonkers.

I'm endlessly grateful to my editor, Brit Hvide, whose guidance is always invaluable and who makes me actually clarify things. (Thank you, I need it.) I love making books with you and look forward to many more.

The whole crew at Orbit is amazing, and I'm continuously thrilled at how lucky I am to work with them.

To my Pod—wouldn't be here without you.

To all the wonderful friends who have been in all my acknowledgments before and will continue to be—Sarah, Liz, Nicole, Ashley, Chelsea, Jensie, Steph, Leah—I love you endlessly.

And to Caleb—you're a dreamboat and I'm glad you're mine. Gonna keep you.